'This book had me kicking my feet and screaming, it was wonderful and a joy to read. Vampires, slow burn but not like slug slow, a good slow pace that leaves you wanting more.'
⭐⭐⭐⭐⭐

'This book was SO fun. If you love fake dating, ridiculous family drama, and a slow-burn romance where both people are terrible at lying to each other, you'll love this. 10/10 would recommend for a laugh, a swoon, and just pure, unapologetic fun.'
⭐⭐⭐⭐⭐

'I'm a sucker (pun intended) for anything vampire based, so throw in fake dating and I'm absolutely sold! Overall, this was a really joyful read that would be perfect for Halloween, or Valentine's Day, or in my case a beautifully sunny day!'
⭐⭐⭐⭐⭐

'This was SUCH a fun read, I found myself giggling so many times it's not even funny - I actually almost fell off my treadmill because I was so engrossed in the book, I forgot I was bloody walking on it. Honestly there's not a single second of this book that I didn't enjoy.'
⭐⭐⭐⭐⭐

'This is a cute, fluffy and tropey romance that happens to also include vampires. I thought it was so much fun, and the perfect light-hearted read.'
⭐⭐⭐⭐⭐

'*My Big Fat Vampire Wedding* is a wonderfully fun, cozy and romantic read. Pandora is lovely and I really enjoyed seeing her and Victor's relationship unfold. Her family is brilliant, the vampire references were great, and her best friend was so funny.'
⭐⭐⭐⭐⭐

'This is a delightful five-star read.'
⭐⭐⭐⭐⭐

'This book was the exact kind of chaos my romantic heart needed. It's delightfully campy, sharp-witted, and filled with just enough angst to make you feel things under all the laughter and fang-flashing flirtation. The romance is exactly my kind of slow-burn-to-sizzle.'
⭐⭐⭐⭐⭐

'I was honestly hooked from the first few chapters. I loved all the characters especially the eccentric aunties and uncles. I was rooting for pandora and victor the whole way through.'

MY BIG FAT
Vampire
WEDDING

Jessica Gadziala is a *USA Today* bestselling author who lives in rural New Jersey with her parrots, dogs, and an ever-growing collection of houseplants. A lifelong dreamer, she's been writing stories since childhood and published her first book in 2015. When not at her desk, she's usually feeding backyard birds, rewatching crime dramas, period pieces, and 90s supernatural TV shows, or adding to her towering stacks of unread books.

JESSICA GADZIALA

MY BIG FAT
Vampire
WEDDING

avon.

Published by AVON
A division of HarperCollins*Publishers* Ltd
1 London Bridge Street
London SE1 9GF

www.harpercollins.co.uk

HarperCollins*Publishers*
Macken House, 39/40 Mayor Street Upper
Dublin 1, D01 C9W8, Ireland

1

A catalogue record for this book is available from the British Library.

ISBN: 978-0-00-876228-5

Set in Sabon LT Std by HarperCollins*Publishers* India

Printed and bound in the UK using 100% Renewable
Electricity at CPI Group (UK) Ltd

To the bloodthirsty romantics, this one's for you.

1

The whole situation was hopeless.

Pandora wiped the counter for the twentieth time in as many minutes, frustrated that the overnight shift at the coffee shop didn't give her the rush of customers to distract her from the swirling thoughts stirred up by the impromptu meeting with her family just before her shift had started.

Wasn't it just like immortal creatures who'd had, oh, a hundred and twenty-four years to outline the exact parameters for inheriting her rightful fortune to wait until three months before her birthday to give her the news?

"You know, darling, this is the way things have always been. I don't know why you are acting like it is such a surprise," her mother had said. The words came out slurred, thanks to unusually large fangs that Pandora suspected were surgically enhanced, though her mother would never admit to such a thing.

"All right," Pandora's manager, Lucy, said, interrupting the whirling thoughts that were threatening to work themselves up into an outright cyclone. "What's going on?" She reached up to pull her thick sable hair into a clip. Pandora had long envied that hair, wondering if the thickness and its ability never to frizz even in the relentless autumnal London rain were due to Lucy's werewolf genes.

Pandora's own deep-red hair threatened to puff up just from standing over the milk steamer for too many mixed drinks.

"It's nothing." Even Pandora heard the defeat in her own voice.

Lucy's brows rose above her golden-brown eyes. Pandora knew her friend well enough to know that she would never let something go when her curiosity was piqued. *A dog with a bone, if you will.*

"My parents," Pandora said.

"Uh-oh. What did they do now? Replace your bed with a coffin again?"

That had been a whole month-long ordeal where her parents had gone on and on about how important traditions were, while Pandora had insisted that coffins just weren't comfortable. *Was it her fault she liked to sleep on her side?*

"No, they just told me that there's some fine print on my inheritance."

"What kind of fine print?" Lucy asked as she straightened the coffee syrups. They were running dangerously low on spiced chai.

2

"Oh, you know, nothing crazy. Just that I have to be married to receive it."

"Wait. What? Married? Your birthday is in—"

"Three months. And I'm, you know, single. Hopelessly, miserably single."

"Well," Lucy said, smirking. "At least you'll have eternity to enjoy your upcoming poverty."

"What is the point of living forever if I am going to be working for minimum wage? Can you picture it? Me, three hundred years old, scavenging around the shops for discount blood."

"Type O-So-Pathetic." Lucy laughed.

"It's not funny," Pandora grumbled as she smacked Lucy with a tea towel.

"It's actually hilarious. Don't they say that love strikes when you least expect it? Given your recent dating record, maybe you're due to actually find someone."

"Gee, thanks," Pandora said with a miserable little laugh.

She had to admit that Lucy was right about her love life. Or complete and utter lack of it, to be more accurate. What could she say? It wasn't easy to meet people when you were of the nocturnal variety. Unless, of course, she wanted to date a fellow vampire.

She didn't, for the record. At least not any of the vampires that she'd met so far. Much to her family's dismay. They'd spent the last fifty years trying to set her up with everyone, from some slimy vamp who'd claimed to be a direct descendent of Dracula himself – *yeah, right* – to some random vampire they'd met at a blood bar who'd been old enough to be Pandora's grandfather.

Was it too much to ask for sparks and butterflies? And

3

not having to try to figure out the schematics of trying to get all glandular with each other in a coffin?

"Just trying to be realistic here," Lucy said. "You know what? I think I just found the perfect guy." She gave Pandora ridiculously cheesy eyebrow wiggles and a nod toward the front of the shop.

Pandora turned around, trying not to seem too obvious. Her gaze slid out of the front windows.

The sun had been set for hours, but the lights lining the street illuminated the steady trickle of rain, soaking the colourful leaves scattered on the pavement.

Droplets slipped down the windows as Pandora finally spotted the man Lucy was talking about.

It took everything in her not to burst out laughing.

Because there, sitting at his usual table near the front of the shop, was one of their regulars. A man with a personality as dry as a sheet of paper and a tendency to noisily blow his nose into a filthy-looking handkerchief every few minutes.

Not to mention that he had a love of blue polka-dots and green-and-red tartan. Often at the same time.

Or the fact that he had not only a crop of white hair on top of his head, but also no small amount growing out of his nose and, somehow, his ears.

"Listen," Pandora said, turning back to Lucy, pressing her lips together to keep from smiling. "I might be desperate, but I haven't quite hit rock-bottom yet. If I propose to anyone, it'll be someone . . . someone like—"

"Like the guy you're secretly obsessed with?" Lucy shook her head at Pandora. She'd made her feelings known about Pandora's crush and adamant refusal to do anything about it. Often.

4

"Shh!" Pandora's head whipped around, making sure no one, least of all said guy, was hanging around, listening to them. "I'm not obsessed with anyone!" she said, even as her mind filled with images of a certain someone who was almost an hour late for his usual trip into the shop. "I'm just going to have, you know, some standards here."

"Yeah, I mean, maybe it's better if it isn't the young, handsome, smart guy you've been drooling over for the past few months, who doesn't know you're a vampire. The old dude is definitely the better bet. With any luck, he'll slip away peacefully in his sleep before you even have to consummate the marriage."

"You're so mean."

"I like to think I'm practical," Lucy said. "A dead husband means you technically got married, like your parents want, so you get your inheritance. But you also are free as a bird to pursue Caramel Macchiato Cutie," she added, using the nickname Pandora had coined for the customer who'd been coming in every night for months.

Pandora shook her head. "I'm not going to pursue anyone."

"Even though you're hopelessly, miserably single?"

"Even though," Pandora said. "Being unhappily single doesn't mean I'm not going to be, you know, a little selective."

"Should probably be more than a little selective." A third voice joined the conversation, making Lucy's golden eyes brighten, and a strange shiver moved up Pandora's spine. She knew that voice.

She'd had many steamy dreams featuring it, his lips near her ear as he whispered words that had her pulse thrumming and butterflies swooping in her belly.

That was Caramel Macchiato Cutie's voice.

All baritone and rumbly.

Pandora whipped around to find him right on the other side of the counter. They really needed to get some bells on that door or something.

Caramel Macchiato Cutie stood there in all of his rain-soaked glory. He was tall and lean under the dark jeans and emerald-green jumper that made his light green eyes pop all the more.

Pandora would bet good money – that she didn't have – on there being some delicious muscles under those layers of clothes. Or, at least, that was what her fantasies suggested. Often. In great detail.

He had a sharp jaw, generous lips that were prone to frowning, and a brow that could be called nothing other than "broody". Looking very much like a dreamy Mr. Darcy had stepped out of the pages of the Jane Austen novel and into a little all-night coffee shop in modern-day London.

In short, the guy was Pandora's dream man come to life.

And there he was.

Three feet away.

While she talked about her embarrassing little predicament.

"Oh, uh, didn't realize you were . . . right there. Hear much?" Pandora asked, stomach twisting in knots, begging him to have just walked up right then.

"Just the part about you being miserably single."

Those were more words than she'd ever heard him speak. Normally, he gave out one- or two-word answers at best. She'd never got to appreciate just how appealing his voice was. The sound of it shivered down her spine, despite her humiliation. Her fantasies were going to get some updating.

"Oh, fantastic," Pandora said, feeling a little queasy. And vampires weren't even *supposed* to get nauseated.

"This is going great!" Lucy said, beaming, looking close to clapping her hands, like this was one of the beloved rom-coms they were both always reading. And not Pandora's embarrassing real life.

"Your usual?" Pandora managed to squeak to Caramel Macchiato Cutie, desperate to get this awkward interaction over with.

He gave her a nod before walking over to his table, pulling off his backpack, and unpacking a laptop, several books and a notebook full of colourful tabs. She had no idea what he was working on, but she loved to watch him deep in thought, the way his brows pinched in concentration as he flipped the pages of a book while his other hand moved frantically over the page.

"Kill me now," Pandora grumbled under her breath as she reached for a paper cup featuring a seasonal flock of bats. The irony was not lost on her.

"You're already dead." Lucy passed Pandora the caramel syrup. "Besides, I changed my mind. You're not going to marry Charlie," she said, glancing back over at the sound of the older gentleman blowing noisily into his handkerchief. Then, as if that wasn't bad enough, inspecting the fabric before shoving it into his pocket.

"No, I'm definitely not," Pandora said, wrinkling her nose as Charlie ran his, likely snotty, hand over the table, tapping his fingers lazily on the surface.

Lucy smiled. "You're going to marry Caramel Macchiato Cutie."

"I am definitely not marrying Caramel Macchiato Cutie," Pandora said, catching a glance at herself in the windows as she passed, her stormy blue eyes looking a little too sad at that declaration as she actively tried to ignore the way that her words caused a pang in her chest.

2

The first rays of sunlight pierced the horizon, golden and amber shards slicing through the indigo of the fading night, like the day itself was unfurling, when Pandora finally made her way out of the coffee shop.

The rain had finally relented, but puddles dappled the pavement, making the orange, red, and yellow leaves too soggy to step on and get that satisfying crunch.

Pandora sighed as she took the stairs down to the Tube, her footsteps sounding as sluggish and heavy as her spirit felt right then.

It was bad enough that her parents had dropped this bomb on her right before her shift, but then Lucy had spent hours gushing about her happily ever after with Caramel Macchiato Cutie. A future that Pandora knew she could never have.

First, because he was a human. While Pandora was

very much a modern vampire who thought the world was ready for vampires to "come out of the coffin", the fact of the matter was that wasn't the reality. There were vampire laws and stuff. Most of them having to do with the fact that vampires couldn't let the humans know they existed.

The Council wasn't exactly clear on why. And everyone was too scared of getting in trouble with them to question further. Word on the street was that the Council members were ancient. Almost primordial. With crazy powers. Sure, all vampires were super-fast and strong, and had acute senses. But the rumors were that the oldest vampires could turn you to dust with their bare hands, could practically hear the whispers of your internal thoughts.

Though it was impossible to tell if that was just hearsay or based on any kind of truth.

Still, the rules existed. Humans couldn't know. Or, at least, they couldn't know for *long*.

If, for some reason, someone needed a human to know about vampires – for blood donation, for example – they had to be glamoured again afterwards. Which, basically, was some weird trick done with the eyes to make a human do or think whatever the vampire wanted.

And the Council wanted humans to only know about vampires momentarily.

Anything else was against their laws.

Caramel Macchiato Cutie could never know she was a vampire.

And, second, because, well, he had never shown any interest in simply interacting with her, let alone any desire to ask her out.

That idea, of course, brought with it a barrage of insecure thoughts. She couldn't help but pick herself apart. The way her deep-auburn hair was always either frizzy or in a tangle; how her curves weren't quite as pronounced as her mother's were; how she was always kind of awkward and shy when she longed to be extroverted and bold.

"Enough," Pandora mumbled to herself as she felt the vibration of the train making its way toward the platform.

She'd always liked the Underground in the wee hours of the morning – full of serious early risers ready to head out and seize the day, rubbing shoulders with the night owls who were stumbling home from clubs or parties in their short dresses and smudged make-up, all bleary-eyed yet punchy from lack of sleep.

"Repent!" a voice bellowed, making Pandora squeeze her eyes shut as she tilted her head back.

Not again.

"The day of reckoning has come!" His shouts startled the nearest commuters, making them scurry away from the man with the unruly beard and tattered clothes as he threw his arms in the air. "The wicked must be cast into the fire! Demons walk among us. Do you hear me? Demons! You!" he hissed, his voice dropping to an eerie whisper.

Here we go, Pandora thought, pulling her jacket more tightly around her. She wasn't cold. She couldn't feel the cold. But she attempted to feel less exposed in the face of the man who saw her for what she really was.

"I see you, demon. How dare you wear the skin of the living?" he snarled at her. "You will burn in the fires of judgment."

11

A ripple of discomfort passed through the small crowd, every one of them averting their eyes and pretending not to notice. Londoners were practiced in the art of avoidance.

Pandora set to ignoring him as well.

But the man kept approaching, holding out a Bible toward her that was making her skin start to crackle at its nearness.

"I see you, demon. You can't have my soul!"

Like she wanted his soul.

Though she was getting hungry enough to want a little nip and sip.

But she didn't eat people. No matter how ravenous she felt.

She ducked her head to avoid eye contact as the train pulled up, kicking up a cool wind.

"Be gone, demon!" he shouted from just behind her as the train doors opened and a crowd hurried inside, happy to be away from the man with the crazed eyes. "Back to hell!"

She was already there, she thought, as she moved with the rest of the crowd into the train, finding a seat and keeping her gaze down, paranoid that someone might look at her and see the truth of the man's words.

"She will feast on you all!" he yelled through the doors, making a few people shift in their seats, likely hoping he wouldn't come on the train with them. "May God have mercy on your souls!" The doors finally slid closed, silencing the man as he continued to rant.

Pandora leaned back in her seat as the train started to surge forward.

That had been the fourth time this month that someone had shouted at her from the train platform or in the street.

12

Or, once, while she'd been passing a church as people had been leaving.

It was definitely on the rise. Pandora suspected that it was a sign the world was changing: people were becoming more aware of the fact that they weren't alone, that the creatures they read about in their novels and watched in their films weren't just figments of someone's imagination, but actual beings who walked among them.

Though, so far, the only ones who seemed to spot her for who she really was were those that society considered crazy. That inclination worked in her favor.

Pandora reached into her purse, pulling out the well-worn paperback, its pages soft from time, its once crisp edges now rounded and frayed from countless hands. The cover of the book, a bodice-ripper straight out of the late twentieth century, featuring a woman with a generous heaving bosom and a shirtless man with long, glorious hair, was faded and creased with a web of fine lines. She lovingly stroked her hand over them, thinking of how the outside hinted at the countless stories of its travels that were just as vivid as the story within.

The spine was woefully cracked, each break a testament to a reader who'd been unable to put it down, who'd been too engrossed to treat it with care.

Pandora had picked it – and others just like it – from a box she'd found on the street, the previous owner's family ready to just throw the goldmine away.

Once she finished it, she would use a specialized book tape to fix the spine as best she could. Then it would go on the shelf with all of the others. Ones she desperately hoped she could share with the masses, each one a little piece of a dream she wasn't sure she could see becoming a reality. At least not without the inheritance it now seemed unlikely she was going to be able to receive.

She forced the thoughts away, trying to concentrate on the story at hand. There was a kidnapped maiden to be found by the roguish hero, after all. Lucy said they had some of the best steam she'd read in a historical romance in ages.

And Pandora couldn't help but keep inserting herself as the maiden and Caramel Macchiato Cutie as the moody, dirty-talking hero.

"Ugh." Grumbling, she slipped the sugar packet functioning as a bookmark back in between the yellowed pages, then put the book in her handbag as the train came to a stop.

She had a long walk ahead of her.

Sure, she could grab a black cab. But it would cost precious money that she couldn't quite afford.

Besides, the walk might help to clear her head before she got home to face her parents.

She definitely couldn't talk to them when her emotions were high, or she would say something that would upgrade the cyclone to a category-five hurricane.

But why couldn't they just adjust to the changing times? Her mother was a modern woman in many ways. Why was she OK with this ancient, patriarchal, vampire bullshit?

Clearly, the walk wasn't helping at all. Only to make her even hungrier. She had a nice pint of relatively fresh blood waiting for her in the fridge, hidden by several bottles of wine. Because if her parents came across a container of pig's blood, they would dump it down the drain. They were purists. The only "good" blood was fresh from the vein of a human. Them finding out she wasn't consuming human blood would just lead to yet another argument.

An argument that she didn't have the energy for.

Hopefully, a little sustenance would help the situation. Then – *then*, she could sit her parents down and try to talk some sense into them.

3

The Von Ashmore estate loomed like a shadow against the sky, casting a threatening gloom across the grounds. Spired turrets clawed at the heavens, their ornate wrought-iron accents tangling with the thick green ivy that coursed along the stones like veins.

The mansion's façade was weathered by centuries of wind and rain, bearing the scars of time, little cracks that bloomed across the grey stone surface.

There was something truly beautiful about its imperfections. Dignified and timeless, it wore its age like a cloak.

Though, to humans, it had all of the spooky and none of the charm. There was some sort of glamour on it that kept people from getting too close. Just a glance at it would send a shiver down their spines, would nudge their fight-or-flight instincts until they felt the need to flee.

The cobblestone path snaked up toward the heavy oak

front door. The stone surfaces were slick with the recent rain and the moss that crept across them, making Pandora slide a bit as she walked.

Tall, skeletal trees loomed overhead, their limbs twisted and gnarled as if they were writhing in pain. The last few orange leaves still clinging to them rustled with quiet promise as the wind swept across them.

Pandora made her way to the entrance, the door groaning under its own weight as she pushed open the brass doorknob.

The inside was cast in shadows, like a secret that didn't want to be revealed.

The foyer stretched upward toward the vaulted ceiling, and heavy velvet burgundy drapes cascaded from the windows, blocking out even a hint of daylight. Only the flicker of candlelight illuminated the space, dancing behind glass sconces lining the walls, casting trembling shadows across the space.

The floor beneath Pandora's feet was gleaming black-and-white marble that led toward the grand staircase, its balustrade carved from dark mahogany, the spindles shaped into figures of coiled snakes, their teeth sharp and gleaming, ready to strike. Pandora could swear that sometimes you could practically see the venom glinting from those fangs.

She had lived through nightmares about those snakes suddenly coming alive, slithering up into her room, then wrapping around her limbs, coiling tighter and tighter until the pressure made her implode.

The air in the space always seemed oppressive, like the house itself was holding its breath.

Above her head, the chandelier hung lazily from the

ceiling. Whenever someone walked across the floor above, the chandelier would sway, its crystal pendants clanking lightly. It was a sound that made Pandora think of bones knocking together.

To the right of the staircase, an arched doorway opened into the sitting room. Everything was upholstered in black velvet, the furniture all stiff and angular, the kind of seating meant to be looked at, not necessarily sat upon.

A massive fireplace yawned at the far end of the room, the grate in front of it a pattern of vines and thorns. When a fire was lit, the shadows of those vines crept across the walls like some spooky children's story.

Above the mantel was a timeless painting of a woman, her skin ashen and framed in deep auburn hair, her distinguished grey-blue eyes on display.

That was Ambrosia Von Ashmore, Pandora's great-great-grandmother. A woman so revered in their household that they spoke her name with awe. Despite the fact that no one had ever even met her.

Pandora hated that painting. And the way Ambrosia's eyes seemed to follow her around the room. She swore that if she could just look over quickly enough, she could catch the painting blinking.

Dark wooden bookshelves lined the walls, their shelves bowing under the weight of ancient leather-bound tomes.

These were not the kinds of books that Pandora enjoyed. These were her mother's books. Grimoires, alchemical texts, and records of family bloodlines long forgotten to anyone but their current caretaker.

Near one of the windows was her father's chess set, the pieces carved from bone. The white king was lying on its side in forfeit.

Not her father's.

He never conceded.

The game was never done until he'd won.

Dante, Pandora assumed, had given up. Her younger brother hadn't inherited their father's competitive spirit.

Down the hallway, the dining room was a cavernous space dominated by a table nearly as long as the room itself, its wooden surface polished to a mirror shine.

Pandora walked through the doorway into the kitchen. If it could even be called that. The space was fully functional, but devoid of the clutter of domesticity. Long, empty stone worktops sat unblemished by bowls of fruit, coffee makers, or microwaves.

The walls were lined with open shelving featuring glass jars full of herbs and powders.

Hanging over the island, a threatening display of knives hung like a butcher's chandelier, their edges menacingly sharp, their surfaces catching even the faintest slivers of light.

Pandora walked over to the fridge, reaching behind the bottles of wine until her fingers closed around the small plastic container of pig's blood.

She pulled it out, giving it a little shake, then removed the lid before taking a long swig.

She cringed as she sipped. At the taste. At the texture. But there was no easy way for her to heat up the blood, so she was just going to have to choke it down.

She could feel the vigor coming back as it absorbed into her system. She felt sharper and more alert as she walked over to the sink to rinse the plastic container, then drop it into her purse, so she could bring it with her to the butcher's shop where she bought her blood.

Sure, she could sometimes find some donated human blood to drink. But it was hard to come by and far too expensive for her budget. These days, she saved that for special occasions.

And learning she was about to lose her rightful fortune was certainly not a cause for celebration.

Pandora let out another long-suffering sigh before making her way up the servants' stairs at the back.

There was no use staying awake now. Her parents had likely been in their coffins for the past hour. Better she drag herself to her bed and get some sleep herself before confronting them again.

The second-floor hallways were narrow and labyrinthine, and the air was colder there, the silence thicker. The only sound to be heard was the creak of the floorboards as Pandora walked.

Everyone, even the house itself, seemed to be asleep.

Pandora passed endless doors. More bedrooms than they could ever use. Not even when the extended family came to visit.

But all of them felt cold and lifeless to her.

By contrast, she swore she could feel the pulse of her own room from several feet away. A small hint of life within the mausoleum they called a home.

She eagerly moved into her room, taking a figurative breath of fresh air.

There was brightness there.

She'd invested some of her salary after she'd started at the coffee shop on a specially-made film to cover her windows, so she could walk safely around her room in the daylight without concerns of getting burned or outright combusting from the unyielding sun.

There were no heavy drapes in here. Just thin sheers that allowed her collection of plants to get the light they needed to thrive, taking over nearly an entire wall of the room. More life. More things her parents didn't understand.

Her room actually had a bed, instead of a coffin. And what a bed it was. A colossal king-sized bed was centered in the space, with a golden four-poster frame featuring a canopy with drapery. But not in the somber shades of black, grey, and red that her family adored. Instead, it was all light, happy yellows and pinks, purples and blues.

"Oh, hello, Vlad," Pandora said when she heard the flutter of wings, making her turn to see her family's undead raven perched on the bed's canopy. "What are you doing in here?" She moved over to offer him her hand, waiting for him to step up before bringing him down.

He was a gorgeous bird, his feathers so black they seemed to drink up the surrounding light. As she shifted him around, he shimmered with hidden depths – iridescent swirls of purple and blue rippled across the surface of his feathers like oil spreading across water.

But the effect was fleeting, disappearing as soon as it appeared, leaving only shadow behind.

"How was your night?" she asked, reaching up to rub his head, loving the way he always leaned into the touch and let out little gurgling sounds.

"Got called *emo* by a bunch of stupid pigeons," Vlad said, making a snort escape Pandora.

"They're just moody because everyone calls them flying rats." She set him on the ornate brass perch her uncle claimed had once belonged to a king. But seeing as that same uncle also claimed to be in possession of several tomes from the actual Library of Alexandria before it had burned, she was dubious.

"Then I sat on a headstone and stared ominously at the groundskeeper for an hour or so. When he was good and spooked, I cawed at him. He dropped his rake and ran. It was a real highlight."

"You've been busy," Pandora said as she stepped inside her ensuite bathroom, closing the door so she could strip out of her work uniform and slip into a pair of pyjamas featuring festive jack-o'-lanterns.

"Saw a magpie stealing a ring off of a table," Vlad continued chatting as she made her way back out of the bathroom. "Considered starting a side hustle."

"What do you need a side hustle for?" Pandora asked as she climbed into her bed, sighing as the mattress curved around her frame. *Who would choose a coffin over this luxury?* "Mum spoils you rotten."

"For you," Vlad said, picking at the nuts in the food bowl at the end of his perch. "Since you're going to be disinherited."

"Gee, thanks for the reminder, Vlad," Pandora grumbled before breaking off into a big yawn.

"Someone has to help you pay for all those hideous pyjamas." Vlad started to preen his feathers.

Pandora pulled the covers up over her body, then rolled onto her side to hug her squishy pillow in the shape of a capybara.

It was right then that she heard the creak of the door across the hall.

Listening, she heard the distinct sound of footsteps making their way along the hall, then down the grand staircase.

Then, finally, the front door groaned.

Curious, Pandora climbed out of bed and crept into the hallway, pulling the curtain slightly to the side to see out into the grounds at the front of the house.

There, decked out in heavy layers and carrying an umbrella, despite the lack of rain, was her younger brother, Dante.

Where was he sneaking out to in the middle of the day?

Was that why he was always looking so exhausted recently?

The flap of wings had Pandora pulling away from the window. Turning, she saw Vlad making his way down the hallway, then around the bend, likely to perch outside of her parents' room, where he would sleep the day away and wait for them to emerge at dusk.

Pandora made her way back into her room, got back into bed, and started to drift off to sleep.

As she did, her mind was consumed with thoughts of Caramel Macchiato Cutie.

Inevitably, those same thoughts invaded her dreams as well. But those were scandalous, private little dreams that had her tossing and turning in her sleep.

4

Pandora woke up in the early afternoon, ready to shower, dress, and get herself mentally prepared for the discussion with her parents.

She was just making her way down the staircase when the front door creaked open, making the golden sun illuminate the foyer and casting the figure in the doorway in shadow.

"Dante?" Pandora said as he pulled the hood down from his head and looked over at her.

Dante had inherited his good looks from both their parents. He had their mother's flawless skin and her piercing blue eyes, but their father's sharp jaw and prominent brow.

It was a misconception that vampires only had "families" by biting and turning humans. Well, that was true enough. For most vampires. But the Von Ashmores were old-school. Interested in things like lineage and legacy. And they were wealthy enough to invest in the expensive magicks that would allow them to conceive. Sure, it was a lengthy and often difficult process. And then there was the awkward and rapid growth from baby to full-grown adult vampire, but it was possible.

Pandora and Dante were proof of that. As was much of their extended family.

"Were you out all day?" Pandora asked as her brother moved down the hallway toward the kitchen.

He ignored her question, though, as he went right to the fridge, digging around behind the bottles of wine.

"What are you looking for?" she asked.

"Nothing," he said, snatching his hand back and closing the fridge. "What are you lurking around for?" he asked.

"I'm waiting for Mum and Dad to wake up."

"Why?"

"To try to talk some sense into them." She sighed. "I don't have a lot of faith that it'll work, but I have to try."

"What do you need to talk sense into them about?" he asked, making her recall that he'd been suspiciously absent from the house when her parents had sat her down to break the bad news to her.

"My inheritance," she said. "And the specific clause around it."

"The one where you have to be married to receive it?"

"How did you know about that?" Pandora asked, throwing up a hand.

Dante furrowed his brow. "Because that's how it has been for centuries?"

Apparently, Pandora was the only one not paying attention. In her defense, there were spicy books to read. Tens

25

of thousands of them. It was actually one of the things she most looked forward to when it came to immortality.

"You know how they are, Pandy," Dante said, shaking his head. "They're not going to see reason about this."

"They have to," she said, a hint of panic sneaking into her voice. "I need that money."

Dante turned away from her for a moment, staring off at the house in general.

"So, get married."

A laugh burst out of Pandora at that. He couldn't have been so distracted by . . . whatever the hell he was doing all the time that he hadn't noticed she'd been single for, oh, ages.

"Oh, right. Just get married. To my invisible boyfriend. No big deal. Won't be suspicious at all."

"So, get a boyfriend."

"Maybe it's that easy for you, Dante, but I haven't dated anyone in forever. There's no reason to assume that string of bad luck is going to change in the next year, let alone three months."

"Fake it," Dante said, shrugging.

"Fake what? Dating?"

"Yeah. Find someone to date, then marry. Get your inheritance, then just break it off."

Pandora thought for a moment. That wasn't . . . outside the realm of possibility. Fake dating was the main plot of at least three-quarters of the romcom novels Lucy passed to Pandora once she was done with them.

But how did one realistically find someone willing to get into that sort of arrangement?

"Why would anyone ever agree to that?" Pandora asked, since Dante seemed to be full of answers.

"Pay him," Dante said.

"I don't have any money."

"From your *inheritance*, Pandy." Dante rolled his eyes at her. "Get someone to agree to it. Maybe someone who needs the money. Agree to some terms. Then parade him around the family like some epic whirlwind romance. Really sell it," he added. "You know how Mum is."

If by "how she is" Dante meant almost alarmingly perceptive and great at sniffing out a lie, then, yes, Pandora was painfully aware. Like the time Pandora had claimed she'd gone out all night hunting prey, only to have her mother take one sniff at her and know she'd spent the night at a coffee shop sipping chamomile tea and reading a book about rival dog groomers falling in love and living happily ever after.

"Then, once everyone is convinced, plan the wedding, get married, stay married for a while, get your money, and get a divorce. Claim things just didn't work out. You weren't compatible after all. Very sad and all that. Then just . . . take your money and live your undead life."

He made it all sound so doable. Easy, even.

And, hey, there had to be an endless pool of men who needed some extra cash just like she did.

She would have to work fast if she was going to do this.

"Dante, I think you may have just saved . . ." She trailed off at the sound of heels clicking across the tile floor.

Their mother was awake.

Awake and in heels within moments of climbing out of her coffin.

Ophelia Von Ashmore was nothing if not the most elegant woman in every room.

Pandora turned to see her mother move into the space,

27

her heels clicking, but she seemed to glide over. Her body was clad in a floor-length crimson velvet dress that hugged every curve. Her hair cascaded down her shoulders, perfectly styled even after a full night of lying in a coffin. Her porcelain skin contrasted stunningly against her inky brows and lashes, making her brilliant blue eyes stand out all the more.

Every time she looked at her mother, Pandora understood why their father remained so enamored with her even after centuries at each other's side. She was easily the most beautiful woman Pandora had ever seen.

"What have we here?" Ophelia asked in that smooth, sultry voice of hers, looking between her children, making Pandora resist the urge to squirm.

"Good evening, Mother," Pandora said, determined to act as if nothing was wrong at all. And, more importantly, that she wasn't scheming against the terms her parents – most especially her mother – had spelled out the night before.

"Pandora," Ophelia said, inspecting her eldest daughter from head to toe, making Pandora painfully aware of her jeans and simple black work T-shirt with Luna Bean's logo across her chest. And, perhaps most grievously in her mum's eyes, her white canvas trainers, complete with a coffee stain on one toe. "Have you recovered from last night's dramatics?"

"Hello, Mum," Dante said, drawing Ophelia's attention away from her daughter.

"Dante, my dear," Ophelia said, walking over toward her son with her hand outstretched, her stiletto-shaped nails painted the colour of fresh blood. She leaned in to press a kiss to his cheek, leaving red stains on his skin.

28

Ophelia had always had a soft spot for her son. Indulged his every whim. Forgiven every trespass.

Thankfully, Dante didn't use that favor against his sister. If anything, he attempted to distract their mother's attention away from Pandora whenever possible.

"Good evening, family." Pandora's father's voice boomed as he moved into the kitchen.

He, unlike their mother, had yet to dress for the day, moving into the space in black silk pyjamas and a cinched maroon dressing gown.

Lucian Von Ashmore was an intimidating man. Tall and fit, with dark brown hair, nearly black eyes, and classic, aristocratic features.

To others, Lucian was terrifying enough to make perceptive humans turn and run when faced with him in a dark alley.

To Pandora, he was a doting, loving father. Who indulged his daughter the same way their mother indulged Dante.

"My love, my eternal life," Lucian said, grabbing Ophelia, bending her backward, and placing a kiss on her lips.

A long one.

Long enough for Pandora to look away uncomfortably and Dante to reach up and rub a hand down his face.

"What are we discussing?" Lucian asked once he set his wife back onto her heels.

"I have yet to ascertain that, darling," Ophelia said, running a hand up her husband's chest.

"We were just catching up," Pandora said.

"Yep. Catching up."

"While on that topic," Ophelia said. "We will be having guests this weekend."

29

Pandora resisted a sigh, wondering which eccentric aunt, uncle, or distant cousin would be coming to stay.

Their last guest had been with them for two years and had had an alarmingly elaborate feeding ritual that included hours of chanting at the moon in dead languages before finally making his way out to find a vein to tap.

"Who?" Dante asked when Pandora was too consumed with the memory of some third cousin twice removed who'd shown up at their door with an entire suitcase full of teeth. Human? Animal? She'd had no idea. And he'd refused to explain further.

"Your aunt Anastacia and Uncle Alexander, along with that lovely daughter of theirs."

Lovely?

Pandora barely contained a scoff at the idea of that snobby, competitive, arrogant, tattling cousin of hers being considered "lovely".

True, it had been many decades since she'd seen that particular relation. But the last time her cousin had been there, she'd run to Ophelia to tell her that Pandora was playing with the human children instead of feeding on them like she was supposed to.

"I presume you will still insist on being out every night?" Ophelia asked, looking at Pandora.

"At work, yes."

"With that . . . dog." Ophelia sniffed.

"Mum, Lucy is a werewolf, not a dog. That's so . . . speciesist."

Her mother sighed dramatically at that but said no more, and Pandora made her excuses to get going before they could all start arguing again.

"Think about it," Dante said as they passed each other

in the hallway. "Then you're not under anyone's thumb anymore."

Oh, she was thinking about it, all right.

In fact, it was all she could think about as she walked toward the train, the leaves drifting lazily down around her.

It was the perfect plan.

If only she could find the right man for the job.

Caramel Macchiato Cutie immediately popped into her head – but, fine, she totally imagined him dressed in a parted white linen shirt à la Colin Firth, as Mr. Darcy, when he walked back after taking a dip in the lake.

She was quick to squash that fantasy, though.

He would never go for it.

He was so serious and studious.

That was not the kind of guy who would agree to some absurd fake-dating scenario. Even if she offered a ton of money for the inconvenience.

She was just going to have to find someone else.

No matter how much her heart ached at the idea.

But there it was, nestled on a narrow, cobblestoned street that looked untouched by time. The abandoned shop stood as a quiet monument to faded dreams. Its once-bright façade had been dulled by grime and streaks of soot, the peeling green paint exposing patches of weathered wood underneath.

A hand-painted sign hung precariously above the doorway, its cracked golden letters spelling out *Greyson's Toy Museum* in elegant script. Beneath it, the arched entrance was blocked by rusted shutters, locking it down tight.

The windows were the shop's saddest feature – large panes of glass fogged with age and smeared with streaks of dirt, revealing only faint shadows of the interior. There were spiderweb cracks branching out from one corner, like the store's heart was breaking with its own neglect.

A battered old noticeboard clung to the brick wall beside the door. Layers of faded posters with yellowing pages for events long past were still situated behind the protective glass.

Above it, a wrought-iron lantern leaned slightly to the side, but Pandora couldn't help but imagine it straightened, the glass cleaned, and the bulbs replaced, thinking of the romantic glow it would create in the evenings.

Pandora had always felt it was the kind of place where stories belonged.

She imagined the paint restored, the windows polished and sparkling, allowing passersby to look through and see the rows of carefully arranged bookshelves and displays featuring bookish merchandise. She thought of customers pulled inward with the promise of comfy chairs to sink into while they got lost in their next adventure.

Pandora forced her gaze away, the thought of reviving the shop filling her with a pang of longing, a bittersweet ache for the life and community she could build there if only she had the means to unlock its full potential.

If she couldn't find the right man to use to convince her family she loved him enough to marry him, any chance of her opening her dream bookshop would disappear.

Her gaze moved around the streets, wondering how she might pinpoint the kind of man she could approach. And what she could possibly say to them as an opener.

Hey, want to get married and inherit a fortune? was probably not the way to go.

Maybe she was going about this the wrong way. Surely,

the best person for the job was someone who was a really good liar. A professional liar, even.

An actor.

That would be the most convincing man for the job.

She could get Lucy to help set up auditions or something like that. That was the kind of thing that would be right up Lucy's alley. She would probably spend the whole shift working on the ad to put up online and deciding what questions they would ask Pandora's future husband.

Husband.

It was going to take some work to wrap her head around that idea. Time she didn't have. Because, with only a three-month deadline, she needed to meet, "fall in love with" – i.e. learn everything about and become really good at faking chemistry with – someone, and then plan and execute a wedding.

While, hopefully, staying sane.

Which, she thought, was not going to be easy once her family got wind of things.

But that was a bridge she could cross when she got to it.

She could only cross one at a time.

And right now, she needed to find her fiancé.

5

"I think we need to ask the hard questions up front," Lucy said, using the company clipboard to scribble her plans. "Your parents will sniff out a fraud in minutes. So we have to dig deep."

"Oh, please enlighten me, oh wise one," Pandora teased her friend as she refilled the tea caddy. "What are these hard questions?"

"Well, first," Lucy said, holding up a finger. "Can he hold a brooding stare for longer than thirty seconds without looking thick? Or, you know, constipated." A snort escaped Pandora. "Because you vampire types, you love a good brood."

Despite herself, Pandora's mind flashed to Caramel Macchiato Cutie. Who, she'd noticed on many an occasion, had the hot brooding-guy thing down pat.

But he wasn't in the running. And she needed to stop thinking about him.

"OK. Second question?"

"Can he deliver grand romantic lines and make them believable?"

"Like what?"

"Oh, maybe, 'My love, you are the moon to my eternal darkness.' But not be cringy about it. It's a critical skill."

"I don't talk like that," Pandora said, rolling her eyes at her friend.

Lucy ignored that, tapping her pen against her clipboard. "Third, what are his dance skills? The wedding is going to require dancing. And your parents are old-school. They are going to expect him to be able to do a standard waltz. Maybe a tango. Bonus points if he can do the spinny bit and doesn't get too green in the face."

"I concede that he needs to know, or learn, how to waltz," Pandora said. "But even I don't know how to tango."

"You've been alive one hundred and twenty-four years, and you haven't learned to tango?" Lucy asked, shaking her head. "What's next? You never learned to Cha-Cha Slide or the Macarena?" At Pandora's guilty look, Lucy sighed. "Well, I guess I know what we are doing on our next girls' night."

"I think I'd rather listen to one of my uncles talk about the 'good old days'," Pandora said.

"All right. Anyway. Back to our list. We can't forget possibly the most important skill of all. The smolder. Because all of this will be for nothing if he can't pull that off. I mean, if he doesn't look at you like the last drop of water in the desert, then what's the point? Your parents will never buy it."

That was fair.

Even just a normal vampire would pick up on there being no real chemistry between them. But before Pandora's mother had fallen in love with her father and agreed to become a vampire for him, she'd been a powerful succubus.

That meant she was not only insanely beautiful and alluring, and capable of using lust and love to entrance her targets, but she was also able to sense things like love and sexual attraction between others.

Sure, when her mother had become a vampire, some of her succubi powers had weakened. But Pandora was reasonably sure Ophelia could still sense attraction.

"Fine, yes, smolder. Anything else?"

"Plenty," Lucy said, checking her list. Which looked like it was three full pages. Front *and* back. "Let's talk fashion. Can he rock a waistcoat? Pull off a cravat? Gothic-chic is going to be needed at some point. Being able to wear it comfortably, so he doesn't seem like he's cosplaying, would be important."

Pandora would like to claim that things like clothing didn't matter. But her family was big on their fashion. Sure, that fashion was stuck in the Victorian period for many. And the Renaissance or Medieval periods for others. Still, it mattered to them.

Her mind flashed back to her mother's obvious displeasure about her work uniform earlier that evening. "All right. Maybe we can buy a nice suit and make the finalists try it on."

"Now you're getting on board," Lucy said, grinning.

"Are we setting the bar too high?" Pandora asked.

"Hey, if we are going to do this, we are going to do it right," Lucy said. "And when you are super rich and powerful, don't forget who helped you get there."

"Oh, I won't forget. Yours is the couch I will be sleeping on for eternity when all of this falls apart and my parents completely disown me."

"OK. Someone is getting grumbly. Are you hungry?" she asked. "I think your fangs are looking a little longer. You're probably hungry."

Pandora reached for her mobile, bringing up the camera and pulling up her lips to inspect her teeth. They looked perfectly fine to her.

"I'm going to go get some dinner," Lucy said. "A nice, juicy steak for me," she added, her eyes seeming to flash a little yellow at the idea of some relatively fresh meat.

Pandora noticed that her best friend's werewolf tendencies got stronger as the moon cycled toward full. From her estimation, they were two days away from the hunter's moon. Which meant that, for three nights in a row, she wouldn't see Lucy as she went and wolfed out with her pack.

"And a pint or so of some vein-vino for you," Lucy said, leaving her clipboard on the counter and going to grab her handbag. "Hold down the fort. And start to think about features. Do you want a brunette? A blond? Maybe even a redhead?" She made her way toward the front door, pulling it open and allowing the wind to send a small flurry of dried leaves into the shop, then disappeared out into the night.

Pandora was truly thankful for Lucy in times like these. She would normally be in an anxiety spiral, if not for Lucy's upbeat enthusiasm. But thanks to her encouragement,

Pandora was almost starting to believe she could pull this off.

Her best friend had spent the better part of an hour discussing all of the plots of the arranged-marriage books they'd read, and the mistakes that had made the situation-ships fall apart, so that Pandora would be smart enough to avoid them.

Even just ten minutes after Lucy had left, her uncertainty started to creep back in, making her set her mind to deep-cleaning to avoid overthinking things.

That was why she missed it when someone walked in.

"What is this?" a familiar voice called. She popped up so fast she whacked her head on the underside of the countertop, making pain ricochet across her scalp.

"Ow." She rubbed her head as she stood and turned to find Caramel Macchiato Cutie standing there.

With the clipboard in his hand.

Pandora squeaked. "Oh, um, notes."

He started to read out loud. "*Good at waltzing. Smoldering . . . delivering romantic lines . . .*"

"It's for a . . . er . . . play!" she said.

"You're putting on a play?" he asked, brows pinched.

"We're considering it." She took the clipboard out of his hands and stuffed it under the counter, hoping her embarrassment wasn't written all over her face. "The usual?" she asked, forcing her gaze to stay on his pretty eyes and not, under any circumstances, slip to those generous, frowning lips of his.

And she certainly couldn't let herself imagine reaching across the counter, grabbing him by the front of his shirt, dragging him halfway across the counter, and sealing her lips to his.

Or, at least, she couldn't let herself imagine that for long.

"Ah, yeah," he said, making her gaze flick up, realizing with no small amount of humiliation that she had, in fact, been watching his lips.

"Coming right up." Pandora slipped some extra cheerfulness in her voice, hoping it might distract him from the aforementioned ogling. "I was starting to think you weren't coming in tonight," she said as she pumped caramel syrup into his cup.

"Actually, this is going to be my last time," he said, making her head whip up.

"What?" she gasped out.

"Yeah, I, ah, it looks like I am going to need to drop out of UCL," he said.

"But why?"

"Out of money," he said, clearly trying to shrug it off, but Pandora could see how gutted he was.

Clearly, the guy was dedicated to his studies, whatever they were. He was there every single night, poring over his texts, writing endless notes, working hard toward whatever his goal was.

"I had held out hope for some grants to finish my PhD," he went on. "Just heard that the last one fell through. I'm already in debilitating debt. I can't take on any more loans. Gotta pack it up and head back home to live with my parents until I figure things out."

"I'm so sorry . . ." Pandora trailed off, hating that when he was admitting something so personal, she didn't even have his real name to try to comfort him with.

"Victor," he said. "What can you do? That's life, I guess." He tapped his card, then made his way over to his table.

Victor. Pandora had mused over what his name might be more times than she cared to admit. "Victor" had never made the list. Somehow, though, it was better than anything she'd dreamed up. But now she wouldn't get a chance to use it.

Pandora kept sneaking glances over at him as she went through the motions of making his macchiato for the last time.

Her heart twinged at that thought.

At the idea that this would be the last time she would ever see his face.

Unless . . .

No.

No, absolutely not.

Victor didn't seem like the kind of guy who would be willing to even entertain the thought of such an absurd plan, let alone actually go through with it.

But it would solve both of their problems, wouldn't it?

Pandora thought of Lucy's list, thinking that Victor certainly had the brooding thing down. And if his face in her fantasies was anything to go by, he could absolutely pull off a convincing smolder.

He was always dressed rather smartly, never coming in wearing something as casual as a tee like your typical university student. Pandora could absolutely see him rocking a waistcoat. Maybe even a cravat.

He didn't seem like the dancing sort, but she was sure that he could be taught a basic waltz. And she totally didn't want him to learn just because she wanted to feel his hand at the small of her back, his other one holding hers, their bodies pressed close as he moved her around the floor . . .

Pandora shook her head, trying to stop getting swept up in fantasies, so she could focus on the potential reality.

Victor needed money.

Pandora was just months away from having an astronomical sum of it.

A marriage could solve both of their problems.

It couldn't hurt to ask him, right?

The hot macchiato in her hand was excuse enough to go over and test the waters, see if he would even entertain a conversation about it.

He looked so dejected.

He didn't pull out his laptop or notebook, just sat there at his table, a closed book on the surface, his hand resting on top of it curled into a tense fist. His gaze was fixed on the wall, all of his defeat and disappointment etching sad lines in his forehead.

If there was one thing Pandora could relate to, it was the feeling of everything you ever wanted your whole life slipping away – all your dreams shattering around you.

The only good thing that came from that kind of destruction, by her estimation, was a bone-deep sort of desperation.

The kind of desperation that made her open to a fake marriage, to lying to her family, to living a lie herself.

The same kind of desperation she hoped might make Victor willing to hear her out. And not laugh in her face.

Rolling the tension out of her shoulders, Pandora moved out from behind the counter and made her way toward Victor's table.

It took him a long second to snap out of his own mind and notice she was standing there.

When he did, she could have sworn she saw something warm flash in his eyes. Though that was almost certainly her own wishful thinking.

"Victor," she said, passing him his coffee and then pulling out the chair opposite him to sit down. "I was wondering if I could discuss a potential . . . arrangement with you."

6

"An arrangement?" Victor asked, reaching for his macchiato. Their hands brushed on the paper cup, making a shiver course down Pandora's spine. She tried not to squirm in her seat. Or rub her thumb over the back of his hand like some creep.

"You see, those notes you were reading, they weren't actually for a play," she said, feeling like her belly was wobbling, knowing how she was opening herself up to ridicule if Victor thought she was peculiar.

"OK," he said, taking a sip of his coffee.

Pandora absolutely did not watch the way his Adam's apple bobbed as he swallowed. Because that would have been insane.

"What is it, then?" he said when she didn't immediately tell him.

"They're notes my friend Lucy and I are making up

for the perfect . . . OK." She paused, sucking in a deep breath. She didn't actually need to breathe, of course, but the more time she spent around humans, the more she picked up on the many ways they used breathing to express themselves.

Sighs, deep exhales, sucking in a deep breath to prepare to do or say something uncomfortable.

Besides, if she was going to be out in public with humans, she needed to act like them. She had long since made herself take occasional breaths in case anyone was watching her too closely.

"I just want to preface this by saying that I'm not, you know, bananas or anything."

"Always a great opener," Victor said, deadpan, starting to look like he was regretting agreeing to hear her out.

"It's going to sound ridiculous," she told him. "But I'm serious. The situation is serious."

"OK. What were the notes for, then?"

"We were compiling a list of potential traits for a husband." Pandora watched as Victor's brows rose and his eyes widened, clearly thinking she was not only ridiculous, but one of those pathetic, needy women who bordered on stalkers. "Not a real husband," she added hurriedly. "A fake one."

"For a book?" he asked, frowning. He clearly wanted to give her the benefit of the doubt here, but she was mucking it up.

"No, for the arrangement I mentioned," Pandora said. Then, resting her arms on the tabletop, she leaned forward. "I'm looking for someone to act like my fake husband."

To his credit, he only raised one brow at that.

"What for?"

"Well, see, my birthday is coming up. And, according to my parents, it's a very important birthday."

"Which one is it?" he asked.

"My one . . ." she started automatically, before catching herself. "My twenty-fifth."

"What's so special about that one?"

"It's when I'm supposed to get my inheritance," she told him, watching as surprise flashed across his gorgeous eyes. It wasn't every day that you heard someone was from that kind of wealth. Most people were just trying to get by.

"You're some kind of heiress?" Victor asked, likely trying to figure out why she was working at a coffee shop, then. But also probably assuming that wealthy people could be quirky and expect her to prove she was responsible enough for her wealth by working a normal job for a few years.

Pandora wanted to deny that.

But it was the best way to describe her situation.

"Yes," she said, nodding.

"I don't understand how a fake husband factors into any of this."

"Well, my family just informed me that to inherit my fortune, I need to be . . . married," she said, almost choking on the word. "I know." She shook her head at Victor's scrunched brows.

"That's some patriarchal bullshit," he said.

"That's what I said!" Pandora said, smiling at him for a second before trying to get serious again. "But my parents are . . . very traditional. They really dug their heels in about this. They won't hear of me inheriting if I'm not married."

"So you are going to *fake* being married?" Victor asked.

"Well, no. I actually have to be married. But the relationship itself will be, you know, fake. All for show, kind of thing."

"That's . . . a lot to take in," Victor said, twisting his coffee cup in slow circles on the surface of the table.

"I know. And it has to be convincing, which is why Lucy and I drew up the list."

"He has to . . . smolder?" Victor asked, a hint of teasing slipping into his tone.

"We kind of meant that he has to try to look at me like he's attracted to me," Pandora said.

"That shouldn't be hard. And waltzing?"

"Well, you know, like . . . wedding dances and such?"

"Guess that's also why there was a note about waistcoats and cravats?"

"Exactly," she said, nodding.

"And he has to have a tragic backstory?"

"What?" Pandora asked, brows raising. "No. No, that's not . . . mandatory. Lucy went a little crazy with her notes. We'd only gone over a few of them."

Victor nodded at that before sitting back.

"Why are you telling me all of this?" he asked, watching her with those verdant eyes of his. She'd imagined just this moment countless times before, what it might feel like to have his undivided attention, to see his gorgeous eyes looking at her like he was truly seeing her, not just glancing at her from the other side of the counter.

It was better than she'd imagined.

She had a sinking feeling, though, that what she was about to say was going to make him roll those eyes, tell her she was absurd, then rush out of the shop.

"Well, after hearing about your . . . predicament,

I was starting to think we might be able to work together toward a common goal."

"What goal is that?"

"My inheritance."

Victor shook his head at her, making her stomach bottom out before he spoke. "I think I'm missing something here. Why does your inheritance have anything to do with me?"

"Well, you clearly need some money so you can go back to university. I'm about to come into a lot of money."

"Wait . . . You want to pay me to—"

"Marry me, yes." Pandora watched him, half expecting him to burst into laughter.

"You're serious," he said, leaning forward, bringing with him the scent of his cologne that she'd never been close enough to catch before. It was a cozy, warm scent. Leather, vanilla, and a hint of cinnamon. Pandora wanted to press her face into his neck, to breathe him in, to . . .

No.

Nope.

She couldn't let her mind go there.

"I am very serious," she told him. "I need my inheritance. My parents aren't budging. And I am single. I really can't think of any other way to handle this."

Victor sat with that a second, his gaze moving past her, staring at the back wall, giving Pandora the opportunity to gaze at him without being seen as a complete creep.

She could see the gears turning in his mind, could picture him trying to sift through all of the reasons this was a terrible idea. He didn't know her. She could be lying to him. He might waste precious time of his life all for nothing.

But she thought she could see the moment when he latched on to the possibility of this arrangement.

Going back to uni. Finishing his PhD. Which, in turn, would likely mean he would be able to work toward his dream job, whatever that was.

Not having to go back and live with his parents. *Not* being stuck in a dead-end job. *Not* having all his dreams shatter down at his feet.

His green eyes cut back to hers.

"What is the catch?"

"There is no catch. Well, I mean, obviously, there are, you know, things we would need to iron out."

"Such as?"

"Getting to know each other. This has to be convincing. My mum is really good at sniffing out lies. We have to have some 'getting to know each other' dates, so we can stand up to any sort of questioning."

"That makes sense," he said. "What else?"

"We would have to go through all of the wedding planning together. Decor, cakes, engagement parties, the whole thing."

"OK. What then? We fake a relationship, convince your family, what then?"

"Then we get married," she said, watching something flash across his eyes, but it was gone too quickly to pin down just what it had been. "For a set period of time. A year seems . . . fair. Long enough to convince my family we gave it a real chance. Short enough that it doesn't feel like we're losing a chunk of our lives."

To her utter amazement, Victor just nodded at that. He wasn't laughing in her face. Or, worse yet, running out of there while telling her how bizarre she was.

"But how long would the engagement charade go on beforehand?"

"That's probably the best, or worst – depending on how you look at it – part," Pandora told him. "My birthday is in three months. I have to be married *before* then."

"How are you going to convince your parents that you went from single to ready to be married in such a short period of time, though?"

"Well, they're sort of . . . romantics," she said. "They got engaged on their first date." She left out the fact that they'd stayed engaged for fifty years before they'd finally made things official. And that they'd needed to postpone the wedding because the witch trials had been sweeping through Europe and it had been too risky to have so many vampires and succubi gather in one place at one time.

"My parents are . . . less so," Victor said. "They sort of run their marriage like a business," he added, the distaste clear in his voice.

There she was, asking him to do the same thing.

"I understand if that is not something you want."

"But it's not a real marriage. It's just, like you said, an arrangement."

"Exactly," she said. "Though I'll be honest and say I didn't consider the fact that you would also need to lie to your family and friends. I can see that being a dealbreaker."

"It's really just my mum and dad," he told her. "We don't have much family. And my best friend. That's it. It wouldn't be that bad."

He seemed to genuinely be considering it.

Pandora felt hope surge but tried to tell herself not to let it run away with her.

Of course she would prefer to be fake-dating Victor. If

he decided this wasn't for him, though, she was going to have to be OK with it being someone else.

"I . . . er . . . I have a *lot* of family," Pandora said. "Just wanted to give you all of the facts. Half a dozen aunts and uncles. Even more cousins and distant relations. And most of them will likely be attending wedding festivities."

"Consider me forewarned," Victor said, though Pandora thought he seemed visibly less comfortable compared to a few moments ago.

He didn't exactly strike her as a people person. Which was fine. She was usually talkative enough for two. Besides, it wasn't like he would be around her family constantly. In fact, it was in everyone's best interest if they interacted as little as possible.

She would just have to claim that Victor was very busy with his studies, if her family kept wanting to have him over.

"If I agree, how would we go about this?" Victor asked. "I feel like things need to be as official as possible, when we are both going to be spending a year faking this."

"I think it's probably smart if we draft up a document and sign it. I don't know if that is legally binding or anything if we don't go to a lawyer, but it's better than nothing. I mean, we could totally go to a lawyer, I guess. I was just kind of worried about this, you know, getting out, and my parents maybe hearing—"

"An informal contract will be fine," Victor cut her off. "What would that document entail?"

"The exact parameters of the engagement. One-year commitment from the day we are married. What is expected: wedding festivities, living together after the wedding to really sell it, then the dissolution of the marriage and my giving you half of my inheritance."

"I wouldn't be chuffed taking half of it," Victor said. If possible, she just fell a teensy bit harder for him. He didn't even know how much she would be getting and, therefore, how much he was forfeiting. He didn't care. He just wanted things to be fair.

"OK. Well, we can work out exactly how much. How much you will need to finish your PhD, for example. Plus a food, living, and clothing stipend."

"I thought you said I would be living with you."

Pandora felt a warm sensation in her chest at all the images that thought conjured up. The two of them standing side by side in the kitchen, waiting for the coffee to brew. Sitting with each other on the couch, each lost in their respective books. Heading down the hallway toward the bedroom . . .

But just as many negative thoughts flooded her mind. Where would she hide her blood, for example, while she was living with Victor? How much human food that she didn't need, or particularly enjoyed, would she have to choke down? What if he *caught her* drinking blood?

"Pandora?" Victor called out, snapping her out of the tsunami of bad thoughts. That warm feeling crept across her chest again at the sound of her name on his lips. She hadn't realized he *knew* her name.

"Yeah?" she asked, suddenly aware she'd been staring at him. Likely with hearts in her eyes.

"Living expenses."

"Oh, right. So, like, retroactive ones. For this time period between now and when we actually get married. Since, normally, you would be going back home."

"I have some savings," Victor said. "I was going to use them to buy a car to maybe travel back and forth from my parents' place and London. I've really become attached to the area. But I can use it to live on for a few months."

"What about UCL?"

"I'm paid up until the end of the autumn term," he said. "I was just going to leave early, since there seemed to be no use finishing it up if I was out of money anyway."

"That works out perfectly, then. You can keep going to uni. I will keep working here. And then we can move in together once we're married."

"In three months," he said.

"Yes."

"This is mad," he said, watching Pandora with a mix of amusement and disbelief.

"It really is. But?" she prompted him.

"But it seems like it's the answer to both our problems. One year," he said, holding out his hand to shake.

Pandora felt a fluttering sensation move through her belly as she pressed her hand into his. "One year."

"I guess there is only one more thing to say," Victor declared as Pandora saw Lucy walking past the windows.

Her friend froze, turned, and stared at the two of them, with their hands still clasped, her mouth falling open in a comical O.

"What's that?" Pandora asked.

"Will you marry me?"

7

"That's what you're wearing?" Lucy asked the following evening, her gaze panning down over Pandora's work uniform over which she'd thrown a warm red cardigan that had been a gift from her mother – a woman who believed only three colours existed: black, grey, and red.

"What's wrong with it? He's seen me in it every day since he started coming to the shop."

"Therein lies the problem," Lucy said with a huff. "This is your first date. You need to look the part."

"Luce, it's a *fake* first date," Pandora said, reminding her friend.

Lucy frowned. "It's still supposed to *look like* a real first date."

She had a point.

Would her parents be suspicious that she hadn't at least

gone home to run a brush through her hair and slapped on something cute? Maybe a little make-up or perfume.

That was the kind of thing Ophelia would find suspicious. Even with her strange, nontraditional daughter.

Every woman wanted to look as nice as possible for a date, right?

"I mean, you've been alive, what? One hundred and twenty-four years. You've got to have some cute outfits in your wardrobe. But to be clear." Lucy held up a hand, a smirk on her lips. "By 'cute outfit' I don't mean one of those floor-skirting numbers from the nineteen hundreds, when ankles were the epitome of sexy scandal."

To be fair, Pandora had chests full of clothing from her long life. Even her first pair of pants, when those had finally become acceptable for women to wear.

But, well, she'd also always been a creature of comfort. Meaning almost everything she did have was of the casual variety, not the kind of things she'd wear on a first date.

"OK, come on," Lucy said, slinging her handbag up on her shoulder. The two of them had swapped shifts with the afternoon staff because of Pandora's date and Lucy's need to head out of town for the full moon. Thankfully, the awnings on the windows made it possible for Pandora to be inside without burning when the afternoon sun beat down on the street. "I'll give you a ride home before I head out to the country."

"OK." Pandora grabbed her own bag before following her friend toward the front door.

Lucy was parked on the street right out front, having nabbed a coveted spot between the lunch and afternoon rush, and the sun had just about set, so Pandora didn't need to duck and run like hell.

"What?" Pandora asked when Lucy just sat there behind the wheel.

"I've never been to your house," Lucy said. "I need directions."

"Oh, right." Pandora shook her head at herself before telling Lucy which way to go.

She wondered if she should invite Lucy in, as they made their way down the street toward her house. Her aunt, uncle and dreaded cousin weren't supposed to be there for another day, but they could have shown up while Pandora had been at work. And the last thing she wanted to worry about right then was her family potentially showing prejudice toward Lucy because she was a werewolf.

In Pandora's opinion, the whole vampire–werewolf-rivalry thing was completely overblown and ridiculous. But she knew some of her family would have things to say.

She knew she would have to deal with that eventually, since Lucy was going to be her chief bridesmaid. She just didn't want that kind of thing to sour her mood right before her first, very important, date with Victor.

"I hope you don't mind me just dropping you off," Lucy said. "I'm racing the clock here." She looked down at her watch.

"That's totally fine," Pandora said, thankful not to have to find an excuse for why she wasn't inviting Lucy in. "That's it right there." She pointed toward the Von Ashmore estate.

"That's your house?" Lucy gaped.

"Technically, it's my parents' house," Pandora said, nodding.

"It's a castle."

Having visited many a castle in her travels with her

parents, Pandora couldn't agree with that, but it was definitely much larger than the average London home, that was for sure.

"Out of curiosity, is there a hunched man in the belfry?"

"We don't have a belfry," Pandora said with a little chuckle. "But we do have an undead raven who likes to recite poetry."

"I mean, who doesn't?" Lucy smiled at her friend. "All right. Go. Get something pretty on. Preferably something that shows Victor your *hunter's moons*." she purred as Pandora climbed out of the car.

"Have a good full moon," Pandora called to her friend, eyes rolling, before rushing up the cobblestone path toward the front door.

"Whoa," she said a moment later, nearly trampling Dante as she made her way inside.

Her brother jolted, turning around to look at her with oddly guilty eyes.

What *was* he up to these days?

It looked like he'd been out all day again.

And he looked a little paler than usual.

"What are you doing coming in at this time?" he asked, sounding accusatory. Meanwhile, he was the one being sneaky.

"I have a date," Pandora said, feeling herself straighten a bit with her excitement.

"A real date?"

"It's a real date with a real man, yes," she said.

"A man?" Dante asked, brows lifting. "A human man?"

"Yes . . ."

"Good luck with that," he said, wincing, then rushed up the stairs before she could ask him to clarify.

56

Trying to shake off the interaction, Pandora made her way up to her room, immediately starting to fret over her wardrobe.

She didn't want to put on one of the many floor-length, figure-hugging, silk or velvet dresses her mother had gifted her over the years. But she didn't want to be wearing jeans and a tee, either.

Eventually, she settled on a simple plum-coloured dress and leggings with some low-heeled boots and a heavy cardigan to complete the look.

Dressy, but not trying too hard.

She fiddled with her hair and make-up, spritzed on some perfume, then rushed back out of her room, knowing she had to take the Underground back toward Luna Bean to meet Victor.

"Well, don't you look lovely?" her father called from the sitting room as she rushed past, making her pause and turn to give him a smile.

"Thank you."

"Where are you going?" Ophelia asked, her gaze sliding down Pandora's outfit with more approval than usual.

"I have a date," she said. She didn't even have to fake the smile that tugged at her lips.

"A date?" her mother asked, perfectly arched brows lifting. "Why is this the first I am hearing about it?"

Because I am one hundred and twenty-four years old and don't share everything in my life with my parents.

"We just set it up last night. We've . . . known each other for a while." Pandora knew she needed to lay the framework for a believable relationship moving forward. "I always kind of . . . had a thing for him, but I didn't think he returned my feelings."

"Why wouldn't he?" Lucian asked, stiffening. He was a man who believed the moon rose purely for the enjoyment of the women in his life, and couldn't fathom anyone not feeling the same way.

Pandora felt her mother's probing eyes watching her, looking for any sign of deception. But there was none to be found. Because Pandora genuinely had been dealing with a crush on Victor for months. She was also much more excited about this date than she should have been, given the fact that it wasn't a real one.

"Is he coming to pick you up?" Lucian asked.

"I am meeting him back at work," Pandora told him, knowing he would be disappointed not to get the chance to scare her date. "I just wanted to run home to change. I have to get going."

"Have a good time," her father said.

"Yes," her mother said, but Pandora didn't like the way she was looking at her. "Have a good time. I expect to hear all the details."

That was absolutely not happening.

Pandora had to run to catch her train back to Luna Bean and as she made her way down the street, she saw that Victor was already on the pavement, waiting for her.

He was dressed smartly in a cozy burnt-orange jumper and a pair of black trousers, with a black peacoat.

"Sorry I'm late," Pandora called out as she approached, watching Victor turn at the sound of her voice.

His green eyes moved over her, taking in her legging-clad legs and the way her dress clung a bit to her chest.

She wouldn't say her *hunter's moons* were on display, per se, but they were definitely peeking.

And she felt a warmth tease over the areas of her body

that Victor's eyes had roamed, making desire pool in her lower belly. She hoped it wasn't reflected in her eyes, as his gaze finally held hers.

"I haven't been here long," he told her, tucking his hands into his front pockets and making his shoulders hunch forward in a way that had no right to be as charming as it was. "So, did you just want to . . . walk?" He looked down the street.

"Sure." She fell into step with him.

The street cleaners had been out in force earlier that day, but the trees had already dumped piles of more orange, red, and yellow leaves all along the streets and pavements, and Pandora couldn't help but smile at how Victor seemed to go out of his way to step on them, clearly enjoying that crunch as much as she did.

"So . . . what should we be talking about?" he asked.

"The basics, I guess. Full names, ages, families, interests."

"OK. You first."

"I'm Pandora Von Ashmore." Technically, she was Pandora Louanna Morrigan Van Ashmore. But she wasn't about to open up that can of worms. "I'm twenty-four. I work at Luna Bean because I'm a bit of a, you know, night owl. I like bright, happy colours. I have a pet raven named Vlad. And I have a mother named Ophelia and a father named Lucian. As well as a little brother named Dante."

"I should probably be taking notes," he said, glancing over at her.

"Maybe it will be better if we also come up with some stories about our families to really make them stick in each other's heads. Like my parents once caught Dante sneaking a toad into his room. But when they confronted him about it, it turned out that it wasn't just one toad. He

59

had twenty-seven toads in his bathroom. He fancied himself some kind of toad king or something."

"What'd your parents do about it?"

"My father ordered him to get rid of them immediately," Pandora told him. "But my mother has a soft spot for Dante, so she had a pond built in the back garden where he could visit them. They're still there, all these years later. Well, maybe not them. But their grand-toads maybe."

Victor gave her a small smile at that and Pandora noticed for the first time that he had a slight dimple in his cheek when he did.

"Dante is the toad king. Got it," he said, nodding. "I don't have any siblings, so I don't have any toad-king stories. I'm twenty-nine. Working toward my PhD. Have a best mate named Sebastian. We met in primary school. We bonded over hating PE. Have been friends ever since. He lives in Manchester now, but we catch up a lot."

"Sebastian the PE-hater. Does he like football?"

"Who doesn't?"

"Fair enough. What about your parents?"

"Both my parents are in education. My mother is a primary school teacher. My father is a secondary school teacher, in maths. What do your parents do?"

"My mother is a . . . homemaker," Pandora said, despite her mother never lifting a finger to cook or clean. "My father is in . . . business." It was as true as it could be. He'd always been good with numbers and investments, always seeming to know which human invention was going to take off and becoming an early investor. Then he'd make a killing and cash out.

It was impressive and obscene the kind of wealth that

immortals could amass over the course of their endless lives.

"What about your brother? Does he work?"

"He's still figuring things out," Pandora said. It was true enough. She'd never really heard Dante talk about what he wanted for his future. To them, there was truly nothing but time.

"Any other prominent family members to know?"

"I don't think you'll be expected to remember any of the others, given how many there are. It'll be easier to get to know them when you have faces to go with names."

"True. So, what about hobbies? What do you do when you're not working at the coffee shop?"

"Mostly, I am reading. Or going to the shops for books. Or library or estate sales to get more books."

"We have that in common, then," Victor said, the edges of his lips curving up, making charming little creases form in the corners of his eyes.

"Yeah, I noticed you always have books on you."

Victor gave her a sheepish look before reaching into his coat pocket and producing a small, well-worn paperback.

Pandora, completely taken by that, pulled her bag off of her shoulder and tugged it open to reveal three well-loved paperbacks.

"May I?" he asked, pointing toward them.

Pandora felt a surge of unease, knowing how many people looked down on romance books, especially ones with scantily-clad models on the cover. But she tamped that down, reminding herself that there was nothing to be embarrassed about.

"Sure," she said, watching him reach for them all, then flipping through them.

"They make special tape for spines like this," Victor said when he got to her bodice-ripper with the worn cover.

"Yes! I was going to fix it once I finished it."

"These books from, what, the eighties, are hard to come by."

"They are. I lucked upon a whole box of them. Lucy and I have been working our way through them since."

"Lucy is your co-worker?"

"Technically, she's my manager. But also my best friend. Though my family hasn't met her yet, actually. So you and she will have that in common when the time comes."

"Why not?" Victor flipped the romance novel over to read the blurb on the back.

"Oh, I don't know. Different schedules, I guess."

And a millennia-old rivalry.

No biggie.

"So, what about favorite foods and films? Or music?" Pandora asked.

"Foods? All things Italian," Victor said.

Oh, great. Italian. Where almost every dish was heavily flavored with garlic, which could potentially kill her in large doses.

"I like going to see films based on books I love. Then complain how much better the book was." Victor's admission made Pandora smile.

"Always a fun pastime," she said.

"As for music, I'm afraid I seem to be stuck in the eighties."

Pandora smiled. "A staple genre." Her brother was more of the audiophile in her family, having strong feelings on every genre and the best artists within each. While her parents basically thought that anything that postdated Beethoven was basically "noise."

"What about you?"

"I like the stuff we play at the coffee house. Coffee-house music, I guess. Singer-songwriter stuff. It's great background music for reading."

"What is your go-to coffee or tea order?" Victor asked. "Since you already know mine."

"I like chamomile tea." She didn't mention that the calming effect of it worked wonders when her vampire urges were getting a little out of hand.

"Chamomile. Not a caffeine addict, then?"

"Sometimes, but I'm sensitive to it."

"Working the overnight shift can't be good for your sleep cycles either," he said, nodding. "Caffeine would only exacerbate that."

"Yeah. So, what else should two engaged people know about each other?"

"Do you have any idols?"

She nodded. "Basically, anyone who can actually write. I tried once. I felt like I was typing for ages and ages. I was sure there were five thousand words. At least."

"How many was it?" Victor asked, lips twitching.

"Two hundred."

That got an actual laugh out of him, dimple and all.

"I also admire artists," said Victor. "I have no artistic skills myself. But I often wish I did."

"OK, what else? Do you drive?"

"I can drive, but I don't have a car right now. You?"

"No. Pet peeves?"

"Open-mouth gum-chewers," Victor said with the kind of immediacy that said he really couldn't stand that.

"People who dog-ear pages in books that don't belong to them. Close talkers. People who stop suddenly on the pavement, then act like you're the problem for ramming into them. Interruptions when someone is clearly in the middle of something. Group projects. Meetings that could have been emails or texts. Too much?" he asked when he caught Pandora smiling at him.

She couldn't help it, she was charmed by his curmudgeonly nature.

"Not at all," she said.

"What about you?" he asked.

"I guess people who are always thinking things were better in the 'good old days'," she said, thinking of her parents, of how inflexible they were to new ideas or customs. Especially when it came to human–vampire relations.

"Your parents." Victor assumed correctly.

"Yeah."

"Well, in a way, this is you rebelling against that mindset," he said.

"That's true," she agreed. "If we get away with it."

"Having doubts?"

How could she explain to him that she had a mind full of all of the failed fake-dating plots in the books she'd read? That she could immediately come up with over a hundred ways it could go wrong. And she wasn't even factoring in the secret-vampire element.

She turned to look up at him, ready to give him assurances she didn't feel. Which was how she missed the cyclist swerving to avoid something in the cycle lane, making him veer right toward her.

Victor's arm grabbed her around the lower back, curling

her toward him, out of the way, but right up against his body.

Time seemed to stutter and then surge forward all at once at the startling closeness, at the way his nearness overwhelmed her senses.

Pressed against him, she felt the quick thud of his heartbeat against her chest, making Pandora wish her own could echo the same confusion and exhilaration.

Victor's arms were encircling her as she breathed in that vanilla, leather, and cinnamon scent of his, making her mind a chaotic jumble.

For a second, she didn't let herself look up, allowing herself be overwhelmed by the warmth radiating from him and the way his peacoat scratched against her cheek.

"You all right?" Victor asked, his voice low and gruff, his breath stirring her hair.

She nodded mutely, words feeling impossible right then.

The world around them slowly resumed its noise and motion, but, in that moment, she was caught in the cocoon of his presence – suddenly, achingly aware of how easily he could affect her, even without trying.

When she finally forced her head to tilt up, she found him tantalizingly close, his features framed by the golden glow of a nearby street light. The sharp line of his jaw, the slight curve of his lips, parted as though he wanted to say something but hadn't decided what yet, and his eyes . . . They snatched every thought from her mind.

They were an intense, unguarded mix of concern and something else that made her stomach flip-flop.

His gaze seemed to search hers, trying to reassure himself that she was unharmed when she didn't answer.

But beneath that, she could swear she saw a flicker of heat.

A whooshing sensation thundered in her ears as a comforting warmth enveloped her.

He was close enough for her to see subtle flecks of gold in his irises, to feel his breath whispering over her hair.

For one short, fleeting moment, the world around them blurred back to irrelevance, leaving only him and the sense that this was the first time they were *truly* seeing each other.

"Careful," he murmured, voice low, almost soft, and the sound of it sent a shiver down her spine.

She wanted to think of something witty to say, some way to laugh it off. But her thoughts were still tangled into an incoherent mess. All she could manage was a quiet, "Thanks."

Those charming little creases formed next to his eyes at that, like her reaction amused him. Or – dare she hope – pleased him.

But then, little by little, he released her, making her arms fall from his.

The absence of his nearness was almost startling. The crisp autumn air washed over her, leaving her feeling shaken and unsteady, while Victor lingered for just long enough for Pandora to wonder if he felt the same way too.

"Perhaps we should head back," he said, gaze sliding away, like he was examining the horizon, seeing things she didn't.

"OK." She tried not to allow the disappointment to take root and grow.

But with each awkward, silent stride back toward Luna Bean, it was hopeless. Not only did the roots grow deep, but the vines twisted around her, squeezing until she felt like she might burst.

"So . . . tomorrow?" Victor asked, his voice after a lengthy silence making her jolt.

"Tomorrow?"

"Second date."

"Oh, right. Yeah."

It would be the first time they'd interact in the daylight. Except, of course, she'd checked the forecast. There wasn't supposed to be any sun. It was going to be a rainy, dreary day. The kind that made her want to curl up with some tea and her romance novels in front of a window.

"Three?" he asked. "I have a lecture until half past two. I can be here shortly after."

She had no plans, save for her usual shift at the coffee shop later that evening.

"Are we going to just sit here and talk?" she asked, waving back toward Luna Bean.

"No. I'll plan something," he said. "It's . . . been nice getting to know you, Pandora."

Then he was turning and striding away.

Taking another piece of her heart with him.

8

"What is *that*?" Pandora grumbled as she was pulled from a particularly vivid dream of Victor pushing her up against a building and kissing her long and deep, instead of releasing her and putting distance between them, like he had the night before.

The sound drifted upward from somewhere else in the house, each note swelling and ebbing, a clawing noise that made her think of a cat yowling in the night.

"That . . ." Vlad said, and she rolled over to see him perched on his stand, waiting for her to wake up. How he managed to get in through a closed door had always perplexed her. "Is your cousin Bellatrix."

"What is she doing? Dying?" Pandora curled her pillow up to the sides of her head, pressing it against her ears to try to muffle the racket.

"She has, apparently, picked up opera."

"Great." Pandora huffed, giving up on the idea of sleeping in and placing her legs off the side of the bed. "The floorboards are vibrating. Has anyone checked the glass downstairs? I half expect it to all be shattered."

She wasn't typically so unkind.

But she was restless from fleeting sleep, thanks to her mind racing with thoughts of Victor. And the awkward silence between them after he'd saved her.

And, well, Bellatrix was probably her least favorite person. So waking up to her vibrato wobbling and warbling, pushing its way under the door, and through the walls and floors, was making her extra grumpy.

Pandora went through the motions of showering and putting herself together. She didn't dress up. It hadn't seemed to make a bit of difference anyway. So she put on her usual work uniform with a cardigan over it.

Then she reached for the stainless-steel tumbler she had hidden under her sink. She'd picked it up in the hopes that it would keep her blood fresh enough to last the night, since she didn't dare risk keeping it in the fridge with Bellatrix snooping around.

The last thing she needed was some big confrontation with her mother about her stubborn refusal to drink human blood. Especially with family visiting. And when she was about to try to float a fake engagement right in front of their faces.

Best to just fly under the radar for the time being.

Pandora chugged her blood then brushed her teeth before making her way out of her room. Vlad perched on her shoulder, looking as pained by the singing as Pandora felt.

They were just about to round the corner to the stairs,

when Dante came shuffling toward them. Like he was coming home. In the middle of the day. Again.

What was going on with him?

As if sensing her thoughts, Dante's head jerked up.

The sleepless smudges under his eyes looked even more intense than they had the day before.

And when she'd been restless in her sleep earlier, she could have sworn she'd heard some strange banging and almost . . . gurgling sounds coming from his room.

But before she could open her mouth to ask him about it, he was wincing at a particularly egregious missed note, making his shoulders pull up by his ears.

"Who told her she could sing?" he asked.

Her indulgent parents, no doubt, Pandora thought.

"Is anyone else awake?" she asked.

"I'm sure they are," Dante said. "Who could sleep through that?"

"But are they downstairs?"

"No. Why?"

"I'm heading out," she told him.

"It's early for work."

"I have another date. Could you possibly tell Mum and Dad that, when you see them later? Maybe tell them how excited I looked."

"Why *don't* you look excited?" he asked.

"I am!"

"Come on, Pandy," he said, shaking his head at her. "You look tired and tense."

"I just didn't sleep well. I'm actually super excited to go on a date with my future fiancé," she said, lying. "I have to get going. I don't want to be late. Is it raining?"

"It's bucketing down." He reached up to push his wet hair out of his face.

"Good," she said. "I'll take an umbrella. Maybe I'll see you later."

"Maybe," he said, in a way that made her think he didn't plan on it.

She was worried about him, but she didn't have time to press him on it. She was on too much of a time crunch with her engagement and marriage.

So she made her way to the servants' stairs, rushed down, and went out the back door to avoid her cousin who, thanks to not needing to breathe, seemed to have endless abilities to hold the wrong note.

When she arrived at Luna Bean, she found Victor waiting inside, sipping his usual coffee with one hand, but holding another drink in the other.

"Chamomile tea?" he asked, holding it out toward her.

"Yes, thank you," she said, smiling at him.

He didn't seem as distant as he'd been the night before. She decided not to overthink that and just be happy about it instead.

"So, where are we having our date?" she asked.

"One of my favorite places in the world," he told her.

But he refused to explain further as the two of them walked under her umbrella toward the Tube.

Instead, he veered the conversation toward the more boring aspects of their contract. Exact dates, contingencies, et cetera.

"What about our living arrangements?" he asked.

"What about them?"

"Will we be living together?"

"Oh, right. Yes, of course," she said, trying to tamp down the warm feelings she got at the idea of sharing a home with him. "After the wedding."

"And what about the divorce?"

"What about the divorce?" she asked, ignoring the pang in her stomach at the idea.

"Would we both move out of the flat?"

"Oh, uh, I haven't given that a lot of thought, actually."

"I guess there's time. Might want to actually *find* a flat before we talk about who lives in it after the . . . contract is over."

She was glad when the train pulled into the station, ending the practical – and oddly sad – conversation as they made their way down the waterlogged streets until they came to a door.

"A bookshop?" she asked, smiling up at him.

"The best one London has to offer." He beamed as he reached for the door.

"That is quite a claim."

"It will live up to it, trust me." He followed her in after lowering the brolly, putting it in a designated spot just inside the door.

Pandora was immediately met with that distinct, layered aroma of old books. She'd always thought that aged paper had the same scent as fallen leaves – rich and slightly musty.

The store was absolutely labyrinthine, with endless bookshelves crammed into the small space, forcing shoppers to walk single-file between them. The shelves bowed with the weight of all the tomes stacked on them.

"Fair warning," Victor told her. "Nothing in here is in order, save for by genre. It's hell if you're looking for a specific book, but heaven if you are just here to browse and find a buried treasure."

They walked through the stacks then, reaching for books, discussing favorites, choosing a few to sit down with in the only two chairs at the very back of the store.

They seemed to forget all about consulting the questions Pandora had jotted down the night before, when sleep had been elusive. Little things she felt that real lovers would know about each other.

Instead, they just talked.

About books and artists. About the things they each loved or hated in stories.

Pandora tried desperately to defend the use of miscommunication in romance novels, insisting that sometimes people were too hurt or too insecure to express themselves the way some readers would want, that it was actually more realistic to have people miscommunicate than it was for them to have fully adult and productive conversations all of the time.

Victor railed against "plot armour", where the main character was constantly thrown into increasingly dangerous situations but somehow managed to survive, despite having no real skills to speak of.

"I hate it more when a character is put in one of those situations and just magically develops new powers that so conveniently can be used for that specific problem. I hate-read a whole YA series once that had it happen so often it was hilarious."

In fact, Pandora and Victor got so wrapped up in casual, in-depth conversation that they seemed to accidentally learn more about each other than they would have, had they followed Pandora's list.

73

She couldn't help but watch his profile as he spoke long and deep on topics that mattered to him, his face animated with his clear passion.

Pandora knew her gaze was likely too soft and lingering, but she couldn't seem to make herself care. She hung on his every word, feeling like it was a rare and special treat to have someone who seemed as quiet as Victor open up so much for her. She actually felt a little frustrated each time he batted a question in her direction, wanting to be able to focus fully on him. But he seemed just as invested in peeling back her layers as she was in exploring his.

"Victor," she said when he finished speaking, watching as he turned to look at her.

"Yeah?"

"What are you studying?"

"Victorian English Literature," he told her, not surprising her in the least, given his passion for the subject. Until, of course, he spoke again. "But I am working on my thesis on literature that focuses on vampires."

Pandora felt like the floor had just opened up beneath her: she was falling into it, her belly swirling, her mind racing.

Vampire literature?

He was doing a thesis on vampire literature?

How, *how*, had she ended up not only having a crush on, but also entering into a fake-dating-and-marriage scenario with the one man who might be able to pick apart her family's odd habits and eccentricities, and conclude they were the very creatures from his books?

"Pandora?" Victor's voice sounded far away while her head was spinning off in a million different directions.

"Yeah?" Her voice came out in a squeak. Then, trying to calm herself down, she said, "I, uh, didn't realize that was a topic for a thesis."

"I don't know if it's been done before. I think that's what will be so compelling about it; publishing takes forever, but I'm hoping it will be out in the summer."

"Why vampires?" Pandora asked, hoping Victor didn't pick up on the panicked rasp in her voice.

"I think they're the most complex of all the possible supernatural creatures that have been created in literature. The fact that all vampires start out as humans, how their death and new life explores immortality and morality. I think an argument can also be made for vampirism being an exploration of the human psyche and our innate dark sides. Plus, from a more academic standpoint, it is interesting how many different cultures had depictions of vampires at the same time."

Because those cultures likely encountered actual vampires.

This was a complete and utter nightmare.

Pandora desperately needed Lucy to get back from her hunt. She needed someone to talk to, to discuss this with, to talk her down from the cliff. Because she was seconds away from calling this off and submitting to an eternity of poverty.

"Pandora?" Victor watched her with scrunched brows.

"Sorry. Just . . . thinking."

Victor's head tipped to the side and Pandora watched his brows pinch, regarding her with a mix of surprise and confusion.

"I didn't have you pegged for a book snob."

"*What?*" She straightened in her seat.

75

"I thought that someone who reads so much of a genre that a large majority of the book world looks down on would be above judging science fiction."

"I'm not judging science fiction." Hell, it wasn't even *fiction*. But she couldn't tell him that. "I was just wondering, uh, why you didn't choose, you know, *Frankenstein*," she said, proud of being able to think on her toes. If this carried on, she was going to need that skill more than ever. "You know, since it is arguably the beginning of science fiction as a genre. Besides." She tried to make her tone light. "You get the fun of exploring how a teenage girl wrote it as a challenge. And likely to avoid another threesome with Lord Byron and her own clueless husband."

To that, Victor's lips twitched up slightly. "I think Mary Shelley has been covered a lot in thesis work. Besides, I think that her story is perhaps better told by another woman, who might have more insight into what it may have been like for a young, talented woman like Shelley to try to make a name for herself among the male 'greats' of her time. While trying to balance motherhood and being the wife of a poet who was also a drunk and a philanderer. And, yeah, what it must have been like to know her husband likely had a relationship with Lord Byron. And herself. It's a thesis that writes itself. Just not one I want to put my name to."

"I guess that makes sense." Pandora was glad to clear up that misunderstanding.

She intentionally asked him about his favorite vampire books, wanting to know if they were the ones that were closest to the reality of vampires.

In the end, though, she had no idea, because he'd mentioned a dozen or so books, some of which she'd never read. Though, she figured, it might be worth picking up some copies and pore over them. Just to know where his mind might be when it came to her kind.

"So, how do we pay?" Pandora asked a few moments later, when they made their way to the end of the rows of books and wound up at a long, time-warped desk. It was cluttered with what looked like thirty years of newspapers, books, and paperwork. Not to mention no fewer than fifteen mismatched teacups.

There was a spider plant sitting near a window, its leaves droopy and parched. It was silly, but Pandora's heart ached a little over its neglect.

"The owner lives upstairs," Victor said. "He's ancient. Ninety if he's a day. Sadly, I don't imagine this place will be open much longer, as he doesn't remember to make it down here most days. I just write a list of the titles I bought and stick the money in that box over there." He gestured to the other side of the counter, where a locked wooden box was situated.

She waited as Victor wrote down all the titles, then put money and the list into the box. As he was distracted, she grabbed a small cup of water sitting on the desk and poured it in the spider plant's dirt. It wasn't much, but those plants were practically unkillable. It would make that drink last a week or two, at least. And maybe she could pop back in to give it more . . .

"Wait, I have to pay," she said when Victor started to move away.

"Already done," Victor told her as he picked up his books. "Think your handbag is big enough for all our books?" he asked, since there was an obvious lack of bags to carry them in. "Don't want them getting wet," he added as she placed her bag on the counter, rearranged the contents, then stuffed her books in before piling his on top.

"Perfect," she said when she just barely managed to get the zipper to close.

Victor checked his mobile for the time. "Probably should be heading back. Your shift is starting soon."

Was it?

Pandora felt like only maybe an hour or two had passed. But when she looked, sure enough, Victor was right. Four hours had passed. And, she had to admit, they'd probably been the most enjoyable four hours of her entire, er, life.

"Yeah," she said, trying not to feel too disappointed for the date to be ending.

It was a *fake* date, after all.

Only, suddenly, it didn't feel quite so fake anymore.

9

"What do you *mean* his thesis is on vampire literature?" Lucy was slack-jawed in the break room of
Luna Bean a couple of nights later.

Pandora noted that her friend looked better than ever.
She always did after the full moon, in fact. Her sable hair,
which was always thick and gorgeous, looked extra shiny.
Her skin was glowing. Her energy seemed revitalized.

Lucy had rushed through the employee entrance just ten
minutes before – twenty minutes late for their shift – and
thrusted a half-dead red maranta plant at Pandora that
she'd "forgotten existed" for several weeks. She had hoped
Pandora could bring it back to life, and had immediately
started to demand details about the date with Victor.

"I know," Pandora said, wincing as she put the poor
wilted plant under the tap, watching its drooping leaves
start to lift with just a proper drink.

"God, the irony is so thick I can't breathe." Lucy pressed a hand to her chest.

"It's a disaster waiting to happen," Pandora said.

"Especially once he meets your family."

"Exactly. How long until he starts piecing it all together?"

"This is too good." Lucy laughed as she pulled her hair up into a clip. "I mean, the man is studying *you* and he doesn't even know it."

"It's not funny!" Pandora said. "I don't know what I will do if he figures it out."

"You'll just have to fess up. And then he will fall madly in love with you."

Pandora shook her head. "It's not a book, Luce. My whole future is depending on this working. And Victor *not* figuring out what I am and running scared."

"Well, my first bit of advice would be not to chug down any artery-ale while he's around."

"Ha ha." Pandora followed Lucy out of the back and into the coffee shop.

"Oh, come on. It's an adventure," Lucy said.

"What's an adventure?" Victor asked, making the two women turn. He was standing at the counter, his usual backpack slung over one shoulder.

"Oh, nothing," Lucy said, recovering first. "Just this whole fake-marriage thing you two are working up. I wish I could be a fly on the wall when Pandora tells her family."

If only Lucy could tell them for me, Pandora thought.

"Oh," Victor said, looking a little worried. "Would I need to be there for that?"

"It's probably better for me to do it alone," Pandora

said as she started to make Victor's macchiato. "Let them come to terms with it first. Then you're going to need to meet them, of course."

"Of course. When do you plan to tell them?"

"Well, she's been laying the groundwork," Lucy said. "She even has her brother in on it, talking about how excited she's been to go on dates every day. I think you could tell them in the next few days, right?" she asked, looking at Pandora.

Pandora's stomach clenched at the idea of that discussion. Especially with her aunt, uncle, and cousin still visiting. For the most part, Pandora had managed to avoid their company. But she knew that once the news got out about her engagement, every relative was going to be crawling out of the woodwork to congratulate her and to meet her fiancé.

But she was going to have to tell them sooner rather than later.

"I think I'm going to tell them on my next day off," Pandora said, mostly to keep herself accountable for actually doing it. "They're probably going to want to meet you pretty quickly after."

"That's fine," Victor said, but Pandora could swear he looked a little ashen at the idea. At least they would be together in their misery.

"OK, so while we're on the topic of wedding stuff," Lucy said once Victor had made his way to his table to start working on his notes again. The only difference now being that Pandora knew exactly what he was studying. And it put her nerves on edge. "We need to discuss my chief bridesmaid dress. Namely, that it can't be hideous. Or peach."

"What's wrong with peach?" Pandora asked.

"Only that it clashes with my colouring and washes me out."

"Noted," Pandora said, pretending that she wasn't casting glances over at Victor. Partly to admire him. But also partly to see if he'd read some chunk of text that had made things click in his brain and was now looking over at her like he'd figured her out. "Don't worry. My mother will likely want a hand in picking dresses. Which means they will be black or red, skintight, silk or velvet, and likely displaying a large amount of cleavage."

"Well, what's the point in having all this," Lucy said, gesturing toward her chest, and, yes, Pandora had to admit that the universe had been generous when forming that particular part of Lucy's anatomy, "if it's not going to be shown off a little? Especially at a wedding. I mean, maybe I'll find some hot groomsman to spend the weekend with."

"It sounds like Victor only has one close friend," Pandora said.

"Well, he might have some hot cousin or something . . . No?" she asked when Pandora shook her head.

"No. Victor said he has a really small family. It's really just his parents and his best friend."

"Well, luckily, it seems like you have more than enough for the two of you."

She had no idea.

Pandora suspected that her wedding would be the event of the century. Which didn't make her want to throw up or anything. But there was no way Ophelia Von Ashmore was going to have some small backyard exchanging of vows with just the immediate family.

Oh, no.

That wasn't her style in the least.

Pandora was imagining all the guest rooms in their house full. Plus the basement that would be lined with dozens of coffins for extended family and friends.

Pandora felt like she was getting hives just thinking about it.

But it would all be over in less than three months. Then she could finally move out of her parents' place – and away from the revolving door of guests – and start working on her dream.

It wasn't that she didn't love her family. She did. She was just overwhelmed at the idea of lying to them all, and trying to keep Victor from seeing something he shouldn't and couldn't. There were so many ways things could go wrong. She was just looking forward to being on her own so that no one could find them out while they finished out the charade.

Though, as her gaze slid to Victor again, this time catching him looking in her direction then quickly away, she had to admit that the larger part of her didn't want the part with him to be over.

In fact, the more time she spent with him, the more time she wanted to spend with him. Even if it did open her up to being found out by him. Especially after the wedding when . . .

"Wait," Pandora said, looking over at Lucy, who was rearranging the disorganized tea caddy.

"What?"

"I'm going to have to live with him."

"Ah, yeah, genius," Lucy said with a laugh. "That's what married people do."

"I'm going to be living with a vampire expert," she whispered.

"Yeah." Lucy nodded. "Only about a thousand ways that could go wrong."

"I really didn't think this through."

"In your defense, you didn't know he was a vampire expert when you made him the offer."

And now she had paperwork signed that she was reasonably sure held some sort of legal weight. There was no going back.

"Look, we will be all stealthy about it. Get you a place leased, then get some of that nifty film for all of the windows. Maybe get a mini fridge that you can hide somewhere to keep your blood in. Those are the two big things, right?"

"Right." But her mind had already moved past all the ways living with someone who could find out her secret could go terribly wrong and shifted to all the ways living with Victor could be a dream come true.

No one complaining about books hiding in the strangest of places. Since he would likely accidentally leave one in the cabinets or in the laundry basket on occasion as well. No more oppressive black and grey. She could fill the space with colour.

"Earth to Pandora," Lucy said, snapping her fingers in her friend's face.

"Sorry, what?"

"You were totally fantasizing about getting all glandular with Victor, weren't you?"

"What? No!"

"I'm not buying it. Your eyes were all dreamy and faraway."

"I was thinking about how our book collections would fill up our flat," Pandora said.

"Suuure." Lucy rolled her eyes. "Wait, are you going to be getting all glandular with him?"

"What? No!" No matter how much she wished she could.

"Don't you have to, though?"

"Why would we have to?"

"To make the marriage official," Lucy said. "Right? Like, marriages aren't official until they're consummated."

"Is that still the rule?" Pandora asked, a mix of panic and excitement flooding her system.

Excitement, because she'd done little but fantasize about that very thing since the first time she'd seen Victor.

But panic because, well, what if Victor didn't want that? Didn't want *her*?

He'd sure been quick to move away from her, to put distance between them, after he'd saved her from that out-of-control cyclist.

"Why do you look like you're going to be sick? Haven't you been dreaming about getting between the sheets with him since you first laid eyes on him? I mean . . . he looks all buttoned-up and reserved," Lucy said, looking over at Victor. "But I bet once you get him unbuttoned, he's all commanding and assured. I bet that man loves to give an Aussie kiss."

"What is an Aussie kiss?" Pandora asked as she took a sip of her chamomile tea, definitely needing something to slow down her nerves that felt ready to fly right off the tracks.

"You know . . . like a French kiss. But . . . *down*

under?" Lucy said, making Pandora choke on her tea as she laughed.

"I know. I'm hilarious," Lucy said, rapping hard on Pandora's back.

"You all right?" Victor called across the café.

"Look at you, being a concerned fiancé," Lucy said, beaming at him. "She's fine. Just . . . wrong pipe. Speaking of pipes . . ."

"Stop!" Pandora said, charmingly scandalized by her friend's outrageous comments.

"What?" Lucy asked, the picture of innocence. "I was just going to say that it's, you know, really important for pipes to be long and firm, and—"

"You've got no shame, have you?" Pandora asked, shaking her head.

"You can't blame me. I've been DJing my own party for ages now. I have to live vicariously through you until some hot groomsman sweeps me off my feet."

"I will pray for your sake that Victor's best friend, Sebastian, is as hot as you are hoping."

"Make him hotter. My standards are on the floor lately," Lucy said with a wince. "Though, you can't pray, so I guess I will have to settle for him retaining at least half of his hair and having decent dental hygiene."

"Reaching for the moon there," Pandora said as a small crowd of customers came in.

She managed to spend some time with Victor before he headed home to get some sleep, their conversation helped on by the constantly interjecting Lucy.

But, eventually, it was time to go home.

She truly had no intention of letting the cat out of the

bag about her engagement as she reached to open the front door of the Von Ashmore house.

She genuinely was going to stick to her own plan.

Until, suddenly, the words were tumbling out of her mouth.

Really, it was all her cousin Bellatrix's fault.

10

"Pandora, darling," Ophelia called out, making Pandora tilt her head back and fight the urge to run.

Those squeaky floorboards had given her away.

But she'd put off seeing her aunt, uncle, and cousin for long enough already.

"Mum," Pandora said, plastering a smile on her face as she moved into the sitting room.

Where Lucian, Ophelia, Pandora, and Dante were all dark-haired and robust, Aunt Anastacia and Uncle Alexander, as well as their daughter, Bellatrix, were all fair-haired, wafer-thin, and pale, making them seem to Pandora like specters haunting her home whenever they were around. She half expected to wake up to one of them standing over her in bed, speaking to her in hushed whispers.

"There you are," Ophelia said, and Pandora could sense

a hint of censure in her tone even as she held out an arm to draw her daughter further into the room. Ophelia ran a hand over Pandora's hair, which had gone a bit frizzy from another rainy day. The Von Ashmore house was ancient and drafty. The moisture had a way of sneaking in through the stone façade and around the window frames, its sole purpose seeming to be to ruin any possible good hair day she might have. "Were you on your way out again?"

She was.

But not to work or on a date with Victor.

She had a pint of fresh blood waiting for her at the butcher's and if she didn't get there soon, the place was going to close. Which meant she was going to go hungry. And start doing dangerous things like staring at people's necks at work later.

She couldn't, however, tell her mother that, so she lied.

"I was just looking for Dante. I haven't seen him much lately. Hello, Aunt Anastacia. Uncle Alexander. Bellatrix," she said, trying hard not to let her voice go hard on that last name.

Bellatrix had grown to be a beautiful woman, with her pin-straight hair that seemed immune to the effects of the humidity in the air, a delicate face, big stormy blue eyes, and a long and lean figure with just the barest hint of curves.

"Hello, Pandora," her aunt greeted her, offering her cheek for kissing. Pandora broke away from her mother to do just that. First to her aunt, then to her uncle. But she couldn't bring herself to do the same for her cousin.

"You seem well, Bellatrix," she said instead, internally wincing at how much she sounded like her parents just then.

"You . . ." Bellatrix gave Pandora a slow once-over, then clearly decided she couldn't afford Pandora the same civility, instead saying, "You haven't changed."

"Bellatrix was just telling us all about her travels to France and Italy," Ophelia said as Pandora moved as far away from her extended family as possible. Which put her right next to her father.

Over the rim of his goblet full of thick, fresh blood that made Pandora's stomach tighten at its own emptiness, Lucian widened his eyes at her as if to say he knew how she felt.

"Really? Fascinating," Pandora said, watching her father's lips twitch slightly at her words and tone.

"She has picked up a passion for opera," her aunt said, sitting up straighter in her chair. If there was anything a parent loved, it was the ability to brag about their child. Even if that child was one hundred and twenty-six years old.

"I've heard." Pandora nodded.

"Brilliant, isn't she?"

"She has no equal," Dante said, appearing in the doorway to save Pandora from choking on a lie.

Pandora pressed her lips together to keep from laughing at the hidden message behind her brother's words.

"Dante!" Ophelia rushed over to her son to press a kiss to his cheek. "I'm so pleased you could join us," she said, dragging him into the room. Even if Dante looked like all he wanted to do was go upstairs and find his bed.

After their parents had relented and let Pandora keep her own bed, Dante had got one for himself as well. Though that, it was clear, was their family's dirty laundry. Not something they should ever share in mixed company.

"Aunt, Uncle, Bell," Dante said, making Bellatrix's eyes go a little hard, clearly not liking the nickname. "Pandy, I'm surprised you're here," he said, making Pandora's brows scrunch, not sure where else he thought she was supposed to be.

"Where else would she be, dear?" Ophelia asked.

"With her boyfriend," Dante said.

Pandora could have kissed her brother in gratitude.

She knew how hard it was going to be to sell a serious relationship if no one else had ever seen him or heard Pandora speak of him.

"Boyfriend?" Lucian grumbled, eyeing his daughter.

"Yeah, they've been attached at the hip lately," Dante confirmed, eyeing the goblet in his father's hand, his pupils blowing wide with hunger, but he didn't go and pour himself some from the decanter.

"*You*," Bellatrix looked Pandora up and down again with a wrinkled nose, "have a boyfriend?"

Pandora went temporarily insane at the disgust in her cousin's voice and face. That was the only explanation for what burst from between her lips right then.

"Well, actually, I've been waiting to announce this, but he's actually not my boyfriend anymore," she said. "He's my fiancé."

You could have heard a pin drop.

Until Dante managed to break the silence, making his way to her and wrapping her up in a hug. "What's his name?" he whispered in her ear.

"Victor," she whispered back.

"Congratulations, Pandy," Dante said, really selling it. "I don't know if any guy deserves you, but Victor is as close as a man could get."

"You've met this boy?" Ophelia asked, looking between her children, a mix of stunned and upset.

"Ran into them one night." Dante said the lie effortlessly.

"Congratulations, Pandora," her aunt said, but there was a chill in her tone as well.

"If you're engaged," Bellatrix said, "where is your *ring*?"

Pandora snatched her hand up, covering her ring finger with her other hand. "Oh, it . . . it was too big," she said. "It's being resized."

She had to add going ring-shopping to her list asap. She knew neither of them had the money for a new one, but maybe she could find something nice at an estate sale or antique store. Whatever it was, it had to be real. Her mother could sniff out costume jewelry from a mile away.

"Why didn't you say something sooner?" Ophelia asked, more suspicious now than confused.

"About the engagement? It's new," Pandora said. "I haven't had the chance to yet."

"How long have you been seeing this . . . Victor?" Lucian asked, tone going dark, slipping into overprotective-father mode.

"Oh, about . . . six months? Maybe a little longer." It wasn't a lie; she'd technically been *seeing* Victor at Luna Bean for approximately that long. "I didn't want to say anything until I knew it was serious."

"Doesn't get more serious than a proposal," Dante said, giving her a wink when no one else could see.

"Well, this is cause for a celebration." Her uncle stood up, blessedly oblivious to the tension in the room and the dozens of questions Ophelia was just barely holding in. He went to the decanter of blood, poured glasses for Dante and Pandora, the only ones without a drink, then handed them their goblets. "To Pandora and Victor!" he said dramatically. "May they know an eternity of love and happiness!"

They all raised their goblets, but Pandora didn't let the blood touch her lips, no matter how tempting the pull of it.

She had no idea where the blood had been sourced. If it had been acquired ethically or not.

When she lowered her goblet, she saw that Dante didn't have any red staining his lips or teeth either.

"Thank you, Uncle," Pandora said, giving him a grateful smile.

"Pandora, darling." Ophelia's tone sounded a bit shrill. "Can you help me in the kitchen? It seems we need more blood," she said, gesturing toward the decanter.

"Of course." Pandora handed her goblet to Dante, who shot her a sympathetic wince. They both knew Pandora was about to be put through the wringer in private.

It was OK, she assured herself. She'd been anticipating this, no matter when she finally let the news slip.

Ophelia barely waited until Pandora took a step into the kitchen before she turned on her.

"How could you announce this news in front of company?" she said accusingly.

"Mum, I thought you would be pleased." Pandora tried to appear wounded.

"I am stunned," Ophelia said. "Why the dramatics over your inheritance clause if you were already dating someone seriously?"

"Because I had no idea if he was ready to propose," Pandora said. "It wasn't like I could tell him to hurry up so I could get my inheritance."

Ophelia's lips pursed at that, seeing her daughter's logic.

"And who is this boy? Who is his family?"

This was the part where she knew her mother would go from stunned, suspicious, and maybe a little hurt, to outright scandalized.

"His name is Victor. And he's a PhD student at UCL."

She watched as understanding dawned on her mother.

"He's a *human*?" Ophelia gasped, her hand flying to her throat.

"Yes, Mother, he's human."

Ophelia's mouth opened and closed several times, not sure what she wanted to say.

It was then that Lucian made his way in.

"Where's the bl—" He picked up on the tension in the room. "What's wrong?"

"Tell your daughter she cannot marry a *human* boy," Ophelia said.

Her father frowned. "A human?" Pandora could see the struggle on his face. On the one hand, he agreed with his wife – he didn't believe humans and vampires should mix. To him, humans were food and nothing else. But he also loved his daughter. He didn't want to say anything to wound her.

"Does he know?" Ophelia asked, not at a loss for words like her husband.

"No! Of course not," Pandora said. There were rules about that sort of thing.

Sure, there were human donors to vampire blood-banks, but they were always heavily glamoured to forget all about vampires and their existence. But the pull toward the centers seemed to be something that no one could shake, so they would find themselves back, donating, getting paid, and getting glamoured over and over again.

It was an ethical grey-area for Pandora. But she supposed

that if it was given freely, and they walked away afterward, then it was far better than people getting drained in back alleys somewhere.

Pandora imagined there were humans out there who knew about vampires. Perhaps even vampire–human marriages. But it was definitely not the norm. And it was frowned upon in traditionalist families like her own.

"A human," her father said again.

"Yes, darling, a human. How very . . . modern," Ophelia said.

"Was there a clause I wasn't aware of?" Pandora asked, starting to panic. "For my inheritance? That he can't be human?"

Her parents looked at each other for a moment. It was her father who turned back first. "No, there is no such clause. You are free to marry who you choose."

"Like you did with Mum?" Pandora asked, figuring that using their own unconventional marriage for comparison could only help the situation.

It hadn't exactly been acceptable for a vampire to marry a succubus back when they'd got together. But that hadn't mattered to them.

Lucian, taking the bait, reached for his wife, pulling her against him. "She has a point."

In her husband's arms, Ophelia's coolness melted a bit and she nodded. "Love will endure." She turned back to Pandora. "We need to meet this fiancé of yours."

"Of course. He's excited about that, actually," Pandora said. Even if she thought Victor would probably rather get a thousand paper cuts from his books and have someone pour vinegar on them than meet her parents, who were going to be chilly toward him.

But they were in this for the long run.

Besides, she'd done the hardest part.

Breaking the news to them.

While she was on the topic, though . . .

"Oh, one more thing," Pandora said, watching both her parents' faces tighten, bracing for what she might say next.

"Yes?" Ophelia prompted her.

"My chief bridesmaid? It's Lucy. My colleague . . . the werewolf. Just wanted you to know that too. OK. I have to go and meet Victor," she said, lying, but needing to get out of the oppressive mood in the kitchen, as her parents tried to figure out where they'd gone so wrong with their daughter to make her not only fall in love with a human . . . but befriend a *werewolf*.

There. Pandora made her way out of the house. The most stressful part was behind her.

Or so she thought.

11

"I don't know," Lucy said, head tilted to the side as she inspected Victor as he came out of the dressing room. "Is it trying too hard?" She eyed the black suit he was wearing. With a black shirt under. And a black tie. "Does he look like he's cosplaying a creature of the night?" she said musingly.

Pandora's eyes bugged out at that, but Lucy ignored her as Victor let out a small huff of a laugh.

"It is very dark," he said, glancing down his reflection.

"Here." Lucy jumped up to pass him trousers and a smart button-down shirt. No jacket, no tie. "Try this instead," she said, pushing Victor back toward the dressing room.

"Easy with the vampire stuff," Pandora whispered to her.

"Victor thought it was funny," Lucy said.

"It won't be funny when he's got vampires on the brain and then meets my family full of them."

"His thesis is on vampires. They're always on his brain," Lucy said. "I just think this will go better if it doesn't look like he's trying to emulate them, y'know? That he shows up as himself. It will make him more comfortable. And that's better for the both of you."

That was fair.

Pandora was already having daily panic attacks at the idea of Victor meeting her parents. Would they remember not to serve blood? To actually serve *food* if it was a dinner party? It had been so long since they'd been human that she was terrified they wouldn't be able to fake it even halfway believably.

She'd forgotten to mention it to them.

And now it was too late.

They'd all been kind of tiptoeing around one another since the announcement. It should have eased some of Pandora's nerves. But it was having the opposite effect.

Now, she was overthinking every little thing.

Hence sitting in the men's department with Lucy just an hour before they were due to show up at her parents' house for the official introductions.

She was overthinking *everything*.

"I'm less concerned with what he's wearing," Lucy said, gaze moving over Pandora. "And more concerned with you. This is what you wear to introduce your fiancé to your parents?" She shook her head at Pandora's casual jeans-and-sweater ensemble.

"They're *my* parents. I'm not trying to impress them."

"No, but you need to *sell* this, right? And I think a real

woman who was recently engaged would be all excited and dressed up to reflect that."

New anxiety unlocked, Pandora pressed a hand to her chest. "I'm gonna have a heart attack."

"Your heart doesn't beat," Lucy said, laughing.

"Then why is my chest so tight?" Pandora asked, hunching forward to try to ease it. "I can't . . . breathe."

"You *don't* breathe."

"That's not helpful," Pandora said miserably just as the dressing-room door opened.

Lucy nodded. "Oh, that's the look."

"Are you OK?" Victor asked, and Pandora could feel his gaze on her.

"She's a little nervous," Lucy answered for her. "I'm going to go pick out something more appropriate for her to wear. You two have a little chat," she said, completely ignoring Pandora's pleading eyes, begging her not to leave.

"What are you so worried about?" Victor asked, sitting next to her in his ultra-starched new outfit.

That her parents would serve blood. That they'd say something careless like "humans" or "mortals". That they'd ask him inappropriate questions. That her mother would sniff out the lie.

"Everything," she said.

He smiled. "We've been preparing for this."

"I know." She nodded, but it still felt like someone was sitting on her chest. While simultaneously choking her from behind. Regardless of how anatomically impossible that was.

"Here. How about a distraction?" He stood to move back to the dressing room, grabbing his trousers, and then came back.

There, in his hand, was a ring.

No, not just any ring.

The ring.

Her engagement ring.

When she'd mentioned going to antique stores to try to find one, he'd insisted on doing the ring-shopping himself.

With everything else she had to worry about, she'd forgotten all about the ring that was supposedly "getting sized".

Victor hadn't forgotten.

And he hadn't just gone out and bought some cheap, ugly ring from somewhere. He'd found the most gorgeous vintage ring she'd ever seen.

It was a stunning cushion-cut emerald with floating bubble halo diamonds to each side, set on a simple gold band.

"*Oh.*" She exhaled, feeling that warm sensation sliding across her chest like it often seemed to do when Victor was nearby.

"Do you like it?" he asked. "I know a diamond is traditional. But I thought colour suited you better." He reached with his free hand for hers.

The second he touched her, she felt a tingle move across her hand, up her arm, then across her chest. Her gaze slid to his face, trying to ascertain if he felt the same tingle, if it was slowly working its way up to a flame across his skin like it was for her.

But with his head ducked, she was finding it hard to figure out what, if anything, he might be feeling as he slid the ring up her finger until it settled at the base, a perfect fit.

"It's beautiful," she said, looking down at how the

100

dark-green emerald contrasted with her pale skin. "Where did you find it?" she asked, trying to draw her own attention away from the way he was still holding her hand.

His gaze cut up to hers, his light-green eyes soft. "It was my grandmother's," he told her, making that gooey sensation spread across her chest.

His scent was thick in the air between them, overwhelming her senses. His lips were so close. If she just leaned slightly forward . . .

"Your hands are freezing," Victor said, looking down at her hands as he moved both of them between his, trying to warm her skin for her.

"Oh," she said, noting the concern etched between his brows. "I have, uh, circulation issues."

"We need to get you hand warmers," he said, chafing her skin.

It was meant to be kind.

It wasn't supposed to stoke the flames of desire within her until it caught, spread, and took over her completely.

Victor's gaze flicked up again and it was impossible for Pandora not to let her eyes drift to his lips before moving back up.

It was right that second that Lucy came back, though, making the two of them break apart almost guiltily.

"I got the perfect . . . Did I interrupt something?" Lucy asked, picking up on the way they were shifting away from each other. And how Pandora couldn't quite meet her eyes.

"No. Well, yes," Pandora said.

"Which one is it?" Lucy asked. "Because I could go . . . take a walk. Or you two could get a room." She gestured toward the dressing rooms.

101

If Pandora could blush, she was pretty sure she'd be flaming right then.

"Victor gave me an engagement ring," she said, thrusting her hand out in the way any newly engaged woman would.

"That makes this dress all the better," Lucy said, after ogling the ring for a second.

She lifted the hanger.

And there it was.

The perfect dress for the occasion.

It was a long silk slip dress in a deep shade of emerald green.

"I can't wear that," Pandora said.

"Don't be silly." Lucy reached down to grab Pandora's hand, then pulled her into the changing room with her.

"How come Victor gets to be himself, but I have to dress like . . . like . . ." Her mother. Like her mother.

"Indulge me here," Lucy said, hanging up the dress. "If you hate it, you can just wear what you have on. But give it a chance."

With that, Lucy exited the room to stand a few feet from Victor as Pandora stripped in the dressing room, mumbling under her breath the whole time.

She slipped into the slinky material then turned to look at herself in the mirror. She hated to admit it, but she did look more like an excited, newly engaged woman. Even the fact that the ring matched the dress seemed intentional, like she knew she would be showing off the ring all night.

Rolling some tension out of her neck, she reached for the door.

"OK, I don't hate it, but . . ." She trailed off as she exited.

102

She'd only been expecting Lucy.

But Victor was still sitting where she'd left him a few moments before. And as soon as she walked out, his head lifted.

Her hand, which was tugging self-consciously at the fabric, fell at the way his easy posture faltered as his eyes traced over her in a slow, deliberate sweep.

Gone was his usual broody exterior. Instead, his gaze carried the weight of something unspoken, something that made her stomach flip and her chest feel tight.

If her heart could beat, she swore it would be hammering against her ribcage.

The dress suddenly felt much tighter than it had inside the dressing room.

Did she look ridiculous?

Was it too much?

She opened her mouth to ask, but the words caught in her throat as his eyes met hers, dark and focused, like the entire world had fallen away, save for the two of them.

"You . . ." His voice came out low, husky, before he cleared his throat and straightened up. "It suits you."

It suited her?

Pandora almost laughed. Nothing had ever felt less natural on her skin. But the intensity in his gaze made the laugh freeze in her throat.

"Is it too tight?" she managed to murmur.

To that, Victor's lips twitched. It wasn't quite a smile, but it was close.

"No," he said, before his eyes did one final sweep.

"Too tight? With that figure? No," Lucy said as Victor excused himself back into the dressing room.

Twenty minutes later, they had paid and were back at

Luna Bean, each changing into their outfits for the night. Victor was left waiting for Lucy to fuss with Pandora's make-up for a while.

Pandora was thankful for anything to distract her from her own nerves, and Lucy's bubbly, incessant talking made it possible to get through the hour-long wait, before it was finally time for Victor and Pandora to make their way toward the Tube.

"Demons walk among us!" A voice carried across the platform as they waited for the train.

Pandora grumbled under her breath, "Not now."

"What was that?" Victor asked, looking down at her.

"Oh, nothing," she said, willing the train to pull up before the unwelcome orator noticed her again.

"They wear the skin of humans and they feed on your souls!"

Victor cast the man a sympathetic glance and Pandora saw him slide his hand into his back pocket, likely reaching for some spare change.

Until the man suddenly rushed toward them, making Victor straighten. "Demon! I see you! She will feed on your soul and drag you down to hell with her."

"Hey." Victor stepped forward, moving himself between the man and Pandora. "No, you need to step back," he said, pulling himself up to full height.

"Repent now, before she devours your soul!"

"Back off." Victor took another step toward the man.

"Victor, it's OK," she said, grabbing the back of Victor's shirt, trying to pull him back.

"It's not OK. He was in your face."

Pandora couldn't help but be charmed by his protectiveness.

When the man came back once again, Victor's arm went around her, ushering her into the train car once it stopped and its doors opened.

"Don't follow her," he said to the man, who was on a mission to warn the world about her true nature. Then Victor stood between her and the man until the doors closed.

Pandora almost didn't want to speak, didn't want to do anything that would make Victor realize his arm was still draped protectively around her and release her. But as the silence stretched between them, she felt she had to be the one to break it.

"It's sad that he has nowhere else to go," she said, meaning that. Sure, he might be trying to out her and he wasn't as crazy as society likely thought he was, but no one should be living on the streets or in the tunnels. Especially as the weather was getting cold.

"It is." Victor glanced down at her.

"Thank you for getting between us," she said.

"Of course."

Then, noticing he was still holding on to her, his arm fell away. Pandora found herself aching for the warmth of him, but she sat in the seat he found for her, pretending she wasn't getting more and more anxious with each passing moment.

"Are you cold?" Victor asked as they walked, the wind whipping them as they progressed forward, sending dried leaves flying around in little tornados.

"I'm OK," she said, though Victor gave her a dubious glance.

"I should have bought the suit. At least I would have had the jacket for you."

"We're almost there," she said, seeing the turrets of the Von Ashmore estate up ahead.

She didn't point out her home, knowing that the glamour would give him the heebie-jeebies if she pointed it out now.

"This is your home?" Victor asked as they entered the grounds a few moments later, their shoes crunching on freshly fallen leaves.

"Yes," she said, watching his wide eyes, the way his posture went a little tight again.

Feeling like he needed support every bit as much as she did right then, Pandora reached for Victor's hand, giving it a squeeze. He squeezed back, looking down at her and giving her a nod.

"We can do this," she said.

Then they started to move toward the cobblestone path.

Where Pandora froze as voices – far, far too many voices – drifted out of the old house.

She gasped. "Oh . . . oh, no."

"What is it?" Victor asked, as Pandora's gaze flew toward the street, seeing something she had missed.

At least a dozen very familiar cars.

This was supposed to be a small meet-and-greet between her parents and Victor.

Why the hell was her whole family there?

"Pandora, what's wrong?" Victor asked.

She couldn't answer, though, not as her mind swirled with about a million ways this night could go epically, monumentally, wrong.

She was about to suggest they turn back, walk away, do this some other time, when the front door flew open and there was her great-aunt Ravenna.

Ravenna was a force of nature wrapped in layers of crimson velvet. She was short and delightfully round with wild, silver curls that seemed to have a life of their own, springing out in every direction as if perpetually caught in an invisible wind.

Ravenna was dressed, as usual, in a deep-red velvet gown, with billowing sleeves embroidered with golden threads and cut scandalously low in front, revealing a generous amount of décolletage that defied both gravity and propriety.

Around her neck was a large ruby that danced upon her cleavage whenever she gestured with dramatic flair. Which was often.

Ravenna was the kind of woman whose presence filled every room she entered, whose over-the-top personality demanded to be noticed.

Even from yards away, Pandora caught a whiff of her great-aunt's heavy-handed perfume, notes of amber and patchouli drifting to them on the breeze.

Here's the happy couple!" Ravenna threw her arms up in the air.

"I'm so sorry," Pandora whispered to Victor.

"Come! Come!" Ravenna called out. "You're late to your own engagement party!"

12

"This could not be happening.

It was supposed to be a low-key affair.

But through the open door where Ravenna was standing, Pandora could hear laughter echoing off the high ceilings and the animated hum of conversations drifting out into the night.

"It's gonna be all right," Victor said, sensing her rising panic and giving her hand a squeeze before starting to pull her forward.

Ravenna turned and made her way into the sitting room, waving her arms out toward the crowd, her long sleeves dangerously close to gliding into someone's glass that Pandora hoped to hell was filled with wine, not blood.

To the side of the room, her cousin Jasper, pale as death, (because, well . . .) was trying to excuse himself from a conversation with Ravenna's husband, Reginald. A man who, once he got you cornered, never ran out of things to talk about.

Pandora's gaze swept around the rest of the crowd, trying to find anything out of place enough for her to need to step in.

There was Uncle Reginald, decked out in a full-on 1850s military uniform – all red material, gold buttons, and gilded shoulder fringe.

As if that wasn't bad enough, he was speaking animatedly to Vlad, whose beak was moving as well, as he answered whatever questions Reginald was asking him.

She supposed she should at least be thankful that Reginald hadn't worn his shakos cap, complete with its foot-and-a-half-tall feather on top.

Ravenna clapped loudly, making most conversations halt.

"They're here! The happy couple is here!" Ravenna said with such gusto that Pandora tried not to cringe.

Victor's hand gave hers another squeeze as Ophelia and Lucian moved out of the crowd, making their way over toward Pandora and Victor.

"Mum, Dad, this is Victor," Pandora said as soon as they were close. "Victor, this is my mum and dad."

"Mrs. Von Ashmore," Victor said, using his free hand to reach for Ophelia's hand, since Pandora was clinging to his other one. "It's so nice to finally meet you," he said as her mother's keen gaze moved over him to land on their hands.

Pandora panicked, thinking she was picking up on the fact that they clearly weren't doing it or anything. Instead, Ophelia cleared her throat and bulged her eyes slightly making Pandora look down and realize she was squeezing Victor's hand so hard that it had turned white.

"Yes, Victor," Ophelia said as soon as Pandora had eased her hold on Victor's hand. "We are glad to make your acquaintance. Even if we have just recently learned about you," she said.

"Mr. Von Ashmore," Victor said, giving Pandora's father a firm shake, keeping eye contact. Which Pandora knew couldn't have been easy because her father was, arguably, the scariest man in any room.

"Victor," Lucian said, his gaze moving over his daughter's fiancé.

"Is that a *ring* I see?" Ravenna rushed up beside Ophelia, ramming into her in the process and sending Ophelia crashing into her husband.

"Oh, yes," Pandora said, about to lift her hand. Ravenna was faster, grabbing Pandora's hand and yanking it hard enough to make her stumble forward.

"Oh, this is a beaut," Ravenna said, pulling the ring up close. Then, and Pandora couldn't make this up, producing one of those little jewelry magnifying glasses out of some hidden pocket to inspect the ring more closely. "Yes, *very* nice. You know, I've always said you can judge a man by how fine his taste in jewelry is. The vam . . . man," Ravenna caught herself, "I dated before my dear Reginald didn't know the difference between an emerald and a ruby. Clearly, that was a courtship due to fail. But you, my dear," she said, looking from Pandora to Victor. "You have found a keeper. Reginald!" Her shout made Victor, unaccustomed to her loudness, jerk. "Get over here and meet Pandora's fiancé."

Reginald untangled himself from his conversation with

the raven, shuffled over, then gave Victor a hearty handshake. "Nice to meet you, old boy," he said, trying to straighten himself up to full height, despite being a solid six inches shorter than Victor.

"You too, sir," Victor said, perfect manners on display. "Is that a real sword?"

"This?" Reginald asked, reaching for it and then brandishing it with wild abandon, making everyone take a step back from him. "It sure is, my boy. I took this thing off of the bod—"

"Hey!" Pandora cut in, voice high and tinny. "Is that Dante?" She looked across the room, desperate to get Victor away from Reginald, who'd just been about to tell the story of roaming the fields of battle, looking for some easy necks to sip from, when he came upon the uniform he was currently wearing and decided he needed it for his own collection.

On any given day, Reginald could be wearing the cloak of some forgotten king, a Roman toga, or, once, a full-on hippie costume straight out of sixties California. And with each of those outfits, there was the story of the poor human who'd lost their life.

As Pandora physically pulled Victor away from that crowd, she could hear Ravenna whisper-yelling at her husband.

"He's a mortal, remember? You can't go around talking about killing his kind."

"Dante," Pandora said, a desperate edge slipping into her voice as they approached her brother, dodging another dozen or so family members in the process.

"Going well?" he asked with a little smirk. "Victor, nice to meet you."

"Why didn't you warn me?" Pandora asked, glancing around the room to see one of her cousins pour something thick and viscous into a glass.

"Mum took my mobile, so I couldn't," Dante said, shaking his head. "Tried to sneak out once or twice too. But you know Mum."

"She looks so young," Victor said, making Pandora stiffen.

"Oh, uh, yeah. Really good genes," she said.

"And your father is . . ."

"Scary as hell?" Dante filled in for him. "I would say he's a big softy underneath it all, but that would be a lie. He's got a soft spot for Pandy, but that only means he's gonna hate you all the more."

"Not helping," Pandora said, wincing.

"Pandy?" Victor asked, shooting Pandora a smile.

"Here, dear," Ravenna said, shoving a goblet toward Victor. "You must be parched!"

Panicked, Pandora's hand shot out, grabbing the goblet before Victor could lift it to his lips.

He shot her a scrunched-brow look as she sniffed the liquid.

But it was wine.

"Just wine," she said on an exhale.

"What else would it be, dear?" Ravenna asked, looking at Pandora like she was the crazy one.

"Thank you," Victor said, pulling his glass back and taking a polite sip.

It was virtually impossible for vampires to get drunk. But Pandora was moments away from testing that theory.

"Of course, my dear. Dinner should be ready shortly," she said, making Pandora's stomach sink.

"Dinner?" she asked, looking at Dante. "Please tell me they ordered in."

"Afraid not," he said, giving her a pained look she didn't quite understand.

"What's the problem?" Victor asked, looking between the two of them.

"Oh, nothing. It's just . . . no one in my family is a good cook. We're, er, cursed that way, I guess. So maybe just . . . take a couple of small, polite bites."

Dante nodded. "Or spit it discreetly into your napkin."

"It can't be that bad," Victor said.

That was where he was wrong.

As he would find out after a few more tense introductions, mostly only on Pandora's part. Victor seemed to be handling things effortlessly. Even occasionally shooting her reassuring smiles.

"Can I ask you something?" he asked as everyone started to file into the dining room.

"Sure," she asked, instantly on edge.

"Your family . . . the way they dress and speak . . ."

"Oh!" she said, mind racing. "They're, you know, part of a historical reenactment society. They really get into character sometimes. It's hard for them to, well, turn it off. Uncle Reginald especially," she added, glad to plant seeds of doubt for when Uncle Reggie eventually said something that wouldn't make any sense. "He's kind of a . . . What do they call them? When an actor really commits to a part?"

"A method actor," Victor said.

"Right. That. He once went around telling us that he was a close personal friend of Socrates," she said, rolling her eyes for emphasis.

"That explains it," Victor said. Pandora thought she

113

heard a false note in his voice, but they'd just made their way into the dining room. And, well, there were other, more important problems at hand.

Like the fact that there was an entire *roasted pig* sitting in the center of the table like decor, an apple in its mouth.

Ravenna was still standing, waiting for them to enter, proud and puffed as a peacock as she waved at the *feast*. "We have all of the best here! Suckling pig, swan pie, jellied eel, ox tongue in claret sauce, lamprey in blood sauce, pottage, butter-basted turnips, and honeyed parsnips!"

Pandora's gaze searched the table for Dante, suddenly understanding the sick, almost green, look he'd given her when speaking of her family cooking.

They'd certainly cooked, all right.

Delicacies, even.

By medieval standards, maybe.

Victor looked a bit grey at the selection.

He leaned in close to Pandora's ear. "Isn't it illegal to kill swans?"

"Oh, um, I'm sure it's just, like, actually chicken," she said, sure of no such thing. "Stick to the veg and pottage," she whispered to him before Ravenna rushed forward, breaking them apart to sit them across from each other at the table.

"Reginald, dear, if you could do the honors," she said, waving toward the pig.

And then her uncle stood and proceeded to draw his sword and attempt to carve with that, knocking over a decanter of wine in the process.

Pandora almost brought up her elbows on the table and held her head in her hands. It was her mother's intense, perceptive gaze that kept her spine against the chair back and her chin lifted.

The mess was cleaned up and Dante grabbed an actual carving knife from the kitchen and began to carve the meat himself, as everyone else started to add food to their plates.

"You need to eat, dear," Ravenna chided Pandora, tapping her arm.

Pandora was getting the impression that her great-aunt was fancying herself the family's expert on humans and human customs. It was both endearing, because Pandora had to appreciate how much she was clearly trying, and hilarious, because Ravenna and Reginald lived in a castle on a coastal cliff overlooking Devon. Where she and her husband rarely, if ever, interacted with humans, preferring to have a revolving door of guests hole up with them in elegance and seclusion.

"Men love a woman who can keep her curves," she said, giving her shoulders a shimmy, which, in turn, made her bosom dance around jollily – and nearly spill out of the low-cut bodice of her gown.

Victor shared an amused look with Pandora as he passed her some of the turnips.

"You know what this meal reminds me of?" Uncle Reginald asked as he heaped the lamprey in blood sauce onto his plate. Pandora didn't even know where the plates had come from. "The meals at the palace directly before the Black Death started," he continued, making Pandora sigh to herself. "Lampreys were abundant then. Though, the blood sauce was a bit richer."

Victor's brows pinched at that.

"He's a big history buff," Dante, at Victor's side, said,

saving Pandora from trying to rack her brain for another excuse.

"Well, if you like that blood sauce so much more, perhaps I shouldn't ever make it for you." Ravenna huffed, flicking her silver curls, offended.

"Everything looks lovely," Victor told Ravenna, making the woman soften immediately.

"See? This young man knows how to speak to a woman who sweated over a stove for seven hours today."

Pandora imagined that was true – the sweating aside – because she couldn't imagine her own mother standing at a stove mixing stew or chopping up lamprey.

"So, Victor," Lucian spoke, making Pandora tense yet again, worried her father was going to try to say something to scare off her fiancé. "I hear you are a student." Pandora hoped Victor didn't pick up on the coolness in her father's voice at that last word.

"I am, sir," Victor replied, seemingly glad to have a reason to put his fork down.

Down the table, Pandora's cousin Jasper was plopping chunks of lamprey back into the serving dish so he could sip the blood right out of his bowl.

With Victor distracted, Pandora leaned down, suddenly paranoid about what kind of blood had been used to make the sauce. But all she caught were hints of fish, tomato, and wine. No actual blood at all.

Down the table, Jasper learned this at the same time, choking and spluttering as Bellatrix scowled and wiped a splash of sauce off her bare arm.

"You all right there, my boy?" Uncle Reginald asked, rapping Jasper hard on the back, making him nearly faceplant into his plate piled with jellied eel.

116

"And how do you plan to take care of my daughter when you are a student?" Lucian asked.

"I will be finishing up university within the next year, sir. Then I plan to become a lecturer myself," Victor said, pulling himself up to full height, proud of his future plans.

Pandora knew her own father would not be impressed, though. Not when he believed Pandora should be pampered by her husband and his fortune.

She probably should have been trying to think of a way to interject, to guide the conversation toward more neutral ground. But she was too busy imagining walking into a lecture hall to see Victor standing there at the front, looking studious in a sweater vest and maybe some glasses that he would take off when he was passionate . . .

Lucian's next question made Pandora groan. "Are you aware that my daughter is about to inhe—"

The heavy metallic clang of the door knocker echoed through the house, its weighted thud carrying a hollow resonance that seemed to shudder through the very walls.

It cut cleanly through the hum of conversation, the clinking of cutlery, and the heavy tension in the air of the dining room.

"Now, who could that be?" Ravenna asked, glancing up and down the table as if to figure out who wasn't in attendance.

Though, thanks to their massive extended family, Pandora could think of at least two dozen cousins, aunts, uncles, or friends that weren't currently taking up seats at the table.

"I will see," Ophelia said, rising from her seat like a queen from her throne.

If Pandora had been paying closer attention, she might

117

have noticed the devious smile tugging at the corners of her mother's lips. But she found herself suddenly occupied by the empty chair directly beside her.

Why had they stuck Victor across the table if there was an empty seat right next to her?

As if answering her question in real time, Ophelia moved into the doorway of the dining room.

But she was no longer alone.

Standing beside her was a man who commanded all the attention in the room.

It seemed as if his very presence made the air in the room shift, demanding everyone turn to look at him.

He was tall and impeccably dressed, his tailored suit fitting him like a second skin, every stitch screaming wealth and refinement.

His dark hair gleamed under the chandelier's light, swept back in effortless waves that framed a face that seemed carved from marble.

He had high cheekbones, a strong jawline, and lips that were curved up in the faintest smile.

It was the eyes that commanded the most attention – a moody grey full of intelligence, their intensity softened only by a slight glint of amusement.

He stood with the easy grace of someone used to being noticed, his posture impeccable, but with an ease that belied his outward formality.

Not a single human in existence exuded that amount of charm and self-possession.

This late stranger?

He was a vampire.

"Everyone, it is my great honor," Ophelia said, giving a genuine smile, "to introduce to you Elias Thornwell."

She reached to touch the arm of the man at her side. "Elias, this is my family." Ophelia waved down the table. "My husband, Lucian. My son, Dante." Then, with much more emphasis, she said, "And, of course, my daughter, Pandora."

"The pleasure is mine," Elias said, pressing a hand to his heart as his gaze swept the table, landing on Pandora. That lightness in his eyes increased, but Pandora was too confused by his presence to notice.

At least until her mother led Elias over to her side.

And Pandora finally picked up on that mischievous look in her mother's eyes.

"Pandora," Elias said as he slid into the seat beside her. She could smell his cologne, something rich and spicy, yet understated. It should have been overwhelming in a pleasant way. But all she could think was that Victor smelled so much more delicious. "I have heard so much about you."

It was right then that Pandora put it all together.

This wasn't just a random dinner guest.

And the seat beside her hadn't just accidentally been left empty.

This had all been planned.

By her mother.

Who didn't approve of her daughter's plan to marry a human.

So she'd brought in the most handsome, wealthy, and charming vampire she could find as another, more suitable, love interest.

"Funny," Pandora said, aware of Victor's intense gaze from across the table. "I haven't heard a thing about you."

13

"She didn't!" Lucy gasped in Pandora's ear.

Shortly after Elias had joined the table, he'd proceeded to compliment everything, from the room to the food, charming everyone with an ease that Pandora had both admired and hated in equal measure. Since he also seemed to be making Victor uncomfortable, Pandora had offered to go get more wine in the kitchen.

And had promptly grabbed her mobile and called her best friend to tell her what her mother had done.

"She did," Pandora said, checking the labels of the bottles of wine. "And now Victor seems tense and broody, while Elias just lays the charm on thick. My father is half in love with him already. Mostly because he's a brilliant businessman and can 'take care of' me."

"You're about to be an heiress. You don't need to be taken care of."

"I know, right?" she said, pulling three bottles of wine to the center of the island to bring back into the dining room.

"What are you going to do? Confront your mum?"

"Not in front of everyone. But I can't just let her think this is OK."

"Darling, are you hiding away?" Ophelia called out.

"I have to go," Pandora whispered to Lucy.

"Call me later! And get me a picture of the hottie."

Pandora quickly tucked her mobile back into her handbag as her mother's heels clicked into the kitchen. Unsurprisingly, Elias was right behind her.

"Yes, my love?" Ophelia looked back toward the dining room, as if hearing her husband call for her. But Pandora knew her game. "Elias, can you help Pandora with the wine?"

"Of course," Elias said, even giving Ophelia a proper little bow.

"Happy engagement," Elias said, his gaze slipping to Pandora's hand. "The human?" he asked.

"Obviously," Pandora replied.

"Not your mother's first choice for you, I take it." Elias reached for the corkscrew and started to open the first bottle of wine.

Pandora gave him a tight nod as she passed him the next bottle to open.

It was right then that she smelled vanilla, leather, and cinnamon wafting toward her, the scent immediately comforting.

"Dante sent me in here," Victor said, giving Elias a hard look. Victor made his way to Pandora's side, making the two of them a united front against the interloper. "Your

121

cousin Jasper was trying to tell me about some bar that I supposedly walk past every day," he continued. "But I swear there's nothing there . . ."

Pandora shared a look with Elias, knowing what Jasper was likely referencing. A vampire club. The kind of place that was glamoured so humans couldn't see it.

"Jasper's probably drunk," Pandora said, shrugging it off. "You didn't have to choke down too much of that food, I hope."

"No." Victor winced a bit. "But no one is really eating," he added with a casual shrug. "Not even Ravenna."

"I'm so sorry about that," Pandora said. "My family has really . . . unusual tastes."

Across from her, Elias's lips twitched.

Victor shrugged that off. "All families have their food quirks. My mother refuses to ever use garlic in her cooking."

At least Pandora wouldn't die if she ate at Victor's parents' house.

"That's handy," Elias said, making Victor's brows pinch.

"How do you figure?" he asked.

"Oh, because of Pandora's garlic allergy, of course," Elias said.

Victor looked confused by that, likely mentally flicking through all of the questions they'd shared, trying to figure out if he'd forgotten something that important. "Of course."

Pandora couldn't figure out Elias's motivation for that comment. Was he trying to make it sound like he knew her better than Victor did? Or was he simply trying to save Pandora from an extremely uncomfortable – if not fatal – meal?

"I have the same allergy," Elias said. "In fact, isn't it . . . genetic for you, Pandora?"

"Oh, er, yes, actually," she said. "I think I forgot to mention that." She looked at Victor. "We're all allergic to garlic. Weird, but true."

"Victor, dear, you are missing the most amusing story." Ophelia appeared in the doorway, pointedly waiting until Victor moved away from Pandora's side.

Victor looked back at Pandora.

"I'm coming too," she said, snatching the two opened bottles of wine and following him out. She refused to give in to her mother's scheming.

In fact, she even took her seat next to Victor at the table instead of staying next to Elias. His leg brushed against hers, and she could swear a jolt of electricity coursed up her thigh and sneaked across her belly.

"Elias is going to be staying with us for a few weeks," Ophelia said, making Pandora turn her stunned look to her mother.

"Why?" she asked before she could think better of it.

"What a strange question," Ophelia said. "Because we look forward to enjoying his company."

Pandora glanced over toward her brother, silently asking if he knew anything of this. But Dante just gave her a small head shake. This was the first he was hearing about it as well.

Pandora was half tempted to declare that now that she was engaged, she was going to be moving in with Victor. She was all too aware, however, that her future was still in her parents' hands. If she wanted to inherit her fortune, she had to play nice. Or, at the very least, not outright goad them.

"Victor, Dante, do you mind helping Ravenna clear the table?" Ophelia asked, knowing she was taking away Pandora's only back-up at the table.

"Victor is a guest, Mum," Pandora said. Normally, her parents were nothing if not well-mannered.

"Nonsense," Ophelia said, waving an elegant hand. "He's practically family now, isn't he?"

"I'll help too," Pandora said, pushing her chair back.

"It's OK," Victor said, giving her hand a squeeze. "Of course, Mrs. Von Ashmore." He got to his feet, then reached for the nearest serving dishes. "I'm happy to help."

Pandora watched Victor follow Dante and Ravenna out of the dining room, before turning back with a sigh.

"So, Pandora," Elias said, either oblivious to her sour mood, or not caring, "I hear you work at a . . . coffee shop."

"I do."

"Why?" he asked, gesturing toward the house.

She couldn't exactly tell him that she worked there because she actually liked humans; she found that their mortality made them seem to just live more fully. They knew they only had a certain number of years, so they tried to fill that time with as much laughter and joy as possible.

It was endearing and refreshing.

"I like it," she answered simply.

Ophelia prompted her. "Dear, this is where you ask Elias what he does for work."

Pandora couldn't care less. But she couldn't be that rude. "What do you do for work, Elias?" she asked obediently.

"I deal in rare artifacts," he said. Which, thankfully,

prompted about three hundred questions from Uncle Reginald, who, apparently, had about a thousand items he might be interested in selling.

The discussion lasted long enough – despite Ophelia's constant attempts to steer the conversation and get Elias and Pandora talking – to allow Victor to finish helping with the clearing of the table, whole pig and all, and take his seat beside her again.

"Never . . . more," Vlad declared this into a sudden gap in the chatter, making Victor look over, brows raised as he inspected the raven.

"That's impressive," he said, nodding at the bird.

Pandora didn't tell Victor that Vlad could actually recite the entire one-hundred-and-eight-line poem. In dramatized fashion. Or that he claimed he was the raven from the famous poem. That taunting Edgar had simply been another of his many pranks during a short stint their family had spent in the States. Nor that, despite all of that, Vlad's favorite Edgar Allan Poe poem was actually *Annabel Lee*.

"He's a chatty bird," Pandora said, figuring there might be a time when Victor overheard the raven speaking, and not wanting him to be surprised by it.

Though, even she had to admit that the chances of Victor finding out that undead ravens existed, let alone that her family had one, were slim to none.

"Shall we take drinks in the parlour?" Ophelia asked, rising to her feet, prompting all of the men to immediately follow.

Victor reached for the back of Pandora's chair and then waited for her to step out, before following her out into the hallway, then down the hall toward the parlour.

"Wow, that's an impressive clock," Victor said as he noticed the cherrywood grandfather clock with its ebony inlays and brass Arabic numerals. The swan-neck pendant sat unmoving.

"It's a shame it hasn't rung since 1832," Lucian said in passing, forgetting the situation for a moment.

Victor shot a confused look in Pandora's direction. "How does he know that?"

"Oh, er, it was . . . in the owner's manual," Pandora said. "Very detailed," she added with a nod.

"Mind if I take a look at it?" Elias asked, making Lucian straighten.

"By all means," her father said. Pandora tried not to roll her eyes as she led Victor further into the room, pulling him down with her on a sofa.

"You're still freezing," Victor said when her hand brushed his. He reached for it, holding it between both of his as Ravenna asked him no fewer than fifty rapid-fire questions, barely giving him enough time to answer before shooting him another one.

Pandora was endlessly thankful for Ravenna, though. She was clearly trying. To be accepting. To make Victor feel comfortable.

While her own mother tried to insert a new love interest into her life. Right under her fiancé's nose.

"There we go," Elias said a few moments later, waving toward where the pendulum was now swinging lazily.

Who was this guy?

Pandora thought he was starting to seem like one of those Mary Sue characters in books that were universally hated because they were just too good at everything. Too pretty, too smart, too talented. With no real depths,

126

vulnerabilities, insecurities, or flaws to even out all that perfection.

What was the male version of a Mary Sue called, she wondered. A Larry Stu? Gary Stu?

If they were taking suggestions for new names for the male version, Pandora would love to volunteer Elias Thornwell.

No, it didn't roll off the tongue quite as easily, but it would sure make Pandora feel a lot better if a hated characterization was named after the vampire who was currently schmoozing her mother and father without any effort.

"Pandora?" Victor's voice snapped her out of her thoughts.

"Yeah?" she asked, horrified that Victor might have seen her staring at Elias and assumed she might be ogling him, instead of imagining what it might be like to stomp over there and push him into the fireplace. "Sorry. I'm getting tired."

It wasn't a lie per se.

She was tired.

Exhausted, actually.

But mentally, emotionally. Not physically. If she went up to bed, she was sure she would toss and turn endlessly, replaying the events of the night, beating herself up for things she'd done, or hadn't done, to make the evening go more smoothly.

"Maybe we should call it a night," Ravenna said, looking concerned.

"Oh, no!" Aunt Anastacia got to her feet. "My Bellatrix was just about to honor us all with a song."

As if the night hadn't been painful enough.

Pandora turned her head so she could speak without anyone reading her lips, and whispered to Victor, "I apologize in advance for this."

Victor turned his head closer, his lips nearly brushing her ear, his warm breath teasing over her skin. "For what?"

He found out soon enough, though, as Bellatrix got to her feet, clasped her hands in front of her, elbows out wide, opened her mouth, and made them all regret the great acoustics in the room.

"Victor," Anastacia said afterward, beaming. "What did you think?"

Victor paused for the barest of seconds before saying, with a straight face, "I have no words."

A laugh built in Pandora's throat before she could fight it off, making her cover it with a hard cough instead.

"Sorry," she said as Victor patted her on the back, his green eyes bright with barely contained laughter himself. "Wine went down the wrong pipe," she said, despite not having taken a sip.

"Bellatrix," Elias called out, making everyone turn to face him. "Wherever did you learn to sing?" he asked, making Pandora wonder if his one true flaw was being tone-challenged.

"Oh, my Bellatrix is entirely self-taught." Aunt Anastacia beamed at her daughter.

"You wouldn't want a vocal coach to ruin such . . . raw talent," Elias said smoothly, making Pandora put a hand over her mouth, looking like she was covering a yawn, not suppressing a smile.

Maybe he wasn't as boring and annoying as she'd first thought.

Still, that didn't mean she was going to fall for the guy, no matter what her mother wanted.

She was with Victor.

Just then, Victor's thumb started to absentmindedly tease over the back of her hand. She felt that familiar sizzle of interest, of attraction, of longing moving up her arm and across her chest, making that newly familiar heat warm her from the inside once again.

At that same moment, across the room, Ophelia's smile fell as she looked at her daughter.

14

"OK. What else?" Lucy asked in Pandora's ear as she rushed around her room, trying to get together for her shift.

"It was mostly tame after that. I mean, as tame as my family can be anyway. They wouldn't let me walk Victor to the Tube, though, which was ridiculous."

"As if any mere human could overpower you, even running on pig's blood and anxiety."

"Right?" Pandora asked, pulling her hair back into a clip, shrugging on her coat, then making her way to the door.

Where she almost plowed right into Elias, who was standing there with his arm raised, poised to knock.

"Pandora," he said, glancing at her work place logo, then back up at her face.

"Is that him? The vampire?" Lucy asked.

"It is," Elias replied.

"What are you doing here?" Pandora asked, glancing past him into the hall, but not seeing anyone else lingering around.

"Your mother asked me to escort you to work this evening," he told her.

"Ooh. This is getting juicy," Lucy said in Pandora's ear. She could barely think with her own thoughts in her head, let alone Lucy's.

"I'll see you in a bit, Luce," she said, hanging up and dropping her mobile into her pocket.

"I don't need an escort. But thanks anyway," Pandora said, pushing past him to make her way down the steps before Elias could say anything further.

She felt him following her, but he said nothing until they were on the first floor.

"I'm afraid I must insist."

"Why are you doing this?" Pandora asked, whirling on him.

"Taking you to work?"

"No. Yes."

"Which one is it?"

"Both," she said, throwing up a hand. "Why are you here? Why are you playing this game?"

"I can assure you it isn't a game," he told her.

"It has to be a game. You don't even know me."

"Which is the purpose of escorting you to work."

"I'm *engaged*," she said, turning and walking toward the door, ignoring Bellatrix and her mother in the sitting room as she went. She was too angry to speak to her mother right then. She would end up saying something she'd regret.

131

"I noticed." Elias followed her down the cobblestone path, then along the road, staying half a step behind her, despite being longer-legged with a bigger stride.

"And yet you are following me to work."

"Are you concerned you might cheat on your fiancé with me?" Elias asked, making Pandora turn and gape at him.

"Of course not."

"Then why does it matter if I tag along?"

Oh, only because she was lying to her whole family and also lying to her fake fiancé, and she really needed to be able to talk about it openly to the only person who knew the whole story. And his presence was only going to make that harder.

"Suit yourself," she said, turning away. "But you have to buy something to sit there all night."

"That will not be a problem."

"And you can't eat any of the customers."

"Not even a little sip?" he asked, making her grumble until she realized he was teasing.

They made their way down to the Tube and Pandora couldn't help but marvel at how he seemed incredibly out of place, but also perfectly blended in.

A group of women seated across from them on the train kept checking him out, whispering and giggling to one another, and one even got ballsy enough to snap a picture of him.

"What?" Elias asked when he caught her staring at his profile.

"That entire group of girls is mooning over you."

"They're not exactly subtle about it."

"They're all very pretty," she said.

"I suppose." He shrugged, not casting them another glance to check.

"Prettier than I am," she added.

"You sell yourself short," Elias said, shaking his head.

"Fine. Then they're at least on the same level."

"Is there a point to this line of conversation?"

"Why are you so intent on spending time with me when there are plenty of other pretty and, the most important part, *willing*, interested women around?"

"If you're so happy with your fiancé, why does it bother you so much?"

"Is it because of my inheritance?" she asked.

"You insult me," he said.

"That's not a no."

"It's certainly not a yes. I have my own fortune. I don't need your inheritance. Your mortal, however . . ."

"Don't insult him," Pandora said crossly, though she was well aware of the irony.

"You don't find it the least bit suspicious that he proposed shortly after you learned the terms of your inheritance?" Elias asked.

"How do you even know that? What else has my mother told you about me and my life?"

"Only what she believed was pertinent, I imagine."

"Like what?"

Elias watched her for a second before deciding to answer her. "She mentioned that you have an unnatural affection for humans."

"It's not *unnatural* to like humans."

"They're your food source."

"So what?" she asked. "By that logic, it is unnatural for a human to like cows or pigs or chickens?"

133

He didn't want to get into a debate with her on the topic, though. "She also said she felt you were making a foolish choice based on a deadline and limited options."

"Wow," Pandora said with a huff. "That's . . . really insulting."

"To be clear, there is no earthly reason you should be short on suitors," Elias said, watching her face for a moment. "Save for your aversion to dating your own kind."

"Have you met most male *vampires*?" she asked, dipping her voice low. "Having centuries to let their egos inflate? Not my type." She made her way out of the train and up the stairs.

The rain was starting to pelt down on them as they made their way toward Luna Bean.

She was glad to get inside, to walk into the break room to get away from Elias for a few moments as she hung up her jacket and fixed her wet hair.

Lucy came shuffling in through the side door a few minutes later.

"Girl, you can't just leave me hanging. What did the hot vampire have to say?"

"Ask him yourself," Pandora said, waving toward the near-empty café, save for Elias, who was standing at the counter perusing the options.

"Oh my God." Lucy gasped, her mouth falling open. "You really didn't do the guy any justice. Holy crap. He's downright lickable."

"I have no interest in licking him."

"Not even a little bit?" Lucy asked, dubious.

"Not even."

"Can *I* lick him, then?" Lucy asked.

"Knock yourself out," Pandora said as they both moved behind the counter.

Pandora was about to ask Elias what he wanted, when she noticed him sniff the air then turn his keen grey eyes on Lucy.

"Smells a bit like *wet dog* in here, don't you think?" he asked, making Pandora gasp as Lucy stiffened.

"Excuse me?" her friend said.

"No need to snarl," Elias replied, only managing to both tick off and frazzle Lucy further.

"What is the *matter* with you?" Pandora asked, glaring at the vampire who had been an annoyance, but not overly offensive, just moments before.

"Nothing," Elias said, tone still light. While Lucy was practically vibrating with rage beside Pandora. "Just surprised that this is a pet-friendly establishment, is all." Pandora's brows pinched at the light dancing in his eyes. Was he just teasing Lucy?

Lucy missed it, though, and Pandora watched her friend's eyes flash yellow, knowing she was close to losing control.

As a whole, werewolves were able to control their impulses. Especially if they allowed themselves to run wild during the full moons, giving in to the beast inside completely for a few days.

But high emotions could trigger the transition if they weren't careful.

"Easy there," Elias said, lips twitching up as he looked at Lucy. "Your inner puppy is showing. Do you need a chew toy to calm down? Perhaps a game of fetch?"

Lucy wrestled with her wolf for another second before finally winning the battle, taking a deep breath and reaching out to grab the container of stir sticks.

"Wow, look, so many pointy wooden objects," she said.

"OK. OK," Pandora said, holding up a hand. "Can we get past all this vampire/werewolf nonsense? Aren't we all more evolved than this?"

"Hey, it's not my fault," Lucy said, head tipped to the side, deceptively calm, "that he lives forever and *this* is the best personality he could muster. Talk about wasted potential."

Elias clapped back, "At least my kind has evolved past marking their territory."

"This is who your mother thinks is a better choice than Victor?" Lucy asked, looking at Pandora. "I've met corpses with more charm."

"Is she always this grumpy or is she just hungry?" Elias asked. "I think I saw a fox across the street." He waved out the window. "Go, fetch."

Pandora spotted another twitch to his lips, convincing her that what she worried could be speciesist dislike was something a lot less antagonistic.

"Aw." Lucy gave him a saccharine smile. "Such big talk for a glorified mosquito."

"What is happening here?" Pandora asked, looking between the two of them, sensing an undercurrent of heat.

And, of course, it was right at that moment that Victor decided to come walking into the shop, shaking rain off of his jacket before freezing mid-stride when he saw Elias standing there.

"Hey!" Pandora immediately reached for a cup and pumped in some caramel syrup. "Just give me one second." She rushed through the process of making his macchiato as Lucy and Elias mostly glared at each other.

"Can you get me my drink?" Elias asked her. "Or do you need to go wash your paws first?"

"We don't have your preferred *drink* here," Lucy said, as Victor watched the two of them with scrunched brows as he sat down at his usual table.

"A black coffee will suffice," Elias said as Pandora hurried over to Victor just to get away from the two of them for a minute.

"What's going on there?" Victor asked as she sat across from him.

"I have *no* idea," she replied, giving Victor wide eyes. "I can't tell if they're going to fight . . . or kiss," she added, making Victor smile. "All they're doing is trading jabs. But they literally just met."

She couldn't tell him, of course, that some vampires and werewolves took that age-old rivalry seriously. Even if no one really even knew why the two didn't get along in the first place.

Apparently, Elias was one of those vampires.

As for Lucy, she was just responding to his energy. Since she was close with Pandora, she clearly didn't care about ancient nonsense like that.

"What is he doing here?" Victor asked, casting a hard look in Elias's direction.

"He insisted on walking me to work," Pandora told him.

Victor let that sit for a second. "Your mother doesn't like me."

"It's not . . . that," she said, even though it was. "She's just . . . She has very specific ideas of the kind of guy she wants me to be with. Regardless of what I want."

"I would understand," Victor said, watching Elias and

137

Lucy get tenser each passing second, "if you changed your mind and wanted to marry him instead. If there's . . . something going on there."

"There's not! I mean . . . he's nice enough."

"And good-looking."

"You're good-looking too," Pandora said.

"And rich."

"*I'm* going to be well-off."

"And your mother loves him."

"My mum will come around," Pandora said. Although she didn't know if that was the case. "I chose you. I'm sticking with that decision. No matter how many times my mum tries to throw Elias and me together."

Victor nodded at that.

"So . . . what now?" he asked.

"What do you mean?"

"We're engaged. We had a little party. What is next?"

"Oh. Well, I guess . . . wedding planning, right? Invitations and cakes and venues . . ."

"And my parents," he said.

"Oh, right. Of course. Have you told them?"

"Yeah. That's how I got the ring," he said, glancing down at Pandora's hand.

The ring had already started to feel like a part of her. She was anxious to take it off for the short amount of time she spent in the shower. Whenever she thought about how she was going to need to give it back to Victor when they divorced, she felt an unexpected pang. Despite knowing she would have the money to have an exact replica made, should she want to.

It would be different.

It wouldn't be from *him*.

138

"Will we be having dinner at their house?" she asked.

"If anything, I think they would come to London," Victor told her.

"Maybe we could arrange a dinner somewhere. For me to meet your parents and for both our parents to meet. I imagine they will all ask about that eventually." At Victor's tense look, Pandora rushed to add, "I will have a talk with my parents about being on their best behavior."

"It's silly to be worried about what your mum thinks of me when we aren't even going to genuinely be—"

"What are we discussing?" Elias cut in, making Pandora jump so much that she almost fell out of her chair.

"Our parents meeting," Victor told Elias, pointedly not bothering to move his jacket and backpack off of the chair at his side.

Pandora wasn't as quick, so Elias slid in beside her.

"That should be . . . interesting," Elias said, making Pandora glare at him.

"You're not invited," she told him.

"I did not expect to be. So, Victor," Elias said, making Pandora's stomach clench.

"You walked me to work," Pandora said. "Why don't you head back? I'm sure Mum would love the opportunity to fawn over you some more."

Elias shot back, "I'm just as certain she would be happier knowing I am here."

"Why are you so—"

"Pandora." Lucy's raised voice made Pandora turn to look at her friend, who was jerking her head toward the break room.

"Go ahead," Victor said, giving her a soft look, then Elias a much colder one. "We're fine here."

139

She didn't want to leave the two of them alone. Both had secrets of hers that she desperately needed to keep.

She rose from her seat and made her way over toward Lucy, who promptly hooked her arm through Pandora's and half dragged her into the break room.

"From under *what* rock did that asshole crawl out?" she asked, cheeks flushed with frustration. "And can we shove him back under it? And roll it over and over him until he becomes vampire goo?"

"Yeah, that was so unexpected. He's been really cordial to me. Kind, even. What did he say when I walked away?"

"More of the same, really. He's annoyingly collected when he's being a jerk too."

Lucy's anger ran hot and wild, like her true nature.

Pandora supposed the same could be said for Elias; his nature was cold and controlled. So his anger was the same.

Oil and water, that was what he and Lucy were.

"I don't like him talking to Victor." Pandora moved into the doorway to watch the two. Elias had his back to her, but she really only cared about Victor anyway. While his posture was tight, he seemed relatively calm.

"It's the perfect storm, isn't it?" Lucy asked. "Victor knows about the fake-marriage scheme. And Elias knows about the you-and-your-whole-family-being-vampires thing. What could possibly go wrong?"

"Don't remind me."

"What's his deal? Like, what is he getting out of this?"

"That's what I asked," Pandora said. "But he didn't really have an answer for me. Maybe I can get Dante to get some answers out of Mum. She's not going to tell me, but maybe he can at least figure out what is in it for Elias."

"Do you think he's going to keep on . . . tagging along?"

"Honestly? Yeah."

"Maybe you can hook him up with that bratty cousin of yours."

"I wish. I think Bellatrix ruined the chances of that when she sang last night. Would you hate me forever if I took a little walk with Victor? He's playing it cool, but I think he's a little insecure about Elias being here."

"Go on. If you come back to me sweeping up a pile of dust, just know . . . I really enjoyed staking that guy through the heart."

"Victor, want to take a little walk with me?" Pandora asked when she went back to the table to find both men eyeing each other up.

"Absolutely," he said, getting to his feet and grabbing his jacket. "Can I leave my things here?" He waved toward the backpack with his books, notebook, and laptop.

"Lucy will keep an eye on it, right, Luce?"

"Of course," Lucy said, coming out from behind the counter to snatch the backpack, casting a suspicious glance at Elias in the process.

Pandora was pretty sure, as she walked through the door, that Lucy whacked Elias around the head with the backpack before making her way behind the counter.

15

"Figured you might want a break from Elias," Pandora said as she handed Victor the umbrella to open.

The rain had slowed to a slight drizzle, the kind that shimmered under the glow of the street lamps and left a light sheen on the pavement under their feet.

The air was cool, carrying with it the scent of damp earth and wet leaves, mingling with the distant aroma of woodsmoke.

London felt hushed, the rain and cold sending people indoors.

Pandora watched a couple at a window seat in a restaurant, sitting close and looking into each other's eyes lovingly.

She felt a stab of longing in her chest as she glanced up at Victor, wishing he could look at her like that. Just once.

Sensing her inspection, he glanced down.

"What were you and Elias discussing?" Pandora asked.

"He was mostly talking business and your family."

"Did he say how he knew my family? He's kind of skirting around every question I ask."

"He wasn't specific. He just said he's known your mother for a long time."

"Maybe he sold her something once," Pandora said.

It just didn't make any sense. Her mother had been trying to hook her up with eligible – yet completely undesirable – vampires for ages. Why, if she had someone that was as handsome, charming, and successful as Elias in her back pocket, would she wait so long to introduce them?

It didn't make sense.

She was still trying to mull that over when she saw a flash out of her peripheral vision, making her stiffen and stare off into the distance.

Was it Elias?

No human could move that quickly.

"What is it?" Victor asked, following her gaze.

"I thought I saw someone."

"Really?" he asked. "I was looking that way and didn't see anyone."

What was she supposed to say to that? *You just don't have super speed, so you wouldn't have noticed.*

"Hm. Weird," she said, but she went ahead and peered down the spaces between buildings as they passed.

"So, how long is Elias going to be staying with your family?" Victor asked.

"My best guess? Until the wedding is complete," Pandora told him, not wanting to lie.

"Is he going to be coming with you to work every day?"

"For Lucy's sake, I hope not," Pandora said, grimacing.

143

"I'm sure he'll get bored of following me around. No matter what kind of arrangement he and my mother have."

Just then, she jolted, seeing the flash again. But as soon as she saw it, it was gone.

"See something again?" Victor asked, this time straightening, tensing, becoming more aware of their surroundings.

"Yeah," she said, wishing the street lights would cast a wider glow, hating all the dark shadows that anyone could hide in.

"Want to go back?" he asked.

"It's probably not . . ." She stopped when she saw it again.

But this time, it was closer.

Pandora stiffened when she saw a flash of moonlight-blonde hair.

Not Elias.

Bellatrix?

Why would Bellatrix be following them around?

"It's my cousin," Pandora said in a hushed whisper.

"Jasper?" Victor asked, looking around.

She'd caught the two of them seeming to have a relatively casual conversation at the engagement party.

Pandora didn't know Jasper well, only that he was a bit of a moody guy, prone to broody stares and sour moods. And endlessly embarrassed by their family's antics.

As he was one of the younger vampires, she also figured he was the least likely to mess up and say something about the Spanish Flu or claim to have been close family friends with one of King Henry's many wives.

"I wish," Pandora said. "It has to be Bellatrix."

"Why would she be following us?"

144

That was the question, wasn't it?

But since Bellatrix and Pandora barely tolerated each other, she could only come to one conclusion.

"I'm worried she might think there's something . . . up with us." Pandora kept her voice low, knowing that vampires have acute hearing.

"Up?" Victor looked down at her with those gorgeous green eyes, his dark brows scrunched.

"Yeah, like, I don't know . . . maybe we weren't convincing enough?"

"It was a family gathering," he said. "What were we supposed to do, have our hands all over each other?"

Pandora's skin tingled at the very idea of Victor's hands all over it, especially in that thin, barely-there dress from the party. She could have felt his warm skin through the material, shivered at the way the fabric would have slid across her overly sensitive skin.

"Pandora?" Victor snatched her out of a lovely little fantasy that left her feeling heated and achy.

"I don't know. Some of my family members can be really . . . perceptive. She could have just picked up on there not being, you know . . ." She trailed off, not sure what to say. Heat? Because she sure as hell felt a lot of that toward him, if not the other way around. "I guess just . . . physical contact," she said, shrugging it off.

To that, Victor nodded, looking off in the distance as they started walking again.

"Do you still see her?" he asked, voice low.

"Yeah," Pandora said, but she tried not to be obvious about it. She didn't want Bellatrix knowing she'd seen her. At least not until she knew how to handle the whole situation.

"Good," he said.

Then he was turning toward her, the umbrella tipping to the side, the fine mist of rain cool on her cheeks, contrasting the warmth suddenly crackling in the air between them.

His free hand slid to the small of her back, steadying her as he leaned down. "Just go with it, OK?" he asked, voice low enough for only her to hear, his breath warm on her skin.

"OK," she agreed, happy to have more of . . . whatever this was.

Then his head ducked and his lips claimed hers.

It was firm at first. Deliberate. Part of an act he wanted to sell to an audience.

But the moment their lips met, everyone and everything else fell away.

Suddenly his touch wasn't calculated, but electric – a surge that melted her immediately.

Her hand instinctively slid up to rest on his chest, feeling the steady thrum of his heartbeat beneath the damp fabric of his coat. And suddenly, for her, there was nothing about that moment that was for show.

His grip on her tightened, pulling her closer instead of steadying her, like he couldn't let her move away. Not just yet.

Her own response betrayed her, lips parting under his.

If it was fake, it wasn't supposed to feel like this. Her chest felt tight, her knees weak, as his lips slanted over hers again and again, dragging a soft sigh out of her.

Her hand moved around to the back of his neck as she leaned in, their bodies pressing close so she could feel the beat of his heart reverberate into her own chest.

Victor's teeth nipped her lower lip, making her head fall back, inviting more. Needing more.

Desire was burning through her veins, a wildfire whose flames threatened to consume her completely.

Another whimper escaped her then and the sound seemed to sober Victor.

He pulled back, his hand falling away. She felt embarrassingly unstable without his touch, even as she forced her own hand to fall.

When her lashes finally fluttered open, he was already gazing down at her. His expression was unreadable but changed.

"There," he said, a faint rasp in his voice. "That ought to do it."

As they walked on, they both refused to look at each other.

Pandora couldn't help but wonder what was going through his mind. If that kiss had been as real for him as it had felt for her. If he was feeling as conflicted as she was.

She was so distracted by her own response to the kiss, and her desire for more, that she was only half paying attention to Victor as he started to talk about different printing places in London where they could get their invitations drawn up and made for them.

Sensing her lack of response, he let the conversation fall away before they even made it back to Luna Bean.

"Where'd he go?" Pandora asked when they walked into an empty café. Save for Lucy behind the counter, looking rather pleased with herself.

"Off to torture someone else with his awful personality, no doubt," Lucy said, shrugging.

147

"I'm going to head out," Victor said as Lucy handed him his backpack.

"Oh. Ah, OK," Pandora said, feeling a little rejected, even if she knew that wasn't logical.

"Text me if something comes up. Otherwise, I'll be here tomorrow night."

With that, and not even another glance at Pandora, he left.

"What was that about?" Lucy asked, watching Victor out the window as he walked down the street.

Pandora rushed closer, leaning over the counter. When she spoke, her voice was airy, her words practically tripping over each other. "He kissed me!"

"What?" Lucy asked, mouth falling open. "You can't drop news like that and not give me a byline, at least."

"Well, it starts with us being followed." Pandora moved behind the counter to wipe down the already spotless surface.

She'd always been a stress cleaner.

By the end of this marriage, she was pretty sure she would rub the sheen off the counters and floors at this rate.

"That weaselly, conniving, arrogant—"

"I would love to hear how that ends," Pandora said. "But it wasn't Elias."

"Are you sure? He headed out not long after you two."

"He probably went to feed," Pandora said. "No, it was Bellatrix. She was moving too fast at first to make out." She left out that Bellatrix had also likely just fed, which had made her so much quicker even than Pandora's own vision. "But then I saw her hair. No one else has hair like her and can move that fast. Except maybe my aunt. But she's probably too busy sitting around my house telling our family how perfect her daughter is."

"Why would she be following you? What a creep."

"I'm worried she picked up on things not being . . . real between Victor and me."

"You said you thought the party went well. Aside from Mr. Tall, Dark and Annoying showing up."

"I thought it had. I mean, my mum was suspicious, but I think that had more to do with Victor being human. Everyone else seemed to, you know, buy it."

"Did she see the kiss?"

"Yeah. I mean, she was there when it started. But I, you know, lost track of her once he started kissing me."

"Did you feel it in your toes? You have the look of someone who felt it in their toes."

"I felt it everywhere." Her body felt warm just from the memory.

"And yet you're speed cleaning," Lucy said, making Pandora freeze, realizing her friend was right. She was so worked up that she was letting her supernatural speed come out.

"He was weird after."

"Weird," Lucy said. "Weird like he was giving you a trouser salute and was uncomfortable. Or . . ."

"Or," Pandora said, sighing. "He was silent and kind of distant."

"But you felt butterflies and heard fallen angels sing?" Lucy asked.

"Pretty much."

"Hmm."

"Do you think he really felt nothing?" Pandora asked, hearing the hurt slipping into her voice.

149

"I don't think so. Maybe he's just, you know, conflicted. You know what? Maybe you just need another kiss to see," Lucy said.

"I can't just kiss my fake fiancé."

"You could if you were doing it to put on a show for your family," Lucy said. "Or in front of Elias to drive it home to him that you two are never gonna happen."

"I think Victor is a little threatened by Elias."

"Which is why you can totally get him to kiss you in front of him. Though I don't think he'd feel in any way threatened if he knew what that guy is really like."

"I'm not saying he wasn't being completely inappropriate. But the way you two were sparring felt a little, I don't know, heated," Pandora said as she moved the stir sticks that Lucy had threatened Elias with back to their rightful spot.

"Oh, it was heated all right."

"You said you wanted to lick him."

"Before he opened his mouth, sure. Even the hottest man on earth can be turned ugly when he starts banging on about things."

"So, you think he's the hottest man on earth?" Pandora asked, loving a chance to tease Lucy like her friend had often teased her about her crush on Caramel Macchiato Cutie before they'd known his name.

"Well, I have eyes, don't I?" Lucy turned away to hide the flush that crept up her neck at the mention of Elias's good looks. "Unfortunately, I also have ears. And a brain. And a modicum of self-respect. So no matter how hot he might be, that's never gonna happen. Anyway, why are we still talking about that arrogant, narcissistic—"

"Aw, talking about me?" Elias's voice interrupted,

making Lucy let out an actual growl that Pandora had to fight not to laugh at.

"Ugh. Great. Count Fangula is back. I'm taking a break," she said before disappearing into the back room.

"Where'd you go?" Pandora asked.

"Thought I saw someone," he said, shrugging.

"Are you working with her?" Pandora asked, suddenly suspicious as she glared at Elias.

"Working with whom?" Elias asked. And he was either a very skilled liar or he genuinely didn't know what Pandora was talking about.

"My cousin," she said anyway, wanting to feel him out some more.

"Which one? You appear to have more of them than most."

That was fair.

"Bellatrix."

"The, and I use this term loosely, opera singer?"

"Yeah, that one."

"Why would I be working with her?"

"You're being just as suspicious as she is," Pandora said, shrugging.

"And to what end?" Elias pressed.

She couldn't exactly say "to prove my relationship with Victor is fake", so she went with, "To break up my engagement."

"I understand why I could be accused of that. But why would your cousin Bellatrix?"

"She's just never liked me," Pandora said.

"I get the feeling she's accustomed to being the person getting the most attention in any room she is in. An expectation not helped, it seems, by her doting parents."

"She definitely likes attention."

"And now you have all of it," Elias said. "How inconvenient for her."

"She followed me and Victor tonight," Pandora said, without really knowing why she would loop Elias in on such a thing.

"For what purpose?"

"I have no idea. Knowing her, though, nothing good."

"Do you think she wants to take Victor from you?" he asked.

She frowned. "That hadn't even occurred to me. I mean, I don't think she'd want Victor. My whole family is just barely tolerating the fact that he's human. I doubt she's into him that way."

"Not necessarily to *have* him," Elias said. "Just to take him."

"That's . . ." Pandora paused. Ridiculous? Insane? Something only a monster would do. "Not outside the realm of possibilities."

Their interactions all through their lives had been riddled with competition. Mostly coming from Bellatrix.

Who was prettier? Who was faster? Who had the nicer fangs? Who could get more attention from fellow male vampires?

History had always shown Bellatrix coming out on top. Or, at least, that was how it had felt to Pandora, since she'd never wanted to play those games in the first place, let alone had cared about who'd won.

"I guess the question here is," Elias said, taking a step away from the counter, "if your fiancé is as in love with you as you are with him?"

With that, he made his way out.

152

Leaving Pandora with her mind reeling.

Because Victor wasn't in love with her.

Not at all.

No matter how much she suspected she was starting to fall for him.

16

"Rise and shine, my dear!" Aunt Ravenna's voice rang out. Too peppy. Too loud. And, most importantly, too close.

Pandora shot up in her bed as Ravenna threw on the lights and came bustling into the room, a flurry of deep-purple velvet, bouncing silver curls – and bouncing other . . . assets – and thick, cloying perfume.

"Oh, a bed!" Ravenna said, stopping short, surprised, but recovering quickly. "When I had a bed last, they were stuffed with hay, wool, and hair." She scrunched up her face. "Lumpy, those beds were. This looks right comfortable." She hauled herself up with a bounce that nearly had her coming out of her bodice as she let out a laugh. "How very modern of you, dear. Oh, you have a pet," she said, reaching for Pandora's stuffed capybara. "Is this a pillow?"

"Sort of," Pandora said, brushing her hair out of her face. "Aunt Ravenna, what are you doing in here?" She didn't want to sound surly. But, well, she'd had a good, long sleep-in planned, since she had the night off. Partly to avoid her family. But also, admittedly, to do some moping over the fact that she hadn't heard from Victor since the night of the kiss, save for a single text for him to approve the invitations. She'd wanted to reach out, but each time, she was reminded of how he'd rushed away from her as quickly as possible and hadn't reached out since. So, while she'd been obsessing over him and longing for him, she didn't want to come off as desperate by bugging him all the time.

"There's much to do, my dear!" Ravenna hopped back off the bed. "Weddings are quite the ordeal. Especially for us ladies," she added. "Your uncle Reginald, all he had to do was show up! I had to fuss for weeks with my mother and sisters. Invitations, menus, fittings, the work is never done. By the time it comes, you will have well-earned your honeymoon."

"Invitations are . . . mostly sorted," Pandora said, hearing a hint of sadness in her voice and trying to shake it off before someone started asking why a recently engaged woman was having the blues.

She couldn't exactly tell them that she hadn't seen her fiancé in days. That she'd picked out the invitations all on her own, trying to figure out which designs Victor would object to the least. And what wording he would prefer.

"And that is important, but what's most important of all, my dear, is the dress." Ravenna went to Pandora's wardrobe, clicking her tongue at the options before selecting a black velvet dress her mother had bought her years before. For a dress from Ophelia, it was relatively casual, with a square neck, empire waist, and a hem that only fell just below the knee. But it felt far too dressy for going shopping.

"I think a nice jumper and some jeans would be more appropriate," Pandora said firmly as she climbed out of bed.

"Appropriate, maybe." Ravenna pushed the dress out toward Pandora. "But when you are getting in and out of clothes all night, trust me, you want to make easy work of it."

Not able to argue with that logic, Pandora went into the bathroom to quickly change and pull her hair into a simple braid.

"Much better. You should wear dresses more, my dear. They do flatter the female figure so much better." Ravenna ran her hands down her ample sides, doing a little shimmy of her shoulders in the process to set her chest jiggling. "The men seem to appreciate them as well."

"I'm sure," Pandora said. "So, where are we shopping at night?"

"Oh, we have our places," Ravenna said with a little nod. "We just have to wait for your little friend to get here."

"My friend?" Pandora asked.

"Lucille? Lucinda?"

"Lucy," Pandora said. "Wait, how is Lucy coming?"

"Well, I called her, of course, my dear. Your chief bridesmaid has to be part of the dress-shopping. And you can have her try on some bridesmaid dresses too while we're there. Along with Bellatrix, of course."

156

Pandora just barely held back a grumble at that. She hadn't exactly been thrilled when her mother had claimed it would be rude not to ask Bellatrix to be part of the wedding party, when she would be staying at the house until after the wedding.

She just didn't have the fight in her to argue about it. So, yeah, Bellatrix would be standing up there next to Lucy on Pandora's big day.

She told herself it didn't matter, since the whole marriage was a farce anyway, but it still bothered her more than it should have. Almost as much as when her aunt Anastacia had insisted that Bellatrix 'gift' them a song at their wedding reception.

There were voices moving down the hallway, making Pandora walk toward the door, hoping one of her crazier relations hadn't met Lucy.

Luckily, it was Dante who was walking Lucy down the hall. He looked worse than ever, the bags under his eyes growing by the day.

She really needed to figure out what was going on with him and where he was going each day, only to come back and make strange noises in his room all night.

There was just no easy way to confront him when there were so many family members lurking in the halls or hiding away in strange corners of the house.

"Did someone leave the front door open?" Elias's voice called, making Pandora sigh as she closed her eyes. "Seems a stray dog made its way inside."

"Go away, fang-boy," Lucy said as she passed him by, a limp snake plant nestled in her arm. "This is a night for the girls. Hey!" She beamed at Pandora as she got to her door. "I killed this." She handed Pandora the plant that was supposedly the hardiest of all. "I hear we are doing some crazy vampire night-time dress-shopping venture. I'm so in. I met your brother," she said, giving Dante a smile as he got to his door. He gave them both a nod, then disappeared inside his room. "What are you looking at, bat-breath?" Lucy snarled at Elias, who was leaning against the wall in the hallway.

"Are you sure you should be going out tonight?" Elias asked, making Lucy's brows pinch. "It's just that I heard animal control is really cracking down hard lately . . ."

"Elias!" Pandora said, putting the plant down to nurse back to health later. She was getting tired of jumping between the two of them.

"Oh, great, we're all here," Ophelia said, coming down the hallway with Bellatrix and Aunt Anastacia at her heels. "Elias, darling, it was so kind of you to agree to escort us this evening."

"We don't need an escort," Pandora said, frowning. "We're a bunch of immortal vampires. What could possibly hurt us?"

"There is always the concern that an ambulance might pass by," Elias said. "Your kind chases those, don't they?" he asked Lucy, that same light dancing in his eyes that Pandora had noticed the last time.

"Children," Ophelia said smoothly. "We can all get along for just one night."

With another couple of barbs thrown between Elias and Lucy, they all headed out onto the streets of London.

Ravenna and Ophelia took the lead. Pandora and Lucy were happy to be at the back, lagging behind the others so they could whisper.

"Why the dark cloud?" Lucy asked.

"I haven't heard from Victor since . . . you know . . ."

"He kissed you silly on the street like some epic romance film?"

The memory, which should have been a fond one, had started to darken around the edges, the joy and pleasure she'd once felt, melting into a melancholy that seemed to settle into her very bones.

"Here's a wild idea," Lucy said as they fell further behind the others. "Why don't *you* reach out to him?"

"I don't want to seem desperate."

"You can't be desperate. You're not actually dat . . . Eavesdrop much?" Lucy asked, making Pandora's head pop up to see Bellatrix had slowed down and wasn't even trying to hide that she was listening to them.

Caught, Bellatrix just huffed and rushed to catch up with her mother.

"Do you think she heard anything?" Lucy asked.

Pandora's stomach tightened, seeing Bellatrix leaning in to speak to Anastacia. Then the two of them looked back at Lucy and Pandora.

"I don't know," she said, watching as a cold wind whipped Lucy's thick hair around. "But we didn't say much. Except that I was desperate, I guess."

"I get why you don't like her," Lucy said, eyeing Bellatrix. "She's trouble."

"Elias thinks she's bitter because she expected to get all the attention when she came to visit and, with my engagement announcement, I stole all of it."

"As much as I hate to agree with anything that Nosferadouche has to say, he probably has a point with that."

159

"Here we are! Here we are!" Ravenna cheered, making several strangers on the street turn to look at them all, their gazes lingering a long time on Ravenna's and Ophelia's outfits.

"Um . . ." Lucy looked at the abandoned storefront.

"Appearances can be quite deceptive, dear," Ravenna said, before doing some sort of intricate knock on the door.

There was a short pause before the door yawned open.

"I thought you guys didn't age," Lucy whispered to Pandora as they faced who must be the shopkeeper.

Admittedly, the woman looked a bit like a reanimated corpse.

She was tall and spindly thin, her cheeks concave, her wrists fragile. Her silvery hair was pulled back in a severe bun to reveal a strong forehead, mercilessly plucked thin brows, and brown eyes so deep they seemed to reject any light trying to reflect off of them.

Her body was dressed in a classic drop-waisted dress in the deepest shade of black. Pandora worried that the thin material might rip from the sharpness of the bones beneath.

"Is this the bride?" The woman's voice, dry as dust, croaked as her gaze moved over Bellatrix's thin frame. "Lovely."

Bellatrix fawned under the praise as Ravenna reached out to grab Pandora's arm, yanking her to the front of the crowd.

"No, no. This is the bride," Ravenna said proudly.

The proprietress's cold eyes slid over to Pandora instead, taking in her body with no small amount of distaste.

160

"You do recall we specialize in vintage gowns," the woman said. "For vintage body types."

At this, Pandora's mother – who was much curvier than her daughter – let out a cutting laugh.

"Sylvia, are you saying this," she said, waving toward her own frame, "is anything but a vintage body type?"

Sylvia, likely realizing that preferred body types varied by generation and location, had nothing more to say about that.

"I suppose we will have a few options," she said, moving inside the seemingly abandoned storefront, leaving everyone to follow behind her.

"Don't you listen to Sylvia, my dear," Ravenna said to Pandora. "You just ask Elias here. Men like all sorts of body types. I've never heard a word of complaint about my curves. *En vogue* or not."

Elias, holding the door open for the women, gave Pandora a smile.

"I've never known your body type to be out of vogue," he told her, but it wasn't the boost to her ego it might have been if she wasn't fretting over her fake fiancé's newfound aversion to her.

"He's been right twice in one night," Lucy said as she walked into the storefront with Pandora.

Inside, they moved through a room full of abandoned racks and an alarming number of spiderwebs to get to the back room.

This bridal shop was a relic from a bygone era. Stepping inside was like walking into the 1950s, where time had paused to preserve its elegance.

Plush carpet in a soft, creamy hue muffled every footstep

161

as the women moved inside, adding an air of quiet reverence to the space.

A round, mirrored platform dominated the center of the room, framed by posts artfully draped in ivory and champagne silk, just begging the women to ascend and swirl for the enraptured onlookers.

The seating area was a collection of vintage armchairs and loveseats adorned in rich mauve velvet and fringed pillows, arranged like a Victorian living room.

Glass-topped side tables bore delicate vases full of freshly cut roses, their petals red as fresh blood.

Scattered around the room, mannequins stood dressed in timeless styles ranging from dramatic ballgowns to sleek, understated sheaths.

The lighting was soft and golden, casting a flattering glow over everything it touched, as if conspiring to make every bride look as radiant as possible.

The walls were lined with floor-to-ceiling mirrors, creating the illusion of endless space, the gowns stretching into eternity.

Though there were also several amusingly unconvincing fake plants scattered around, dust gathered on the plastic leaves. In Pandora's opinion, using fake plants when the gorgeous real ones existed was crazy.

"Well, I feel underdressed," Lucy said, looking down at her jeans, trainers, and long-sleeved tee featuring a rock band that was secretly made up of werewolves.

"Bride," Sylvia croaked at Pandora, waving toward the raised platform, wanting her to climb up onto it. *What, to be inspected and picked apart?*

More so than lying to her family and to Victor, this was the part of the whole charade that bothered her the most. Being the center of attention. Having all eyes on her.

"We should have had some drinks before we came," Lucy murmured. "If it makes you feel better, she's probably going to say all sorts of things about me getting my wolf scent all over the gowns."

"It doesn't," Pandora said, sighing, then going up on the platform, trying not to squirm under not only Sylvia's inspection, but her mother's, aunt's, and cousin's.

The only ones looking at her truly fondly right then were Ravenna and Lucy.

As expected, Sylvia eyed her from all angles before joining her, using a measuring tape to judge every inch of her body. Then she grabbed several styles that "could possibly be suitable" and shoved her into a dressing room.

Blessedly alone, if for just a moment, Pandora sank down on the floor, reaching into her handbag for her mobile and snapping a picture of herself with a background of endless gowns.

Current Status: Drowning in silk, satin, and lace while being told how wrong my body is for every one of these dresses. Tell me you're doing something more fun.

She shot off the text before she could think better of it, shoving her mobile in her bag after, then stripped out of her dress to slip into the first gown.

That one was, apparently, too tight.

The next made her look too "hippy".

The third reminded all the women of a nightgown.

She was debating which one to try on next when her mobile started ringing in her bag.

163

She dug for it, saw Victor's name, and swiped her finger across the screen.

"Oh, hey," she said, cringing at how lame an opener that was.

"I tried to text."

"I was trapped inside a lace dress that didn't want to let me go," she said.

"What's wrong with your body?" Victor asked, sounding impatient for an answer, like the question had been bothering him.

"Oh, it's not . . . 'Vintage' is the chosen word."

"What time does yours not fit in with?"

"From the looks of this place, the fifties."

"So, you look like you're not starving yourself on grapefruit and yogurt while addicted to legal speed? Think I'd call that a win."

"Try telling that to the shopkeeper," Pandora said grumpily.

"Do *not* tell me we need to cut you out of a dress," Sylvia called through the door, craggy voice setting Pandora's nerves on edge.

"Wow," Victor said, overhearing. "You know what I think you need after this?"

"What?"

"A revenge meal. Something fatty and calorie-dense," he said. Then, "I know a place. Text me when you're done."

On the one hand, she really didn't care about food.

On the other, she really wanted to see Victor again.

"You're on," she said, smiling for the first time in hours.

She emerged a few moments later to wide eyes all around. Clearly, the mermaid-style dress was *not* the one.

"Who were you speaking to, my dear?" Ravenna asked as she walked a circle around Pandora, giving the dress the fair shake that none of the others had.

"Victor," Pandora said, feeling her lips curve up once again. "We are going to meet up after this," she added.

"To do what?" Ophelia asked, tone sharp.

"Spend time together," Pandora said.

"Where are you two going?" Lucy asked, trying to slice through the tension building in the room.

"We're going out to a restaurant," she said, ignoring Sylvia mumbling to herself about "not needing any food".

"A *human* restaurant?" Ophelia asked.

"Yes, of course, Mum. What other kind of restaurant would we go to?"

"I'm sure Elias would love to explore your . . . human interests," Ophelia said.

Across from Pandora, Lucy's eyes widened, her lips parted, clearly shocked to find that her friend's stories about her mother weren't exaggerated in the least.

"I haven't had much of an opportunity to explore all London has to offer," Elias said, dashing Pandora's hopes that he would read the room and say he had other plans.

"So, go on a guided tour," Lucy said, shooting daggers at Elias. "Don't be a third wheel on someone's date with her *fiancé*."

"It would be rude not to show a guest around," Ophelia said.

"Then we'll make it a double date!" Lucy said, forcing some cheer into her voice as she shot the fakest smile in Elias's direction.

"Do you think the restaurant will have dog bowls available?" Elias asked.

"Probably not," Lucy said through clenched teeth. "But I doubt they'll have crimson Kool-Aid for you either."

Pandora took herself back into the fitting room, closing her eyes tight.

This was going to be a nightmare.

But there seemed to be no stopping it now.

17

"Sorry about this," Pandora whispered to Victor as she rushed ahead of Elias, her best friend, and their endless bickering. "My mum invited Elias along, then Lucy volunteered to come so it wouldn't be so awkward."

Victor glanced over Pandora's shoulder before suddenly sliding his arms around her, pulling her flush against him.

His hand rose, his fingers warm against her chilled cheek, before his lips softly landed on hers.

Logically, she knew it was just for show, that he wanted them to greet each other the way any happy, engaged couple might.

Either way, it wasn't *personal*.

But the second his lips pressed against hers, she forgot all about that. It certainly felt real, the way all the stress from the last few days fell immediately away, the way his arm slid around her lower back, pulling her more tightly against his body, the way his fingers slid from her cheek to cradling her jaw just under her ear.

It definitely felt real when he didn't immediately break away, instead deepening the kiss until she felt her insides turn to mush as her arms went up to twine around his neck, holding him close as his lips pressed deeper and deeper.

Just when she felt like she was floating, his lips pulled away and his forehead rested against hers for a moment.

"I hope they were watching," he said, voice raspy, making Pandora's heart plummet.

It was an arrangement, for goodness' sake, nothing more. She needed to stop projecting her feelings for Victor onto the situation at hand.

Speaking of hands, he slipped his in hers before turning to look at the others.

"Lucy. Elias," he said, his tone a bit sharper as he greeted the other man.

"Hope you didn't mind some company," Elias said.

"Doesn't seem like it would have mattered even if I did," Victor said.

"Ophelia doesn't seem to get the concept of third wheels," Lucy said, shrugging apologetically.

"There are four of us," Elias said.

"Because someone needed to tag along to keep an eye on you." Lucy rolled her eyes at him as the four of them walked toward the restaurant.

It was a cozy little exposed-brick-wall establishment with warm, golden lighting and a menu offering a mix of British and American fare.

When Victor ordered a burger and chips, Pandora, not

really caring what she ate, chose the same. While Elias analyzed the menu as if it was of the utmost importance that he pick the right meal. Despite not caring for food any more than Pandora did.

"For God's sake. Just get him the same as me," Lucy said, snatching the menu out of his hand and handing it to the server before Elias could object.

"What if I don't like steak?" Elias asked.

Lucy shot back, "Everyone likes steak."

There was a moment of awkward silence before Lucy – bless her – started talking about the dresses at the shop.

"Why didn't you go to a different place if the shop-keeper was rude?" Victor asked, his arm casually draped across the back of Pandora's chair. She was just barely managing not to lean back, to feel his arm against her.

"Oh, um . . ." Pandora's mind went blank.

Lucy looked similarly blank.

It was Elias who managed to save the moment.

"Old family friend," he said. "They've been going to that shop for lifetimes."

If Victor thought that was a weird way to phrase it, he said nothing. Though Pandora could tell something was bothering him, given the way his jaw had gone tight, a little muscle ticking there occasionally as Elias started talking about the dresses as well. Then segued into the invitations, the possible menu.

"Let's go powder our noses," Lucy said, popping up out of her chair in the middle of Elias speaking, not caring how rude she was being.

She grabbed Pandora's arm and dragged her along until they were in the bathroom. Lucy looked around, making sure they were alone, before letting out a loud growl.

"I can't even think straight thanks to Lieutenant Lip Flap and his war on silence."

Despite herself, Pandora couldn't help but laugh, finding it loosened some of the tension she was holding on to.

"I think he's doing it to goad Victor," Pandora said. "To show how involved he is, while Victor . . . hasn't been around."

"You need to get some alone time with Victor again. Give him some reassurances," Lucy said, digging in her handbag for her eyeliner. She leaned over the sink to get closer to the mirror as she lined her gorgeous golden eyes. Pandora decided not to ask her why she was putting in the effort.

"It's a fake relationship," Pandora said.

"Sure. Yeah. That kiss looked real fake."

"He said afterward that he hoped you guys were watching."

Lucy's gaze slid across the mirror to Pandora's reflection – since modern mirrors no longer had silver backings, vampires did reflect – watching her for a second, then letting out a sigh.

"What?" Pandora asked.

"I think you're both dense," she said, clipping the cap back on her eyeliner and tossing it into her bag with a flourish.

"What?" Pandora asked. "How so?"

"Because you are both very clearly into each other, but you keep insisting on the charade."

"Well, the charade is worth a lot of money."

"You two can still be into each other while pretending you've been into each other for a lot longer to sell the whole marriage thing," Lucy said.

170

"I'm not going to lie. I really wish that was the case, Luce. But there's been no sign of him genuinely having feelings for me. Guys who are into you don't go no-contact for days. Hell, guys who want to acquire tons of pounds to get out of debt don't avoid you for days."

"Well, did you ask him what he was up to?" Lucy asked.

She had.

But he'd called before she could read his message.

Pandora reached for her mobile, swiping it open, then reading the text.

I was visiting my parents to tell them about the engagement.

"Oh," she said, scrunching up her face as she turned the mobile for Lucy to read.

"See? Perfectly good reason."

"But it would have been better to know that before, so I could tell my family. I'm sure everyone is wondering where he's been."

"Especially your awful cousin. Did you see the way she narrowed her eyes when you said you were going out with Victor after the fitting?"

"No," Pandora said. "But I've been trying not to look at her."

"I don't trust her. I'd make sure she's not slinking around eavesdropping at your door or stuff like that."

"Yeah." Pandora tried to flatten her hair. Having no luck, she turned away from the mirror and headed to the door. "We probably shouldn't leave those two alone together for any longer than absolutely necessary."

When they got back to the table, though, Elias was missing.

"Where'd he go?" Lucy asked, glancing around.

"Dunno. He was looking at something out the window, then just excused himself and left."

"Love when the trash takes itself out. Maybe I can get the server to make my meal to go, so you two can get some time alone. Ugh," she grumbled as Elias came striding back into the restaurant. His hair was windswept and there was a hardness around his mouth that hadn't been there a few minutes before.

"Thought we lost you," Lucy said. "I was about to order a round of drinks to celebrate."

To that, Elias gave Lucy a small smile as he sat back down. "Saw someone I knew," he said as Pandora took a sniff, wanting to see if she scented blood on him. But there was nothing but his posh cologne. "But we should order drinks regardless," he said, flagging down the server and ordering a bottle of wine that certainly sounded expensive. "My treat," Elias said, as if sensing that everyone else at the table were on extremely tight budgets.

"I'm fine, thanks," Victor said, trying to put his hand over his glass.

"I insist," Elias said, grabbing the stem of the glass and pulling it away so he could fill it.

"So," Lucy broke in, her voice loud. "How was your visit with your family, Victor?" Victor visibly relaxed, his arm sliding behind Pandora's seat again. But this time, his fingers brushed her back.

"It went well. They're excited to meet you," he said, giving Pandora a smile. "And your family. They were very

172

worried about our parents not having met yet, despite us being engaged."

"Yes, strange, that," Elias said, getting a hard elbow to the ribs from Lucy.

"Oops," Lucy said, not sounding apologetic at all as she raised her glass to take a long swig.

"Well, we can get that arranged," Pandora said, nodding. "My parents have nothing going on."

They batted around dates until they found a few when neither had uni or work, and decided to speak to their parents about a meet-up.

All the while, whether he realized it or not, Victor's fingers were toying with the ends of Pandora's hair, making that warm sensation course through her once again.

The mood had lightened considerably. Until the bill came.

"Elias is paying," Lucy said, cutting through the tension. "It's his penance for making us all endure his company." She gave him a sickly-sweet smile as he reached for his wallet and tossed far too much money into the bill folder before rising from his seat. "And now, he's going to get out of your hair by walking me to the Tube," she said as Elias pulled her chair out for her. "It is a huge sacrifice on my part to suffer his company for another minute. But that's how much I love you two," she said, giving them a wiggly finger-wave before turning and all but shoving Elias toward the door.

"Am I the only one picking up on something . . . strange between the two of them?" Victor asked as he rose and then waited for Pandora to do the same.

"No. There's definitely something weird going on there.

They're annoyed by breathing the same air, it seems," Pandora told him as they moved outside.

Sure, Pandora knew there could be some species-based tensions between them. But since they'd met, Elias had proven himself to be more modern than she'd first thought. He even told the crowd about a particularly amusing interaction he'd had with a local, and particularly grouchy, gargoyle. Who'd tried to sell himself in service to Elias because he was sick of the schoolchildren looking up at him on their walk home and making fun of his missing fang.

And she knew from experience that Lucy had no issues with vampires either.

So the two of them tossing species-based barbs at each other instead of looking for anything personal to gripe about made Pandora think that they actually didn't dislike each other, but were just digging their heels in and sticking to the story that it was hate-at-first-(and every)-sight rather than admitting that as they spent more time together, they saw they had mistaken initial assumptions about each other.

Pandora knew her friend to be hot-tempered and stubborn. She could see Lucy having a difficult time admitting their first impressions were wrong, and letting bygones be bygones. Lucy once held a grudge against a neighbor for years over one small disagreement about parking spaces. After all the snark tossed between Lucy and Elias, Pandora imagined that Lucy was just sticking to the same energy as the first meeting, despite the fact that the zingers they were tossing lately felt a lot less pointed – and that Elias hadn't even been taking any digs at Lucy during dinner.

She hoped for everyone's sake that the two of them would sit down and have an adult conversation where they could both agree to change their opinions of each other based on new evidence.

"Do you think there's something going on with them?"

"Definitely not," Pandora said.

"How do you know?"

"Well, first, because Elias is always at the house," she said, immediately regretting it when Victor's green eyes went dark. "But also because Lucy never keeps anything from me. I know about every bad date she's ever had."

Even the one time that Lucy had woken up after a particularly strong full moon to find herself naked in the woods with a man she'd never seen before.

She'd been reasonably sure they had just encountered each other while on a hunt and that nothing had happened between them.

Apparently, it was a turning point for her as a shifter, wanting to make sure she never went through a full moon alone again, despite not having lived near her own familial pack in many years.

"Do you want me to walk you to the Tube?" Victor asked.

"Do you maybe just want to . . . walk for a bit?" she asked.

"Sure," he said, tucking his hands into his front pockets and making his shoulders curl forward – something that Pandora found almost intolerably adorable.

If this was a real relationship, not a business arrangement, she was pretty sure she would have moved into his path, grabbed the front of his jumper and pulled him down for a long, deep kiss.

But it wasn't.

So she needed to keep her hands to herself.

No matter how much harder that seemed to get each time she was around him.

"How have things been at home? Is your family driving you crazy?"

"Pretty much every moment," Pandora said, but she was smiling. "For the most part, it is good crazy. Three more relatives have shown up since the engagement party."

"Who?" Victor asked, lightly touching her hip to guide her away from a man stumbling out of a pub.

"My uncle Leopold and his partner, Cody."

"Leopold and Cody," Victor said, looking amused by the mix of new and old-fashioned names.

Pandora couldn't exactly tell Victor that Leopold, a man who had been single and lonely for the better part of five hundred years, had happened across a newly made, twenty-something vampire named Cody at a trendy new underground vampire club. Sparks had flown. They'd been inseparable ever since.

"There's a bit of an age gap there," Pandora said. "Then there is Aunt Henrietta," she went on. "If you think Aunt Ravenna is a bit . . . eccentric, Henrietta puts her to shame. She showed up just before dawn in a cloud of musky perfume and sixteen small dogs."

"Sixteen?" Victor asked, aghast. "I like dogs as much as the next Brit, but . . . sixteen."

Henrietta had long been a fervent dog-lover. And she was often despondent over the fact that there were no immortal dogs the way there were immortal ravens like Vlad.

"They're all spoiled horribly rotten, too," Pandora said fondly, thinking of the way Henrietta went to everyone's bedroom to hand them a bag of dog treats, instructing them to give any dog who came to their door a little snack before sending them on their way.

"What kind of dogs are they?"

"She likes them small and fluffy," Pandora said. "She has several different-coloured Pomeranians, Pekinese, papillons, and chihuahuas. And, yes, she will introduce you to each of them. As well as tell you several facts about them."

How Henrietta kept track, with thousands of dogs through the years, of their favorite toys, treats, foods, weather, music, and beds was completely beyond Pandora. But she always found it endearing.

"I will look forward to that," Victor said.

"You don't have pets, right? I don't think I ever asked that."

"No. I had a childhood dog. But once he passed, my parents opted against getting another. And I didn't feel it was right to get one when I'm so busy with uni."

"We've only ever had Vlad."

"How long do ravens live?"

"Oh, uh, I think the average domestic lifespan is forty or fifty years."

"Wow. Maybe I'll get a bird instead of a dog. It would be nice to have something that you can have forever."

Before they knew it, they were at the Tube. And with no other reason to keep walking, they went their separate ways, promising to text once they'd cleared schedules with their families for the in-laws' meeting.

They were both in agreement.

It was going to be an intimate affair.
Just both sets of parents.
Maybe at a nice restaurant.
At least, of course, that was the plan.
Until Ophelia got her nails into things . . .

18

"Oh, well, hello," Pandora said as she opened her bedroom door to see a merle Pomeranian standing there like he was waiting for her. "I'm supposed to give you a treat, right?" she asked, reaching for the bag as the dog came rushing into her room, sniffing around.

"He's a menace." Vlad came flying into the room to land on his perch, getting a couple of halfhearted yips from the dog. "Just this evening, he ate your mother's favorite shoe, played tug with some of the curtains, and used your father's favorite walking stick as a chew toy."

"I think he's the puppy." Pandora defended the dog, who was sniffing around the bed, likely never having seen one before.

"I suppose I am not one to judge. When I was fresh out of the egg, I used to sit outside the window of a lady who'd had the temerity to shoo me off her feeder once and whisper to her."

"What did you say?" Pandora asked as she bent to try to scoop up the puppy.

"'I know your secrets, Martha. I saw what you did.' Things like that."

"You probably drove her mad."

"Turns out, she'd killed her husband by putting poison in his stew. She turned herself in to the police after being 'plagued by her conscience'."

"You have led quite the interesting life," Pandora said as she finally grabbed the puppy and started to carry him toward the door. "Oh, no. Did they cook again?" she asked, smelling something food-like wafting up from the lower level.

"Your aunt Ravenna said she has done a lot of research since the engagement party," Vlad said, flying to land on Pandora's shoulder as she walked out into the hall.

"I feel like I should be worried," Pandora said.

"Might want to prepare for having to call the paramedics," Vlad said before flying down the stairs ahead of her.

"Oh, there you are, my sweet Maxwell!" Aunt Henrietta called, arms out, snatching the puppy out of Pandora's arms. "Oh, Mummy was so worried about you."

Henrietta was a Rubenesque woman who, in fact, claimed to have been a model for several of Peter Paul Rubens's paintings 'in her day'. She was always dressed in absurd contrasts. That night, it was a green velvet Regency dress underneath a modern faux-fur leopard-print jacket.

Her curly red hair was pulled back in a French braid

and her face was covered in many layers of thick make-up, with false lashes, heavy eyeliner, and bright red lips.

As for shoes, the moment Henrietta had discovered rubber clogs, she'd outright refused to slip her feet into any other shoewear. She even had an entire piece of luggage full of the little charms you could put into the holes of the shoes.

Pandora fully expected Henrietta to wear something truly absurd to her wedding. Like a serving-wench dress from the Renaissance under a punk-style floor-length black leather jacket. And, of course, the rubber clogs.

"He will be the sweetest little ring-bearer – yes, he will," Henrietta cooed at the dog as Pandora tried not to groan at the idea of sixteen little fluff balls with no sense of direction making their way down the aisle toward her.

"Pandora, my darling." Ophelia descended the stairs. "That's what you're wearing?" She clucked her tongue at Pandora's choice of an understated navy-blue corduroy skirt with a white blouse.

"I don't want to make Mary and Robert uncomfortable if they aren't dressed up," Pandora said. "This is probably going to be a little overwhelming as a whole."

Pandora had tried to fight her mother on another party. But Ophelia had claimed that they would have to get to know the family eventually, so what was the point in delaying it.

"Besides," Ophelia had said. "This is hardly the whole family."

It wasn't.

But it seemed like each time Pandora turned around, some other distant relative was showing up and expecting to move in until the wedding.

More family members meant it would be harder for Pandora to keep control over the situation. When it was mostly just Uncle Reginald to worry about slipping up in front of Victor, she felt comfortable handling it. But now it would be Victor, Mary, and Robert rubbing shoulders with other relatives who hadn't sat through the last party.

It would be fine.

It had to be.

"You look like you need it," Elias said as he held out a glass toward her. She reached for it, expecting wine, only to find the liquid thick and viscous. "What?" he asked, watching her with a look that seemed to be seeing far too much.

"There can't be *blood* here tonight!" Pandora said, her voice a low hiss. "What if Victor, Mary, or Robert accidentally pick up one of your glasses instead of their own?"

"When was the last time you fed?" Elias asked, watching Pandora with a frown.

Too long.

She knew it was the reason she was feeling frazzled and unfocused. There simply hadn't been a good time for her to go to the butcher to get her usual bottle of blood. Especially when Ophelia made Elias follow Pandora whenever she left the house.

She was hoping Lucy was going to be able to make it to the house, before Victor and his parents arrived, with a tumbler full of blood that would help her feel more like herself before the night's festivities started. But Lucy was working the afternoon shift at the coffee shop and there was no way she could leave before the nightshift workers arrived. Which left her an extremely narrow window to get to the butcher's, then to the estate.

182

Maybe, if Lucy could run interference when she did show up, she could sneak into the kitchen, chug her blood, then rinse all traces of it out of her mouth. Then she'd be able to maneuver this evening with a lot less anxiety.

She hoped.

"Shoo! Shoo, you nuisance!" Ravenna flapped her hands at one of Henrietta's dogs, who was gnawing at one of the wooden chair legs.

"Kevin, come to Mummy." Henrietta leaned down to scoop up the long-haired chihuahua and snuggle it to her chest. "Don't listen to the mean lady. She's never known the love of a sweet puppy."

"I have a loving *husband*, you bitter old crone," Ravenna mumbled to herself as she attempted to fluff the stiff couch cushions.

"I have had husbands as well," Henrietta said with a haughty chin-lift. "Dogs are more loyal. And they don't assail me with pointlessly long-winded diatribes about how things used to be so much better in the 'good old days'."

"Please, can we get along for just the evening?" Pandora asked pleadingly.

Ravenna and Henrietta, two generally affable women, had some age-old hatchet that refused to get buried. The last thing Pandora needed was one of them to comment on Henrietta's suspiciously deceased five husbands in front of Victor and his parents.

"I can if she can," Henrietta said, nose up.

"I can if she can keep her beasts from destroying the place," Ravenna said, pushing past Henrietta to go into the kitchen to check on – may the universe have mercy on them all – the food.

183

Pandora ran her hands down her dress before continuing into the sitting room, finding her uncle Leopold standing close to Cody near the fire, the two of them listening raptly to some story Uncle Reginald was telling.

Thankfully, Cody had had a bit of a modernizing effect on Leopold. Which meant he was dressed in an understated black suit with a pinstriped shirt beneath. By contrast, Cody wore a pinstriped suit with a black shirt beneath. Both men looked smart and normal standing beside Uncle Reginald, who'd opted to wear full-on baroque extravagance with his knee-length, frilled breeches, square-toed high-heeled shoes with rosettes, and an opened, frilled shirt. Though Pandora was pretty sure his long coat with braid-trimmed button holes was actually from a later period.

She supposed she could at least be grateful that he hadn't opted to wear one of those heinous curled wigs.

Victor would have surely told his parents about her family's 'historical reenactment' and 'method acting', so it shouldn't be the same shock to them as it had been to Victor originally.

"Everything's going to be fine," she murmured to herself.

"What?" Bellatrix snapped at her as she passed by, making Pandora suppress a sigh. She turned to see her cousin in a scandalously tight red silk dress that exposed her entire back, right down to just above the curve of her bum.

Catching Pandora looking, Bellatrix did her own once-over of her cousin. If the curl of her lip was anything to go by, she clearly found Pandora's style lacking. She walked away with an exaggerated sway of her hips.

"Don't pay attention to her," Elias said, passing Pandora

a glass that, this time, was full of wine instead of blood. "Just another ploy to draw attention to herself. You look lovely."

"Thanks. I'm still not leaving Victor for you, no matter how nice you've been," she told him.

During that brief period when she hadn't been in contact with Victor, she'd actually seriously tried to consider it, to make herself see him as a viable romantic interest. But she simply couldn't do it.

"I know," Elias said with a nod. "No one who saw that kiss the other day would think you're anything but head-over for the guy. Save for maybe Bellatrix," he added.

"What do you mean?"

"She was there that night," he told Pandora. "That was who I'd seen and went to try to confront. But she was too fast. Got away from me."

She was about to ask some follow-up questions, when the knocker clacked against the front door, making her jolt.

"Probably Lucy," she said, hoping that was the case so she could get her blood. But when she rushed toward the door and pulled it open, Victor was standing there.

"Oh, hey," she said, surprised. "Where are your parents?"

"They're driving in," he told her. "Traffic was awful tonight, so I told them I would meet them here and take the Underground so they didn't need to fight it to get me. Can I come in?" he asked with a small smile when she kept barring his entrance.

"Oh, right. Of course," she said, moving out of the way, only to find herself secured around the waist and pulled against his firm body, his lips crashing down on hers.

She melted into him, her hands sliding up his arms, holding on as his kiss grew warmer. But just for a moment. Then he was lowering her down onto her feet, giving her a soft smile that made her belly flip.

"You ready for this?" he asked, low enough for just the two of them to hear.

"No," she replied, leaning forward to bump her forehead into his chest.

"It's gonna be fine." His hand went to the back of her neck for a second and she could almost swear she felt the brush of his lips on her hair. But surely that was just her wishful thinking.

"Oh, Victor!" Ravenna cheered, rushing down the foyer, her low heels clicking on the tiles, her arms outstretched.

"Ravenna," Victor said, greeting her back. "So nice to see you aga—"

He lost the rest of his sentence as Ravenna yanked him against her and just about squeezed the air out of his lungs before kissing him hard on each cheek.

"Aren't you a sight for sore eyes? You make me wish I was five hu . . . fifty years younger. Come in out of the cold! We can't wait to meet your parents."

With that, she rushed off to get Victor a glass of wine as Pandora led him into the sitting room.

"You must be Henrietta," Victor said as he immediately spied Pandora's aunt on a sofa with half of her dogs sitting next to her or on her lap and the others on the floor at her feet, chewing at her rubber clogs. "I've heard so much about you," he said politely.

"Charmed, I'm sure," Henrietta said, holding out her hand for a kiss. Which Victor managed to pull off after a moment's hesitation. "They don't like men," Henrietta said when Victor tried to pet one of the dogs, only to get snarled and snapped at. "Smart that way," she added with a little chuckle.

Pandora led Victor across the room toward her uncle and his boyfriend, who had untangled themselves from Reginald.

"You must be Leopold and Cody," Victor said, giving them each a hearty handshake. "You're not historical reenactors?" he asked as he looked at their outfits.

Leopold's brows pinched and he opened his mouth to speak, but Cody was quicker, slapping the back of his hand into Leopold's chest and replying with all of his light, easy charisma. "Oh, not us. We like modern times a little better. Did Reginald tell you about that scene from that Black Death play he worked on?" he asked smoothly.

Thank goodness, Pandora thought, feeling her shoulders relax. She had two more people to act as a buffer against the more eccentric family members.

"That must be Lucy," Pandora said, hearing another knock and pulling Victor along with her toward the hallway.

But Ophelia was already at the door, opening it to reveal another visiting family member.

"Oh, no," Pandora said, eyes going wide as she looked at Great-Uncle Dudley.

He was a tall, thin man who wasn't aware any shade other than midnight existed, so he wore it from the top of his top-hat-covered head to his leather shoes.

He looked like he'd stepped out of some gothic novel.

Or, Pandora thought with rising panic, like a stereotypical vampire.

"What's wrong?" Victor asked. Then, when she didn't immediately answer, "Is that a cockatoo on his shoulder?"

187

Yes, yes, it was.

And there was the problem.

Well, Dudley himself was a bit of an odd duck. But not worse than the rest of her family – just in a different way.

It was the bird that was going to be a problem.

Because if she thought the feud between her aunts Ravenna and Henrietta was bad, it had nothing on the decades-long bone-deep hatred between Vlad and Uncle Dudley's cockatoo, Elizabeth.

Unlike Vlad, Elizabeth wasn't immortal. But birds like her easily lived eighty or more years naturally with good care. And Elizabeth had spent every one of her fifty-six years becoming an absolute menace to society. And trying to mate with a very uninterested Vlad.

"Vlad hates that bird," Pandora told Victor as Elizabeth let out an ear-splitting squawk.

Pandora's head turned to the side to find Vlad suddenly lift off of his perch, flying into the foyer, his wings ruffling her hair as he mumbled something that sounded a heck of a lot like a particularly nasty curse as he went.

He wasn't quick enough, though. Elizabeth saw him, took flight herself and went after the poor raven, her yellow crest up high, ready to start some trouble.

"Was that Elizabeth I just saw?" Dante's voice sounded from behind Pandora. He looked like he'd just emerged from bed, but clearly hadn't had a restful sleep, judging from the purple smudges under his eyes.

"Yeah," Pandora said, grimacing.

"That's going to be fun." Dante nodded at Victor. "Hey, Victor. Your parents here?"

"Should be any minute," he said as Henrietta came

bustling out of the back of the house, cradling one of her dogs to her chest as she made a beeline for Dudley.

"That rat with wings of yours!" She rushed to catch up with Dudley as he actively tried to avoid her. "Don't you walk away from me!"

"Just breathe," Victor said, rubbing a hand up and down Pandora's spine.

She'd been so distracted that she'd forgotten to pretend to breathe. She tried to humor Victor as she took a few slow, deep breaths. But mostly, she was just enjoying the feel of him casually touching her. Even if her body was having anything but casual thoughts.

She might have even leaned into him and let out a little mewling sound, if the knocker hadn't sounded through the house at that very moment.

"Just keep breathing," Victor said as they both moved together, as a couple, toward the door.

"Mum, Dad." Victor greeted his parents.

Victor was the perfect melding of them both. He was tall and fit like his father, with the same strong jaw and broody brows. But he'd inherited his mother's thick, dark hair and gorgeous green eyes.

"This is Pandora. Pandora, this is Mary and Robert," he said, waving toward his parents.

"It's so nice to meet you," Mary said, reaching to shake Pandora's hand. Robert did the same. Everything about them was a little stiff, standoffish. Pandora couldn't tell if it was simply their nature, if they were feeling shy about the party, or if they just didn't like her. Though she went ahead and latched on to the last one. For funsies. Because she wasn't stressed enough.

"Mary, Robert, these are my parents, Ophelia and

189

Lucian. Mum, Dad, this is Mary and Robert." Pandora introduced them when her parents made their way into the foyer.

Pandora couldn't help but see the contrasts between the couples.

Mary and Robert were dressed nicely, but in an understated way, in simple slacks. Mary had on a jumper; her husband had opted for a sleeveless jumper over a button-up shirt. They stood with a few feet between them, never once touching.

Then there was Ophelia and Lucian. Ophelia was in another of her velvet, floor-length gowns in a wine colour that hugged every curve. Lucian was in an all-black suit, complete with some fine gold jewelry. And the two clung together as close as newlyweds, as if being apart from each other physically hurt them.

Pandora knew she wanted a relationship like her parents had. Deep. Everlasting.

But she'd chosen one like Victor's parents. A little cold, detached, businesslike.

"It's going well. Chin up," Victor said, his breath teasing the shell of her ear as he turned to whisper to her, his hand sliding across her lower back.

Still feeling a bit depressed over the whole situation, she let herself lean into him. She even allowed her hand to slide up to rest on his chest as their parents exchanged pleasantries.

"Oh, why didn't anyone tell me they were here!" Ravenna came rushing out of the kitchen, her curls bobbing. "Oh, Victor looks just like you!" she said, barreling forward to wrap the unsuspecting Mary and Robert in a spine-crushing hug. "It is so good to meet you," she added as Victor's parents' faces were mirrored masks of surprise and discomfort.

"Let them breathe, woman, would you?" Uncle Reginald said, pulling his wife back so he could thrust his hand toward Robert. "That's my wife, Ravenna. I'm Reginald."

Clearly, Victor had told his folks about her family's "acting" careers. They seemed less shocked by their outfits and more amused. Or even, on Robert's part, impressed.

"Nice to meet you. That is *quite* a costume," Robert said, nodding. "Very accurate. Though, mismatched," he added, making Reginald frown.

"Dad's a bit of a history buff himself," Victor said.

"Are you now?" Reginald asked, using Robert's hand, which he was still holding, to pull him toward the sitting room.

"Dante," Pandora whispered, then nodded her head toward the two retreating men.

"On it," Dante said, giving her a wink, then following behind the men.

"Oh, my. Is someone screaming?" Mary asked as the sounds of Elizabeth's squawking carried through the house.

"Oh, that's just Elizabeth," Victor said. "Pandora's uncle's cockatoo." Ophelia's brows pinched, likely wondering how Victor knew about such a distant relation.

Good, Pandora thought.

Maybe she would stop being suspicious or trying to sic Elias on her as if she truly believed they had a deep connection.

"Mary, can I get you a drink?" Ravenna asked. Then, before waiting for an answer, she grabbed the other woman around the waist and pulled her along to the dining room.

"Victor," Lucian said, his face no softer with regard to a man he wasn't sure he approved of yet.

"Lucian, Ophelia, may I borrow you for a moment?" Elias suddenly butted in, making Pandora's posture relax.

"Of course," Ophelia said without another glance in Victor's direction.

"What was that about?" Victor asked as Pandora reached down for his hand and drew him with her toward the oversized storage cupboard at the end of the hallway.

"I think Elias just became an ally," she said, reaching up to flick on the low light above their heads.

"What does . . . What the hell . . ." Pandora turned to see what he was looking at.

"Oh, that," she said, eyeing the suit of armor set a foot or so behind her. "Dante hid it in here ages ago. Said he was getting the creeps from it."

"Yeah, I can see why." Victor eyed the suit of armor the same way Pandora always eyed the painting of her great-great-grandmother Ambrosia over the mantel. "Anyway, what did you say about Elias?"

"He said he's accepted that we're together and happy. So I think he's kind of . . . helping out now."

"Wait. Does he know?"

"No! No. I mean, he's just . . . helping with my parents and their coldness. As well as the rest of my family and their . . . eccentricities."

"They're really not that bad," Victor said as she sighed hard. "Hey, it's fine." His voice had softened as he watched her. She was all frayed edges. Her hunger was making her bloodlust increase. She was alarmingly aware of the pounding sound of Victor's heart, of the whooshing sound as the blood moved through his veins, just begging her to lean in and take a little nip, maybe a sip or two . . .

No.

No, she had to keep it together.

She was just so hungry.

What was taking Lucy so long?

"You're trembling," Victor said, suddenly reaching for her, pulling her flush against his chest and wrapping her up tight. "Oh, you're freezing." His hands started to chafe over her skin, trying to bring some warmth to her. "Pandy, everything is going to be all right," he said as she let herself lean into him, letting out a little whimper at the sound of the nickname on his lips.

She knew she should feel guilty for accepting his comfort when she was mostly upset about wanting more from him. And, yes, maybe the fact that she really needed to feed.

But she let him run his hands all over her, meaning to warm her up and succeeding. She felt like a wildfire was raging through her.

Before she could talk herself out of it, her hands were sliding up his chest, the sides of his neck, framing his face and pulling him down toward her.

She saw the confused pinch to his brows, but he let her close the distance, let her lips claim his.

For a moment, she was worried she'd overstepped, that he wasn't interested.

But then his hand slid up her spine to grab the back of her neck, tilting her a bit as he claimed her lips more fiercely, until she felt it down to her toes.

A low moan escaped her as Victor pressed her back into

the wall, his body warming hers, his tongue teasing the seam of her lips, then claiming hers as the desire grew.

She had to ball her fists to keep from grabbing his shirt and peeling it off. But just as she was about to give in to the need, it was Victor's hands that slid down her back, sinking into her ass and pulling her more firmly against him.

If there was any question of his desire for her, for this, it was erased at the feel of his hard length against her own need.

A long moan escaped her, making a rumbling sound move through Victor. It vibrated into her own chest, bringing with it a little shiver of need.

Pandora couldn't stop herself from shimmying her hips against him, a move that had his hands digging into her flesh a little harder.

His teeth nipped her lower lip as his fingers started rucking up the fabric of her skirt, drawing it up inch by inch, letting the air kiss her exposed skin.

Once he had the skirt up high enough, he fisted the material at one of her hips with one hand, then allowed his other to tease up the skin at the side of her exposed thigh.

A needy tremble coursed through her as his touch whispered upward, tracing the barely-there edge of her panties across her upper thigh.

Victor's lips pulled from hers, his heavy-lidded gaze holding hers as his fingers suddenly pressed between her thighs.

Pandora's head fell back, the moan escaping her as her hips rocked against his touch, begging for more.

That rumbling sound moved through Victor's chest

194

again, pleased by her reaction, by the desire he felt beneath his fingers.

Pandora's fingers dug into his shoulders as her hips did another involuntary rock against his touch.

She whimpered. "Victor, please."

Heat flashed across Victor's eyes as his fingers pressed in again. Once. Twice.

Frustrated with the barrier, Victor's hand shifted up, slipping under the waistband of her panties, then sliding beneath.

The feel of his touch against her bare skin had her thighs shaking. In pleasure. In the anticipation of more.

Victor's finger slid up her cleft, finding her clit and working it in slow, soft circles.

Pandora's head fell forward, her forehead to his shoulder, breathing in his familiar scent, as his finger kept working her, kept driving her up.

She couldn't seem to stop herself from turning her head in, from nuzzling into the pulse point on his neck, feeling the frantic thud of his own desire as he continued to tease her.

Her fangs felt longer, thicker.

Her tongue flicked out, teasing the spot where she felt his heart beating. And maybe she let her teeth graze his skin, just a scrape of the sharp edges, regardless of how strongly her body was screaming for her to press in, to nip, to taste.

A groan escaped Victor at the sensation.

Then his fingers were slipping down, sliding inside her.

Her lips against his skin muffled the moan that clawed its way out of her as his fingers settled deep, just an unmoving fullness.

On a whimper, her hips moved in a circle, getting the movement her body was begging for and pressing her cleft against his palm, creating a friction that had little sparks of need spreading, catching, burning through her.

Victor sucked in a deep, steadying breath.

Then his fingers were moving inside her as his thumb slipped up to keep working her clit.

Pandora's fingers dug into his arm as he drove her up, as he worked her achingly slowly, tormenting as well as pleasing, never quite giving her what she needed to get the release that she felt coiled in her core.

"I need to taste you," he murmured, voice thick.

I know that feeling too well, she thought, before his other meaning sank in.

By then, his fingers were already sliding out of her.

A whimper escaped her, the need for release an acute ache, almost a pain.

But then Victor was lowering down in front of her as he pressed her back against the wall, letting it support her weight as he disappeared under her skirt.

Pandora reached down with frantic, shaky fingers, pulling the skirt up out of the way, not wanting to lose sight of him for a second. Especially when he tilted his head back to look up at her with hunger in his gorgeous green eyes.

His fingers moved up, grabbing the waistband of her panties and drawing them down slowly, seeming to enjoy her longing as her thighs shook, as her hands curled into fists around her skirt, wringing the material.

It fell around her feet and Victor lifted each foot, freeing the material.

Then his lips were pressing into the inside of her knee, blazing a heated path up her thigh.

Pandora's chest felt tight, her head fuzzy, by the time her leg was draped over his shoulder and his tongue was tracing the crease of her thigh.

So, *so* close.

His breath was warm on her cool skin, the contrast sending butterflies swooping through her belly.

Then his head finally shifted.

A current shot through her body at the feel of his tongue teasing up her cleft. The shock of pleasure was searing, sizzling, smoldering, making her head fall back as a long, ragged moan escaped her.

Against her, Victor made that rumbling sound again, like he was just as excited by her pleasure as she was, the vibrations of the sound against her creating an entirely new dimension of sensation.

He worked her with the pressure and speed she was craving, driving her up as she struggled to keep her moans down.

His fingers slid back inside of her once again, stroking as he continued to tease her with his tongue.

He drove her right to that edge, then sent her flying over, continuing to lick and stroke as she crashed, as the pleasure overtook her completely.

The aftershocks were still racking her system as Victor's head shifted, pressing a kiss to her other inner thigh, working his way back down toward her knee.

It was right then that Pandora heard Lucy's voice calling through the house, her tone becoming a little frantic when she didn't locate her immediately.

Victor pulled away, exhaling hard as his head ducked so she couldn't see his face.

"Go," he said, voice rough, as he reached to rake a hand through his hair.

She really needed a moment to pull herself together too. Or, better yet, to forget all about the party, take Victor upstairs, and finish what they started.

But she couldn't do that.

So, instead, she moved out of the storage closet.

Without her panties, she realized a moment too late.

But there was nothing she could do about that when Lucy finally spotted her, waving the bottle full of sustenance at her.

Pandora hoped it would help with her frayed nerves.

Even if, with each passing moment, she suspected her hunger had less to do with needing to feed and a lot more to do with her fiancé himself.

19

"You look flushed," Lucy said as the two crept into the kitchen, finding it blissfully abandoned, save for whatever foods were sitting under cloches. Pandora was afraid to look. "How do you look flushed? You can't flush, right?" she asked, eyeing her friend with a quizzical head tilt. "Or maybe you're just . . . not as pale as usual?"

"I'm just a little overwhelmed. And underfed," she said, struggling with the too-tight lid on the stainless-steel tumbler hiding her meal.

"I saw Victor's parents on the way in," Lucy said, seemingly completely unbothered by the whole thing, as Pandora finally got the top off and took a long swig. "They seem . . . quite prim and proper, yeah?"

Pandora nodded. "Very. Luckily, Dante and Elias are running interference for me. And my uncle Leopold and his boyfriend are as normal as a couple of vamp—"

"There you are," Victor said, pulling to a stop as he looked at Pandora standing there, a bit of blood still staining her lips.

"Is something wrong with that wine?" Lucy asked pointedly when Pandora simply froze.

"Yes," Pandora said, turning to make a show of spluttering into the sink. "I think it's turned." She quickly filled her mouth with tap water, swooshing it around to get the red out of her mouth.

"Even smells off," Lucy said, sniffing the contents of the tumbler and starting to put the lid on it.

"Why not dump it if it's bad?" Victor asked.

Pandora's stomach dropped at the idea of wasting perfectly good, and very needed, blood.

But what other choice did they have?

With her back to Victor, Pandora flashed her rinsed teeth at Lucy, who gave her a little nod to let her know they were clean, then proceeded to dump the rest of the blood into the sink drain, the water running over it until all traces were gone.

At least she'd gotten a big sip.

She could feel it moving through her system, calming some of the anxiety she'd felt growing all day. And even as Victor came closer, she could no longer hear the blood moving through his veins.

"Is everything all right?" Pandora asked, hoping her breath didn't smell metallic.

"Yeah, I was just looking for you. Figure we should, you know, have a united front."

How did he seem so unaffected? As if nothing at all had just happened? While she felt like a completely different person than she'd been when she'd gone into that closet?

"Oh, right. Of course." Pandora moved toward him as Elias suddenly came into the kitchen.

"What's going on in here?" he asked, and Pandora could swear she saw him sniff the air. Could he still smell the blood? Worse yet, could he tell it was pig's blood? Might he tell her mother?

"Oh, great. You," Lucy said, capping the tumbler but keeping a death grip on it.

Pandora hoped Lucy would stash it somewhere that she could find later, after anyone who might be suspicious was long gone.

Victor started to pull Pandora into the hall, so she had no choice but to follow. She was trying to focus on not letting her mind wander back to the cupboard, so she missed the reason Victor had come to a sudden stop.

"Victor, what—"

"Is she sharpening her teeth?"

Pandora's stomach dropped as she whirled around to find, sure enough, Aunt Henrietta filing one of her fangs.

"What? No! Silly," she said, forcibly pulling him forward as he tried to keep looking. "It's, uh, a new form of flossing," she said, proud of her quick thinking. "From . . . France. It's all the rage," she added, really trying to sell it. "My family is all really into dental hygiene."

Maybe he would have questioned her further.

But Elizabeth chose that moment to crash down onto his shoulder, a flurry of white feathers and heavy breathing.

"Oh, hello," Victor said as the cockatoo turned to look at him before letting out a shriek that could nearly burst an eardrum.

"Elizabeth!" Pandora scolded the bird.

"Better you than me," Vlad murmured from his hiding place behind a vase in the dining room.

"What was that?" Victor asked, looking around.

"I didn't hear anything," Pandora said, lying through her teeth, reaching up toward the cockatoo. "Step up. Elizabeth, step up," she said in a firm voice.

Elizabeth didn't want to, however, and decided to take a nasty bite of Pandora's hand instead.

"Told you that thing was a nuisance!" Aunt Henrietta said, her dogs yapping in agreement, excited by all the hubbub.

The evening was getting away from Pandora, fast.

She needed to rein it in a little.

"Look, Elizabeth," she said, pointing toward Vlad's hiding place. Elizabeth zeroed in, then took flight just a second after Vlad did, trying to get away before she got to him.

Pandora felt bad sacrificing him. But she would give him some scratches later. And some extra treats. He'd forgive her. If he'd got over the one time when, as a young little vampire, she'd plucked one of his tail feathers because she simply didn't know any better and wanted to have one to play with, then he could forgive her for using him as a distraction for the troublesome cockatoo.

"My, your family has quite the pet collection," Mary said as they moved into the sitting room.

"Some more well-mannered than others," Ravenna said, glancing down as one of Henrietta's dogs started using her skirts as a tug toy. "Anyway, no matter. Don't they make such a lovely couple?" She smiled at Pandora and Victor, standing close, hands clasped.

"They do." Mary agreed and looked between Pandora

and Ophelia. "You can see where you get your looks from." Then, she looked a little closer at Ophelia, close enough to make Pandora squirm.

Because, well, when two women who were supposed to be the same age were standing so close, it was impossible not to see the differences between them.

Whereas Mary's cheeks had thinned a bit with age and there were fine lines around her eyes, mouth, and forehead, Ophelia, by contrast, had flawless, ageless skin.

"Your skin is remarkably smooth," Mary said, leaning in a little closer, like she was trying to find a wrinkle. But there were none to be found.

"Oh, yeah," Pandora said, panicking. "It's, you know, a tea. An old family recipe."

"I would love that recipe," Mary said.

Well, Pandora had walked right into that one, hadn't she? She was just going to have to throw something harmless together and pass it off as their family's old youth elixir.

"Of course," Ophelia said with an easy smile, recovering more quickly than her daughter.

"Oh, and who is this?" Mary asked, looking past Pandora toward where Lucy and Elias were entering the room.

"Oh, this is my best friend – and chief bridesmaid – Lucy," Pandora said. That part was easy. Explaining Elias, who was neither family nor a friend, was less so. So she just blurted out the first thing that came to mind. "And her boyfriend, Elias."

The look of shock and betrayal on Lucy's face made Pandora immediately remorseful, as Elias effortlessly played into the lie, wrapping an arm around Lucy's shoulders and hauling her against his body.

"Yeah, can't get enough of this one. Isn't that right, pup?" he asked, making Lucy's eyes flash yellow for the quickest of seconds. Too fast, Pandora was sure, for anyone except the vampires gathered around to notice.

"Yeah," Lucy said through gritted teeth. "Sometimes, I love him so much that I just want to suffocate him."

"Been there," Henrietta said with a knowing nod, making Pandora stifle a groan.

"But what a way to go, my darling," Elias said with a mischievous glint in his eye at the innuendo Pandora prayed no one else caught on to.

Lucy's cheeks, however, went brilliantly red, making Elias chuckle as he pulled her closer and planted an affectionate kiss on her head.

"Oh, absolutely," Reginald said from across the room, making everyone turn to look at him as he reached for a fire poker and started to demonstrate some sort of fight stance, prompting Robert to grab the fire shovel and follow Reginald's instructions. "Very nice. Yes, that's how we did it!"

Pandora debated getting involved, but figured it seemed harmless enough. Just two "history buffs" demonstrating their shared knowledge. There was no reason to assume Robert would come to the conclusion that Reginald had firsthand experience of such things.

So she stayed where she was, trying to keep the conversation light between her mother and Victor's mum.

Until, suddenly, Ravenna appeared, to announce dinner. "If you can all step into the dining room," she said, waving everyone in the right direction, practically bouncing in excitement.

"I don't know if I can eat eel again," Victor whispered to Pandora, making her let out a small laugh.

"It smells . . . different from last time," she said, though she was having a hard time placing anything.

"Here, my sweet pup," Elias said, pulling a chair out for Lucy, who looked daggers at him as she slid onto it.

Pandora made Victor sit next to her, regardless of what her mother might have preferred.

Robert sat next to Reginald, with a less-comfortable-looking Mary at his other side.

"There's no pig this time," Victor said.

"No dogs at the table," Ravenna told Henrietta as she came into the dining room, all of her dogs at her heels.

"They'll be under the table," Henrietta said, taking a seat next to Mary.

"Tonight, we have baked feta pasta," Ravenna said, pulling the lid off one of the dishes. "Spicy vodka pasta," she went on, pulling off another lid. "Sweet pepper sandwiches stuffed with cream cheese and bagel seasoning . . ."

"Is it just me or are these dishes all the ones trending on social apps?" Victor asked.

He was right about that.

Ravenna, realizing her mistake with the food from too long ago the last time, had done her research and decided to make every trendy food dish that had recently gone viral.

Pandora was touched, again, at Ravenna's effort to try to do right, to welcome not only Victor, but his parents too, into their family. No matter how tense some others were about the arrangement.

The meal itself went off with a surprising lack of catastrophes. Sure, Pandora's cousin Jasper was caught staring at Victor's mum's neck more than a few times. And, yeah, at some point, Elizabeth, frustrated with not being able to locate the clever Vlad, instead decided to run around under the table, chasing Henrietta's sixteen dogs. And, sure, Reginald got into far too many details about some minor war that Pandora was pretty sure wasn't even in any history texts.

But other than that, everyone seemed to enjoy the food. Dante, Elias, and Lucy managed to keep Mary distracted from any oddness.

It all went well. Better than she ever could have expected.

But then there was another knock at the door.

Looking back, Pandora was pretty sure she could pinpoint that as the moment the night took a sharp turn and then veered completely off the tracks.

20

Pandora's gaze went to her mother, but she looked just as perplexed as Pandora felt, as Lucian rose from the table to ascertain who was at the door.

"How much more family do you have?" Victor asked, looking down the table. Which, despite the many people gathered around, was only half full.

"Well, let's put it this way. When everyone is here, there's not only no room at the table, but we usually have people standing around."

"Wow," Victor said, shaking his head. "Are they all as . . . colourful as everyone here?" He glanced over at Dudley, who was feeding his cockatoo pieces of pasta out of his own mouth.

"I wish I could say not," she said, wincing.

The sound of footsteps drawing near had her attention turning to the doorway.

Really, if she'd been given a thousand guesses as to who might be at the door, she still never would have landed on the right person.

Because right there, standing next to her father, was the woman whose eyes had followed Pandora around the sitting room her entire life.

It was her great-*great*-grandmother.

Ambrosia Von Ashmore.

She couldn't exactly say that the quite youthful, stunning woman standing just a few yards away was her great-*great*-grandmother, now, could she?

But no one else seemed capable of coming up with a good lie on the fly either.

"Well, don't you look just like your mother," Ambrosia said, those haunting grey-blue eyes pinned on Pandora.

"I . . . Thank you," Pandora said, not really seeing the resemblance herself, but knowing that was meant as a compliment. Even if Ambrosia's cool tone didn't suggest as much.

"Wait," Victor said, brows scrunching as he looked at Ambrosia.

He'd seen the painting in the sitting room.

And there was a spark of recognition in his eyes.

"Aren't you the woman from the painting?" he asked.

"There is no painting, young man," Ambrosia said, her tone sending a shiver down Pandora's spine. But not so much as the way her eyes seemed to glow as she spoke to Victor. Almost as if . . .

"No," Pandora said, jumping out of her seat so quickly that her chair overturned, knocking onto the wood floor, making half the table jump.

"Whoa. That was fast," Victor said, looking at her, seeming a little drunk.

208

Of course he did.

Her great-great-grandmother had just *glamoured* him. That was completely out of line.

"Pandora," Ophelia said, her voice a hushed warning.

Sure, Pandora had been raised to respect her elders. And you literally couldn't get any older than Ambrosia. But that didn't mean she had the right to go around glamouring whoever she wanted. Especially Victor.

"Is there a problem?" Ambrosia asked, brows lifting, the picture of innocence, like she genuinely couldn't understand what she'd done wrong.

Maybe that was the case. The last Pandora heard, Ambrosia lived in a castle in Scotland, far removed from society as a whole.

"No, no, of course not," Ophelia said, gesturing toward an empty seat. "Would you care to join us?"

"I would like to speak to my grand—"

"To Pandora," Ophelia butted in. "Of course. Of course. Pandora," she added, her tone tight.

"I'll be right back," Pandora told Victor, then gave Lucy big eyes so she knew to keep an eye on things, before following her great-great-grandmother out of the dining room and into the sitting room.

"News got to me that you are to be married," Ambrosia said as soon as they were alone.

"Yes. I'm engaged."

"To a mortal."

"Yes, the one you glamoured," Pandora said, unable to keep the anger from seeping into her words.

"Does he know what we are? What *you* are?"

"No."

"Then what is the problem with a little glamour?"

209

"It's wrong," Pandora told her.

"Why?"

"Because it's . . . It's like brainwashing."

"Yes, that is the point of a glamour. To wash the brain of things we don't want the mortals to know."

"There's no need for it. We've been managing just fine without needing to glamour Victor or his family. That's not how I want to go into this marriage."

"But with lies about your very nature is fine?" Ambrosia asked.

That wasn't a bad point, Pandora had to admit. No matter how she didn't like being reminded of that truth.

"It's different. I'm not messing with his memory," Pandora said. "He looked drunk after."

"Perhaps my glamour is stronger than I realized. I have only ever used it on my familiar."

"You have a familiar?" Pandora asked, not having heard of anyone else in her family having one. Generally, they didn't want humans in their homes, in their lives, which was why some were struggling to accept the fact that Pandora wanted one in her home, life, bed, heart.

"Yes, of course."

"So, you don't hate humans?"

"Why would I hate my life source?" Ambrosia asked, frowning.

"So you don't disapprove of my relationship with Victor?"

"Well, I have to admit it is quite . . . unconventional. But I would be lying if I said I didn't enjoy the company of a mortal man. Their egos tend not to be as overwhelming as a man who has had centuries to become intolerably arrogant."

"But?" Pandora asked.

"However," Ambrosia said. "The point being you would have centuries with one of our kind."

Pandora couldn't tell her that she only planned to have a year with him, no matter how much that thought made her heart hurt. "I understand that."

"Is everything all right in here?" Lucian asked, lurking in the doorway, clearly wanting to protect his daughter, but also wanting to show the appropriate amount of respect for his great-grandmother.

"You have raised an interesting daughter," Ambrosia said, and Pandora wasn't entirely sure that was a compliment.

Lucian seemed to pick up on the same thing his daughter did, because his brows raised.

"Pandora, can you give us a few minutes?" he asked.

She didn't ask why.

She was happy to get the heck out of there. Better to let her father handle it. She had enough on her plate.

With that in mind, she hurried back into the dining room, hoping there were no fires that needed putting out.

Only to find Victor missing.

"Where's Victor?" she asked Dante.

"Oh, I think he was going for more wine," Dante said, clearly distracted by trying to keep an ear on the conversation between Uncle Reginald and Robert. It seemed as if Ravenna and Lucy were speaking to Mary.

Everything seemed all right.

Until Pandora noticed another empty chair at the table. Bellatrix's one.

There was no logical explanation for the way panic surged through her system – for the bone-deep certainty that something had gone wrong.

No, not just wrong.

Horribly wrong.

Unable to shake the feeling, she made her way along the chair backs, making a beeline for the kitchen, not sure what she was going to find, but knowing she needed to find Victor.

She moved into the kitchen, but found it empty.

There were several bottles of wine gathered on the island, the corkscrew still sticking out of the top of one. As if whoever was uncorking it had got ten distracted by something.

Or some*one*.

"Why are you marrying Pandora?" Bellatrix's voice carried to Pandora during a slight lull in conversation in the dining room.

"I . . . like her," Victor answered, voice slow and thick.

Were they in the pantry?

Pandora rushed over in that direction, but paused as her hand went for the doorknob.

Yes, eavesdropping was wrong.

But so was cornering Pandora's fiancé when she wasn't around.

"Fine," Bellatrix said, sounding frustrated. "But there's something else you're not saying. What are you two keeping from everyone?"

"It's a secret," Victor said in that same slow, slurred voice. Like he was drunk.

No.

Like he'd done with Ambrosia.

When she'd glamoured him.

Bellatrix was glamouring Victor. To try to get information out of him.

212

"Yes, but what is the secret?" Bellatrix asked.

Pandora threw open the door, knocking Bellatrix in the back with it, making her stumble forward toward Victor.

"What the hell do you think you're doing?" Pandora snapped at her cousin as Victor visibly jolted when the glamour broke.

"Pandora," Victor said, brows scrunched as he looked at her. Then he cast a confused glance around the pantry. And, finally, at Bellatrix. "This isn't . . . It isn't what it looks like," he said, but he seemed uncertain.

"Victor, can you please bring the wine out to the table?" Pandora asked, glaring at Bellatrix.

"OK," Victor said, looking upset.

But she couldn't deal with him right then. There would be time to comfort him later.

Right then, she needed to deal with her cousin.

Pandora waited until she heard someone speaking to Victor in the dining room before she slammed the pantry door behind her and took a threatening step toward Bellatrix.

"What the hell do you think you're doing? You don't get to go around glamouring my fiancé."

"If you weren't both hiding something, I wouldn't need to."

"You don't know what you're talking about."

"Oh, I think I do," Bellatrix said, flipping her pale hair over her shoulder. "He even admitted that you two have a secret."

"We have lots of secrets," Pandora said. "Like any couple."

"Nope. Something is up. And I'm going to figure out what it is."

"You know what it is, Bellatrix? You are pea-green with envy. You just can't stand anyone getting attention other than you. It's sad, really."

Pandora thought she had her for a moment.

Anger and embarrassment flashed across Bellatrix's gaze.

But it wasn't long before it was replaced with an icy sort of reservation.

"I'm going to find out what's going on. Then I'm going to expose you to everyone."

With that, she moved toward the door, slamming into Pandora's shoulder as she went.

Pandora stood there for a moment, trying to pull herself together, to stop her mind from spiraling.

It wasn't until she stepped into the kitchen, finding Victor waiting for her, that she realized something else she'd overheard in that pantry. Before she'd even gone inside. When Victor was being glamoured, so he couldn't have been lying.

"Why are you marrying Pandora?" Bellatrix had asked.
"I like her."

He liked her.

21

"Well, on the plus side," Lucy said as the two of them hauled bags of coffee beans out of boxes, restocking them under the cabinets in the front of the shop for easy access when they ran out. "Now that all the meetings are over, there's really no reason for Bellatrix to even run into Victor."

Lucy was a lot more optimistic than Pandora about that.

"Except she could track him down at uni. On the Tube. Leaving here at night. At his flat." There were a thousand ways her conniving cousin could find Victor alone, glamour him, and get all the answers she was seeking. All the while, Victor had no idea what was being done to him or what he was saying.

"True," Lucy said, sighing. "Isn't there some ancient

vampire talisman or magic or something that can prevent him from being glamoured?" she asked.

"I might know that," Pandora said. "If I, you know, applied myself to my vampire history studies. Which, I didn't. And neither did Dante, so I can't ask him. Anyone else would get suspicious."

"What about Lord Fangsworth? Wouldn't he know?"

"Elias had a business trip to go on. Mum wasn't happy about it. But I think now that he knows there's no connection between us, he doesn't see the need to be around all the time. I could wait until he gets back, but I just don't want Bellatrix to get a chance to get to Victor."

"Hmm," Lucy said, glancing out the windows as the wind kicked up leaves in little cyclones for a moment, before they died down and fell back to the pavement. "Hey, what about a magick shop?" she asked. "Not like one of the ones for the general public, which sell gemstone rings and do basic tarot readings. But one of the more serious ones. Wouldn't a witch know more about this sort of thing?"

It was certainly worth a shot.

"I don't know of any, though," Pandora said.

"I think I passed one on a run one day."

"What makes you think it's one of the non-touristy ones?" Pandora asked.

"There wasn't even any real signage telling you what they offered. And when I looked in the window, the place was packed with ancient-looking artifacts, leather-bound books, and stuff like that. Not shelves full of tarot decks or anything like that. What was it called? Arcane something," Lucy said, reaching for her mobile and trying to plug it in.

"What?" Pandora asked after helping a customer and finding Lucy still frowning at her phone.

"It's not listed," Lucy said. "But look." She turned her mobile so Pandora could see the street view of the shop she was talking about. And it was there. It even had a small, wooden, handwritten sign above the door.

Arcane Emporium.

"Well, I guess maybe we can take that as a sign that it is one of those legit places, right?" Pandora asked.

"We should go. Tomorrow," Lucy said. "We're both off. You can sneak out by saying you are going to Victor's place. Where *is* Victor's flat?"

"I have no idea," Pandora said. "But maybe that's a good thing. If I don't know, chances are no one else does either."

"True. OK. So tomorrow, sunset."

Sunset came in what felt like the blink of an eye, despite no fewer than a dozen run-ins with the many members of Pandora's family staying at the house. Including her great-great-grandmother, who always seemed to be watching her a bit too closely.

Paranoid, Pandora watched Ambrosia back when she wasn't looking, wanting to know if she was maybe in cahoots with Bellatrix, the two of them trying to figure her out.

But from what she could tell, Ambrosia seemed more interested in spending time with the older members of the family – Ravenna and Henrietta, along with Lucian – and didn't seem to spare Bellatrix, Dante, or Jasper much mind.

"Whoa," Pandora said, when Dante nearly plowed into her as she started to head out.

He looked awful.

Those smudges under his eyes seemed to be getting darker with each passing day, despite his spending most nights up in his room, presumably sleeping.

If she hadn't been on her way out, she would have followed him, demanded some answers. But, for the moment, Victor was more at risk as far as she could tell, so she had to handle that first.

After that, though, she was going to figure out what her little brother was up to.

Dante barely even seemed to register her existence anyway as he lumbered inside, leaving Pandora watching after him.

Which was how one of Henrietta's dogs slipped out the door into the night.

"Pepper! Pepper, get back here!" Pandora chased after the little fluff ball as he tore off into the front garden, excited for some freedom. "Pepper!" Her shouts became more frantic as she lost sight of him.

It was just then she heard a snarl that had the hairs on her arms raising. Not two seconds later, Pepper came running back, tail tucked, letting out little cries.

"What was that?" Pandora asked, scooping him up.

"Sorry, that was me," Lucy said, stepping out of the shadows. "It was a little nastier than normal because his little fluffy butt was about to run into the street."

"That's . . . a handy skill," Pandora said, scooting the dog back into the house and closing the door behind him.

"You ready?" Lucy asked, producing two insulated mugs in her gloved hand. "Coffee for me. Circulation sippy for you," she said, making Pandora let out a little laugh. "I know it's been hard for you to get to the shops to even get the blood, let alone any privacy to drink it. I passed by it on the way here."

"You're the best," Pandora said, looking around, then taking a sip, feeling like she was coming alive again immediately.

Lucy, now completely fascinated with Pandora's crazy family, asked for endless updates as they took the Tube across town, before setting out on foot toward the little back street that wasn't well lit and, therefore, not much of a stop for tourists nor locals.

The Arcane Emporium was tucked into an unassuming corner storefront down the cobblestone street. It was painted a deep-forest-green color and its front window was half obscured by dried plants and flowers hanging down by their stems.

As they approached, the heavy wooden door began to shimmer, catching the light to reveal some sort of sigil that seemed to dance in and out of sight. Like it was recognizing them, or maybe revealing them to the proprietor within.

Lucy shared a look with Pandora before she reached for the brass door handle and pushed. It opened with a groan as the women stepped inside.

The air within was thick, heavy with scents of old parchment, herbs, metals, and incense.

Dim light flickered from the many wrought-iron wall sconces and candelabras, casting part of the shop in shadows thanks to the labyrinth created by towering shelves that weaved through the interior.

Pandora had a fleeting thought that whispered that if she walked into one of those rows, that she might never emerge again. There was almost something vaguely threatening about the aura in the building. But, she reminded herself, that was likely simply wards created to keep wrongdoers out. She was probably feeling it so strongly because she was, by nature, evil, so the wards were pressing on her a bit, even if they were allowing her to move inside.

Closer inspection revealed that many of the shelves were stuffed and bowing with heavy leather-bound tomes, jars of various substances – dried petals, glowing liquids, bones of different sizes and origins – and ancient-looking scrolls, complete with unbroken wax insignias.

On all other surfaces – shelves, tables, countertops – artifacts fought for space. Rune-etched stones and boxes, tarnished astrolabes, figurines, and heavy-looking wands.

The shop itself felt alive to Pandora, like it had its own pulse and soul, as if all the items gathered within hummed with their own latent energy.

Each creak of the floorboards as they walked echoed with whispers of forgotten rituals.

In a glass case toward the back of the shop, items were hidden behind locks that glowed and flickered, that seemed to whimper softly.

There was nothing about this shop that invited any novice to move inside, to play around with a craft they knew nothing about. The entire establishment seemed to actively try to scare you away from practicing the dark or forbidden magicks they offered supplies for.

Then, emerging seemingly out of nowhere, the shopkeeper stepped in front of their path.

She was a striking woman of indeterminate age whose presence commanded notice, but also oozed mysteries.

She was dressed in layers of deep, shadowy velvet in shades of black, midnight blue, and plum, reminding Pandora of sorceresses in many books she'd read. Intricate embroidery of unknown symbols adorned the chest and cuffs of her gown. The threads caught the light and shimmered, in much the same way as the sigil on the front door had, charged with some sort of magick.

The woman's hair tumbled in waves of blonde and white over her shoulders, framing a face of sharp cheekbones and piercing eyes the colour of storm clouds, keen and forbidding.

Her hands, adorned with an array of rings, moved with a precision that suggested a lifetime of practice as she drew something in the air before the two women.

Another sigil, Pandora thought.

A chain hung around the woman's neck, holding a vial of something that seemed suspiciously alive, undulating and shivering behind the glass containing it.

"I don't believe I've ever had a vampire and werewolf in here at the same time," she said, her voice low and deliberate, each word imbued with the weight of ancient knowledge.

While Pandora didn't feel she was unfriendly, there was something guarded about her as she looked over them.

"Yeah, that vampire–werewolf rivalry is totally overblown," Lucy said, waving a hand, trying to play off the discomfort that Pandora could feel emanating from her.

"It is not," the proprietor said, brows furrowing, as if trying to figure out why Lucy was being dishonest with her.

"Well, I mean, for us it is," Lucy said, waving toward

Pandora. "We're best friends. Supernatural creatures have more in common than they don't, I think. Even her crazy family seems to be OK with me. Well, more OK than they are with humans, I guess. Why am I babbling?" she asked, looking to Pandora with panicky eyes.

"I think she's making you," Pandora said, watching the shopkeeper closely, feeling it herself. It wasn't a glamour, per se. She didn't feel drunk the way Victor or other humans sounded when a vampire put the whammy on them. This was more like being drawn forward, like there was a warm hug enveloping her, making her feel comfortable enough to open up, to spill all of her secrets.

"Very good," the woman said, nodding. And just like that, Pandora felt released. "What would bring a vampire and a werewolf here together?"

"Well, that's about my friend here," Lucy said. "She's engaged."

"Congratulations." The woman's gaze slid to the ring. "The former keeper of that ring had a long, happy marriage," she said, making Pandora's brows lift.

"Yes, well, her fiancé is of the warm-blooded variety. And, well, he can't know they're vampires. And her family can't know . . . some secrets they're keeping," Lucy said, waving toward Pandora again.

"And?"

"And she's got this nightmare of a cousin who is trying to glamour the truth out of her fiancé. So, we decided to come here to see if maybe there's a way to prevent him from being glamoured."

"There is nothing to prevent some glamour but allow for other glamour," the woman said, eyeing Pandora.

"Oh, no. No, I don't glamour him. That's just . . . wrong.

I just want to protect him from it in the future. It's really gross that it can happen to him in general. But especially from my family."

To that, the proprietor nodded.

She turned in a swoosh of coloured velvet then quickly disappeared in the maze of bookshelves, leaving Lucy and Pandora to rush to catch up, lest they lose track of her completely.

They found her standing in an L-shaped formation of glass cabinets, the contents looking slightly less ominous than the ones in the back that were glowing and pulsing and shrieking.

As Pandora drew closer, in fact, she discovered that within these glass cases there were only types of jewelry.

"He can just wear a nice little accessory and it's all good?" Lucy asked, looking down at the jewelry but not getting too close. Because of that pesky werewolf/silver thing.

"It's a bit more complicated than that," the shopkeeper said as she unlocked one of the glass cases. "Here we go." She produced a gold chain with a pendant hanging from it. The pendant was also gold, and bullet-shaped, with a small window in the front revealing the glass vial hidden within.

"Let me guess," Lucy said, eyeing it. "Blood goes in there."

"Indeed, it does."

"Whose blood?" Pandora asked, knowing there was no way she could get any of Victor's without him knowing. And with his studies in vampires, she really didn't think she could risk being any more suspicious than she already was.

"Yours," the woman said. "Given willingly. While saying a specific enchantment."

"That's it?" Lucy asked, almost sounding disappointed. While Pandora was thankful. Though a bit worried about how much that kind of jewelry might cost. Because she was relatively sure it wasn't just a normal glass-vial pendant. There had to be some sort of magic forged in it.

"Most of the work is already done," the woman said, flexing her fingers as if she was the one to imbue it with magic. She probably had been.

"Will it work immediately?" Pandora asked. "Or is it something that has to be done on a full moon or otherwise primed?"

"The original spell was cast correctly," the woman said. "You are simply activating it with your blood and words."

Pandora nodded at that. "What reason could I possibly give Victor for why I'm giving him a vial of my blood?" she asked, looking at Lucy.

"Hmm," Lucy said, squinting at the pendant. "I think if you fill it enough, you might not even be able to tell it's blood. Will he be able to open it?" she asked the shopkeeper.

"Once it is sealed, it is sealed forever."

"If he asks, you can just say it's a family heirloom. I mean, the contents in it have certainly been . . . handed down."

More lies.

The guilt had started to become a gnawing sensation in Pandora's stomach that no amount of blood could satiate.

But this was for his own good.

To protect them both.

"OK," Pandora said. "Yeah, I'll take it."

After shelling out a painful amount of sterling for the pendant, the shopkeeper jotted down the spell and told Pandora she should go outside under the moonlight and, with her bare feet in the earth, fill the vial and say the incantation.

"How will we know it worked?" Lucy asked.

"You will know," the woman said.

Then, just as quickly as she'd appeared, she was gone.

Pandora and Lucy made their way back outside, walking until they found a semi-private patch of grass.

Pandora slipped out of her shoes and gave the piece of paper to Lucy to hold out for her to read.

"Oh, shoot. We don't have a knife . . ." Lucy said, looking around like she might find one lying around.

"It's fine," Pandora said, uncapping the vial, then lifting her wrist and using one of her fangs to break her skin.

"Oh, gross. I mean . . . handy," Lucy said, wincing as the blood flowed. "All right, as you drip, say the words."

"*Through my veins, a shield is cast.*

"*Your mind's your own, your will holdfast.*

"*No glamour shall cloud, no spell ensnare*

"*My blood's protection is yours to wear.*"

"So mote it be," Lucy said as the last drop filled the vial.

"OK." Pandora reached for the cap. "But she said we would know it worked. Nothing . . . Oh." She gasped as the cap clicked on, then the entire pendant heated to the point of burning as a light seemed to explode from it.

Then, nothing.

The light was gone, the pendant cool to the touch.

"Well, then," Lucy said, nodding. "Insane amount of money well spent."

Pandora was apt to agree.

"Now you just need to text Victor and ask if you can pop over and give it to him," Lucy said as she fished in her bag for a spare tissue to clean up the outside of the pendant with.

Pandora reached for her mobile to shoot him a text while her mind raced.

She was going to give a spelled pendant full of her own blood to someone who knew more about supernatural things than the average human.

What could possibly go wrong?

22

Victor lived just a few streets away from UCL. Lucy's flat was in the opposite direction, so she and Pandora parted ways at the shop. Pandora walked the rest of the way alone, the cool wind kicking her hair up, and she tried not to fret over the tangles it had likely twisted itself into as she made it to the block of rooms that Victor shared with a few mates.

"Sounds worse than it is," he said as he met her outside the grey-brick building. "Mike has a girlfriend, so he's over her place more often than not. Grant works two jobs on top of uni. Tate doesn't go to uni and he currently sleeps on the couch in the living room. But since Mike, Grant, and I all have our own rooms, it doesn't bother us much."

"I have, like, a dozen people at my house right now, so I can't speak," Pandora said with a shrug.

"Ignore Tate if he says anything dense," Victor said as he led Pandora up toward his door. "He can be a bit of a git. But he gets all the leftover food at the restaurant he works at, which means we basically don't spend anything on food, so we put up with his crap."

With that, Victor led Pandora into his living room. A.k.a. Tate's bedroom. It wasn't a large space and it was dominated by a blue couch covered in pillows, a sheet, and a duvet. As well as its occupant, Tate.

He was average height and build, with wavy, messy blond hair that had an indentation from his headphones.

He was sitting on the edge of the sofa in boxers, a rumpled white tee, and socks with holes in both big toes. A bowl of sugary cereal was in his hands as he watched the rugby game on the telly.

"Tate, Pandora. Pandora, Tate," Victor said as he closed and locked the door.

"Right. The fiancée we never heard about until, like, two weeks ago."

"Didn't want to scare her off by letting her meet you," Victor said, eyes dancing as his hand went to Pandora's lower back, guiding her toward the hall.

"I'll put my headphones on. Won't hear a thing."

If Pandora could blush, she would be crimson right then. Victor simply ignored him, though, as he led her to the last room in the hallway, right past the center bathroom that was remarkably clean, considering how many guys lived there.

"This is me," Victor said, opening the door to his bedroom and stepping inside.

It was a small space dominated by an extra-long twin-sized bed and the antique writing desk butted up under the window, which served not only as the work station but also the nightstand.

Instead of a headboard, there was a row of shelves overflowing with dozens of books. Across from the bed itself, there was a telly mounted on the wall beside the wardrobe.

Otherwise, the space was neat. His backpack was hung on the door. His desk was organized. His bed was made.

Clearly, he was on a limited income but he was making the best of it.

Though, in her opinion, the whole space would feel a lot more alive and cozier if he had some hanging plants in front of the window.

"Is everything all right?" Victor asked once they were behind a closed door.

"What? Oh, yeah, fine. I just wanted to pop by. I, um, have something to give you," Pandora said, suddenly kicking herself for not concocting a convincing story on her way to his flat.

"To give me?" he asked, pulling the chair out from his desk and turning it to sit.

"Yeah, it's . . . it's kind of a family heirloom," she told him, proud of her quick thinking. "I was hoping you could start wearing it. You know, like, daily? That way, if we happen to see my family, they will see it. And it might . . ."

"Help sell how serious this is," he said, making Pandora's shoulders relax slightly.

"Yes, exactly."

"What is it? Some kind of jewelry?"

"Yeah, it's a pendant," she said, reaching in her purse

to produce the chain. "It's not too crazy. You know, given my family's sort of eccentric taste." She let the pendant fall into view.

"Yeah, that's not bad at all," he said, reaching for it.

"Here," she said, snatching it back. "I'll put it on for you." She wedged herself into the small space behind the chair, then opened the chain to slide it on for him. "There." She caught herself starting to rest her hand on his shoulder, then pulled away. "Just make sure you always have it on, OK?" she asked as she sat on the edge of the bed.

Victor looked puzzled at that but he nodded. "OK. I don't have to worry about damaging it?"

"No. It's pretty well-crafted," she said.

The silence stretched long enough to get uncomfortable. "How have things been at home?" he asked. "I still can't believe I got so drunk so fast," he added, looking embarrassed.

"My family's wine can be kind of potent," Pandora said, feeling guilty about his embarrassment. And the fact that her cousin had taken advantage of his mind. "No one noticed." Since, by the time he'd got back to the table, he'd been pretty much back to normal. "We'll just water it down next time or something."

"Yeah, I . . ." A litany of curses came crashing through the walls from the living room. "Sounds like he switched from rugby to video games," he said. "Want to go for a walk? Get some air?"

Pandora knew her mind was going to go into an inappropriate place if they stayed in his room. With a bed in it. That she would love more than anything to pull him

230

down on, claim his lips with hers, feel his hands sliding down her . . .

"Yes," she said, popping up at the same time that Victor did, making both of them collide in the tiny space, his whole front brushing against hers.

The electricity sizzled across Pandora's skin as her head tipped up, seeking him, wanting to know if he was as impacted as she was.

But Victor stepped back before she could read his expression, turning his back to her, and made his way to the door.

Having no choice but to shelve her own desire, she followed him out to the living room where Tate was trash-talking someone he was playing in his game.

"That was quick," Tate said, making Pandora's eyes go round. "Gotta work on your game, man," he added, getting a growling sound out of Victor.

But Victor didn't engage, just grabbed his coat, then pulled open the door and waited for Pandora to step into the hall.

They walked in silence for a few moments, each lost in their own thoughts. Until Pandora found herself turning automatically down the street that would lead to her bookshop.

"Toy museum?" Victor asked when she stopped out front as she always did, reality slipping away, her imagination taking the reins.

Her mind chased away the cobwebs, refreshed the paint, filled the space with colour, plants, little suncatchers in the windows to refract the light and create little rainbows through the store.

She could practically hear the giggles of children in their section, could see the teen girls gushing over the latest hot fae king, could feel the excitement of someone who'd never liked reading finding the book that sucked them in for the first time.

She'd always seen it in her head as a place where everyone was welcome. Humans, vampires, werewolves. Maybe she could ask that witch shopkeeper lady to create some sort of talisman or spell to make the place a sanctuary for all creatures, a place where they could put down their prejudices and bond over their shared love of stories.

"Pandy?"

The fantasy had pulled her in as it always did. She was smelling fresh paper, and hearing the coffee-house music, and feeling the leather spines of a book.

"Sorry, Victor," she said, shaking her head.

"Where'd you go?"

"Hopefully, into my future," Pandora told him.

"What do you mean?"

"This place has been vacant for ages. And for just about as long, I have been dreaming of buying it and turning it into my own bookshop."

"That's why the inheritance is so important to you."

"Yeah." Her gaze slid over to Victor's reflection in the glass. "It's really not about just . . . having money. To buy posh clothes or get a fancy flat. It's about making this dream come true."

"Tell me about the dream."

Then he stood there with her, his shoulder brushing hers, as she talked about the colours, the plants, the books, the merchandise, the vibes she wanted the place to have.

232

"And coffee," Victor said when she was done. "There has to be coffee."

Pandora nodded. "And tea."

"And cozy chairs," he said.

They went on like that for a while, each coming up with items that the perfect bookshop would have, since they both loved books and the places that sold them.

And it was the first time she ever felt like someone else was sharing in her dream.

Sure, Lucy knew about it and they would sometimes discuss the obscure, but best, books that had to be on the shelves. But it was the first time someone was seeing it with her, improving it, getting excited about it.

"Just over two months," Victor said.

"Hm?"

"Just over two months until you can make an offer on this place," he said, gesturing at the building. As she looked over, the tree overhead shook in the breeze, sending some orange leaves cascading around him, one landing on his shoulder. She reached out, brushing it away.

"It really is that soon," Pandora said, giving him a small smile as she forced her hand to lower, not slide down his arm, maybe take his hand . . .

"Just about ten thousand things to arrange before then," he said, wide-eyed.

"Don't remind me. My mum and aunts really dug their claws into the reception and flowers and . . . everything else. My head spins just thinking about it."

"It's good you have the help, though. They've all done it before."

233

Some many times.

The issue was that they'd done it hundreds of years ago. When trends and customs were wildly different.

But she couldn't tell him that.

"Yeah." She nodded. "It'll all work out."

If there weren't any more nasty surprises to worry about.

23

"What is going on here?" Pandora asked when she walked into the sitting room to find Vlad on his antique perch. With Elizabeth the cockatoo cozied up next to him. No, not only cozied up. She had her wing wrapped around him.

"Don't judge," Vlad said, stifling a yawn.

"But you can't stand her," Pandora said.

"She's grown on me."

"Grown on you, or worn you down?" Pandora asked as Elizabeth turned to start preening Vlad's feathers.

"Both," he replied. "But she makes that arrogant crow that's always in the garden jealous. So there's that."

Pandora broke into a knowing smile just as the knocker sounded, making her brows scrunch. It was still morning. Her entire family was upstairs sleeping. Including, of course, Henrietta's dogs, who she'd somehow trained to be mostly nocturnal as well.

"Probably another package," Pandora said, waving toward the tower about to topple over in the foyer.

Once Cody had introduced Ravenna and Reginald to the wonders of online shopping, it had been a steady stream of boxes showing up at the door.

Some contained things Ravenna insisted were "vital" to the wedding planning. Others had replicas of things that Reginald missed about the "old days". Mostly, though, he liked to order costumes meant for Renaissance fairs or cosplay. Then spend hours telling everyone what was, and was not, historically accurate. From the design to the threads used in the stitching.

Pandora reached for the knob, expecting to just find a retreating parcel carrier and a box on the front steps.

Instead, Victor was standing there, backlit by the sun, making her notice flecks of gold and red in his dark hair that she'd never noticed before.

"Oh, hello," she said, giving him a surprised smile.

"Sorry to just pop by. I figured it would be smarter to discuss things in person than try to answer . . ." He looked at his mobile. "Seventeen separate texts."

"Sorry about that. My family has been a bit overbearing about some of the planning details," Pandora said, moving back so he could step inside, glad for the opportunity to have him inside without worrying about her family saying or doing something absurd.

"I imagine they just want it to be nice for you."

"For us," she said. "Which is why they want me to consult you on all of these things. I am practically expecting Aunt Ravenna to require your actual signature on all these decisions."

"I like Ravenna," Victor said, taking off his backpack as they sat down at the dining table.

"She's the best. OK, so, for the meal . . ." she said, ready to get down to business.

But it was right then she heard footsteps making their way down the staircase. Given that everyone else had just gone to bed, there was only one person it could be.

Dante.

Pandora put her finger to her lips.

Victor's brows drew down but he didn't say a peep as she slowly rose to her feet, making her way to the doorway to see, just as she'd expected, Dante making a beeline for the front door.

He paused, reaching to grab a coat from the hanger, pulling up the large hood, then reaching into the pockets to produce gloves.

Then he pulled open the door . . . and moved out into the daylight.

"Hey," Pandora whispered, rushing back toward Victor, picking up his backpack. "Come on. We have a little mission today."

With that, she rushed to the door, grabbing her own coat and gloves, then reaching for an umbrella.

"Oh, it's not supposed to rain," Victor said.

"It's for the sun," Pandora said, pulling open the door, then opening the umbrella. "I get burned very easily. Even on a cloudy day, I can get a little burn." She made her way down the front path, trying not to run, while keeping an eye on her quickly moving brother.

"What are we doing?" Victor asked.

"Following Dante," Pandora said in a whisper, not wanting Dante, who had super-hearing just as she did, to overhear.

237

"For what reason?"

"He's been acting strange lately," she told Victor. "Sneaking off, not telling anyone where he is going." *In the daytime*, she added silently. "He's looking more and more run-down, so I just want to make sure he's OK."

Victor's gaze softened at that.

He might not have siblings of his own, but he clearly understood her concern as they followed Dante down the streets of London, then to the Underground, where they stood at the train car at the furthest end, their backs to Dante.

Not that he seemed to notice them. Or even seem worried about being followed.

Why would he?

None of his family went out during the day.

They could, of course. There were many times Pandora had needed to go out in the daylight over the years. Precautions had to be taken. Long sleeves, gloves, oversized hats, and umbrellas or parasols. Sometimes, especially in the summer, you could still feel the threatening burn of the sun through your protective measures, but Pandora had never been singed, let alone caught fire, before.

That said, Dante had no reason to think their family would even want to be out in the daylight. They took pride in being creatures of the night. Of being the shadows lurking in dark corners. Of being the whispered sounds that haunted humans as they walked down alleys or alone on the pavement at night.

"Going quite far out there, aren't we?" Victor asked as Pandora admired a particularly gorgeous garden, still alive with late-blooming dahlias and asters.

"Oh, sorry. Do you have to be at uni?" she asked,

suddenly worried that she'd pulled him away from something important.

Really, she should have just made an excuse and gone her separate way from him back at the house. There was no telling what Dante might be up to – what she might need to protect Victor from.

She hadn't been thinking straight, clearly.

Though, the larger part of her thought she simply wanted him there. With her. Especially when potentially uncovering something upsetting.

"No. No, I'm done for the day. I was just going to do the washing. This will be more fun than that."

Eventually, Dante got off the train.

"Hampstead," Victor said as they made their way through the station, following Dante at a safe distance as he made his way out onto the busy streets.

Pandora ignored the sideways looks from passersby as she walked under her umbrella.

"It's been a while since I've been out this way," Victor said as they moved from the busy city streets toward a more residential lane, the leaves crunching under their feet as they walked. "But . . . there's not much out here now, is there? Now that we're past the shops?"

"Not really," Pandora said, watching Dante pause to pet a passing golden retriever before continuing on.

"Maybe he has a mate out this way. Or a girlfriend."

Pandora hadn't even considered that possibility.

It would make things make sense, wouldn't it? If he'd perhaps got himself a human girlfriend. Why he was out all day and stayed holed up in his room all night. Why he was so supportive of her fake relationship with Victor.

"Maybe."

But as they turned down the road that went from residential to rural, she was pretty sure that wasn't the case either.

It wasn't until she saw Dante take a turn into a car park that she realized where he was heading.

"Is he going to the pond?" Victor asked, looking over at Pandora for confirmation.

"Seems like it."

What the heck was he up to?

"Meeting with some friends?" Victor asked, suddenly sounding more hesitant, like he felt bad for following Dante if he was doing something so casual.

"I understand if you don't want to go any further," Pandora said. "But I'm already this far. I want to see what he's doing."

She couldn't tell him it was because this wasn't normal behavior. That he shouldn't be out in the daytime at all, let alone out by the pond where the sun was even stronger.

"How about we take a stroll around the lake?" Victor said. "If you want to confront Dante, I will just hang back."

She gave him a grateful smile. "Sounds like a plan."

If they'd been there for any other reason, Pandora might have soaked up the moment. The riot of colours of the leaves on the ground. The scent of the fresh earth. The way the water rippled gently with the breeze as it picked up.

And, of course, sharing that with Victor.

But she was too busy searching for Dante.

She was about ready to give up when she suddenly saw him emerge from the lifeguard station.

Wearing the typical red-and-yellow lifeguard colours.

240

Only, he had sports leggings on and a jacket. As well as a massively wide-brimmed hat.

In short, he looked outright ridiculous.

But he was clearly there with a purpose.

Being a lifeguard.

"Um, can you give me a few minutes?" Pandora asked.

"Sure," Victor said. "Got some books in here." He patted his backpack. "Take your time. I'll be right here."

As if to cement his point, he pulled out a book and sat down on the ground. He seemed engrossed in his reading before Pandora had even started to walk away.

Weeks of the weight of her concern fell away with each step, replaced with absolute confusion.

But before she could even come up with any plausible explanations, Dante spotted her, his face going from shock to anger in a blink.

Then he was rushing toward her, making her anxiety shoot up when she noticed that, in his anger, he was moving at vampire, not human, speed.

A quick glance around, though, showed no one really noticed. It wasn't exactly swimming season for most people, so the pond wasn't as busy as it would have typically been a month or two before.

"Pandy, what the hell are you doing here?" Dante asked, grabbing her around the upper arm and dragging her off the path and into the woods.

It wasn't until they were out of sight that he released her. "Did you really *follow* me?" he asked.

"You've been off for weeks. Months, maybe," Pandora said. "I've been worried about you, but anytime I try to bring it up, you change the topic. You're out all day, then holed up in your room all night. But you aren't getting any sleep, judging by the bags under your eyes. You look . . . unwell."

It was then that she realized just how true that was.

There were the bags and bruises, sure. But more than that, he seemed a little gaunt, so thin in the face that his cheekbones had hollowed out.

If it were possible, she would think he was sick. But vampires didn't get sick. At least as far as she knew. Some members of her family mentioned some sort of vampire plague thousands of years back. But Pandora was suspicious of the validity of that story since those particular family members were known for stretching the truth.

"I've been coming here during the day," Dante said, waving back toward the pond.

"I've put that part together. But . . . why?"

"I love it here," Dante said, shrugging. "I love swimming. I love being out in the daytime. I . . ." He looked off into the distance. "I hate being a vampire."

"Oh, Dante," Pandora said, her heart aching for him. No, she didn't love every aspect of being a vampire, but she didn't hate it exactly, either. She sure loved the idea of eternity to read all the books she still had on her to-be-read shelf.

"You don't love it either," Dante said, looking back at her, willing her to agree with him. "You don't feed. I know you don't. And you haven't for a long time."

"No," she replied. "I don't feed. I drink pig's blood. It's more like . . . like a human being vegetarian, though. It's kind of a moral thing for me. Not that I hate who I am. Just that I don't want to hurt anyone just to feed myself."

"There are human donors."

"But they're glamoured," Pandora said, shrugging.

242

"That just feels wrong too. Pig blood is a good substitute. It's just . . . not something I want to share with the family. You know how they are."

"I can't stand any blood most of the time now. But, yeah," he said, shaking his head. "That's part of the reason I'm working here too. I want to take care of myself. Provide for myself. I don't want to be jumping through hoops to get an inheritance from Mum and Dad."

"I get that," Pandora said. "I really like working too. But . . . you could get a night job. Or a job at an indoor pool. This is so dangerous," she said, waving up, indicating the sun above her umbrella.

"Is it?" Dante asked, something strange in his eyes that Pandora wasn't sure she'd seen there before.

But then, he was reaching out, grabbing the sleeve of his jacket and pulling it up, then thrusting his hand out toward the sun.

"What are you doing?" Pandora squeaked, trying to stay under her umbrella but also push it out far enough to cover his hand.

"Just watch," he said, wiggling his pale fingers in the sun's rays.

Pandora's stomach twisted in knots. But he didn't spark, let alone catch fire. He didn't even . . . burn.

What was going on?

Confused, Pandora threw out her own arm.

She was mostly covered, but there was a small sliver between the top of her glove and where her jacket reached down.

Immediately, though, she felt the sizzle on her skin, saw the smoke, smelled her skin starting to burn.

"Ow," she said, snatching her arm back.

Dante looked sympathetic as he just stood there with his arm not sizzling or smoking.

Then he used that arm to reach into his pocket, producing a tube that looked a bit like a lip balm, but at least twice that size.

"What is that?" she asked.

Instead of answering, Dante reached for her arm, turning it so the unburned underside was showing, then uncapped the tube to rub some of the thick white contents onto her skin.

"Now try," he said. When she didn't grasp his meaning, he pulled her arm back out from under the umbrella and into the sunlight.

This time, though, she didn't sizzle, didn't smoke, didn't burn at all.

"What?" she said, frowning at her arm, then looking at her brother's skin. "What is in that tube, Dante?"

"Something I've been working on in my free time."

In his free time when he was supposed to be sleeping after working all day?

"That's what you've been doing in your room? With the door locked?"

"Yes," he said, nodding.

"What is it? Some kind of extra-thick sunblock?"

"Not really. I mean, yeah, there is some zinc oxide in it like normal sunscreen. But it's more than that. In a, you know, magickal way."

"Like what?" Pandora asked, mind flashing back to the esoteric shop she'd visited with Lucy. Had Dante been there too? Talked to the same woman she had?

"Ground moonstone, activated charcoal, herbs picked under a full eclipse, infused nightshade . . . lots of things."

"You've been working on making your own vampire sunblock? So you can swim and lifeguard?"

"So I can have a normal life, yeah," he said.

"How did you know what to use in it?" Pandora asked, taking the stick and rubbing it on her fingers so she could use them to put the sunscreen on her face.

"Trial and error. A *lot* of trial and error," Dante said, looking exhausted even at the mention. "I did a lot of research. Went to some shops for obscure supplies. Burned myself thousands of times."

"Does it always work? How long have you been testing it?"

"All summer," he told her. "I've been tweaking it here and there, wanting to see if I could improve it just a little bit more each time. I especially wanted to see if I could get it to be more waterproof."

"But you're still all covered up," Pandora said, looking at her brother's absurd outfit.

"When I started here, I may have kind of told them I'm a little allergic to the sun."

"Not a lie, really," Pandora said with a laugh.

"Exactly. But I can't just be like, 'Oh, hey, by the way, I'm not allergic to the sun anymore,'" he said. "And it really isn't completely waterproof, which wouldn't be so bad if I was sure I would always get a chance to re-apply, but things can get crazy around here sometimes. I mean, not so much right now." He waved at the pond, empty, save for a set of kayakers. "But in the summer for sure."

"This is so cool, Dante," she said, sticking her hand out again, feeling the comforting warmth the sun supplied. Without all the burning flesh and bursting into flames.

"How difficult is it to make? And how obscure are the supplies?"

"It's a lot of work, but it's doable. Worth it, at least. Some of the supplies are harder to find than others, but none of it is stuff I would run out of."

"So, what is your plan? Just keep this for yourself, so you can try to live more of a human life?"

"Originally, yes."

"But?"

"But now I'm wondering if there is maybe a market for it. Not for every vampire," he rushed to add. "I don't think it's right to take away the only protection humans have. But for vampires like you and me. Ones who don't want to feed on humans. There's more of us than you'd think."

"How do you know that?" Pandora asked, always having felt very alone in her desire not to eat humans.

"There's some forums for vampires like us. Ones who don't want to use humans like that, who wish we could all coexist peacefully."

"You want to see about marketing this product to them?"

"It's risky," Dante said. "There's always the chance of it falling into the wrong hands. I just . . . I feel bad for everyone like us who can't live the lives they want because of what we are."

"I wonder . . ." Pandora said, trailing off as her mind wandered.

"Wonder what?"

"I wonder if maybe you could . . . spell it?" she said.

"Spell what?"

"The sunscreen. Could the product have a spell on it that would make it so that, I don't know, anyone with the wrong intentions can't use it?"

246

"I have no idea," Dante said, frowning. "But it's an idea, isn't it?"

"You could try to find a witch. Bring the plan to her. See if she could help you out. Maybe for a share of the profits or something to make it worth her time. Or . . . when I get my inheritance – if we can pull this off – I can invest."

Dante's eyes brightened. It was the first time in a long time he'd looked so hopeful. "I can look into it. There's got to be a witch somewhere who could make that kind of spell."

"Until then, I expect one of these," Pandora said, waving the stick at her brother. "I mean, Victor already thinks I get horrible sunburn." She indicated her umbrella. "And terrible circulation. And a garlic allergy. But it would be nice to have this just in case of anything . . . unexpected."

"Only a few more weeks to go, right?" Dante asked.

"Yeah, the past few have kind of gone by in a flash," Pandora said.

Things had been back to normal, she supposed, with Victor. She went to work. He showed up to study, work, and drink his macchiatos. Sure, they talked more these days, since they had a lot of planning to do for the future.

Not just the wedding, but things like life *after* the wedding. They'd both been doing a lot of flat-shopping online, trying to find a place close to uni for him, but also Luna Bean and the bookshop Pandora hoped to open. So they would sit and pore over the options on her breaks, then talk about how many bookshelves they'd need, what colours they'd paint the walls, all that stuff.

Admittedly, it meant there was a lot of daydreaming going on for Pandora. Imagining their lives together.

Making coffee and tea in the morning. Sitting in the living room at night, each reading their books.

Did those dreams also veer off into fantasies, ones where they might brush each other as they flipped pages, where one, then both of them might lean in, kiss, touch, head to one of their bedrooms, and make their fake marriage a real one? Yes, yes, they did.

But back in the real world, Victor kept his distance physically from Pandora now that they weren't around their families together.

So Pandora had been trying not to let herself harp on that one thing he'd said to Bellatrix in the pantry while being glamoured.

It clearly hadn't meant what she'd thought.

Of course he *liked* her. If he hated her, there was no way he would be going through this bollocks plan with her. Especially when it was going to involve living with her for a full year.

"Yeah?" Dante asked. "I'd have thought that it would drag, with how much the aunts and Mum are all over you."

"Don't forget the cousins," Pandora said.

The train of family members coming to stay had not stopped with the appearance of her great-great-grandmother Ambrosia.

There had been a day or two of peace before the cousins started rolling in.

Though, for once, Pandora was pleased with the company of the younger female cousins who gushed over her ring, who asked her all sorts of questions about Victor. No judgment or weirdness about her choice to marry a human.

They worked as a nice buffer between the older women's often antiquated or crazy wedding-planning ideas.

There'd been a particularly worrying suggestion of some sort of full-moon blood ritual.

But the cousins put a quick end to that. Which also meant Pandora didn't have to be the bad guy all of the time.

"We're about bursting at the seams," Dante said. "Wonder when it will stop."

"The night before the wedding, I suspect," Pandora said. "The rooms might be full, but we have the whole basement and attic to fill with more coffins, if needed."

"Yeah. Been worried Mum was going to try to make me share. My whole room looks like a science laboratory."

"Dante!" a voice called in the distance.

"That's the other lifeguard," Dante said. "I have to be getting back."

"Right. Of course," Pandora said, handing him back his sunscreen. "I'm sorry I followed you. I was just concerned."

"It was good to talk to someone about things," he said.

"I'm really proud of you," Pandora said. "For knowing what you want and working toward it. But, please, get some rest. And get some blood. You're wasting away."

"I've just been busy. I will take better care. You've got enough to worry about. Don't need to go adding myself to that list." His colleague called his name again. "Coming!"

"Go ahead," Pandora said. "I'll see you at home."

With that, she watched her brother rush back toward the jetty, smiling and laughing with his coworker.

Sure, he looked ridiculous, covered head to toe.

But he was also happier than she'd ever seen him.

For a moment, she watched him in his element, getting down on the jetty to dangle his legs just over the water as he watched the shoreline and the kayakers.

Finally, she moved out of the woods and made her way back toward Victor. She stopped a few feet away from him as well, watching him as he sat there engrossed in his story.

The wind kicked up, making his hair fall into his face a bit. It was in need of a trim. She just barely held herself back from reaching out, from brushing the soft strands back. The edge of his book curled in, making his hand spread out to flatten it so he could continue reading.

Her mind immediately thought of that hand. When it was holding hers with gentle pressure. Of it teasing the edges of her hair when they'd sat at the restaurant. Of it pressed into the small of her back in a way that always felt comfortingly possessive to her. Or, of course, as it moved over her body in the cupboard, sparking little fires of need until her body was an out-of-control wildfire.

"Oh, hey," Victor said, looking up and catching her standing there watching him.

"Hey," she said.

"Everything all right?"

"We had a good talk," she told him as he stuck his book back in his backpack then got to his feet.

"I don't want to pry . . ."

"It turns out he just has this job that, I guess, he doesn't think our parents would approve of. And he looks so tired because after he comes home from work, he's been working on building a sort of business that has been consuming all of his extra time. He really wants to become independent. And not have to rely on our parents' money."

"That makes sense. Strange how he felt the need to keep it from you."

"He probably figured I was overwhelmed enough as it

250

was," Pandora told him. "Did I tell you that we have more family visiting?"

"More?" Victor asked, eyes widening. "How many more can there be?"

"Quite a few," she said. "This crowd is younger, though. And they've been helping me out when the aunts or my mum are being a little crazy."

They walked back to the Tube, discussing the many things Pandora had messaged him about when it came to wedding planning.

She was pleased to realize they agreed on pretty much every point. And the only one he differed on was about a menu item that he learned Ravenna really wanted to include. Since he had a soft spot for her, he went ahead and sided with her on that. Pandora, charmed by his affection for her great-aunt, wasn't bothered about giving in on that one point.

"Oh," Victor said, patting down his pockets when they were climbing the stairs from the Tube.

"What is it?" she asked.

"I've misplaced my phone," he said, turning his backpack to dig around in it. "Maybe I left it in your house?"

He had put it on the table when they'd sat down to discuss her texts. He could have easily forgotten it.

"We'll check," she said as they walked back to the house.

It was still too early for her to worry about any of her family. Or so she thought.

Until they walked into the dining room to find her great-great-grandmother standing there.

"Oh, hey," Pandora said, stiffening.

Things hadn't exactly softened between the two of

251

them since the night of the in-laws' meeting. She couldn't help but blame Ambrosia for giving Bellatrix the idea to glamour Victor.

"Hello," Ambrosia said, looking over Pandora, then Victor as he found his phone on the table.

She saw her great-great-grandmother zero in on the pendant hanging from Victor's chest. Pandora could tell by the way Ambrosia stared at it, brows slightly lifted, that she knew exactly what it was.

"It's good to catch you two," she said, making a strange shiver move down Pandora's spine.

"Why's that?" she asked, moving closer to Victor.

"I never got a chance to give you your engagement present."

"That's not necessary," Victor said before Pandora could think of anything to say.

"Of course it is," Ambrosia said. "Traditions are important."

"Do you need to go get it?" Pandora asked.

"It isn't a gift so much as an . . . experience," she said.

"What kind of experience?" Pandora asked, back going even straighter.

"Oh, just a little . . . lovers' getaway," Ambrosia said.

Why did Pandora get the feeling that there was some sort of catch?

24

"Why are you looking a gift horse in the mouth?" Lucy asked the following night when Pandora showed up for work to request the next three shifts off so she could go on this getaway that Ambrosia was insisting on.

"There has to be a catch," Pandora said.

"Why? This is your family. Even if they might not love your choice of a significant other, they love *you* and want you to be happy, right?"

"I guess," Pandora said, but she still couldn't shake the feeling.

"You're just getting paranoid as the day approaches . . . Oh, God, did someone lift the lid on your crypt again?" Lucy asked, looking past Pandora toward the door. "Because I've got some industrial-strength duct tape, if needed."

253

Pandora knew it was Elias before she even turned.

"Sweet as ever, pup," Elias said with a charming smile.

"What are you even doing here? Your job, as pathetic as it was to begin with, is over."

"I want to be there for the wedding. Sounds like it will be a hell of a time," Elias said. "You must be the life of the party. So long as no one brings a vacuum out."

Despite herself, Pandora let out a little snort.

"Traitor," Lucy said under her breath, even though her eyes were dancing a bit. "Isn't there anywhere else you could be? A support group for men who peaked in the Victorian era, perhaps?"

"Alas, I find myself without my private jet at the moment," Elias said. "I hear it is being borrowed so you and your fiancé can take a trip."

"Where is the trip?" Pandora asked a little desperately.

"I'm forbidden from telling you."

"I need to know if it is some sort of trap."

"Honestly, I don't know exactly where you are heading. I just know why your family wants you out of the house."

"See!" she said, pointing at Lucy. "I told you there was some sort of catch."

"A small one, really. And I probably shouldn't ruin the surprise, but this is a situation that, unfortunately, I feel like you might want your little furball here to be in on." Elias shot a little wink in Lucy's direction.

Lucy growled. "I am not furry."

Elias's gaze slid over Lucy in a way that Pandora felt was just shy of suggestive. "Perhaps not at the moment. But the full moon will be here again soon, won't it?"

"Elias, focus," Pandora said. "What is my family up to that I can't be around for?"

"They're planning stag and hen parties."

Pandora groaned. "Oh, no."

There were only about five thousand ways that could go wrong.

"Relax," Lucy said, holding up her hands. "I will get all over it. And I'm assuming Count Blech-ula can handle the stag part."

Elias, eyes bright, pressed a hand to his chest and gave her a small bow. "See? We have it covered."

"Except the two of you are still taking digs at each other."

"Hey, our tense feelings for each other will motivate us to each try to out-do the other at every turn and make sure that everything that could possibly go wrong has been subverted," Lucy said.

"So you and Victor can go and enjoy your getaway," Elias said.

"It's just three days!" Lucy sensed her friend's unease. "If anyone deserves a little relaxation, it's you. You've been stressed out for weeks. Go. Enjoy some time with Victor."

With no actual choice in the matter, Pandora made her way home to attempt to pack a bag without having any idea where she was going or what she might need.

There was a knock at her door, making her suppress a sigh. There was never a moment alone in a house bursting at the seams with family.

She hadn't decided whether to answer it yet, when she heard Dante's voice. "It's me, Pandy."

"Sorry," she said, unlocking it to let him in. "I'm . . . screening my visitors."

"I just wanted to bring you this," Dante said, holding out a tube. It was similar to the one he'd had at Hampstead Heath ponds, but easily three times the size. "Now that I got it right, I figured it was wasteful to keep making small ones."

"This is great!" she said, still so excited for his invention and the possibilities it had for his future.

A life of his own.

Exactly what she was working toward as well.

"It's going to be so strange here without you," Dante said.

"Will you keep an eye on Bellatrix for me?" she asked. "I don't think there's anything she can find out around here. But you never know."

"Did you hear she had a screaming match with Kora and Maribelle?" he asked.

"What? When? How'd I miss that?"

"It was when you were at Luna Bean. Bellatrix decided to wake the house with her . . . let's call it 'singing'. Kora and Maribelle ran upstairs, thinking someone was being sacrificed. Bellatrix got all offended. It was brilliant." Dante smiled.

He'd been just as horrified as she'd been to learn that Bellatrix had tried to glamour information out of Victor. So neither of them felt guilty for enjoying Bellatrix getting at least a little bit of a comeuppance.

"I'm sorry I missed that," Pandora said. Kora and Maribelle were visiting without their parents, so they had no qualms about getting in their cousin's face when she was being especially intolerable.

They'd already gone at her over some mean-spirited teasing of Pandora and her terrible gown-shopping fiasco.

And some comments she had to make about how weird it was to date your food source.

"And you'll help Elias with the stag party?" Pandora asked. She'd already asked Kora and Maribelle to team up with Lucy against anyone else and their crazy plans. They'd been charmingly open and excited to be working closely with a werewolf. Pandora was relieved to realize she and Dante weren't the only vampires who didn't buy into that bullshit about vampires and werewolves hating each other.

"Yeah. Don't worry about it. We've got this all handled. Go and enjoy your time with Victor."

"We're not really together, remember?" she asked in a whisper.

Sure, she'd had some hope after the events of the cupboard. That things had changed for them. That he was possibly as interested in her as she was in him.

But there'd been no other incidents since then.

No accidental touches, let alone deliberate ones. No innuendos or lingering glances.

She was starting to think she'd imagined it all.

One thing was for sure, though. It had clearly just been a spur-of-the-moment thing. A moment of charged feelings, of mutual built-up desire. Not necessarily personal. Definitely not a sign that Victor wanted to make their relationship real. No matter how much that might have hurt her.

"Sure, yeah," he said, but there was a false note in his words. "What time is your flight?"

Pandora glanced at her mobile. "Oh, no. Only two hours. And I don't know where we're going or what I need to pack."

"Layers," he said, shrugging. "Books. That should cover it for you."

He wasn't wrong about that.

So Pandora took two pairs of shoes out of her suitcase and added in a few more paperbacks instead.

To save time, she was meeting Victor at the airport, so she grabbed her bags and made her way out into the hall.

Where she almost collided with Bellatrix.

"She's not fooled, you know," Bellatrix said.

"I don't know what you're talking about."

"Ambrosia. She's not fooled. That's why she's sending you away."

"Sure, Bellatrix. Whatever you need to tell yourself to feel better," Pandora said, even if her stomach was twisting itself into knots at the idea of her cousin being correct.

She pushed past Bellatrix before they could get any further into an argument.

"What's wrong?" Pandora asked, coming to a stop when she found Vlad sitting on a perch in a dark corner.

To that, the raven let out a long-suffering sigh.

"Elizabeth."

"What happened? Last I checked, you were feeding her almond slivers and dancing for her."

"That's private," Vlad said, puffing up. "She was watching the crow from the window today. Saying things like, 'Love you, pretty bird.'"

"Vlad, that's all she *can* say," Pandora said. "She's not like you. She has a very limited vocabulary." And because she was such a sweet, snuggly bird to her owner, Dudley, all he said to her were sweet words. "That's literally all she can say."

"Well, it hurt," Vlad said, flicking his inky head and refusing to talk about it any further.

Pandora figured that, before the end of the night, he would be treating the whole family to a recital of the saddest, most heartbreaking poetry ever written.

"If you two haven't worked it out by the time I get back, we will talk about it, OK?" Pandora stroked his soft feathers for a second before making her way downstairs and out, doing so quickly, before anyone could drag her into conversation.

She made it to the little private airstrip just moments before Victor's car pulled up.

"Wow," he said as he moved up beside her, shifting a beat-up tan weekender bag further up on his shoulder. "That's what we're taking?" He stared at the sleek jet.

"Seems like it," Pandora said, still unable to shake her anxiety, even if Victor's excitement was becoming clearer by the moment.

"Alone?" he asked, still unable to wrap his head around that.

"Yes. This is Elias's private jet," she said, figuring the windows featured the same tint as those she had in her bedroom, so they could travel at all hours without him having to worry about getting scorched or bursting into flame.

"Never really understood the appeal of aspiring to certain levels of wealth . . ."

"But you're starting to reconsider that stance?"

"Something like that," he said as they both made their way toward the jet, going through the motions of speaking to the one gentleman who served as the cabin crew, the captain, and the co-captain.

259

"Can you tell us where we're going?" Pandora asked, figuring she would have hours on the plane to come to terms with whatever she might be dealing with when they landed.

"I'm afraid I can't until we are in the air," Mikhail, the one-man cabin crew, told them as they made their way into the cabin.

"Oh, wow," Pandora said, turning in a circle.

Sure, she'd been in a private jet once or twice. It was impossible for her family to travel commercially. So when there was necessary travel ahead of them, they used a family jet, or rented one.

That said, this jet was incredibly customized. Gone were all the typical champagne colours and cherry wooden accents Pandora had come to expect of private jets. In its place were deep grey walls, velvet-covered seating, and black lace sheers covering the windows. Despite the fact that they were covered in the film Pandora had been expecting.

"There's so little seating," Victor said, looking around.

He wasn't wrong about that. Replacing the typical club chairs was one oversized lounge.

Then, toward the back, half hidden by some thick drapes, was a single seat for the cabin crew.

"Seems roomy enough," Pandora said, making her way over and sitting down, excited at the prospect of sitting close to Victor for, she assumed, several hours of travel time. Both of them reading.

They were getting dangerously close to her fantasies coming true as they got comfortable, listened to the spiel from Mikhail, then each reached for their books and settled in.

"What has you so engrossed?" Victor asked, pulling her out of her story to find him watching her. There was a soft look in his eyes that made her heart feel all gooey.

"What? Oh," she said, slipping her bookmark into place. "This is a highlander romance."

"Got a thing for kilts, do you?" Victor said teasingly.

"I always like the dichotomy of the fiery-tempered highlander and the very prim Englishwoman falling for each other. It allows for a lot of personal growth for the two of them."

"Want to read it to me?" he asked.

"What? Really?" she asked, surprised he would be interested.

"Yeah. My book is a bore. Yours sounds better."

With that, Pandora moved back to the beginning of the book and started reading. All the while reminding herself that they were surely going to be on the ground before she got to the spicy bits that would be too difficult for her to read aloud to anyone, least of all Victor.

At some point, her own voice getting hoarse, Victor took over, his voice moving smoothly over the words, making her feel warm all over as she pulled her legs up onto the seat and maybe leaned a little closer to her fiancé.

Slowly but surely, she felt her eyelids getting heavy, lulled toward sleep by his soothing voice and close, warm body.

She wasn't asleep long, though, before the plane hit a bit of turbulence, making her eyes shoot open. To find she'd curled into Victor in her sleep. Her head was on his strong shoulder, his heartbeat a steady thud against her ear.

Up that close, she could hear the whoosh of the blood in his veins again, could feel her fangs lengthening with how close she was to his neck.

"This does not bode well for my future career in lecturing if my voice puts you right to sleep," Victor said, voice soft, his breath rustling her hair.

"I haven't had someone read to me in a really long time," Pandora said, not moving. Not yet. "It was very soothing. And mixed with the smooth ride . . ."

"Speaking of, I think we know our location." Victor nodded toward the windows directly across from them.

Curiosity piqued, Pandora reluctantly moved away from Victor to look out the window.

And as she did, she felt her belly knot up.

In the distance, she could see rugged peaks standing in contrast to the rolling hills dotted with olive groves and villages.

The coastline sparkled to the north, turquoise waters meeting golden beaches.

There weren't many places in the world with water like she was seeing.

This was clearly the Mediterranean.

And that village full of blue-washed buildings?

That could only be one place.

Chefchaouen.

The Blue Pearl of Morocco.

Ambrosia had sent them to Morocco.

"Ma'am?" Mikhail interrupted her thoughts, making her turn. "Your gran—"

"Ambrosia," Pandora cut him off.

"Yes, Ambrosia wanted me to give you this," he said, passing her a small envelope.

262

Ignoring the sloshing sensation in her stomach, she tore it open, finding a small card inside. Within the card, just a simple message from her great-great-grandmother.

You need to see how incompatible you are with a human.
Enjoy the next three days with your betrothed.
In the unyielding sun.

25

"Morocco, wow," Victor said as they watched a car pull down the airstrip, as if waiting for them.

As Pandora tried not to panic.

Three days in sunny Morocco.

No trusty London fog or rain to make it easier for her to move around without worrying about burning or incinerating.

What the hell was she going to do?

Even as the thought formed, though, she remembered the visit from her brother right before she'd left. The large tube he'd given her. The same tube she'd stuffed into her bag before zipping it up.

She had the vampire sunscreen.

So while she hadn't had room to pack a parasol, she could slather herself in the sunscreen, wear long layers for her "circulation issues" and wear her big, wide-brimmed hat.

It would be OK.

"Just give me one second," Pandora said as the jet stopped and Mikhail opened the door. "I want to freshen up." She grabbed her bag and rushed into the tiny bathroom.

Alone, she grabbed the tube of sunscreen, then started to slather it across her face, neck, hands, and the portion of her arms that could possibly peek out from beneath her shirtsleeves.

She had a bit of a white cast on her skin, but, hey, Victor already thought she was prone to sunburn, so he would understand her putting on some thick sunscreen.

Satisfied, she dug around for her hat, stuck it on, then made her way back out to meet Victor.

To be fair, Ambrosia had a point. She'd never considered the idea of having to leave London with Victor, that they might happen to go to places in the world where she wouldn't have the same protections she did in London.

That said, it wasn't a real relationship. She didn't have to travel with Victor if she didn't want to. In fact, they were both going to be too busy to travel for the year of their arrangement. She would be busy building her bookshop. He would be working on his thesis and getting a job once he graduated.

So this challenge was just a little hiccup in their plans. It wasn't going to be the lesson Ambrosia was trying to teach her.

"Ready?" Victor asked. "Mikhail said the car should take us to our accommodation. And there will be everything we need there."

"Brilliant," Pandora said, ignoring the pit in her stomach as they started to move out into the sunshine.

They stopped inside the airport, per instructions, to exchange their pounds for dirham, then slid into the sleek black car with heavily tinted windows, allowing Pandora to breathe a sigh of relief.

Victor rolled down the car window, letting in the salty sea air as they drove closer to the blue-washed buildings. Pandora could make out the vibrant life of the medina. Shopkeepers stood near displays of their colourful textiles, local crafts, and leather goods.

"Have you ever been?" Pandora asked, watching Victor as he took in the sights.

"No. It's stunning, isn't it?"

"Yes." Pandora wasn't sure if she was speaking of Morocco or of Victor himself.

The car dropped them off at the bottom of a seemingly never-ending staircase, each step and the walls on the sides all painted in hues of blue.

According to their folder of instructions, they would find their accommodation somewhere near the very top.

"Shall we?" Victor asked, waving toward the stairs.

And so they did, making their way up the steps, occasionally stopping to glance at shop fares or gorgeous tiles that adorned doorways to private residences.

"Oh, brilliant," Victor said, making Pandora turn to see him pulling a pretty red umbrella with white trim out of a holder at a shop. "You didn't pack yours," he said, handing it to her. He fished some dirham out of his pocket and handed it to the woman, who gave them both a soft smile.

While Pandora trusted Dante's sunscreen, she was thankful for the added protection. And incredibly charmed by Victor's considerate nature.

"Thank you," she said, and they began walking again.

"Thought I was in reasonably good shape," Victor said a while later, giving Pandora a grimace as they got to about halfway up the hill. "All these steps have proven me wrong on that." He reached down to rub his aching thighs before starting to climb once again.

When they made it to the top, it was just a short walk toward a private white-stucco home.

It was cozy and neat, set against a backdrop of the mountains with a wonderful view of the Blue City below them.

"This is stunning," Victor said, back to her, his hands on his hips as he looked at their view.

She had to agree.

But, this time, she was sure she meant him. Even if he clearly didn't feel the same way about her.

The inside of the house was small, but not claustrophobic, complete with a fully functioning kitchen with a washer/dryer, a living room with two couches, a nice-sized bathroom that had a basket full of essentials waiting for them, and, finally, the bedroom.

Pandora couldn't help it.

She stopped in the doorway, a laugh bubbling up and bursting out.

It was straight out of one of the books she and Lucy were always reading.

There was only one bed.

It was the oldest trope in the genre.

And one of Pandora's favourites.

Now here she was, experiencing it.

"What's so funny?" Victor asked, watching her with his lips curved up and his eyes warm.

"Nothing," Pandora said. "Just trying to, um, picture Ambrosia here, is all," she said. "This is lovely." She took her suitcase over to the side of the bed she was claiming.

"So, what do we do? Explore? Get something to eat?"

"Sure," Pandora said, really not caring what they did, just kind of excited for some time alone with him without the pressures of her family and the wedding planning.

It was every bit as lovely as she'd secretly hoped it would be. Walking side by side, perusing small shops and wares, stopping when they were tired, to read, sitting beside each other, getting tajine for dinner, trying spiced coffee out of gorgeous hand-painted cups with saucers, soaking in the sights and sounds of this charming town.

Until, eventually, they made their way back to their house.

Where Victor had to go and ruin her excitement about the whole one-bed situation by declaring he was going to let her have the bed to herself and sleep on the couch instead.

She supposed she should be thankful he was such a gentleman, but the ache she felt as she rolled restlessly in the bed alone had other things to say about the whole thing.

When she finally did sleep, she did so fitfully, waking up feeling cranky and tired. Until she smelled the scent of fresh coffee.

It might not have been her favorite drink back home, but she'd taken a fancy to the spiced coffee in Morocco. Enough that she was pretty sure that when she opened her bookshop, they would have to have something like it on the menu.

"Good morning," Victor said as she moved out of the bedroom to find him standing in the kitchen, clothes still rumpled from sleep.

"Morning," she said, giving him a genuine smile. "Did you get us coffee?"

"And baghrir," he said.

"What's baghrir?" Pandora asked, accepting her spiced coffee.

"Pancakes, essentially." Victor produced a plate stacked with golden pancakes. "But made with semolina and then soaked in honey and butter."

"Sounds great," Pandora said, wondering how hungry she was going to be by the time they made it back to London. She didn't think there was going to be an opportunity to find somewhere to buy blood, let alone a way to drink it in private.

She would be fine, of course. She'd have to go a really long time without sustenance to actually have to worry about it killing her for real. But she would get hungrier, would start looking at people's throats, imagining sinking her teeth in.

"Pandy?" Victor asked, making her shake her head and accept the plate he was holding out toward her.

"Sorry. Not awake yet," she told him as they set their food and coffee on the table.

They had breakfast, talking about what attractions they wanted to see before taking off to do just that.

It was one of the happiest days of Pandora's life. Walking around and chatting with Victor, buying little trinkets – some for memories, others as gifts – and ducking into shops when random little rain showers broke out.

If Ambrosia's plan had been to show Pandora how incompatible she was with Victor, the entire thing had backfired epically.

If anything, by the time they trudged all the way back

up to the house late that night, Pandora was more convinced than ever that she had fallen harder than she'd expected for her fake fiancé.

She was still battling with those feelings as she made her way toward the bedroom later, but pulled to a stop when the bathroom door opened, bringing with it a puff of hot air and steam.

And Victor.

In nothing but a low-slung towel.

All of the many hours she'd spent thinking about him without his clothes on had clearly been a waste of time. Her imagination had nothing on the reality.

The breadth of his shoulders, the strength of his chest, the definition of his abdominal muscles – neither too faint, nor too etched – and, she realized with a choked little whimper, those little indents of his Adonis belt that dared you to follow, to seek what was hidden beneath the towel.

"All yours," Victor said.

It took Pandora an embarrassingly long time to realize he wasn't referring to his body, but the bathroom.

"Oh, right, thanks," she said, but she made a beeline for the bedroom, closing the door, then leaning against it as she tried to ease the chaos thrumming through her veins.

There was a knock at the door, making her jolt and whip around. "Yeah?"

When he didn't answer, she pulled open the door. She didn't know if she was disappointed or relieved that he'd changed into a T-shirt and jeans. "Hey, want to read some more of that book?" he asked, giving her a sheepish little smile.

"Really?" she asked, brightening.

"Really. We can't leave the heroine hanging. She's about to uncover who stabbed her husband."

"I think it's the brother," Pandora said, rushing toward her luggage to find the book.

"The brother? No," Victor said, shaking his head. "I think it was the priest."

"The *priest*?" Pandora asked, shocked. "No way."

"All the signs are there," Victor said, plucking the book out of her hands as they both made their way to the living room to curl up on the couch.

Victor read long into the night, until his voice grew hoarse and they were forced to both head to bed.

As Pandora lay alone in bed, she wasn't sure if she was upset, or grateful, that the book they were sharing was a slow burn.

But they had one more night in Morocco.

Who knew what could happen.

26

"What do you mean, *nothing*?" Lucy asked after the private jet had landed back in London, and she had scooped them up.

After they'd dropped Victor back at his flat, Pandora had filled Lucy in on everything that had transpired in the Blue City, while she sipped the blood her friend had procured.

"Nothing," Pandora said, slamming her head back into the rest twice.

"But the book had to get spicy, right? Or was it closed door?"

"Oh, it got spicy all right," Pandora said. "But Victor called it a night before we got to it."

"How soon before you got to it?"

"I didn't know at the time, but when I couldn't sleep and looked at it, it was literally the next page."

"So, chances were, he saw the spice and just called it quits so things weren't awkward."

Pandora grumbled.

"I still can't believe there was only one bed," Lucy said. "And then he slept on the couch."

"I'm pretty sure we have all the proof we need that he genuinely isn't into me in that way," Pandora said, leaning down to dig in her bag to find some mouthwash.

It was then that she came across a small box she was sure she hadn't packed.

"What's that?"

"I don't know." Pandora pulled the box out.

"Well . . . open it," Lucy said, then yelled at someone who cut her off in traffic. "Use your indicators, for God's sake. They're not decorative!"

Pandora flipped the top off the box, finding a set of silver earrings with blue accents the same colour as the stairs they'd climbed several times a day while in Morocco.

On the lid of the jewelry box was a small handwritten note.

Something new and something blue.

"Oh, come now," Lucy said. "That man is in love with you."

"For someone who is in love with me, he certainly does everything in his power not to touch me."

"Maybe you're not giving out the right vibes," Lucy said. "You – hey, it's called driving, not bumper cars!" She slammed on the brakes. "You need to let him know how much you want him."

"I eye-banged his mostly naked body for a solid minute."

"That's a good start. But you could have, you know, touched him. Wild idea, I know," Lucy said teasingly.

"So," Pandora said, looking for anything else to talk about. "How did things go with Elias?"

Lucy's growl was a bit more lupine than usual, hinting at the upcoming full moon.

"That good, eh?" she asked, getting narrowed eyes from her friend.

"Let's just say I'm excited for your wedding. If for no other reason than being able to have that man out of my life for good."

"Were there issues with the family?" Pandora asked.

"Not really, no. I mean, we did have to do some sticking together to get things to shake out the way we needed them to."

"I'm afraid to ask what that might mean."

"Nothing to worry about. It actually worked out perfectly. Your hen party is going to be at Nocturnum," Lucy said.

"Wait. What? Why?" Pandora asked, gaping at her friend, who kept her gaze forward, pointedly ignoring her outrage.

Nocturnum was one of the handful of underground vampire clubs in London. The kind of place Pandora purposely avoided. Where blood was on tap and human donors could be rented for a snack.

"Listen, you're just gonna have to suck it up for the night. No pun intended," Lucy said, smirking at Pandora.

"Why that club?"

"Because there happens to be a human bar right next door," Lucy said. "Elias and I figured the best way to pull this off is if the parties take place right next to each other.

This way, you can pop in and out of the hen party, and go check on the stag end of things."

"That's actually brilliant," Pandora said.

Sure, she had to show her face occasionally so her aunts and cousins and everyone knew she was floating around, having a good time, doing the partying thing that all soon-to-be-married women would be doing.

But she would spend as much of her time as possible at the party next door, keeping an eye on Victor and her male family members.

"Well, I'm glad you think so. Because you have approximately eight hours to get some rest, get dolled up, and get ready to party."

"What? It's tonight? We just got back in."

"I know. The timing is awful. But it was the only time we could get Nocturnum to agree to such a large party. They're booked solid for the next four months. If we didn't jump on this, we were going to have to think of a different plan. Besides, you are probably flying off that blood after three days of starving."

Lucy wasn't wrong about that. The exhaustion that had been pulling at her eyelids just half an hour before had disappeared after just a couple of sips.

"OK. You're right. Better to get this over with. After this, things should calm down. At least when it comes to my family interacting with Victor."

"That's the spirit," Lucy said, pulling up outside Pandora's house.

The two of them climbed out, and Lucy paused to grab two garment bags out of the boot before following Pandora inside.

"Oh, there you are, my dear!" Ravenna said, rushing

toward Pandora to wrap her up in a crushing hug. "So glad you got back in time for your party."

"Me too." Pandora gave her great-aunt a smile.

"How was Morocco?"

"Beautiful. We had a wonderful time." Out of the corner of her eye, Pandora could see Ambrosia watching from the doorway of the dining room. "Victor bought me new-and-blue earrings for the wedding at a little shop there. It was just the stress relief we needed."

Perhaps she would feel guilty about embellishing the truth if it weren't for the fact that she knew her great-great-grandmother had sent them on the trip to attempt to break them up.

"Oh, that is so lovely," Ravenna said. "That is a good man you have there. OK, go, go. Get ready for your party. I can't wait to see this club."

Was it weird to have family members who were hundreds or thousands of years old going to your hen party? Probably. But Pandora didn't have a ton of friends, so she was glad to have family to celebrate her upcoming vows with.

Plus, they could all have a good time. Without, you know, feeding on anyone who wasn't willing.

Pandora, Lucy, Kora, and Maribelle spent a few hours in Pandora's room. Doing their make-up, getting dressed, chatting.

And then they were all piling into a limo as Dante, Elias, and the other cousins and uncles headed out to pick up Victor, who'd been a good sport about the sudden party, despite likely suffering some jet lag and wanting to just rest.

"Elias said they even managed to get in touch with

276

Victor's best mate," Lucy told her as they drove toward the club.

"Sebastian."

"Yeah. Figured it would be nice for him to have at least one person from his life there," Lucy said.

"Here we are!" Ravenna cheered, clapping her hands as the limo pulled up to the curb.

The entrance to Nocturnum was hidden in plain sight, marked only by a worn brass plaque beside the door and a single red bulb casting the front of the seemingly abandoned building in an eerie light.

The group made their way inside and the city sounds – the distant rumble of cars, faint echoes of conversation, the occasional shriek of a siren – faded as Pandora made her way down the narrow spiral staircase.

Each step felt like a deliberate departure from the mortal world above. The very air felt thicker, an intoxicating scent of aged leather, sandalwood, and something darker, more metallic, that Pandora was trying hard not to think about.

At the base of the stairs stood a towering figure in an expensive suit, his handsome features obscured a bit by the club's rouged lights.

The doorman's gaze slid over the eclectic group. From the tight, short, low-cut dresses worn by Pandora, Lucy, Kora, Maribelle, and Bellatrix, to the long, ornate, heavy dresses and gowns worn by the older vampires.

He shook his head a bit at them, but reached to pull apart the thick velvet curtains.

The scene unfolded before Pandora's eyes.

It was a sprawling, dimly lit lounge just about as far as the eye could see. Everything was in shades of crimson and black. Heavy chandeliers dripped from the ceiling, casting muted maroon over the club's patrons, rendering their features otherworldly.

Shadows clung to the corners and Pandora couldn't help but wonder – or fear – what might be happening just out of sight. Especially since, right there in the open on one of the many black leather couches, two female vampires had their fangs stuck into either side of the neck of a male human donor.

A deep, persistent bass reverberated through the floor, felt rather than heard, a rhythm eerily similar to a mortal heartbeat.

Pandora couldn't help but feel drawn to it, this invitation that threatened to bypass her conscious thought, her very morals.

She turned, following the tug she felt inside her, finding the bar spread across one wall. Behind it, a male bartender was pouring the house specialty – a viscous, dark-crimson liquid – into two separate goblets for waiting patrons.

Half of her party broke off to head to the bar. Or, she shuddered to think, find human donors.

Pandora and Lucy pressed deeper into the room.

The atmosphere shifted as she watched the way the humans moved around, captivated and adoring, orbiting the vampires like moths to a flame.

She caught snippets of conversations, mentions of ancient clans, deals being brokered, thinly veiled threats to make good on old rivalries. All around, there were hints of danger wrapped in velvet voices.

Lucy led Pandora toward a raised private section with comfortable seating and tables. "There's a staircase directly back there," Lucy told her, pointing toward a dark corner of the VIP section. "Leads down toward a private feeding room. But beside that is a doorway into the alley that connects this club to the bar next door, so we can sneak in and out without anyone really noticing. Kind of glad how busy this place is tonight."

"Is it a thing that people buy private feedings for others?"

"Yeah. That's how some of the male vampires are trying to seduce the humans." Lucy waved toward where one of the servers was leading a dazed-looking human toward a red-headed female vampire sitting at a table alone. The server gestured toward a man who raised his glass of blood at her before the woman stood, grabbed the human, and led him toward one of the private rooms.

"OK. So . . . you are just buying me a bunch of feedings tonight to celebrate."

"Precisely."

Plan in place, Lucy and Pandora joined Kora and Maribelle on the dance floor, all of them getting lost in the music and the ability to be in public, but also unafraid of moving too fast, of acting too . . . inhuman.

Eventually, though, Lucy linked an arm through a human donor's and led him over to Pandora. Then the three of them made their way toward the feeding rooms. Where they simply handed off the human to another vampire, then rushed out the back door.

The alley smelled rancid, making both women wrinkle their noses as they inched toward the door to the pub.

The inside was in direct contrast to the club.

The lights were a warm white, the floors a light hardwood, the walls an understated cream, but covered in kitschy, mismatched decor. From signed football and rugby photographs to film posters and maps of old London.

It was a rowdy crowd. Loud and brash. A group of young uni guys were in a back corner singing a rugby anthem, their arms swinging with the beat, making their pints slosh over onto their hands, shoes, and the floor. Another duo were arguing about something on the TV. A group of women were laughing at something one woman was showing the others on her phone.

And then, of course, there was her family.

Pandora had no idea if she had Elias or Uncle Leopold and Cody to thank for the fact that none of her family was wearing something out of ancient Greece or some nineties goth club.

"Victor seems happy," Lucy said as the two women watched a man who must have been Sebastian lean in toward Victor and say something that had him throwing his head back and laughing.

As if hearing Lucy speak, Elias turned, honing in on them, then disentangling himself from the crowd and walking their way.

He kept moving past them, though, and out the back door.

"How's it going?" Pandora asked when she reached him.

"Have you managed to keep Victor from overhearing something he shouldn't?" Lucy asked.

"Your faith in me is truly heartwarming, pup."

Lucy rolled her eyes at that, but she didn't snap back at him for once.

"Everything is going as planned. Luckily, only Cody, Leopold, and Jasper know about the vampire club. And they're helping me make sure no one finds out and tries to sneak over."

280

"How's Victor?" Pandora asked.

"Good. His mate, Sebastian, has helped loosen him up a bit. What?" he asked, frowning at Lucy and her faraway look.

"What?" she asked, snapping back. "Oh, nothing. I seem to slip into a fugue state whenever you're speaking." Her lips were twitching, though, like she was enjoying teasing Elias, rather than actually snapping at him.

Pandora snorted.

"Why don't you take the bride back to your own party, pup? Or do you not know how to have fun that doesn't involve chasing squirrels?" Elias asked, eyes dancing.

"OK," Pandora said. "Before this turns into an hour-long flirt-a-thon, we're gonna go."

"We are *not* flirting," Lucy said, but Pandora noticed that she glanced back over her shoulder at Elias.

"No, of course not."

They headed back into the party, where Pandora made her way to the bar.

"What can I get you?" the barman asked. "We've got A, B, AB, O. All positive and negative. Or," he said, watching Pandora with his head tilted, "we have a few . . . *vegetarian* options, as it were."

"What? Really?"

"Seems like times are changing," he said, reaching for a glass, putting it under the tap, and pouring some thick O negative for someone waiting for a refill. "We have two animal blood-types, as well as synthetic."

"Synthetic?"

"New to market. Supposed to taste like AB. I think it has a little bit of an aftertaste, but it provides all the necessary nutrients. Without all the moral guilt."

"OK. Well, I guess I'll give that a try."

To that, he reached for a bottle under the counter. "Don't worry," he said, popping the top, then pouring it into a glass. "No one will know but me. Happy engagement, by the way," he added, passing her the glass before moving on to take more orders.

"Oh, ah, was this too much pressure?" Lucy asked when she found Pandora next, taking tentative sips of her fake blood.

"What? Oh, this? No. This is synthetic blood. Can you believe it? Someone finally made it."

"So, it's like a vampire nutrition shake?"

"I guess that's a good way of putting it. I have to look into it when we get home."

"How's the taste? Is it like real blood?"

"I think it tastes kind of like watered-down blood. And there's a bit of an aftertaste, but it has more of a kick than pig blood, energy-wise."

"Well, that's good news. Especially if it is shelf-stable. You could easily find somewhere to stash that at your new flat. Victor will never have to know."

Pandora had been thinking the same thing as she sipped the fake blood. Between the synthetic blood and Dante's sunscreen, there really was a chance for them to try to live normal, non-vampire lives.

While she didn't believe that vampires as a whole were ready to forsake their old ways, give up feeding on humans, desire to come out of the shadows and live in society – to come "out of the coffin", if you will – she loved that there were options for vampires like her brother and herself. Ones who desired new opportunities to live among humans.

*

"I know you're flying high on your third glass of that stuff," Lucy said a while later as she joined her on the dance floor. "But I think it's time we check on the boys again."

The blood felt like it was vibrating in Pandora's veins, making her feel more alive than she last remembered. She'd spent so many years just barely surviving on occasional pig's blood – since she didn't want the butchers to get suspicious if she ordered too much – that she'd forgotten how good, how strong, how vital she could feel when she was properly fed.

This was the closest to being high she'd ever been.

She now understood why her aunts and cousins were all up in the VIP section laughing and buzzing with life.

"Right." Pandora finished her glass and dropped it down on the bar before following Lucy out of the back door.

"I just don't trust Eli . . . Oh!" Lucy yelped, tripping over something and toppling forward.

Pandora, powered with three glasses of sustenance, was faster than usual. Her hands shot out, grabbing her friend and hauling her back up to her feet.

"What did I trip . . . Oh," Lucy said, eyes wide as she looked down.

"What's the . . . Oh."

All that fake blood seemed to turn to stone in her stomach and veins as she looked down to see what Lucy had tripped over.

No.

Not what.

Who.

"Oh, no. No, no, no." Pandora gasped, her chest feeling

tight as she looked down at the man lying on his stomach in the alley.

"Is he dead?" Lucy asked, eyes gaping as she looked down at the man in his light-blue jeans and green-and-white-checked jumper. "Oh, God. He's not moving, is he? You don't think . . ." She trailed off as her gaze slid to the bar right next door.

Pandora did think, actually.

It was their nature, after all.

And while the vampires in Nocturnum had open access to willing human donors, her male family members at the bar had no food source, only beer and spirits to drink that they couldn't get drunk on or get sustenance from.

If one had been hungry and had perhaps seen someone going out the back for a smoke or some air, there was no reason for Pandora to assume they wouldn't do what was in their nature to do. Bite. Feed.

Pandora didn't see any bitemarks, but some vampires didn't drink from the neck. She had a cousin who exclusively drank from the crook of the elbow, claiming it tasted better there. He could have a bite anywhere. And she really didn't think they should waste time looking.

"What do we do?" Lucy asked, nudging the man's body with the tip of her shoe, grimacing the whole time. "We can't just leave the body here, right? What if Victor decides to come out here?"

She had a point.

If Victor decided to get some air, he would practically trip over the body like Lucy had. Then what? Call the police? And if the police came, they would question everyone in the bar. Which included her family. Her very weird,

284

very eccentric family who didn't necessarily see anything wrong with killing someone.

"We need to move him."

Lucy's gaze scanned the end of the alley, where it opened to the road to allow the refuse collectors access.

"Do you think you're strong enough to lift him into the bin?" Lucy asked, motioning toward the waste container.

He was a pretty big guy. Even with three synthetic blood drinks in her system, Pandora wasn't sure she was that strong.

"I don't think so."

"Well, maybe we could just . . . prop him up on the other side of the bin. Just so he's out of sight. We can even report it after everyone goes home."

"Yeah. Yeah, let's do that," Pandora said. "You take the legs. I'll get his upper body."

With that, they moved around the body, leaning down and grabbing hold of the man.

"Whoa, that stuff really works, huh?" Lucy asked when Pandora accidentally lifted the man upward until he was practically kneeling on the pavement. "Maybe we can—"

"Pandy?"

Pandora and Lucy looked at each other, eyes round. Panic soared through Pandora's system as she looked over to see Victor frozen half a step out of the pub, the door resting against his shoulder. "What's going on? Is he OK?"

"He's, uh, passed out," Lucy scrambled to answer. "Completely pissed," she went on. "Kind of the definition of 'legless', don't you think?"

Pandora had never been so thankful for Lucy's quick thinking as she was right then.

"Yeah. He never could handle his drink," Pandora added.

"Who is that?" Victor asked.

"Oh, it's, uh . . ." Pandora fumbled.

It was a complete stranger? Seemingly drunk dry by one of her family members? Because, oh, right, they're all vampires. Surprise!

"It's her cousin Douglas," Lucy said.

"What is he doing out in the alley?"

"Probably stumbling around, not remembering where he was," Lucy said.

"Where was he drinking?"

"In the pub with you, obviously."

"I never saw—"

"What's going on?" Dante appeared, clapping a hand on Victor's shoulder as he started to push past him into the alley. "Oh." Dante's gaze took in the man's lifeless body, Pandora's arms around him, the look of panic on both women's faces.

"We came across Cousin Douglas," Pandora said.

"Right. Yeah. Doug. Guess he still can't hold his liquor," Dante said, shaking his head.

"Wait. Why are you here?" Victor asked, looking at Pandora.

"That's on me," Lucy said, turning to face the men, wedging her body in such a way to block their view. "See, we were playing a little game of truth or dare," she said.

"Truth or dare?"

"Yeah. And, well, Ravenna is really sloshed on the spirits. And she dared Pandora to come here and, well, shag you in the alley."

"Lucy!"

"Seriously?" Victor asked, lips curving up.

Lucy nodded. "She's a scandalous woman. Probably be

286

around any minute to make sure Pandora made it here. But when we got here, well, we saw Douglas passed out. Decided we had to be responsible adults and get him home. So . . . oh, lovely," she grumbled as Elias moved out behind Dante and Victor as well.

"Doug had too much to drink," Dante said before he could ask.

Elias's gaze moved over the women, the body, and back again before nodding. "Told him to slow it down."

"You saw him inside?" Victor asked, brows scrunching.

"Yeah. Been here a while," Elias said.

"I don't know how I missed him."

"You were busy with Sebastian," Dante said, shrugging.

"That's why I came out. Sebastian just ordered shots," Elias said. "He's waiting for you."

"Oh," Victor said, looking conflicted. "Let me just help Pandy get Doug—"

"No, no," Elias interrupted him. "You're celebrating. Go have your shots. I'll help the girls."

"Great." Lucy continued to grumble under her breath.

With that, Dante gently pushed Victor back into the bar. Elias leaned back against the door, blocking anyone from coming out again.

"You're seriously not going to help?" Lucy asked, narrowing her eyes at Elias.

"You want help with that? Sure, let me go grab my shovel and an alibi."

"You're literally a vampire. You deal with bodies all the time."

"And yet I've never been reduced to this level of amateur hour."

"You're going to just stand there?"

"Someone needs to be the designated sarcastic observer. But if you really want them, my hands are all yours, pup," Elias said, tone warm.

Pandora saw Lucy's eyes heat, but she was quick to tamp it back down. "You put that cold, dead hand anywhere near me and I'll bite it off. Come on," Lucy said, turning her back on Elias to focus on Pandora. "Let's get this done. Your family is going to be looking for you soon."

"All right. On three. One, two—"

"*WhereamI?*"

Pandora and Lucy reeled back, shrieking, as the body slurred and shifted.

"He's alive?" Lucy gasped, then spun on her heel at the sound of Elias's laughter. "What are you laughing at?"

"How did you not know he was alive?" Elias asked.

"You knew?" Lucy asked. "Why didn't you say something?"

"And miss this circus act?"

"Hey, um, you're all right," Pandora told the man as he thrashed around before going slack again. "OK. I think we need to get him in a cab."

"Right. To where?"

"Oh. Right."

Elias piped up. "I'm assuming he has a wallet."

"Oh, now you're helpful." Lucy fished in the man's pocket to find his license with his address. "Huh. His name is Derrick. We were close."

She tucked the wallet back in his pocket, then each woman moved under one of his arms and lifted, half carrying and half dragging him toward the mouth of the alley. Where Lucy flagged down a cab and both women shoved him in, gave an address, and tossed some money at the driver.

With that, they made their way back to the party.

Pandora felt like she was floating for the next several hours, unable to stop replaying the interaction with Victor over and over in her mind.

Because when Lucy fed him that lie about truth or dare, saying Pandora was showing up to shag him, she could have sworn there was something warm, something interested, in his gaze.

And this time, she wasn't going to talk herself out of it, say it was just her imagination.

She knew what she'd seen.

His pupils had dilated and his eyes had warmed.

Maybe the ongoing attraction wasn't as one-sided as she'd thought.

Though, even if that was the case, she had no idea what the heck to do with that information.

27

Luckily enough for Pandora, after they'd got back from Morocco, she was mostly too busy to overthink about what it meant that they'd spent several days in Morocco, curled up on the sofa reading a love story, when nothing had happened.

There were fittings to suffer through, endless magazine-plastered aesthetic boards provided by her aunts and cousins to choose from, arguments about her family's chosen location for the wedding. Arguments she inevitably lost, then had to scramble to make it work somehow.

"That is the twenty-ninth text since we sat down," Lucy said as Pandora reached for her phone, scrolling up through the last three texts she'd received.

"I'm starting to regret letting my family learn how to use mobile phones."

"I guess it beats having to have sit-downs with them

about every little detail, though," Lucy said as she dropped a sugar into her tea.

"That's true," Pandora said after shooting off a response. "The last time we had a discussion at home, Vlad sat on his perch, sighing heavily and reciting Shakespeare's *Sonnet 87* dramatically while Elizabeth sat on the windowsill preening her feathers."

"Why was he reciting sad poetry?"

"Because he thought Elizabeth was preening for the damn magpie eating off the bird feeder."

"His jealousy is both hilarious and sad."

"I know, right? Meanwhile, she's clueless."

"What's he going to do when she eventually goes home with Dudley?"

"Good question. I imagine there will be a lot of pining. Maybe he'll taunt another poet or something. Prompt him to create some awesome new art."

"Something to look forward to. OK. Now, show me the next flat," Lucy said, holding out gimme hands until Pandora passed her the tablet. "This is the one you like best?"

"One look at all of the bookcases and you will see why. And all of the windows for my plants."

Lucy spent the next few minutes reading the description and scrolling through the fifty-plus images that Pandora had looked at so often that she was seeing them behind her lids when she closed her eyes. Some nights, she would even imagine walking through the house, looking at her and Victor's books on the shelves, their art on the walls, their toothbrushes in the holders. Though, in those fantasies, she went ahead and imagined them in the same bed.

"Can I ask you a question?" Lucy said when she finally set the tablet back down.

"Sure." Pandora cradled her chamomile tea between her hands.

"What is the plan after the divorce?"

"What?" Pandora's stomach dropped at the mention of divorce from Victor. Even though their relationship was a sham and that had literally been the plan from the very beginning.

"You know, with the flat," Lucy said, but Pandora was almost certain that wasn't the only thing her friend was talking about. "When you divorce, what happens to the flat?"

Pandora's heart ached at the idea of a home she'd once shared with Victor suddenly featuring the shadows of his absence all around.

"I guess I would keep it if I really fell in love with it. Victor wouldn't fight me on it. Why?"

"Because you were watching me with hearts in your eyes as I flipped through the images. I hate the idea of you losing a place you clearly love already. Without even going to see it."

"What are you doing?" Pandora asked when Lucy reached for her mobile, tapping something in, then lifting it to her ear.

"Hi! This is Pandora Von Ashmore," she said, making Pandora's brows shoot up. "I was wondering if I could do a viewing . . ." She rattled off the address, then listened to the estate agent. "That would be great! Can't wait to see it."

"You don't even know my schedule," Pandora said once Lucy hung up.

"And that's why you are going in half an hour," Lucy said, looking proud of herself. "Since I know you're free. Now . . . let's see what Victor is up to." She scrolled through her contacts, then shot off a text. "Guess he's not busy," she said when her phone pinged just a moment or two later. "He's in. You guys have a date."

"I was supposed to be having a date with you."

"You did. Now you're having time with Victor. Alone time."

"With the estate agent."

"Still. Time to walk around, plan your future, that sort of thing. Without your family involved."

Pandora knew what Lucy's romance-novel-loving heart was trying to do. The same thing authors had been doing for ages. Pushing the main characters together as much as possible until the sparks flew.

But this was real life, not a book.

So Pandora was going to learn to keep her expectations firmly planted in reality. And the reality was, she and Victor had simply shared a couple of heated moments that, clearly, meant more to her than they did to him. She was just going to need to accept that and move on.

"It would be nice to cross this off my list," Pandora said, pointedly ignoring Lucy's eye roll as she shot off another text. "Victor will be meeting us here in ten. Then you two can head out."

"I was supposed to be spending time with you."

"Yeah, but you see me all the time."

Pandora couldn't argue with that. On top of working with her most nights at Luna Bean, she also had Lucy hang out with her and her family when they were making arrangements.

By the time the two women brought their cups up to the service station, Pandora spotted Victor crossing the road toward the shop. A gust of wind made leaves kick up around him and blew the hood back off of his head.

Unbidden, memories of the feel of his soft hair on her thighs flooded her mind.

Desire bloomed through her too quickly to tamp down, leaving her feeling achy and overly sensitive as Victor ran a hand through his hair to brush it back out of his face.

Despite knowing it would only make matters worse, Pandora let herself entertain the idea of her fingers sinking into all that soft hair as his bodyweight pressed her into the mattress, as his body moved with hers . . .

"You're eye-banging him again," Lucy said with a gentle nudge to Pandora's side as Victor made his way into the coffee shop. She smiled at him. "You got here fast."

"Yeah," Victor said, nodding at her, then shooting a soft look at Pandora, who was too distracted by how her body was reacting to his nearness to untie her tongue and greet him. "Hey, Pandy."

"Hello," she said, then winced at how formal she'd sounded.

"Well, I am going to go run some errands," Lucy said. "You two have fun flat-shopping."

With that, she was gone, leaving Pandora standing there staring at Victor, as heat shot through her veins.

"You all right? You look a little . . ."

Turned on?

Ready to rip his clothes off right there in the middle of a crowded café?

"Fine." Her voice came out in a squeak. "It's a little warm in here," she added, fanning her face.

"Want to walk, then?" he asked. "We have time."

"Sounds good." Maybe the activity would work through some of the sexual frustration so by the time they got to the flat, she wouldn't be ready to throw herself at him.

As they walked, she tried not to let herself overthink every casual brush of his hand to her hip or lower back as he guided her through foot traffic and across the street. Or the way his hand closed over hers when they both went for the door of the building at the same time.

They both greeted the overly enthusiastic estate agent before taking the lift up to the second-to-last floor. Given how much the flat they were about to look at cost, Pandora could only imagine that the people who owned or rented the penthouse must be completely minted.

Then they followed behind the estate agent's pristine cream trouser suit, perfectly coiffed hair, and click-clacking heels as she gushed about the light, the features, the recently re-finished floors, and the updated kitchen.

Pandora found herself annoyed by the woman's cloying rose perfume when all she wanted to do was catch a hint of Victor's signature scent.

"Oh, if you'll excuse me," the agent said a few moments later as her mobile started to ring.

She click-clacked away as Pandora watched Victor step in front of the windows, the sun moving out from behind a cloud to shine on his hair, making golden streaks cut through the brown.

"What?" Victor asked, watching her as she looked at him. She was sure her want, her love, was right there on her face for him to see.

"Oh, you won't believe what I did," the estate agent said, bustling back in. "I took my husband's keys with

295

me! He's locked out of our flat. We haven't finished our tour—"

"We could wait for you," Victor said, gesturing around the room with its minimalistic staged furniture as if to say, "There's nothing to steal here."

"Well, maybe if I could just meet him downstairs," the estate agent said, sounding conflicted to even leave them alone for a few minutes.

"We're OK here. Gives us more time to argue over whose books get to be displayed on the shelves in the living room," Victor said, all charm.

"OK. I will have him meet me here," she said. She reached for her phone to shoot off a quick text. "I'm not thinking straight. My in-laws are coming to town," she added with a grimace.

"We know a thing or two about that, what with all the wedding planning," Victor said, draping his arm around Pandora's hips and hauling her against his side.

She didn't even pretend not to melt into him. She even let her hand slip up his stomach to rest on his chest.

The agent's eyes softened before she hurried to the door. "I will be quick."

They both heard the flat door close, but neither of them moved for a long moment. It was Victor who stepped away first, making Pandora feel like her heart was being pulled away with him.

"Obviously," she said, reaching into her bag for a book. "My books go on the eye-level shelves." She stuck the book there, front cover out. "It's because of their superior cover design."

"I can't argue with . . . Is that the one we were reading in Morocco?" he asked, lines creasing between his brows.

"I . . . uh . . . yeah."

"You haven't finished it yet?" he asked, walking over to pluck it off the shelf, opening to the bookmarked page where they'd left off.

She couldn't exactly tell him that she hadn't been able to bring herself to read any further without sharing it with him, but that she also seemed to be carrying it around with her like some sort of security blanket.

"Not yet," she told him. "Things have been busy."

"They're not busy now," Victor said, walking over to the couch, gaze scanning the pages from where they'd left off.

There was no way he hadn't seen that it was the beginning of a detailed sex scene.

And he still wanted to read it. Aloud. To her.

She never crossed a room so quickly in her life.

Her belly was flip-flopping even as her chest felt like a thousand butterflies had started swooping as she lowered herself down on the couch beside him.

It was a small couch, so when she kicked off her shoes and pulled her knees up, she'd shifted close enough that they were touching from shoulder to thigh.

Feeling her, Victor sucked in a breath so deep his chest shook before he slipped a finger behind a page in the book, then started reading.

To be fair, while it was a spicy book, it was a bodice-ripper from the heyday of the eighties. Which meant that while it wasn't closed-door, it didn't have the explicitness that was typical of more modern love stories.

Still, Pandora felt herself pressing her thighs tightly together to ease the ache building between them as Victor read those pages, talked about desire and forbidden touches, of sighs that became moans, of shivers that turned into writhing and ecstasy.

If Pandora needed to breathe, she was pretty sure she'd practically be panting right then.

She was so distracted by her own desire that she barely noticed when Victor stopped reading.

His head turned, eyelids heavy, to look at her.

"You liked that scene, hmm?" he asked. Was it just her, or did his voice sound deeper, thicker than it had a moment before?

Pandora couldn't even try to come up with any sort of intelligible response to that. Nope. All that came out of her was this low whimpering sound.

Victor's eyes blazed in response as the book fell to his other side before his hands were grabbing for her hips, pulling until she had no choice but lift up, turn, and move to straddle him.

He didn't release her, though, until he dragged her hips down, until her need was pressing down on his lap, meeting his own straining desire.

A shudder moved through him at the sensation as a ragged moan escaped her lips just a second before he claimed them, kissing her hard and deep, one hand grabbing the back of her neck.

The other dug into her hip, forcing her to rock once against him. This time, her moan was muffled by his lips as her own hips did another little involuntary wiggle, needing the feel of him, the friction.

Victor's lips broke from her mouth, leaving her lips feeling swollen and tingly as his own slid down her jaw, then her neck.

A shiver racked her system as her hips did another rock

298

against him. This time, she got that delicious little rumble to move through him as well.

If there was any question in her mind that he wanted her to continue, the way his fingers sank into her ass and dragged her against him was all the encouragement she needed.

His tongue and lips and teeth explored her neck as she carried on rocking against him, driving herself up against his hard desire until there was a tightening in her core, until her moans were growing louder.

Victor's head lifted, sensing how close she was, wanting to watch her as she rocked against him one more time, making the orgasm crash through her over and over.

Pandora fell forward, pressing her face into his neck, breathing him in, feeling the thrum of his heartbeat against her lips as the pleasure pulsed through her.

When the fog of her own climax finally pulled backward, she felt the way his fingers were still digging possessively into her ass, how his heartbeat was hammering against his chest, how his need was still straining against her.

She kissed his neck.

Traced the pulse point with her tongue.

Maybe even teased the tips of her fangs against his heated skin.

But then she was sliding back off of his lap, lowering herself down between his spread thighs.

Looking up, she found his eyes molten as he watched her.

Anticipation had her belly flipping as her hands slid up his thighs, moved across his lap, worked his button and zipper free, then slipped inside to take him in her hand.

A little whimper escaped her at the thick length of him as she pulled him free of the material.

At her touch, Victor's muscles tensed, his breath exhaled shakily, his hand slapped down on her shoulder, fingers digging in. But not pulling her closer, letting her lead.

Not that she needed any encouragement.

Not when she had him like this.

Literally in the palm of her hand.

Eyes heated.

His whole body tensed for her touch, for the feel of her tongue as she traced it up his length, around the tip, before letting him slide into her waiting mouth.

Victor's whole body jolted as he settled deep, his hips rocking up into her mouth once as his hands reached to gather her hair, fisting it at the nape of her neck so there was nothing obstructing his view as she started to work him.

She was slow at first, soaking up every sigh, every tensed muscle, the way his eyes went to half-mast as he watched her.

But as his need for release grew, so did her desire to feel him fall apart because of her.

So she worked him harder, faster, getting him panting and groaning, rocking deeper into her throat as she took him in each time.

Then his whole body tightened as a hushed curse escaped him just before the taste of him filled her mouth, making a little moan escape her.

She worked him through it before letting him slip out from between her lips, turning to rest her head against his thigh as Victor's fingers gently sifted through her hair.

Both at a loss for words.

But completely content with the silence.

Until it was interrupted.

The ding of the lift.

The click-clack of heels on the floor in the hall.

Pandora shot back up onto the couch as Victor tucked himself away, both of them fussing with their hair and clothes, making sure nothing was askew as the agent's hand jiggled the door.

Victor grabbed the book, flipping the suggestive cover over so it was against his leg just as the estate agent came rushing back into the room.

"So," she said, exhaling a bit, clearly still flustered by the mishap.

"We'll take it," Pandora said, beaming at the woman, happier than she'd been in weeks.

All that was left to do was sign the papers.

And, of course, get married.

28

"Good evening, everyone," Sebastian said as he stood up from the table. "I'm Sebastian. Victor's best mate. Or, as he likes to call me, *Perfectly Adequate* friend, which I think is his version of a compliment."

There was the rumble of a few laughs around the table.

Pandora felt her own lips curving up as she glanced over at Victor at her side, the warmth of him chasing away the chill inside what was, essentially, a long, ancient, greenhouse.

When Lucy and Pandora had found out that Pandora's family had set up their wedding-party dinner inside a greenhouse on the grounds where the wedding was to take place the following evening, they'd scrambled to find portable heaters and comically long extension cords, just so it was relatively comfortable for the members of the wedding party who actually did feel the cold.

Pandora had to admit that with the long table lined in flowers and fine china, and the flickering candles set in their standing candelabras lining the room, it was a perfectly romantic and charming spot for their little get-together.

Even if it had taken some last-minute maneuvering to pull it all together.

The food had been served by Ravenna and Henrietta. And it seemed that the more practice Ravenna had researching and working on appropriate modern-day human meals, the better her cooking had become.

Lucy had let out a moan that had given Pandora some secondhand embarrassment when she'd taken her first bite of the apple-stuffing pork loin.

"When I first met Victor, we'd bonded over a mutual distaste of all things forced physical activity in school. Little did I know, Victor only wanted to avoid sport so he could spend more time with his nose in books, not slacking off like me.

"But by the time I learned how much he was reading and mumbling about vampires and obscure blood rituals, it was too late – we were best mates. Though, I'll admit, I thought that the chance of him finding a girlfriend, with his particular interests, was about as mythical as the creatures he was studying."

There were a few polite laughs from the crowd that was made up primarily of those "mythical creatures" Sebastian was talking about.

"Victor, you've spent ages studying the undead. Some of us, present company included, were starting to worry there wasn't a single living woman who could attract your attention.

"But then, enter Pandora. Someone capable of looking past the furrowed brows, the thesis-induced caffeine shakes, and his ability to talk about his books in excruciating detail, and see the kind, loyal, somewhat intense, but wonderful man he is. And you've made him happier than I've ever seen him.

"Pandora, you are about to marry a man who will love you with the same intensity he once reserved for seventeenth-century folklore.

"So let's raise a glass to Victor and Pandora – the proof that there really is someone out there for everyone. Here's to your next chapter. May it be filled with laughter, love, and endless arguments about the most fearsome fictional vampire. Cheers!"

"Cheers!" everyone chorused in unison before bringing their glasses to their mouths.

"OK, my turn," Lucy, slightly buzzed and pink in the face, said, as she got to her feet. "Hey, everyone. My name is Lucy. I'm Pandora's best friend, partner in crime, and fellow lover of all things romance novels. Which, I have to say, prepared me perfectly for tonight. Because if there's anything romance novels can teach you, it's to spot a love story brewing.

"And what a love story is has shaped up to be," she went on, smiling at Pandora and Victor. "Filled with all the right tropes, too.

"First, they're clearly the perfect grumpy–sunshine. There's our hero, Victor. The brooding intellectual who can outstare a marble statue. And, of course, our heroine, Pandora. The brightest bit of sunlight in everyone's lives.

"Then, as we know, there is the slow burn. And I mean slow. How many months passed where Victor came into

Luna Bean to study instead of noticing the absolutely perfect woman right before him?

"I have to admit, there were times when I thought all his studying was going to end in a research paper, not a wedding. But I had faith in the plot. And, eventually, Victor looked up. Sparks flew. Hearts skipped. Bellies fluttered. Knees went weak. Like every good romance novel.

"Pandora, you have proven yourself to be the leading lady in your own story. And, Victor, you have shown us that even the most stoic of heroes can fall head over heels for the right woman.

"So, to my best friend and her very own Mr. Darcy – may the rest of your story be filled with grand gestures, witty banter, smoldering stares, and only the absolute best plot twists ever.

"And, of course, may there always only be one bed, notes in the shower steam, and kissing in the rain. Here's to your happily ever after. Cheers!"

"Cheers!" Everyone smiled brightly, buying into the story Lucy had just read to them.

Pandora wanted more than anything for it to be true. And her heart ached at the reality of their situation. Of the *actual* tropes their story featured.

Fake dating.

Marriage of convenience.

Nothing that featured all of the grand romantic gestures that everyone around the table assumed.

Victor's arm slid around the back of Pandora's chair as he turned his head away, so no one else could see what he was saying.

"You OK?"

"Yeah," she said, but she didn't even bother to put any

conviction in her voice as she raised her champagne to her lips and took a sip, the bubbles popping on her tongue.

"Pandy," he said, tone pleading. His breath was warm on the shell of her ear, making a shiver move through her. "Cold?"

"Yeah," she said, lying. Or maybe she wasn't. But it was not the kind of cold that he meant. It was in her heart.

Because, despite her bone-deep belief that things had changed between them since touring the flat, nothing had happened since.

She tried to convince herself it was simply because he was working flat-out to finish his thesis and session at uni. And what little free time he did have, it was full of wedding planning and furniture-shopping, since everyone was going to expect the two of them to want to live together immediately after the wedding. That was what real married people did, after all.

The thing was, she was starting to worry that, to him, all it was between them was the occasional spicy, mutually satisfying stolen moment. And not, as it was for her, feelings. Of the love variety.

While this may have started as a fake-dating marriage of convenience, somewhere along the way, she'd fallen head over heels for her fiancé.

Victor's hand started to chafe her arm for a moment before he shrugged out of his blazer and draped it over her shoulders.

It was still warm from his body and smelled of that perfect vanilla, cinnamon, and leather scent of him. It only made the longing worse.

A little whimper escaped her, despite herself.

"I think you're just exhausted," Victor said, voice low.

"You've been running around at warp speed for months. Working. Planning the wedding. Meet-ups. Dress-shopping. Finding us the perfect flat. You need a nice, long break."

He wasn't wrong about her having been busy.

Sure, any wedding required a lot of work. But hers doubly so because of the shortened timeframe, as well as trying to thwart her family's crazy plans. Including some insane blood ritual requiring the kind of chanting that would have had his family and friends running for the hills.

And, yes, she was burnt out. But not physically, like Victor thought. She was emotionally spent. From pretending to be in a happy, loving relationship, from never so much as letting her smile slip because she knew Bellatrix and Ambrosia were watching her every move, looking for anything to be off, so they could pounce and expose her.

Increasingly, all she wanted to do was curl up in her bed with the covers over her head. Not even with one of her beloved books. Because, suddenly, love stories just made her all the more aware of her one-sided romance.

It was almost over, she had to keep reminding herself. Even if, objectively, this last part of the whole ordeal was the most painful.

Sebastian's and Lucy's speeches had been gutting.

She knew she should have been thankful to her friend for coming up with something so personal and heartfelt, but Pandora's heart ached more with each word she said. Because Pandora wanted them to be true so badly.

And once this event was over, there was the wedding the following day to get through.

It was supposed to be the happiest day of her life.

But it was going to take everything in her not to cry.

"Yeah. Luckily, we have our honeymoon," she said, hearing her own voice getting thick as tears stung the back of her eyes.

"Two weeks of nothing to do but relax." Victor sounded wistful too, excited about a break. Even though he was still working on the finishing touches of his thesis.

"Yeah." She glanced around the table, finding her loved ones chatting, laughing, happy. All of them completely oblivious to her own turmoil.

She suddenly felt more alone than she had in nearly one hundred and twenty-five years.

"Can I steal your girl for a few minutes?" Lucy asked, showing up just when Pandora felt her eyes starting to glisten.

"Of course," Victor said, standing, then pulling out Pandora's chair for her.

She kept his jacket, not needing it, just wanting the closeness, as she followed Lucy out of the greenhouse.

"Needed to get you out of there before you grabbed the tablecloth to use as a handkerchief," Lucy said as the night air bit at their exposed skin.

"Why did your speech have to be so perfect?" Pandora asked, sniffling as the first few tears slipped from her lashes to trail down her cheeks.

"Because it's what I want for you. And I think it's something you can still have."

Pandora scoffed. "Right. In my fake marriage."

"I'm still not convinced it's as fake as you seem to think it is."

"Luce, Victor has barely touched me lately."

"What are you talking about? He's constantly touching you. Arm around your chair. Toying with your hair.

308

Taking your hand. Whispering into your ear. What was he supposed to do? Hoist you up on the table and spread you wide for dessert . . . in front of everyone? You two are never alone."

She wasn't wrong about that; now that Pandora wasn't so wrapped up in her own misery, she could see things more objectively.

Most of the time, they weren't even together. And when they were, it was at Luna Bean. Or at her family's house. And, once, at his flat. Where his roommates were simply too close and too nosy to have anything happen.

Still, she couldn't quite let herself hope things were different than they'd seemed for weeks. She wasn't sure she could survive more hopes being cruelly dashed.

"Why are you so determined to believe he isn't as into you as you're into him?" Lucy asked.

"Because I don't want the heartbreak of realizing he isn't."

"But what if he is?"

"I can't live in a fantasy world. I am going to need to live with Victor for a year. Can you imagine how embarrassing it would be to let him know how I feel, only to get rejected, then have to keep seeing him every day?"

"Can you imagine how wonderful it would be to tell him how you feel, have him return those feelings, and then fall madly in love and live happily ever after?"

"I know why you're saying this, but I need to be practical. And just get through the wedding. I can't be getting my hopes up. At least not right now," Pandora said.

"All right. I understand. I just want you to remember that just because you believe it, doesn't mean that's how it is. There is a chance he's indifferent. But the chance that

309

he isn't is just as high. You have no idea if you don't ask or make a move. That's all I'm saying. OK," Lucy said, coming to a stop. "I am going to go back and get completely pissed on that expensive champagne." She reached out to give Pandora's wrist a squeeze before running back toward the greenhouse.

Pandora wasn't quite ready yet, so she just kept walking endlessly around the grounds until she found herself at the back of the castle that served as the guest rooms for the entire family. Victor's parents included, though they'd gone to bed early, so no one had to worry about babysitting them while the bridal party had a little get-together.

This garden wasn't manicured, but instead allowed to grow wild with endless winding hedgerows that stretched high above Pandora's head, creating little pockets of privacy where no one else would find you.

That was just what she needed.

A little privacy.

A place to get her thoughts and emotions in check.

Then she would need to go back to the party and fake it for another couple of hours.

She found herself in a square of hedges with a giant weeping willow in the center. She was about to sit down, when she heard the crunch of twigs and leaves, telling her she wasn't alone.

A part of her hoped it was some animal, not a vampire or human looking for her.

"There you are," Victor said, making her turn around to find him making his way toward her. "I was worried when Lucy came back without you."

She really needed not to think too deeply into that.

"I just needed some air."

Victor moved closer, his head tipped to the side as he searched her face. "What's wrong, Pandy?"

"Nothing. I'm fine. Just needed some space."

"From the party?" He moved closer. "Or from me?"

"It's not that."

"It feels like that," he said. "It feels like you've been pulling further and further away from me for a week or two now."

"No, I've just been—"

"I know you've been busy, but it's been different. Since the flat," he said, making her insides wobble. "It seems like you've been going out of your way not to be with me."

What could she say to that? It was true. She'd been mostly keeping in touch by text. Even when he'd arrived this afternoon, she'd let Lucy greet him while she pretended to need extra time to get herself ready for the little gathering for the bridal party.

"Pandy, if you've changed your mind . . ."

"I haven't," Pandora was quick to assure him. Because she was sure that the only thing more painful than being near him but not being able to have him the way she wanted, was not being around him at all.

"I know some of your family still hasn't come around," he said.

That was still somewhat true. Sure, her aunts, uncles, cousins, brother, and father had all come around now that the big day was nearly here.

As for Ophelia, well, Pandora had seen some change after her mum realized that she was never going to be with Elias, that she was committed to her fiancé.

And, quite frankly, she didn't really care what Bellatrix

311

and Ambrosia had to say about it, since they'd both done some shady things to try to thwart her relationship.

"It's not that," Pandora said.

"Then what is it?" Victor asked, stepping closer, coming under the tree with her. "Why are you keeping me at a distance?"

"I . . ." She trailed off, not sure what to say, if she had another lie in her.

"Pandy," Victor said, reaching out, his fingers gently taking her chin between his thumb and forefinger to lift her face to his. "Talk to me." His thumb shifted up, starting to trace lightly underneath her lower lip.

The touch scrambled her brain, made it impossible to filter her thoughts. So what came out was the question that had been eating away at her for weeks.

"Was any of it ever real for you?"

"Any of what?" he asked, brows scrunching.

"Never mind," she said, trying to duck her head, but his fingers tightened on her chin.

"Any of this?" he asked.

Then his lips were on hers.

Up so close, he overwhelmed her with vanilla, cinnamon, and leather as his lips pressed harder, demanded more, chased away any concerns that he wasn't as lost in the moment as she was.

One of his hands slid behind her neck as his other arm draped around her lower back, pulling her flush against his body.

The warmth of him was nothing compared to the fire that was burning inside her as his hands moved down her back, sinking into her ass, pulling her against his need as a whimper escaped her.

"It was always real for me," he murmured against her lips before claiming them again, kissing her hard and long, until she felt tingly all over, until the need was a coiled ache in her core again.

Victor's arm tightened around her, bringing her with him as he lay down onto the ground under the willow.

Reaching between them, he pulled her skirt up, allowing him to roll over her, to settle between her thighs.

Pandora's fingers dug into his shoulder as her legs wrapped around his hips just before he bore down on her, dragging his hard length against the material of her panties, making a deep moan work its way out of her.

Her hands were greedy then, yanking at his jacket until it was on the ground beside him, before pushing his buttons through the loops, exposing his skin inch by delicious inch.

Victor went up on his knees to take off his shirt, giving Pandora a lovely view for a short moment before he moved over her again.

Her hands met the bare skin of his back and suddenly her own dress was feeling too hot, tight, restrictive.

As if hearing her own thoughts, Victor rolled to his side, taking her with him. Then, anchoring his arm around her hips, he rolled her over him, then pushed up to sitting, forcing her onto her knees at the sides of his legs.

He said nothing then as his hands started to slide her skirt up, letting the night air kiss her skin little by little. Just this once, though, Pandora didn't need him to say what he was thinking, what he was feeling; it was all there right on his face.

The heat.

The hunger.

The need.

But beneath that, something that had her heart feeling full to bursting.

Just as she placed it for what it was, though, Victor lifted her dress up off her arms, leaving her in nothing but a pair of barely-there panties.

A shiver of anticipation moved through her as Victor let out a deep breath, his gaze moving over her.

His fingers landed at her ribs then slowly drifted up, teasing over her stomach, then upward to cup one of her breasts.

A soft, mewling sound escaped Pandora as his hand tightened, then released before his thumb and forefinger found the tightened point and began to roll.

Her hips rocked down against him again, the ache in her core too strong to ignore.

A low groan escaped him at the feel of her grinding against him.

His other hand moved up, teasing her other nipple as she kept writhing against him, kept driving herself up, too needy to pretend to be anything else.

It was the brush of his soft hair on her skin that had her slowing down. Then his tongue was on her, teasing over the sensitive point until her head was thrown back and she was arching into the sensations.

He sucked it into his mouth, making her groan fill the quiet night air for a moment before his tongue and teeth toyed with her.

He moved across her chest, dragging out the sweet torment.

Then, suddenly, he was rolling her under him once again, his welcome weight pressing her into the cool, soft grass.

314

Her thighs wrapped around him, her heels digging into his ass, holding him tightly against her as her hips rocked.

Victor's lips claimed hers again. Harder. Hungrier.

Then he was moving with her, grinding down into her writhing movements, increasing the pressure, the friction, as his lips muffled her frantic whimpers.

"Victor, please," she whimpered, looking up at him with heavy-lidded eyes, finding his just as intense.

But he didn't pull back just enough to free himself, to slide inside her and give her relief from the pressure in her lower stomach. No, he went back on his knees, running his fingers up her skin, then pressing against the material between her thighs.

Pandora arched off of the ground with a moan at the feel. But the touch was fleeting, leaving her as soon as it found her, as he reached back for her ankles, pulling them forward, and pressing her knees into her chest.

He reached down and grabbed the material of her panties, drawing them down her thighs, over her calves, then off her feet, tossing them to the side with her dress.

A shiver ran through her as his fingers teased back up her thigh. This time, when he touched her, it was without the barrier.

His thumb teased up her cleft to find her clit, rocking gently side to side as two of his fingers slipped down and slid inside her in one languid stroke.

She nearly shattered apart right then.

The feel of his fingers, the look in his eyes, the rumbling sound that moved through him.

But then his fingers were stroking inside her, slowly building speed and pressure as Victor's breath got faster and more ragged.

Her own hand moved down, sliding over his lap to find his hard length straining against the material of his trousers, then stroking her palm around the head at the same tempo as his fingers were teasing her.

That seemed to undo him.

His fingers left her and she was helpless to stop the whimpered objection that escaped her, at the loss when she'd been so close.

But then his hands were moving toward his own trousers, working the material down and off.

The needy ache between Pandora's thighs intensified at the sight of him naked before her. At his hard length proving he was just as far gone as she felt.

Her hand moved out again, closing around him, stroking him until he pushed her hand away, pinning it on the ground above her head as his weight came down on her again.

"Yes," she whimpered at the feel of him against her cleft, rocking, but refusing to press inside her as his lips claimed her again.

With his weight balanced on the one arm above their heads, his free hand moved up her side, closing around her breast, squeezing. Harder this time, almost to the point of pain, dragging another ragged groan from her as her hips started to writhe more restlessly against his slow, steady rocks.

Just when she thought she couldn't take another second of anticipation, Victor's lips left hers as he pushed up to look down at her.

Then, his gorgeous green eyes watching her, his hips shifted back and she felt him pressing against her for a moment, then surging inside.

316

Her gasp of pleasure mixed with his as he slid deep inside her in one long stroke, making her thighs clamp to the sides of his hips and her walls tighten hard around him.

They stayed just like that for a moment, adjusting to the sensation, to the connection, and just then, somewhere in the distance, a clock chimed midnight.

It was the day of their wedding.

But then the need overtook them completely, leaving her hips writhing and her fingernails digging into his hips as he started to move inside her.

It was slow and sweet at first, but, as their pleasure grew, as the need for release built, they both moved together more quickly.

Her moans mingled with his ragged breaths as the two of them rushed toward that cliff, then flew over and crashed in unison.

Pandora's body shook as Victor tensed, and their moans mingled together as the pleasure overtook them completely.

And as their connection deepened, the night drew its curtain around them, shielding whispered promises and vows too sacred for daylight.

29

"You need to get up!" Lucy said, slamming the door to Pandora's room.

The sound seemed to rattle through her bones.

But nothing, not even the interruption of her much-needed rest, could ruin Pandora's mood.

She'd been in the garden with Victor until the sun was kissing the sky. Reluctantly, they'd pulled apart and made their way into the castle, heading toward their own separate rooms.

Pandora lay in bed for hours after, reliving the events of the night, the whispers and sighs, the love she'd felt for him leaching into her bones, into her very marrow, as they'd held each other in a tangle of limbs in the cool grass.

And today, today she was going to marry that same man.

She felt like she was floating.

"Wait a minute," Lucy said, mouth falling open as she drew closer to Pandora's bed. "Is that . . . Is that beard burn on your neck?" she asked, making Pandora's hand slap to her neck, which felt oddly hot and sensitive. "It is! No way. I mean . . . I'm so happy for you and I need all of the details. But your female family members are about to burst in here to primp and prod at you for hours. So you might want to rush into the bathroom to try to cover up that redness."

Pandora threw off the covers and ran into the bathroom, checking her reflection in the mirror. And, sure enough, there was a path of irritated skin down her neck where Victor's lips had been.

"How do I cover this?" she asked, looking at Lucy's giddy reflection in the mirror.

"If we had time, some ice and an oatmeal compress. But we don't, so . . . What do we have here?" She grabbed Pandora's toiletry bag and dug through. "OK. This cream should soothe it." She handed the tube to Pandora, who quickly rubbed it on the spot. "This is Dante's sunscreen, right?" Lucy waved the tube at Pandora.

"Yeah."

"You said it has a white cast, right?"

"Yeah."

"OK. This is as close to make-up as we are going to get since you don't have any foundation."

With that, Pandora slathered it on until it reduced most of the redness.

"They're going to be with you as you get into your gown. Is there anywhere else we have to worry about?" Lucy asked.

319

If Pandora could blush, she would be crimson.

Still, Lucy must have caught a flicker of her embarrassment because she beamed at her friend.

"Oh, my God. I love that. And I want to hear all of the details. But the mob is always here. So . . . cover up your spots. I will stall," she said, just as the click of heels sounded outside Pandora's room.

Pandora rushed to do just that, brushed her teeth, and fished a few twigs and leaves out of her hair before washing it.

It was going to be a long day. She could have a full shower later.

When she made her way out of the bathroom a few minutes later, her room – which was enormous – was packed with women. The noise of their conversations alone almost had her backing into the bathroom for a couple more minutes of peace. Most of the chat seemed to be about her bed, with a couple of the women bouncing on the edge of it and sharing a look that made Pandora think they were starting to reconsider their own personal use of coffins.

But just when she was actually considering that, she was spotted.

And they all . . . swarmed at her. Hugs and cheek pecks came from every direction as she was twirled around and fussed over.

Pandora felt dizzy as her gaze slid helplessly to where Lucy was standing near the door with Vlad perched on one shoulder and Elizabeth the cockatoo on the other.

She noticed with a smile that Vlad had on a little birdie suit vest and Elizabeth had been dressed up with what looked like her own bridal gown vest.

320

"Here," Ophelia said when the crowd dispersed to fuss over the bridesmaid dresses that had just been delivered by Pandora's father. "We may not be able to get drunk, but traditions should be observed." She held out a glass of lazily bubbling champagne.

"Plus the bubbles are fun," Kora piped in.

Pandora reached for the champagne flute. "Thank you," she said, rolling some of the tension out of her shoulders. Her family could be a real sensory overload when they all came at you at once.

"I remember my wedding day," Ophelia said, running a hand down Pandora's steadily drying hair that was likely already starting to frizz out. "I think all of this," she said, gesturing toward all the women, "was more stressful than coming up with my own vows."

Oh . . . oh, no.

She'd forgotten to write her vows.

She had brought a notebook with her, promising herself she would find a few private moments to work on something that would be convincing, but not make her want to cry in longing for the words to be true.

But then, well, Victor. In the garden. Something she wouldn't trade for anything. She would just have to come up with her vows on the fly.

Something must have passed through Pandora then because Ophelia's head tipped to the side. Then Pandora watched in horror as her mother's gaze honed in on the spot on her neck that was covered, but not exactly invisible.

Her gaze flicked from her daughter toward the floor and Pandora realized with a sinking stomach that the dress she'd thrown off before bed was still there.

"There are grass stains on your dress," Ophelia said, looking back at her daughter.

"Oh, right. Um, I . . ."

Her mum's blood-red lips curved up at her daughter's fumbling. "We are all adults here, darling. I remember one time, your father and I were taking a walk through a graveyard, and we—"

"Please. For all that is good in the world, do not finish that story."

To that, Ophelia laughed. "Oh, but what joy it brings to a parent to torment their children with the accounts of their torrid lovemaking."

"I don't want to hear this," Pandora said, putting down her glass to cover her ears.

Ophelia smiled wider and her eyes were suddenly softer than Pandora had seen them since before the whole conversation about the terms of her inheritance.

Suddenly, Pandora knew something had changed.

Her mother's constant and obvious disapproval had melted away. Leaving Pandora to wonder if Ophelia had simply not approved because her succubus senses had picked up on some sort of disconnect between Pandora and Victor's words and their energy together.

Now that things had progressed between them, Ophelia seemed happy for her daughter.

Pandora's gaze slid past Ophelia to find Ambrosia watching them. Ophelia turned, following her gaze, then turning back to her daughter.

"She still does not approve of my marriage to your father," Ophelia said, making Pandora's brows shoot up.

"Really?"

"She never approved of her darling great-grandson

marrying a succubus," Ophelia said. "And, no, the irony is not lost on me," her mum continued. "But my objections weren't simply because of Victor being a human. And all the ways that becomes complicated as your marriage stretches on. I just . . . I didn't feel the connection, darling. How could I approve of that? But anyway, don't worry about Ambrosia. She will disappear tomorrow and you likely won't see her for another fifty years."

That was a bit comforting, actually.

"What are we going to do about her eyebrows?" Aunt Anastacia interrupted them, bringing over several of the other aunts.

"What's wrong with my eyebrows?" Pandora's hand flew up to touch them, terrified they were going to try to pluck them within an inch of their lives.

She'd survived the thin-brow trend twice in her long life – in the thirties, then again in the nineties. She was not going to go through that again.

"We're not giving the girl a makeover," Kora said, making Pandora give her a grateful smile. "She doesn't need one. We're just here to . . . enhance everything."

With that, they began all of the aforementioned "enhancing".

"Good Lord," Lucy said, finally moving in at Pandora's side at the dressing table. "I never thought I would get a second alone with you."

The only reason she did was because one of the uncles had knocked and announced there were some fresh blood bags downstairs.

"Be honest, do I look like a clown?" Pandora asked, refusing to look at her reflection again. She'd been looking at herself for so long that she didn't even recognize herself anymore.

"It's . . . a bit clownish," Lucy said, jumping up and going over toward where she'd brought her own bag into the room to get herself ready for the ceremony. "I don't think it's quite at the oversized shoes and tiny car stage, but let's tone this down a little, shall we?" She produced a package of make-up wipes. "And while I do that, you'll drink this."

Lucy held up a coveted bottle of synthetic blood. Since learning about it, and telling Dante about it, she'd been having a surprisingly hard time keeping a decent stock of it around. She wasn't sure if the demand was high or if the supply was low. But she was thankful for a bottle. If things got romantic after the ceremony and she was hungry, she was worried she might accidentally slip up and nip Victor in the heat of the moment.

"They only had A negative," Lucy said.

"That's fine. Anything is good," Pandora said, uncapping it and taking a long swig, not sure how long she would have before her family came back. She wanted to finish it and get rid of the evidence before they did.

With that, Lucy rinsed the bottle as Pandora swished some mouthwash, before they got started on removing half of the make-up from Pandora's face.

"I mean, really, that was a comical amount of mascara," Lucy said, reapplying it with a much lighter hand. "They should have been more worried about your hair," she added, going in her bag to produce some products meant to tame the frizz and static until, finally, Lucy had Pandora's hair falling in long auburn waves down her back. Her friend stood back and looked at her masterpiece.

"There. Perfect. We had to let them fuss. But I couldn't let you walk up to the altar looking like that. Now, I want some details about the beard burn."

But it was right then that Pandora's family came bursting back into the room, successfully squashing any personal conversation as the discussion went back to outfits and hair and make-up, as the other women fussed over the bridal party with the same enthusiasm they had worked on Pandora.

With some blood in her system, the nerves of the day seemed to trip into overdrive, making her feel racy and fidgety.

There was a soft knock at the door just as the crowd started to talk about getting Pandora into her gown.

Ravenna rushed to the door in a flurry of red velvet, all her assets bouncing as happily as ever.

"Oh, aren't you so handsome!" she said, making Pandora's belly flip-flop. Victor was on the other side of the door. "You know you can't see your bride before the ceremony," she went on. "But I will tell you that she is an absolute vision."

"She always is," Victor said, sending butterflies fluttering through Pandora's chest. "Just wanted to bring this for her. You can give it to her."

"Oh, aren't you just the most thoughtful young man?" Ravenna said, reaching out. "I will give it to her. With your love. Oh, this is such a wonderful day!"

Pandora was smiling even before Ravenna made her way back to her, holding out a large steaming mug.

"Your groom brought you a little present. It smells . . . Well, it smells," Ravenna said, making Pandora burst out laughing.

"It's chamomile tea," she said, taking it in her hands. "My favorite."

He'd known she would be starting to freak out. Then he'd brought her tea to try to fix it.

He really was the best man she'd ever met.

And she was about to make him hers.

Legally.

Since her heart had already been his for a long time.

"Let's get you in that gorgeous gown of yours," Ravenna said once Pandora had the last sip of her tea.

It really was a gorgeous dress. One Lucy had actually found, since the appointments with the judgmental Sylvia had led nowhere.

The garment bag unzipped and all of the women who hadn't yet seen the dress gasped.

It was the perfect gown, one that was traditionally bridal but also a bit gothic as well.

The lace top and arms were black that slowly melted into the white of the rest of the dress, where it was embroidered with black and crimson flowers that got more prominent around the train.

And, best of all, the women at the shop she'd gone to for her fittings had oohed and ahhed at her instead of criticizing her.

"How perfect," Ravenna said, pulling it out of the bag, then working the hidden zipper down the back. "OK, my dear. Time to get in. We are running out of time," she said.

"One second," Lucy said, producing a bag that Pandora had missed before. "I have a little something for her to put on underneath."

With that, she shoved Pandora into the bathroom with

the bag. "It's vintage," she said before closing the door. "Except for the knickers. Those are new, obviously."

Alone, Pandora took the items out of the bag, finding a new pair of black lacy panties with the tags still attached, as well as a gorgeous lace bustier.

Well, at least she wouldn't need to strip down to absolutely nothing in front of her whole family.

Shrugging out of her clothes, she pulled on the new set, then, remembering, put on the earrings that Victor had given her.

New, blue, and old.

She just needed something borrowed.

She made her way out of the room, making Ravenna smile at her.

"Victor is a lucky, lucky man, my dear," she said, rushing Pandora over to her gown, where she and Ophelia helped her into it.

Finished, Pandora smoothed her hands down the front of the gown before turning to look in the mirror.

For a second, she almost didn't recognize the woman looking back at her. She looked more like her lovely mother than she ever had before. Perfectly put together, her features on full display, her hair tamed.

Ophelia moved in behind her daughter, giving her a soft smile, then lifting her arms, moving them around Pandora to rest a necklace on her skin.

"Something borrowed," she said as she clasped it. "Lucy told me she had old handled. And I know you said Victor got you new and blue. I wanted to give you your borrowed."

"It's perfect," Pandora said, reaching up to touch the single teardrop ruby on a delicate black chain that made it disappear into the dress, leaving the ruby looking a bit like a blood drop on her chest. "Thanks, Mum."

Next, Lucy, Kora, Maribelle, and Bellatrix all got themselves into their dresses.

"Have I mentioned how much I love you for picking simple black dresses?" Kora asked. "The last wedding I was at made us wear crinolines that I swore were three yards wide. It was insane."

"The sun is about set," Henrietta said as she tied the final bowtie on her last male dogs. The girls were wearing little pink tutus.

The other aunts had just barely been able to talk Henrietta out of making Pandora and Victor use her dogs as flower girls and ring bearers.

"So exciting! OK. We have to go and get to our places," Ravenna said, shooing the women out of the room.

The sudden quiet made Pandora's ears ring.

"We need more champagne," Kora said, pouring the bridal party another round as they waited for the knock on the door.

It came twenty minutes later.

Lucy opened the door to find Elias standing there. He was acting as a stand-in for Victor's side of the bridal party, since the only friend Victor had was Sebastian.

"Look at you," Elias said, gaze moving over Lucy. "All polished up."

"Wow," Lucy said. "Careful, that almost sounded like a compliment. Are we ready?"

"We are." He offered her his arm.

"Ugh, fine." Lucy chugged the last of her champagne, then grabbed her flowers and allowed him to lead her from the room.

Bellatrix, largely ignored by everyone all day, save for her own mother, followed next.

Rolling the tension out of her shoulders, Pandora followed Kora and Maribelle out of her room.

The castle was a sprawling place. And with each step, Pandora felt her nerves jangling in her bones.

Suddenly, this didn't feel right.

Not only lying to her family.

But more so, lying to Victor.

How could she make the man marry her when he didn't even know who she really was?

She managed to keep her worries to herself as they all walked – leaves crunching under her feet and the cool wind kicking up the ends of her hair – toward the mausoleum. Yes, mausoleum. She was getting married at a *mausoleum*. It was one thing her family had refused to bend on. They'd rambled on and on about traditions and family.

The only reason she'd given in was because the mausoleum actually kind of looked like the place in the *Pride and Prejudice* movie where Mr. Darcy first confessed his feelings to Lizzie.

It was a massive round stone structure with charmingly chipped pillars.

She could hear the rumbles of conversation from the crowd at the other side of the structure, but it was big enough that she couldn't see anyone yet.

"Pandora?" Lucian called to her, waiting for his daughter as the rest of the bridal party moved toward the other side of the mausoleum.

And, suddenly, it just burst out of her.

"I can't do this."

"Do what? Get married?" her father asked, concern etched on his handsome face.

"Marry someone I've been lying to since I met him," Pandora said, her stomach twisting into tighter knots. "It's not right. I can't stand there and say vows and make promises when I'm being dishonest with him. He doesn't even know who I am. What I am." Pandora was ranting now. "How can I possibly marry someone who doesn't even know I'm a vampire?"

"Pandora, stop!" Lucian said, something in his tone making her blood freeze as she suddenly whipped around.

And there, a few feet away, completely within hearing distance, was Victor.

30

He just stood there, looking at her, disbelief and hurt taking turns playing across his handsome features. While it felt like the ground had just opened up beneath her.

"Victor," she whispered.

At the sound of her voice, he turned and strode away.

No.

No, it couldn't end like this.

"Go after him," her father said as she watched his figure disappear into the darkness.

"He doesn't want to see me."

"Yes, he does. He's hurt, but he does."

Pandora wasn't convinced. But the idea of hurting Victor made it feel like someone had ripped her heart out of her chest.

She grabbed handfuls of her skirt so it didn't trip her up and started to rush after him.

As she rounded the mausoleum, she saw Bellatrix standing there, a smug look on her face that made Pandora think she might have had something to do with Victor coming around the back of the mausoleum at the exact right moment to overhear her.

That didn't matter, though.

All that mattered was trying to explain to Victor the whole situation.

Just this once, she was glad for her powers, namely her speed, as she ran through the graveyard to rush ahead of Victor and cut him off mid-stride.

"Right," he said with a scoff as he came to a stop. "Super speed."

"Please, let me explain."

"Explain what? That you've been lying to me for months?"

"Yes."

"How can you possibly explain that? You expected me to marry you with this massive lie between us?"

"How could I possibly tell you?" she said. "Vampires don't exist, right? You would have thought I was crazy if I'd told you that from the very beginning. And don't even try to deny that."

"I would have probably thought you were mad, yeah," he said. "At first. But we've been together for a while now. We've talked about our lives, our goals, our dreams. We've discussed sharing an entire year of our lives. And all the while, you've been keeping something this monumental from me?"

"If I didn't tell you at the beginning, how could I have once time had passed? You would have felt betrayed no matter what."

"So better for me to find out on my wedding day."

"That's not what I'm saying. That's what I was talking about with my father. That this felt wrong. That I couldn't allow you to marry me without telling you."

"You let it get this far, though. Last night . . ."

"Was what made me feel like I had to tell you. It was different after that. We're different. It wasn't fake anymore."

"It was never fake, Pandy," Victor said, voice suddenly heartbreakingly sad.

"What?"

"That night when I came to tell you that I wouldn't be coming back, that I had to drop out of uni – that was the night I was going to try to finally get up my nerve to ask you out. This was never fake for me, Pandy."

"I had always—"

"I've spent the past few weeks thinking that maybe, just maybe, this marriage wouldn't be fake after all. That you would see how good we were together."

"I did see that," she said.

"But you didn't believe it enough to be honest with me."

"It wasn't like I was going to tell you that I'm actually naturally a blonde or something, Victor. How was I supposed to tell you that not only are vampires real, but I'm one of them?"

"Did you think I didn't already suspect?" he asked. "I study vampires in all forms of fiction. And even nonfiction. All the signs were there. You're always cold. You are 'allergic' to garlic and use umbrellas in the sun. You never seem to enjoy food. You're faster than you should be. And that's not even mentioning your family . . ."

"Ravenna and Reginald," Pandora said, knowing they were the most outlandish.

"Your mum, actually. I almost believed the historical actor thing. But your mum looks about the same age as you. And then there's this." He reached into his shirt to pull out the necklace she'd given him. "You gave me a vial of blood after the strange encounter I had with Bellatrix in the pantry. I've read everything about glamours. I knew what she'd done. You could have told me. Instead you, what, put some kind of spell on me?"

"It's a protection amulet," Pandora said, feeling her eyes sting. She would have preferred if he was angry, if he was yelling at her. But he just seemed so hurt, so broken.

"Seems as if the only one I needed protection from was you," he said, tugging hard until the chain snapped, then tossing it on the ground at her feet. "This isn't happening. I can't marry someone who has been lying to me. Not even to get to finish my PhD. Not for any reason." He paused, looking over her. "You look beautiful, Pandy."

With that, and nothing more, he walked away, leaving her there in her wedding gown, crying through her make-up.

"Pandora?" Sometime later, Pandora heard Ophelia calling and the whoosh of the air moving as her mother sped toward her, spurred by the information her husband had likely given her. "Oh, darling."

Then she was wrapped in her mother's arms, crying into her neck like she'd done as a young girl.

Ophelia didn't try to tell her it would be OK. Surely, she knew how she would feel if she'd lost her own love. So she simply stroked Pandora's hair and held her together as she fell apart.

Pandora was sure the tears would never cease.

When they finally slowed, she felt dry from the inside

out. A fragile piece of paper that threatened to turn to dust with the slightest mishandling.

She wasn't really aware of how the wedding reception dispersed. All she knew was that she found herself in the back of a darkened car with her mother on one side and Lucy on the other, while her father and Dante sat in the front.

They half carried her to her bed.

Where she stayed the whole of the next day.

And the day after that.

And after that.

"My dear, you have to nourish yourself," Ravenna, uncharacteristically somber, said as she sat on the bed beside Pandora, holding a cup of human blood.

"I don't want anything." Pandora rolled over and pulled the covers over her head. She wondered what might happen if she never drank again. Would she just dry up and turn to dust? That sounded preferable to living endlessly in her misery and regret.

"Aunt Ravenna, allow me," Dante said as he walked into her room.

"Do try to get her to drink," Ravenna said, reaching out to give Pandora's ankle a squeeze through the blankets before she made her way out, closing the door with a quiet click.

"I don't want it," Pandora said.

"I have the synthetic blood," he said, and she heard the click of the cap being twisted off.

"I don't want that either."

"You have to drink. Mum and Dad want to talk to you. And I don't think you'd have enough strength to walk downstairs at this point."

335

"I don't want to talk to them."

"I know you must blame them for some of this. But they're family. You have to speak to them." Pandora rolled over in the bed, looking at her brother from under swollen lids. He made a sighing sound, pushing the bottle toward her. "Please, just hear them out. Then if you want to rot in bed, so be it."

"Fine," she said grumpily, trying to pull herself up against the headboard, finding the task nearly impossible. Dante was right about her not being able to walk downstairs in her current state. "How long has it been?" she asked as she reached for the bottle of fake blood, finding it almost intolerably heavy.

"Two weeks," he told her, watching as she sipped her drink.

Two weeks.

It felt longer and shorter at the same time.

She'd done nothing but cry and think herself sick, trying to figure out when she should have talked to Victor, told him the truth. But not sure that, if given another chance, she would ever have felt comfortable doing so.

"There, don't you feel better?" Dante asked when she set the bottle on her nightstand.

She did feel much more alive, whether she actually wanted to or not.

"I just want to shower," she said as she threw off the covers. "Then I will speak to them."

With that, Dante left her alone and she washed, put on fresh clothes, and made her way downstairs.

The house was unusually quiet after weeks full of activity and noise. She didn't know how many of her family members were left, save for Ravenna and Reginald. But whoever was still around was staying out of sight as she made her way down to the sitting room.

"Pandora," her father said, sounding relieved. "Come sit down. Your mother and I need to speak to you."

Pandora walked on numb legs, still feeling horribly exhausted. But with blood in her system, she suspected it was more mental and emotional tiredness.

"You were right," Ophelia said. "When you told us that we were being old-fashioned and stubborn and patriarchal. You were right. While we do cling to our old ways, and we both think there is some virtue in that, we also have to understand that you have grown up in a different world than we did, that your ways are going to be different from our own."

"OK," Pandora said, nodding.

"As such, we are going to give you your inheritance on your birthday," her father told her.

It was what she'd always wanted.

But now, it suddenly felt completely pointless.

31

"I think it's absolutely perfect," Lucy said, turning in a circle in the bookshop, taking in the months' worth of work they had put into the place.

Admittedly, even after the talk with her parents and knowing she was going to receive the inheritance, she had stayed in her bed, wallowing in her misery, not able to see a way out of the fog of heartbreak.

It had been Lucy who'd eventually showed up. She'd been fresh off of a full moon, so she'd been full of energy and determination when she'd come in the room, whipping off the covers and all but dragging Pandora into the bathroom while telling her she was greasy and stinking.

Reluctantly, Pandora had showered and changed. She'd drunk the blood bottles Lucy had kept passing her.

"Now," Lucy had said, exhaling hard. "You are going

to stop wallowing in your self-pity and actually do something about it."

Pandora wasn't sure that was possible.

Until they got to talking.

Lucy was quick to put an end to the idea of approaching Victor to give him his share of money, insisting that he would never take it.

Pandora knew in her heart that he wouldn't.

But she refused to allow him to lose his chance to finish his PhD when she had the means to fix the situation.

"Why don't you just . . . invest in his department?" Lucy suggested. "You could fund the whole department. That way, Victor gets to finish his degree without needing to take money directly from you."

After some thought and research, Pandora concluded it was the only way she could make it up in some way to Victor.

So while Victor was likely home for his winter break, maybe trying to figure out what he was going to do with his life since he thought his uni career was over, Pandora was having meetings with UCL, working it out so the whole cohort in his department would be able to have the rest of their schooling for free.

With that squared away, she turned her attention to the bookshop.

True, it felt different.

Her lifelong dream was no longer the same.

She saw him everywhere. In their choice of paint colours, in the wood stains, the art. She smelled him in the coffee brewing in the café as she and Lucy worked overtime to get everything just right. She felt him in the spines and the pages of the books as she slid them into their spots on the shelves.

It was impossible not to think of him in each private nook with its comfy chair. Or sitting at one of the tables at the café, his caramel macchiato set at the corner as his hand scrubbed across the pages of his notebook and his hair fell charmingly over his forehead.

When she was tired enough to allow herself the misery that came along with fantasies, she would picture herself walking over to him, reaching out to brush his hair off his forehead. And maybe he would look up, eyes unfocused for a second as they adjusted to not looking at tiny words. Then he would give her a sweet, soft smile.

If she really wanted to torment herself, she would imagine leaning down to press her lips to his.

She never let it go beyond that, though.

That alone made it feel like someone was stepping on her heart and crushing it to dust, when she came back to reality.

"I guess," Pandora said as she looked around the shop.

"You guess?" Lucy asked, sighing. "We have put our blood, sweat, and tears into this. Literally, I painted over my blood right there." She jabbed her finger toward one of the built-in bookcases. "And you cried into that cushion," she continued, pointing toward the window seat. "And, well, I think I sweated over the entire floor. That's what gives it that nice shine."

"I know you worked hard. You know how much I appr—"

"Oh, God. Don't give me that 'you appreciate me' thing. We both busted our butts because we knew how good this place could be. I know this is a little bittersweet for you because you were planning to work on this place with

Victor. But I want to remind you that this was your dream well before that."

She was right.

But Pandora was still struggling to find her enthusiasm for it.

"And that we nearly died with the amount of blood we had to give to that witch to spell this place."

That, unfortunately, was not that much of an exaggeration. Apparently, to bring forth their desire to have the shop be a haven for all supernatural beings, a place where grudges based on species could not exist, they had to bleed for it. Not only them, but one of every kind of creature they wanted in on the sanctuary truce.

That meant weeks of tracking down down-on-their-luck sirens, succubi, shifters, fae, goblins, and, well, every other kind of creature they could think of, and asking them to donate their blood for a fee.

Pandora estimated that nearly half of the money that went into the bookshop went to getting blood from other creatures.

Lucy, luckily, gave hers for free. Well, no. She wanted a nice steak dinner in exchange for it.

"You know, we never really tested out the spell," Lucy said.

"How were we supposed to test it out?"

"I don't know . . . maybe you should try to hit me."

"I don't want to hit you."

"It's for science." Lucy lifted her arms in a fighting stance. "Come on. Hit me."

"Is that invitation for anyone?" a voice called, making Lucy's eyes widen as she whipped around to find Elias standing in the shop.

341

"What are you doing here?"

"That's on me," Dante said, coming in behind Elias, holding two bouquets of flowers.

"I thought you went back to Transylvania," Lucy said, getting a snort out of Dante.

"Well, the spell doesn't seem to work with arguments," Pandora said, taking the flowers from her brother. "Thank you."

"Congratulations on your dream coming true," Dante said as she put the flowers on a table.

"Thanks."

"Come on, hit me," Lucy said, making Pandora turn around to see her with her fists up as she circled a bemused Elias.

"That is not going to happen."

"Fine. I'll hit you, then," she said, cocking back, then starting to swing.

It was like an invisible wall shot up between them.

Lucy's fist froze a few inches from Elias's face. When she tried again, the same thing happened.

"What does it feel like?"

"Like punching gelatin," Lucy said. "Really thick gelatin. Kind of cool, actually."

"At least we know it works before we open the doors," Pandora said.

"You have your first customer waiting," Elias said.

"What do you mean?" Pandora looked out the windows, but saw nothing except the usual foot traffic moving past.

The grand opening was still a few hours away. And as much as she hoped for success, she wasn't exactly anticipating a crowd. At least not right away.

Elias pointed up, making Pandora's brows pinch. But, sure enough, when she craned her neck up high enough, there was something on the roof that hadn't been there when she and Lucy had arrived before sun-up to fuss with some finishing touches.

"What is it?" Lucy asked.

"A gargoyle."

"What? No way!" Lucy rushed outside to gawk at the snarling stone creature perched on the roof. On a stack of stone books. "That's so cool. Hey, dude. You can come in early if you want."

"I don't think he's going to do that," Elias said.

"Why not?" Lucy asked.

"Because he needs to shift. Do you shift in public?" he asked, his gaze moving over her. "I'm assuming you don't shift with clothes on."

"Oh," Lucy said, going back into the shop. "Right. That makes sense. He will be a nighttime visitor, then."

Pandora planned to have an actual twenty-four-hour bookshop, so it could cater to creatures of the night such as herself. And the occasional insomniac human. But until she was fully confident in her staff, she and Lucy would be working swing shifts to keep an eye on things, since they'd both left their positions at Luna Bean.

Once the dust settled, though, Pandora intended to work the overnight shift. She was excited to see how many fellow vampires came in to browse the shelves. And other creatures who, for whatever their reasons, didn't want to be out in the daytime.

"So, what book are you buying?" Lucy asked, looking at Elias. "I can show you to the self-help section, if you'd like."

The two went on like that for over an hour before Pandora lost track of them, thanks to just about every member of her own family dropping in under their parasols to offer their congratulations ahead of the party.

"Hey," Lucy said, showing up at Pandora's side. Pandora had been standing behind the desk, worrying her earring with her fingers. One of the earrings that Victor had given her. She hadn't let herself wear it, or her engagement ring that she kept "forgetting" to send back to him, since the botched wedding. But just this once, she was allowing it. It felt right, having a part of him there with her on the big day.

"Yeah?" Pandora asked, shaking off the daydream she'd been caught up in.

"It's time," Lucy told her, lining up a stack of books so the edges aligned perfectly. "I'm just going to hit the start button on the coffee machine, then we can unlock. Look," she added, nodding toward the windows.

Where, sure enough, there was a small line waiting for their doors to open.

Pandora's heart swelled as Lucy rushed to start the coffee machine before walking with Pandora toward the door.

"One, two, three." Lucy turned the lock.

Pandora pulled the door open and invited the first customers inside.

It was a steady trickle of customers for the first two hours, people perusing the sections, getting coffee or tea, and chatting with Lucy and Pandora about their favorite authors and genres.

And for just a few hours, some of the misery she'd been feeling for months fell away.

344

A customer even started to get her excited about a new romance that was going to be released later that month, despite the fact that she hadn't been able to pick up a love story since the wedding, her own heart too broken to read about others falling in love.

It was a lovely opening.

Truly, it was.

She couldn't have asked for more.

Still, though, she couldn't quite shake the feeling that something was missing.

No, not something.

Someone.

The bells on the door jingled, making her turn, ready to plaster on a customer-service smile.

But it froze and fell.

Because standing there, just a foot inside the bookshop, was Victor.

"Hey, Pandy."

32

"Victor?" Pandora's voice was half whisper, half sob as she blinked, thinking when her eyes opened again, he would be gone.

But he was still there.

In fact, he was moving closer toward her.

He looked better than she remembered, in his dark jeans and thick forest-green jumper that made his light-green eyes pop all the more.

His hair was a few weeks past needing a trim, but the disheveled look was endearing on him.

"Congratulations," he said as he approached the counter, his gaze moving over her. "I always knew your bookshop would be amazing. Love the name," he went on when she stood there, too stunned to speak. Or blink. Or pretend to breathe. "The Eternal Page." He gave that small twitch of a smile she loved so much. "A little nod to who you really are."

"Y . . . yes," she said, nodding.

"It's perfect. You nailed the vibe you were hoping for in here too. Bright and happy, but cozy and inviting."

The door opened with a chime, making Victor turn to look at the man coming inside. A man so well-built that you could see the muscles through the thin material of his shirt. He had chiseled features and cool, dark eyes.

Something about him had Victor's brows furrowing as he turned back to Pandora.

"Gargoyle," she said, never wanting to lie to him again.

"Gargoyle," Victor said with a little laugh. "Guess there's still a lot I need to learn. Are there other creatures?"

"Well, Lucy is a werewolf," Pandora told him, waving over toward where Lucy was making lattes behind the counter in the café section of the shop.

"A werewolf. Wow."

"And there are fae, succubi, sirens . . . basically all the creatures you read about in fiction are based, at least partially, on reality."

"I should be more shocked than I am," he said. "How have you been, Pandy?"

She knew she was supposed to feed him some platitudes, tell him she was all right, that everything was OK. After all, her misery was of her own making.

But she couldn't force out even a kind lie. Not to him.

"Not good."

To that, Victor's head tipped to the side as he watched her.

"I knew it was you," he said.

"What do you mean?"

"The funding for my department. I knew it was you the second I heard about it."

347

"It was the right thing to do," she said. "I didn't think you would take the money directly from me. But if it came through the school, I thought you would take the opportunity to finish your PhD. You've earned it." When he didn't immediately reply, Pandora leaned forward. "Please tell me you took advantage of it."

"The next term hasn't really started yet, but, yes, I decided to finish."

"Oh, good. I'm so glad to hear that. How have you been?"

"Doing a lot of thinking," he said.

"About?"

"Many things. Not the least of which, going back over every movie, show, and book I've read about vampires, as well as my entire thesis, knowing now what I know."

"Any new conclusions?"

"That you're not purely evil creatures."

"How did you come to that?"

"Because I spent weeks around your family," he told her. "No one who has met Ravenna would think she's evil."

"But she drinks blood," Pandora said, pitching her voice lower.

Victor glanced around. Clearly uncomfortable with the close quarters and possibly eavesdropping ears, he looked back at her. "Is there an office where we may speak more freely?"

"Sure." She led him down the hall, past the toilets and into the shoebox-sized office.

Away from the scents of brewing coffee and sugary syrups, Victor's cinnamon, vanilla, and leather scent overwhelmed her senses, making her chest feel tight and her skin warm.

348

The longing was acute and instantaneous, and she couldn't help but wonder if the need was etched all over her face.

"That's something I've been wondering about," Victor said, no longer whispering.

"What?" Pandora asked, too focused on the nearness of him to keep track of the conversation.

"The blood."

"Oh, right. OK. What about the blood?"

"Does Ravenna drain people? As in dry?"

"Not that I know of, no."

"But it happens."

"Yes, it happens."

"The night of the stag and hen party . . ."

"I thought he'd been drained," Pandora said. "Lucy and I were worried that you might step into the alley, find him, and call the police. We were just going to move him, not get rid of him."

"Have you done that often? Hidden bodies?"

"Never."

"Not even your own . . . meals?"

"I don't drink human blood. Not anymore. I did as a child, back before I knew any better."

"What do you drink?"

"Well, it was pig's blood. Until the night of my hen party. We were at a club next door to your pub."

"There's no club there . . . Oh," he said, putting things together. "It's an . . . underground club."

"Yes. And, well, the barman told me that there's a new blood on the market for 'vegetarian' vampires like me and Dante. It's synthetic, but provides everything we need to survive. I've been drinking that since."

"Wow. Is there a market for it?"

"Seems to be. I think it's a sign of the changing times, the newer generation having different feelings from our parents."

"Your parents are OK with it?"

"They're . . . learning to adjust," she told him.

Since the wedding, she'd become a bit allergic to lying. Which meant she'd started to come clean to her family about not drinking from humans; she explained she'd been drinking pig's blood for years and was now on a supplement. And so was Dante.

"They got over me not wanting to sleep in a coffin, so they'll get used to this eventually."

"So the coffin thing is true, huh?"

"Pretty much across the board. Some of my family members even travel with their coffins when they visit."

"I can . . . picture that," he said, nodding. "Anyway, yeah, the more I've thought on it, the more convinced I am that just like there are good and evil humans, there are good and evil vampires. Bellatrix comes to mind," he added with a small smirk.

She didn't feel like it was a good time to mention that in the midst of her grief over the loss of Victor, Bellatrix had gloated any chance she'd got. As had Ambrosia.

"Yeah, Bellatrix is not a great representative for our kind."

"And no one who has ever met you could think there's anything evil about you."

"I haven't always been good," she said. Sure, some part of her was craving his compliments and kindness. The other part, though, didn't feel like she deserved it.

"I've had a lot of time to think about things," Victor

350

said. "And as much as I was hurt that you didn't trust me with that information, I also understand that it wasn't exactly something you could easily tell anyone. I mean, in some vampire fiction, there are even vampire overlords to make sure no one tells humans you exist. I didn't even stop to ask if that was the case."

"It is actually the law that no one knows. Save for the occasional vampire who keeps familiars, but that's considered a different matter. Though, I'm not sure how they even monitor something like that."

Victor nodded at that.

"Still. Even if there weren't some vampire overlords keeping an eye, I get why you didn't tell me. And I don't know if I would have necessarily believed you anyway."

"You would have. Like you said, you had your suspicions. I should have given you the chance to believe me or not. I'm sorry I wasn't honest with you."

"I know," Victor said. "I'm sorry I didn't give you a chance to explain. How did things go after . . . after?"

"I don't know," Pandora replied. Even just the memory of those moments immediately following their argument made pain slice through her once again. "I . . . ah . . . My mum brought me to my room."

She didn't want to tell him in what state she'd been, didn't want to guilt him for being upset with her. But something in her tone or face gave her away.

"How long?"

"How long what?" she asked. "How long did I stay in bed?"

"No. But, now, yes."

"It doesn't matter."

"It matters to me."

"A while," she said. "What were you originally asking?"

"How long was it not fake for you?"

"I don't think it was ever fake for me. I'd had a crush on you pretty much since you first came into Luna Bean. Had a silly nickname for you and everything."

"Well, now I have to know the nickname."

Pandora scrunched up her face, embarrassed to admit it. "Caramel Macchiato Cutie. Lucy teased me about my crush endlessly. I mean, obviously, it was just kind of, you know, superficial then. But once I approached you and we started talking . . . I was always into you, Victor."

"That feeling was mutual."

Was?

It was naïve of her to hope that it wasn't all in the past tense for him.

"I need to tell you something," she said.

"OK."

"I'm not telling you to guilt you. Or to try to win you back. I'm telling you in the interest of being completely honest." She went to her desk to grab her bag, then reached inside for the ring some part of her had hoped to see on her finger for eternity. "I was in love with you," she told him, holding out the ring. "Senselessly, hopelessly in love with you."

He took the ring, then watched her for a long moment. But she found his green eyes unreadable.

Finally, he sucked in a deep breath.

"Was?" he asked.

"Am," she corrected him. "I don't think I'll ever stop loving you."

"Forever is a long time. Especially in your case."

"I still mean it," she told him.

352

"Well," he said, reaching down to take her left hand, lifting it, then sliding the ring on her finger. "I think this still belongs here, then."

"Victor . . ."

Tears were stinging the backs of her eyes at the feel of his skin on hers, of the familiar weight of the ring on her finger.

"Unless you don't want it there anymore," he said, his gaze finding hers.

"No! That's not it," she said, blinking back the wetness in her eyes. "I just want you to be sure."

"Is there a reason I shouldn't be sure?"

"No. No, I will never keep something from you again. I will even tell you if you get an awful haircut. Or if you have bad breath. Or if I find myself staring at your neck."

"Well, you might not need to be *that* honest."

"I don't want to keep anything from you again. I don't ever want to risk losing you. I barely survived it once."

"All right. Full honesty." He laced his fingers between hers. "And maybe a less rushed wedding."

"Or, you know, a civil ceremony. You, me, Lucy, and Sebastian."

"I dunno. I was kind of enjoying that massive vampire wedding. Though, trying to explain marrying in a graveyard was . . . fun."

"This time, maybe it can be more about us and what we want."

"And what do you want?"

"You."

"You have that," he said, pressing his forehead to hers. "What else?"

353

"A wedding in a giant library. Somewhere cold. Preferably while it's snowing."

"That sounds perfect," he said. "Maybe somewhere with a winding, overgrown garden. With lots of little hidden spots to get lost in together."

Heat bloomed through her at the memory.

And now he was saying she could have that, and so much more, forever.

"Oh, I do have one stipulation."

"Anything."

"We don't sleep in a coffin."

"I don't know. It sounds kind of cozy with you in it with me."

"I'm afraid it's a dealbreaker," he said with warm eyes. "I'm a bit claustrophobic."

"A big, comfy bed it is, then."

"Sounds perfect."

"It does," she said. "So, are you going to kiss me or not?"

With that, his lips claimed hers.

Soft and sweet at first, then growing deeper, more intense, both of them full of the promise of forever.

Some part of Pandora was acutely aware of the store full of people, and Lucy, just feet away.

But as Victor reached over to press the lock on the door, then backed her up to her desk before bending, grabbing her legs, and dropping her onto it, she couldn't seem to bring herself to care.

Her hands were frantic, moving over the body she'd been sure she would never get to feel again, peeling away layers of clothing that were hiding him from her.

Victor was just as needy, his hands roaming up her belly

to close over her breasts. But they were both quickly frustrated by the material blocking his touch.

Her hands went up and Victor was all too happy to slip her shirt up and off, then reach behind her to loosen the clasps of her bra.

Then his hands were closing over her, making her eyes slide shut at the long-wanted brush of his fingers on her bare skin.

"Look at me when I'm touching you," Victor murmured, making Pandora's belly flip-flop as her eyelids fluttered open to find him watching her with an intensity that made her heart feel like it was growing too big for her chest. "There you go," he said as his thumb and forefinger squeezed her nipple just a little harder, the pain–pleasure mix making her whimper as she arched into the sensation, rather than away from it.

She loved Victor in all his forms, but there was something about this version of him – demanding, possessive, so close to losing control – that was making her nearly come undone as well.

Victor's free hand went to her shoulder, pressing until she went flat across her desk – and she was sure she would never look at the big desk calendar the same again. Depending on how this went, she might need to burn the damn thing.

She stared up at him, watching his struggle to regain some of his control.

That was the last thing she wanted.

Her legs moved out, hooking around his hips and pulling him closer. The move had his lips tipping up as his fingers grazed over her ribcage, making a little shiver move through her.

He bent forward, sucking one of her nipples into his mouth, making her arch up off the desk as a moan ripped free from her.

"Shh," he murmured, his breath warm across her breast.

Then his lips and tongue and teeth were on her again, testing her ability to keep quiet as he drove her up without even touching her where she needed it most.

It wasn't long, though, before his fingers were working her trousers down her legs. And her panties weren't far behind.

Then he was spreading her wide for him before leaning down and teasing her with his lips, tongue, and fingers.

There was no keeping her moans down then and his hand slid up to her mouth, muffling her cries as he drove her to that edge, then sent her flying over, her body tensing then shaking with the intensity of the orgasm as it racked her system.

As soon as she came down, he was driving her back up until she couldn't take the anticipation anymore.

Pandora slid off the desk, reaching to free him from his trousers and underwear, then stroking him hard and fast until he was as far gone as she felt, as desperate for more as she was.

Victor grabbed her, turning her and bending her over her desk as he stepped in behind her.

Then his hand was slapping down on her bottom cheek once. Twice. Three times. As he rubbed himself against her cleft, around her clit.

Teasing. Torturing. Refusing to give in until she was begging for it, begging for him.

"Victor, please," Pandora cried out, her fingers curling into fists on the surface of the desk as she wiggled back against him.

On a sound that was almost a growl, he slammed deep inside her, both of them crying out at the feel of her walls tightening around his hard length, at getting what they'd both been aching for for far too long.

They were lost to the world then as they went from slow and teasing to hard and fast until, with a shuddering cry, she came around him, taking him with her until they were both completely spent.

"Well," Pandora said afterward, Victor's fingers softly whispering up and down her spine as they both tested the craftsmanship of the desk, bodies cuddled close. "I think I need to leave early tonight. And then spend all night doing that all around our flat."

"Our?" he asked, tentative but hopeful.

"Yep. But I already stole the best shelves. You're just going to have to learn to live with that."

"Mmhmm. Or sneak out in the morning when you're sleeping to replace them with my books."

"You wouldn't dare."

"Wouldn't I?"

"OK. How about a compromise?"

"What kind?"

"On all the best eye-level shelves, we put the books we read together."

"The spicy ones?" he asked, fingers slipping down her belly again.

"The spicier the better."

Epilogue

One Year Later
Romania

"I think I owe Uncle Reginald an apology," Pandora whispered to Victor as they stood in the center of a cobblestone path. Where, just five feet in front of them, a bat had transformed into a man.

"That's . . . That's not really . . . Dracula, is it?" Victor whispered back.

He certainly looked like the titular character, Pandora decided, as she admired the tall, ghostly-pale man with slicked-back black hair, coal-dark eyes, and a long purple-velvet-lined cape.

At Victor's words, the man before them scoffed.

"It's Drachmar. I don't know why any of those pesky mortals can't get that right. All the books, the telly shows, the movies. Drachmar. How difficult is that?"

Victor stared at him. "So you're not—"

"I am he," Drachmar said. "I am the one. The first. The infamous. The fearsome. The eternal."

"And a man of so few words," Victor said, lips curving up.

Drachmar's eyes narrowed at that and Pandora was ready to step between them.

"Mortal, you will cower before me in fear."

Those weren't just words or a command, but a glamour.

Luckily for Victor, and unluckily for Drachmar, Pandora had been sure to return Victor's protection necklace to him once they'd got back together.

"I'm not much of the cowering type," Victor said, making Pandora have to force her lips into a straight line, not wanting to irritate their host. "So . . . this isn't Bran Castle."

That got a growl out of Drachmar.

"That," he said, with a wave of his arm that made his cape fly out dramatically, pointing to the other side of the hill, "is Bran Castle. Yet another thing the storybooks get wrong. This," he waved at the castle he stood before, "is my true castle. Built by the same bloody Saxons. But better. Not crumbling like in all those ridiculous books."

Pandora and Victor shared a small smile.

"I'm sorry, Drachmar, but we were under the impression that the castle was open for guests. Had we known you were here, we never would have come."

It hadn't been Pandora's first – or fiftieth – choice, in fact. But Victor had been intrigued by the idea of staying in the castle where so many of his fictional vampire stories took place. Even though Pandora had insisted time and again that Uncle Reginald was notorious for embellishing the truth. If not outright lying.

"It is yours," Drachmar said with another wave of his long-boned hand. "I'm afraid I have to track down my familiar."

"Renfield?" Victor asked.

"Raymond! Ray-mond. That is his name. You mortals." Then, before anyone could say anything else, Drachmar shifted into a bat and flew off with an eerie shriek.

"How long until you can turn into a bat?" Victor asked, looking over at Pandora. She whacked him across the stomach. "Shall we?" He waved toward the front door.

"I don't know what I was expecting," Pandora said as they stepped into the castle. "But . . . ah, this was not it." They both looked around, not sure what to think.

Sure, it was a castle. Stone walls. Long, sprawling rooms. Heavy drapery. Fireplaces large enough for families to live inside.

But it wasn't the bones of the place that had their attention.

It was what Drachmar had decorated the space with that had them not quite believing their eyes.

Nearly every inch of the entire lower floor was full of TV and movie posters, thousands of books, even action figures and stuffed animals that were based on the character of Dracula.

"He's his own fan club," Pandora said with a little laugh.

"I'm kind of disappointed I already finished my thesis," Victor said. "Because . . . this would have been an interesting twist. Looks like Reginald wasn't lying, was he?"

"No," Pandora said, running her fingers over the comically large fangs in a full-sized vampire replica she figured must have been from a movie set or museum at some point. "So now I'm wondering if the perch Vlad uses at my mum and dad's house actually did belong to a king."

And maybe he *had* talked about philosophy with a drunken Socrates. And had helped design the Notre Dame cathedral. And had been the one to make the famous Mona Lisa smile while Leonardo da Vinci had painted her.

"Maybe that ancient scroll he gave me really did come from the Library of Alexandria," Victor said, reaching for Pandora's hand. "What a place for a honeymoon," he added, lifting her hand to his face and kissing her on the finger, just in front of her engagement and wedding rings.

This time, they'd actually gone through with the ceremony. Though, it had been touch-and-go there for a while.

For example, they had all almost burned to death because one of her aunts had decided to set up a bunch of candles around the library. The library full of old books loaded with ancient, dry paper.

If it hadn't been for a quick-thinking and moving Lucy, the knocked-over candelabra would have ignited a whole shelf of encyclopedias and trapped them all in a burning room.

Sure, the encyclopedias had been full of old, inaccurate information. But it would have been a real tragedy for everyone to have died on such a lovely day.

Then, well, there'd been the reception. Where Ravenna and Henrietta had got into an argument that had devolved into an actual, real-life food fight. While Vlad had sulked and pretended not to be jealous of Elizabeth's new beau – a lovely Camelot macaw who hadn't seemed to know that Vlad and Elizabeth had ever been an item. And Victor's father almost finally figured out the whole vampire thing.

She and Victor had decided as a couple not to share that information, both believing his parents were a bit too . . . practical to be able to wrap their heads around the idea of supernatural creatures not only existing, but marrying into their family. Most humans wouldn't be able to handle that kind of truth without hysterics or even an outright breakdown as the world they thought they knew fell apart around them.

It wasn't worth the risk. Especially considering how infrequently the families got together. It would be even less often when his parents finally moved to Portugal like they'd been dreaming of after retirement.

As crazy as it had all been, Pandora knew she would look back on it with nothing but fondness for the rest of her life.

Even just thinking back on some of Victor's vows made her feel like she was flying.

Being with you has taught me that real love lies in embracing every part of who we are. Today, I vow to cele-brate all that makes you unique, to cherish your heart, and to love you for all the time we're blessed to share . . .

"I'm afraid to see what's behind this door," Victor said as they followed a trail of dried red rose petals up the grand staircase and toward one of the doors on the second floor. "What are the chances we won't be sleeping in coffins?"

She'd mentioned the need for human beds to Uncle Reginald. But, well, as much as the man had the memory of a steel trap when it came to ancient Greece or every war mankind had struggled through, he had a remarkable ability not to remember things told to him just moments before.

"Worst case, we build a fort," Pandora said, not caring where they slept so long as they were together.

"That sounds quite romantic," Victor said. "Ready?" He reached for the brass doorknob in the shape of a human hand.

She'd thought she was prepared for anything when it came to a vampire home, having spent so much time in different ones throughout her life.

This one, though, was straight out of gothic fiction.

The room was colour-washed – walls, moldings, ceiling – in black. The old windows were hung with thick black velvet drapes that blocked the sun and kept out cold drafts.

The stone floor was covered in various rugs. Likely just for the aesthetic. But it worked to keep the chill from creeping in through the floor as well.

There were massive canvases on the walls with gilded frames, half a dozen gorgeous women looking down at Pandora and Victor as they stepped inside.

"The brides, I presume?" Victor said, looking around at them.

"Kind of creepy, if you ask me," Pandora said, feeling like their eyes watched them as they moved.

"But at least there's a bed."

There was.

It was bigger than any she'd ever seen before, a black four-poster bed with crimson crushed-velvet drapery and black silk and linen bedding.

"We can close the fabric if the portraits get too creepy when we try to sleep," Victor said.

In sconces on the wall, candles flickered as if with a breeze, their wax dripping down their pillars to hang off of their holders. There were even some old drips on the stone floors and carpets.

"The petals are a sweet touch," Pandora said, seeing the way they led to the bed, but didn't cover the fabric.

"Guess Drachmar is a romantic," Victor said.

"Something else I feel needs to be found in fiction about him somewhere."

"Maybe you should write it."

"Hmm?" He reached for her suitcase and brought it to the foot of the bed.

"Write it. I was saying that maybe you should consider writing it yourself."

"I already submitted my thesis."

"I didn't mean a thesis," Pandora said. "Ever since I read that, though, I've been thinking that maybe you should write fiction."

"Fiction? Me? What gave you that idea?"

"Well, I think we can both agree that I've been around a while."

He smiled. "We could say that."

"And in that time, I've done a lot of reading."

"I did see your reading app," he said.

"And before I figured out how much I love a good romance, I tried out all the other genres. I ultimately decided that most nonfiction books weren't for me because they can be so dry. But your thesis was so rich and engaging. It read like fiction, it was so inviting. I just think that if you can make nonfiction that interesting, then something fictional would be unputdownable."

"It's funny you say that," Victor said, sitting on the edge of the bed and patting the spot next to him. Pandora walked over, sitting down at his side.

Even after a year together – mending, building trust, growing as individuals and a couple – she still couldn't get used to being able to be with him so casually. Sitting side by side, bodies brushing. She hoped she never got over the magic of that. No matter how long they were together.

"Why's that?" she asked, tilting slightly so she could rest her head on his shoulder. Because if you couldn't be all lovey-dovey on your honeymoon, when could you?

"Because I've been thinking about some stories. They've been keeping me up at night, in fact."

"Really? What kinds of stories?"

"About vampires, of course," he said, making her lips curve up. "Your family has been . . . quite inspiring."

"I can imagine," Pandora said. "Vlad's tales alone could fill an entire series of stories."

"Now that we have proof that it wasn't all made up, I think Reginald would be the most fascinating."

"Have you written anything?" To that, he gave her a bashful little smile. "You have, haven't you?"

"A bit."

"When?"

"Mostly in the mornings when you're still sleeping."

"Have you been enjoying it?"

"I have. I expected it to feel more like work, but it's been more like a hobby – something fun – than work."

"That's amazing. I hope one day you let me read it. Even if it isn't my usual genre. What?" she asked when his cheeks and ears went bright red.

"It kind of is."

"It kind of is what?"

"Your genre."

"My genre? Wait . . . do you mean you're writing . . . a romance?"

"I've been a bit inspired."

"By me?" she asked, charmed.

"Yes. But also, that book we were reading in Morocco.

I may or may not have been stealing your books here and there. Been devouring them like sweets," he said.

"They are addictive."

"They are. Not quite as good as the real thing, though." He rested his head on the side of hers.

They sat there like that for a few quiet moments, just enjoying the nearness, the silence after so much noise for so long.

Because, as it turned out, planning a second wedding hadn't been any less chaotic than planning the first. In fact, it had involved more work on both their parts, since they'd not let the family have free rein to do whatever they'd wanted.

Though, this time around, they had agreed to the blood ritual that Pandora had put her foot down about the first time.

"OK," Victor said, slapping a hand on her thigh. "How about we explore the rest of this castle before seeing if, in addition to the bed, our host remembered to put food in the kitchen."

"Or my synthetic blood." Pandora took his hand as they made their way out of the room.

In the year after first discovering the fake blood, there had been an uptick of marketing and availability of it in vampire circles. Even diehard traditionalists would sometimes indulge in it once the company, smartly, started to make different "vintages" that would allow even the most snobbish vampire to brag about knowing the different flavor notes.

So, it wouldn't be as crazy to assume Drachmar had discovered it as well. Even if he turned his nose up at it on principle.

They found no fewer than twenty bedrooms in the various wings of the castle. Thirty-five fireplaces. And at least a million pieces of vampire memorabilia, their plastic material or neon colours in stark contrast to the tasteful brass, gold, and black, red and grey tones of the home's original decor.

Pandora had to admit that Drachmar was right about *his* castle being in much better shape than the one on the other side of the hill that was supposedly his "real" home, according to both fiction and nonfiction sources.

There were few cracks and no crumbling stones. The paint on the walls was meticulously maintained, and the carpets and drapes were all pristine with not a single moth hole to be found.

"I was not expecting this," Victor said when they finally found their way into the kitchen.

Pandora hadn't been either.

Judging by the rest of the castle, Pandora had expected to find a room stuck in time. If not a simple hearth to cook by, then at least a range from lifetimes past. But everything in the kitchen was sleek and modern. There was a massive industrial range that Pandora knew, from shopping for their flat, cost an obscene amount of money, all stainless-steel appliances, rich, cherrywood cabinets that went all the way to the high ceilings, and a bowl overflowing with fresh fruit in the center of the island.

"I think I lived in a flat the size of that refrigerator," Victor said as he pulled the doors open to reveal a fully stocked interior. Everything from fresh veg, yogurt, eggs, and meat, to kombucha and condiments.

"Sorry. No blood," he said, giving Pandora a wince.

"Maybe in the pantry? Since you don't usually serve it cold."

"Right. Of course." Victor went to the pantry, walking in and letting out a whistle that had Pandora following.

Floor to ceiling, the shelves were overflowing with every essential from rice and beans to sugar and flour to the strangest types of crisps and snack cakes.

"Choose your vintage," Victor said, waving toward the shelving just behind the door.

And, sure enough, as high as the eye could see, there were cases of the synthetic blood. Every type available on the market. Even one Pandora hadn't seen before.

"Looks like we're all set on food. Want me to uncork you one of these fancy ones?" he asked, pointing.

"Definitely. How long do you think we have before sunrise?" Pandora asked, looking toward the heavily draped windows.

Victor flipped his watch – a wedding gift from Elias – to check the time. "I'd say two hours before we start to see it – why?"

"Well, remember that package I wouldn't let you look inside?"

"I do."

"You can finally know what it is at just about sun-up."

With that, Victor made himself some steak and potatoes while Pandora enjoyed several of the bottles of synthetic blood until she felt like she was buzzing.

Only then did she rush to retrieve the package from the case in their room, grab Victor, and drag him outside.

"You can't be serious," Victor said as they stood facing the lake located not far behind Drachmar's castle.

"How many times have I made you watch the movie?" she asked, handing him the linen shirt.

"Why don't we just watch it again?" he asked, looking dubiously at the lake.

"Just so I can complain about the scene for the millionth time?" she asked. "Come on. Make the fantasy come true."

"It's got to be frigid."

To that, she reached out, grabbing him by the waistband and pulling him close.

"I promise I'll warm you up after."

That was all it took.

Victor shrugged out of his shirt, put on the thin linen shirt she handed him, then, with one deep breath, climbed into the lake.

She watched as he went under the water, then emerged the way fans always wanted to happen in film and TV, but were never blessed with.

But there Pandora was.

Graced with her very own Mr. Darcy climbing out of the lake and making his way toward her.

"Everything you were hoping for?" he asked, looking a little blue in the lips.

"And more." She pulled him down for a kiss. Long and deep. Until the heat was thrumming through them both.

"Go ahead," Victor murmured when he felt her lips on his neck, kissing down toward the pulse point as her fangs started to elongate, begging for a nip.

She didn't need more than that.

They'd learned many months ago that they both enjoyed when she gave in to her impulses, when she let her teeth nip his skin, when her tongue laved over the small beads that appeared on his skin.

A soft whimper escaped her, mingling with his groan.

With that, Victor grabbed her and pulled her up off her feet. She wrapped her arms and legs around him, holding on tight, feeling the cool and wet soak through her clothes by the time they got back to their room, where he lowered her down onto the soft rug in front of the warm fire.

Her hands reached to pull the soaked linen shirt off of Victor's body. Hers followed.

Victor leaned down, his wet hair dripping onto her skin as he sucked her nipple into his mouth, making her arch off of the carpet and deeper into his mouth.

His tongue thrashed and his teeth grazed until the warmth of desire sparked and caught fire, burning through her until she was grabbing at his trousers, yanking them down his hips, then closing her hand around his length.

Victor's eyes closed as she stroked him.

But then he pulled her up onto her knees, before sitting up and positioning her over him.

As she lowered down, his face pressed between her breasts then moved upward, planting kisses up her chest, over her collarbone, up the side of her neck, before sealing his lips to hers.

He drew her down onto his lap and a whimper escaped her as his hardness rocked against her.

Pandora lifted up, then lowered down on him, letting out a little gasp as he filled her.

Victor's hands sank into her hips, guiding her movements until she took over, riding him harder and faster as the need grew, until she was burying her face in his neck, her fangs nipping into his flesh, his taste bursting across her tastebuds as the orgasm soared through the both of them.

They stayed there after, warm and happy.

Until Victor suggested they grab another of her books and read until they both fell asleep.

"Have I mentioned how happy I am to spend eternity with you?" she asked, rolling on top of Victor to smile down at him, her hair falling like a curtain around the two of them. They'd discussed the possibility of Victor being turned one day. But, you know, sometime down the road. There was certainly no rush.

"You may have mentioned it a time or two," he said, his eyes as warm as his smile, as he reached up to tuck her hair behind her ear. "But I could listen to you say it for the next thousand years."

"Forever?" she asked.

He kissed her. "Forever."

Acknowledgements

Writing a book may be a solo act, but publishing one never is (it turns out it takes more than caffeine and existential dread to get a story across the finish line). Luckily, I had an incredible crew doing the heavy lifting while I did the typing.

To my editor, Amy Mae Baxter, for taking a chance on me, cheering me on, and helping shape this book into everything it could be.

To Maddie Wilson, for her eagle-eyed edits that helped me whip this book into shape. (*"I'm sorry about all the action beats—lol," she said, shrugging, sipping her coffee, and exiting stage left.*)

To Jessica and the entire team at Avon UK, for their dedication and hard work in bringing this book to market.

And last but never least, to my readers—you make this wild, magical life possible. Every preorder, review, aesthetic board, message, and comment is a gift that I never take for granted. Thank you for being just as excited about this as I am. (*We made it to bookshelves, dolls! Squeal!*)

Loved
My Big Fat Vampire Wedding?

Don't miss Jessica's next book
Mermaid in Manhattan,
coming May 2026!

Preorder your copy now!